PASSIONATE PROMISE

Mara lowered her head, trying to hide in Nathaniel's embrace. "I wanted it to be perfect. I wanted to . . . seduce you."

Nathaniel entwined his fingers in Mara's hair, pulling out the pins, freeing it. Tangling his fingers in its long, dark waves, he brushed his thumbs back and forth against her cheeks. "If you insist."

She shook her head, missing the teasing caress in his voice. "It's no good."

Nathaniel tilted her chin upward and bent his head until his lips brushed hers. "It could be, Mara," he said against her mouth, "but it has to be both of us. Together, don't you see?"

She shivered at the feel of his mouth on hers. Her hand flattened against his chest, and she ached with the longing to feel his bare skin beneath her fingers. "Love me, Nathaniel," she whispered.

By Laura Lee Guhrke

Prelude to Heaven
To Dream Again

Available from HarperPaperbacks

Harper
Monogram

To Dream Again

⊰ LAURA LEE GUHRKE ⊱

HarperPaperbacks
A Division of HarperCollinsPublishers

HarperPaperbacks   *A Division of* HarperCollins*Publishers*
10 East 53rd Street, New York, N.Y. 10022

Copyright © 1995 by Laura Lee Guhrke
All rights reserved. No part of this book may be used or reproduced in any manner whatsoever without written permission of the publisher, except in the case of brief quotations embodied in critical articles and reviews. For information address HarperCollins*Publishers,*
10 East 53rd Street, New York, N.Y. 10022.

Cover illustration by Vittorio

First printing: February 1995

Printed in the United States of America

HarperPaperbacks, HarperMonogram, and colophon are trademarks of HarperCollins*Publishers*

❖ 10 9 8 7 6 5 4 3 2 1

To my father, Bill Guhrke, the entrepreneur, the dreamer in our family, for his honesty, his kindness, and his vision. Men like him are the true romantic heroes of the world.

And for my mother, Judy Guhrke, who follows him with financial statements and calculator, and whose incredible love and support have helped him make their dreams come true.

I love you both.

If a man does not keep pace with his companions, perhaps it is because he hears a different drummer.

—Henry David Thoreau

1

Whitechapel 1889

Nathaniel Chase heard the loud, rather insistent knock on the open door and the irate voice calling his name, but being rather preoccupied, he did not look up from his task. "Yes, Mrs. O'Brien, what is it?"

The stout landlady followed the sound of his voice, dodging her way around moving men, steamer trunks, furniture, and wooden crates. In the center of the room she paused, unable to find her new tenant amid the chaotic jumble of his belongings. "Mr. Chase?"

"Over here," he called.

Peeking between a tall wooden Indian and a large telescope, she saw him on his knees beneath a table, his back to her, rummaging in a box.

She cast a curious glance at the tools and machinery that littered the table before bending to peer at the man beneath. "*Mister* Chase, sure did I not say to have your things off the stairs by five o'clock?"

Nathaniel stopped ransacking the box and lifted his head to reply, forgetting that he was kneeling beneath the table. He hit his head with a bang, nearly tumbling his equipment onto the floor. "Ouch!"

He caught the legs of the table to prevent it from falling. Once it was stable again, he moved out from under it and jumped to his feet. "I'm sorry, ma'am," he said, rubbing his sore head and doing his best to look contrite, "but moving in is taking longer than I thought."

"Where do you want this one, guv'nor?"

Nathaniel glanced at the two men who stood nearby holding a huge crate between them. "Ah, my trains!" He pointed to an empty space beside the table. "Put it here, if you please. And be careful," he added. "It's somewhat fragile."

He returned his attention to his new landlady. "Mrs. O'Brien, I will have my things off the stairs as soon as I can find a place to put them."

She placed her hands on her ample hips. "You said you'd be moved in by the end of the day. Other tenants will be returnin' from work soon and won't like findin' they can't get up the stairs, yer boxes and things bein' scattered hither and yon. You promised me—"

"Yes, I know," he interrupted. "By the time my neighbors return from work, my things will be out of the way." He looked around with a frown. "I don't know where I'll put them. It seems I have underestimated the quantity of my luggage."

Mrs. O'Brien was never one to miss an opportunity. "I've a cellar you could use. Only two shillings the week."

Nathaniel considered that option for a moment. These were only temporary lodgings, of course, but he wasn't certain how long it would be before he could find permanent rooms. In the meantime, he would have to use his rooms as his laboratory, and he wanted his things close at hand. Mrs. O'Brien's cellar simply wouldn't do. There had to be another solution.

He raked a hand through his hair and glanced up, then paused as an idea struck him.

"The attic is directly above me, is it not?"

"It is." The landlady frowned suspiciously. "But I don't see—"

He pointed to the ceiling. "If I put in a hole, I could use the attic."

"A hole in my ceiling? Heavens, no!"

Nathaniel paid no attention to her protest. "Yes, that would work," he muttered to himself. His decision made, he turned to one of the men who was bringing in his things. "Mr. Boggs, could you come here a moment?"

The burly, bald-headed man stepped up beside him, and Nathaniel pointed above his head. "Could you cut a hole here and give me access to the attic?"

"Mr. Chase, I won't allow it. I won't let you tear me house down!"

Mrs. O'Brien's declaration was lost on the two men, who began to discuss the project. "Very good," Nathaniel finally said. "When can you begin?"

The man rubbed his jaw. "I'd need t'get me tools and buy the goods. And I'll want me boy to 'elp. Tomorrow afternoon be all right, guv'nor?"

"Of course. Before you leave today, would you and your men get the rest of my things off the stairs? Just pile them anywhere you can find room."

A wail from Mrs. O'Brien caused Nathaniel to turn to her. "Are you unwell?" he asked, noting her flushed face and distraught expression.

She placed a hand to her heart. "Holes in me ceiling. Oh, heavens."

She seemed quite upset to Nathaniel. This was a matter of simple carpentry, easily repaired when he moved out, and he couldn't understand her distress—until he looked into her eyes and perceived a shrewd gleam in their green depths.

He pulled his wallet from the inner pocket of his jacket. "If I leave, I will pay to have everything put back exactly the way it was before," he assured her. "And I'll pay you half rent for the attic."

He began to count out money. "And there's five pounds to you, my dear lady, for all the inconvenience."

"Well, now," she said, brightening considerably, "that's somethin' I can agree to." She snatched the money from his hand.

Nathaniel turned and tossed his wallet toward his desk, where it landed in an open drawer. He took the landlady by the elbow and turned her gently toward the door. "Mrs. O'Brien, you are a pearl beyond price. I thank you."

"Will ye be needin' anything else, sir?" she asked, tucking the money into the pocket of her apron as Nathaniel guided her past Mr. Boggs and around a stack of crates. "Breakfast, tea, an' dinner? I'm a fine cook, I don't mind sayin'. Three meals a day for, say, two quid the week?"

"That's a tempting offer. A man does appreciate home cooking. I will consider it." He gave her his most charming smile and pushed her out the door. "I'll have my things off the stairs shortly," he promised. "Good day."

She hesitated a moment, then bobbed her head and turned to go down the stairs. "Very good, sir. If there's anything else you need—"

"I'll be sure to let you know."

"Lad's got more money than sense," she muttered as she descended the stairs and finally disappeared.

Nathaniel turned back around and caught sight of the

huge crate that contained his trains. He grinned. He didn't have much money, and he probably didn't have much sense either. But he had his dream, and that was enough.

Mara Elliot walked along the mezzanine of the factory with a brisk, no-nonsense stride that bounced the ostrich plume of her straw bonnet and caused the heels of her high-button shoes to hit the floor in rhythm with the steam engines on the production floor below.

The six o'clock whistle sounded, a loud squeal over the rumble of machinery, and she turned, leaning over the rail to watch as activity ceased below. Steam engines shut down, conveyor belts came to a stop, and the deafening roar of machinery faded away. People began heading for the doors.

When she caught sight of her secretary beckoning her to come down she turned away from the rail and joined the women leaving the mezzanine.

"If me Alfie thinks of gettin' any tonight, he's off his chump," one woman declared to another, pausing on the stairs in front of Mara. "Takin' me 'ard-earned wages and passing 'em to a bloody pubkeeper! I won't stand it."

"Good for you, Emma," the woman beside her said.

"And shovin' me around. Who's 'e think 'e is?" Emma paused for breath and glanced over her shoulder, catching sight of her employer standing only a few feet behind them. "Evenin', ma'am," she said respectfully and moved back, pressing herself against the wall to let Mara pass. The other woman did the same, and Mara walked between them.

She had never been the sort to fraternize with her employees. She knew other small business operators who did, regarding their workers as a sort of extended family, but Mara preferred to keep some distance between herself and her staff, feeling it gave her more respect.

She was very conscious of her position. She was not the owner, she was the owner's wife. Her authority was always at risk, and she knew the best way to maintain respect was to remain cool and efficient.

When she reached the bottom of the stairs, her secretary was waiting for her. "What is it, Percy?"

"Mr. Finch is waiting in your office. He needs to speak with you."

"Here?" Mara was surprised. She couldn't recall the solicitor ever coming to her office before. "I'll go immediately."

She started across the production floor, and her secretary fell in step beside her. "Did he say what he wanted to see me about?" she asked.

"No, but perhaps it's about the gentleman who was here this morning."

Mara stopped walking. "What gentleman?"

Percy also came to a halt. "I didn't have the chance to tell you earlier, but a man came this morning asking to see Mr. Elliot while you were out. He seemed surprised to find that your husband wasn't here."

Mara's brows drew together in a frown. "James is in America now. At least, I thought he was." One never knew with him. He could be anywhere. "Did the man say what he wanted?"

"No, just that he had business with Mr. Elliot and was expected. Mr. Elliot supposedly had arranged a meeting with him here."

She nearly laughed out loud. It was just like James to arrange a meeting in London when he was probably wandering around the Arizona desert. "Did you tell him James has been away for quite some time?" *Four years.* "And that we don't anticipate his return in the near future?"

"Yes, ma'am. He mentioned that Mr. Elliot had arranged for them to meet here in London, and that he had come all the way from San Francisco, expecting Mr. Elliot to be waiting."

More fool him, Mara thought cynically. Anyone who expected her husband to be where he was supposed to be was doomed to disappointment. "San Francisco? An American gentleman?"

"No, he was British, I believe. I explained to him that you were in charge during Mr. Elliot's absence, and he requested a meeting with you. I made an appointment for him to meet with you Thursday morning at eleven."

She sighed. "Oh, very well. I'll meet with him if I have time. Go home, Percy. I'll see you tomorrow."

Percy walked away, but Mara remained where she was, lost in thought. She couldn't help wondering why someone had come all the way from San Francisco to see James. She didn't like the sound of it. Knowing her husband, it was probably some get-rich-quick scheme. Well, if he thought he was going to take out another loan to pay for it, he was mistaken. It was hard enough to make interest payments on what he'd already borrowed.

With a shake of her head, she dismissed the stranger and her wandering husband from her mind and turned down the hallway leading to her office.

"Mr. Finch," she greeted the gray-haired gentleman as she entered her office and closed the door behind her. "What brings you down here?"

The solicitor rose to his feet, but he did not give her his usual smile of greeting. "A matter of some importance, I'm afraid."

Mara caught the stilted sound of his words and began to feel slightly uneasy as she studied the solicitor's worried face. "Is something wrong?"

Finch tugged at his collar. "Perhaps we should sit down."

"Of course." Mara crossed the small room. "What is this about?" she asked, circling her desk.

"Mara, dear, you'd best sit down."

"What's the matter?" He looked so grave, her uneasy feeling grew into alarm, and she knew something terrible had happened. "Mr. Finch, what is it? You're beginning to frighten me."

"Mara . . ." He paused and sighed deeply. "James is dead."

"Dead?" The news hit her like a punch in the stomach, and she sank into her chair. Numbly, she stared up at the solicitor. "How? When?"

Finch sat down, taking the chair opposite her across the desk. "I received a cable from California a few hours ago. Evidently, he had purchased a gold mine near San Francisco and was there to take a look at it. I'm told there was an earthquake while he was in the mine, and he was killed. Seven days ago. They dug his body out and buried it, but it took a bit of time to learn who he was."

She leaned her elbows on the desk and pressed her fingers to her suddenly throbbing temples. Then she closed her eyes, recalling the last time she'd seen James. He'd been packing to depart for America, babbling rubbish about adventures in the untamed West, and some new deal in railway stocks.

He'd said he would send for her and Helen once he was settled, but she had told him no, that this time she wasn't going to drag their daughter halfway across the world to follow him. She had reminded him of all his past promises to settle down. She'd asked him to stay for Helen's sake. Then she'd thrown pride away and begged him to stay, using the only plea she had left.

If you truly love me, you'll stay. You'll do it for me.

That, of course, had not worked. He'd gone to

America anyway. He had handed over the reins of the company to her and left her with the debts. Alone, she'd had to take care of their daughter. Alone, she'd had to deal with the pain when Helen had died. Alone, she'd been forced to make a living from the tattered remnants of a company he'd tired of after less than a year.

The company. Mara lifted her head sharply. "What about Elliot's? Do I inherit it?"

"Although your husband evidently died without making a will, the company would still come to you as his wife, but—"

"Thank heaven." She breathed a sigh of relief. "At least I have that."

"No, Mara, I'm afraid you don't."

For a moment, she didn't understand. Then the realization hit her, and she sucked in a sharp breath. "The bank. The loan. Dear God."

The solicitor's slow nod confirmed her worst fear. "Joslyn Brothers is calling in the loan on Elliot's. I'm sorry, Mara."

The past repeated itself over and over again. No matter how hard she worked, how hard she fought, it never made any difference. *Think, Mara,* she told herself, fighting to remain calm. *Think.* "What about this gold mine he bought? Wouldn't I inherit that as well?"

"There's no gold in it. Your husband, it appears, had not consulted mining engineers before he purchased it. The mine is worthless."

How characteristic of James to die in a worthless gold mine. It was the inevitable fate of a man who always wanted to find the end of the rainbow. Again, she was the one who had to deal with the consequences. She shook off the bitterness that swept over her. "What do I have to do to keep Elliot's?"

"The terms of the loan James took against the company

are quite clear. The balance and any interest become due and payable ten days after his death. To keep Elliot's, you have to pay off the loan. Within three days from now."

Mara felt sick. The principal was at least five thousand pounds. She could never raise that kind of money in only a few days.

She thought of all the work she had done. All the careful planning, all the worry, all the sacrifices to make a life for herself and become an independent woman. After four years of struggle, Elliot's was finally solvent. The future had actually begun to promise the security she craved.

Gone. In the blink of an eye, it was all gone.

Mara walked slowly through the now quiet factory, moving between the machines and tables. Finch had tactfully left her to grieve in private, but she found she could not grieve. James was dead, but in her heart he had died a long time ago. He had died by degrees, day by day, year by year. She should feel sad, she supposed, but she felt nothing at all.

She should cry, but she remembered all the tears she had shed during her first eight years of marriage to James. Tears of heartbreak as a young bride who couldn't understand why her husband was always leaving. Tears of farewell when she again packed up everything to join him, and friends were left behind. Tears of worry when it all fell apart, when the bills inevitably came due and there was no way to pay them. Finally, tears of bitterness when the fire came, when Helen had died, when James had not been there.

Too many tears, washing away all her love for him until there was nothing. Four years ago, she had run out of tears, and she had not cried since. She could not cry now.

She had to think, she had to come up with a solution to the problem at hand. In a few days, everything she'd spent four years building would collapse, and she had no idea how to stop it.

There was nothing else to be done. She had to find a way to hang on. In the morning, she would go to Joslyn Brothers and try to persuade them not to call in the loan. She went back into her office and gathered the company's account books, placing them in her worn leather portfolio. When she left her office, she found Percy at his desk. He had not obeyed her order to go home. He often worked late, and she knew he was underpaid for the hours he put in, but she couldn't afford to pay him more.

Suddenly, she felt an overpowering urge to confide in him, to ask for help, for advice. He looked up, and the words stuck in her throat. She gave him a stiff nod of good night, and left the factory, but paused a moment to glance at the sign above the entrance: "Elliot Electrical Motors Company."

Not for long, perhaps. She turned away and started for home. A stray kitten, its ribs showing plainly through matted gray fur, hissed at her as it slinked by. She felt like hissing back. She was in that sort of mood.

She walked to her lodging house next door and heard the clock strike eight as she stepped inside. *If only I had the money to pay off the loan,* she thought, starting up the stairs. She shook off the thought impatiently. If only was a silly term, a child's wish. She didn't have the money and all the wishing in the world wouldn't give it to her. But the wistful words followed her as she reached the second level of the three-story building and turned to the door leading into her flat. *If only . . .*

Preoccupied with her thoughts, Mara didn't notice the item on the landing until she stumbled over it.

"Oh!" she cried and pitched forward, dropping her portfolio.

After regaining her balance, she bent down, rubbing her shin and trying to discern in the dim twilight from the window at the end of the hall what had caused her to stumble. It was a wooden crate filled with flat metal disks of varying sizes. What was such a curious item doing in the hallway?

She didn't have much time to ponder the question before a loud pounding began above her head. Startled, she jumped at the unexpected sound.

Mrs. O'Brien must have let the rooms upstairs. She hoped the new tenant didn't intend to continue that pounding all evening. What was he doing?

The noise from upstairs stopped as abruptly as it had begun. Mara picked up her portfolio and fumbled in her pocket for her latchkey. Finding it, she turned toward her room, carefully stepping over the crate. She came to a halt before her door and frowned in irritation at the sight of it hanging slightly ajar. Three days now, and the lock still wasn't fixed.

With a sigh, she pushed the door open and stepped inside her room.

As rooms went, hers wasn't much. The ceiling plaster was cracked, the mattress sagged, and the table and chair were too rickety to be of much use. The view from her window was the brick wall of Elliot's. She had always intended to find better lodgings once the company was profitable, but there never seemed to be any profits.

She had to take stock of her situation. After setting her portfolio on the table and turning on the gas lamp, she opened her window to let in the hint of summer breeze. She carefully lit a small fire in the grate and put on the kettle to boil water for tea. Then she pulled the information she'd gathered from the office out of her portfolio, placing the account books in neat stacks on the table along with pencils and paper.

Her door had swung open again, and she tried to close it, but the latch refused to cooperate. The kettle began to boil, and she let the door go.

After pouring out her tea, she sank down in the chair, feeling its uneven legs rock beneath her. She pulled the account books forward and began looking for some way, any way, to scrape together five thousand pounds.

A little while later, she set down her pencil and sat back, defeated. The cash-on-hand was meager, a tiny fraction of what she needed to pay back the loan. The only alternative was to sell assets, and there wasn't a single piece of equipment they didn't need in the factory. She'd been over the balance sheet a dozen times. The money simply wasn't there.

Leaning forward, she rested her elbows on the table and rubbed her eyes with the tips of her fingers, feeling the cool smoothness of her kid gloves against her lids. If she didn't come up with the money, she would lose the company. If she lost Elliot's, what would she do?

What occupations were there for a widow whose only work experience was managing a factory? No one would hire a woman for that. She lifted her head and stared down at her gloved hands. She supposed she could become a typist, but she imagined work of that nature would require her to remove her gloves.

Mara tugged at the fingertips of her left glove and pulled it halfway off, staring down at the scars on her hand. People would stare at her with pity in their eyes. They might ask questions. She yanked the glove back into place, hiding the scars even from herself.

What was she going to do? Visions of the future hovered on the edge of her mind, a future of poverty, a future born of the past. A dismal future, indeed, for a woman with no prospects and little money of her own.

Desperation began to spread through her, desperation and a hint of panic. She rose to her feet. Walking to the washstand that stood in one corner of the small room, she took her tin bank from its hiding place.

Tuppence for the bank, Mara. Her mother's words floated back to her from years ago. *At least tuppence, every day.*

As a child, she had watched her mother put two pennies in a tin can each day. She'd said if they did that every single day, they'd eventually have enough to buy a home of their own. But her mother had died in a rented shack in a South Africa shantytown without ever seeing her dream come true.

Mara had vowed to do better. She'd married James believing in his grand dreams, hoping to escape the poverty. She'd made her own tin-can bank and dropped pennies into it with all the optimism of a child bride. During the good times, it had been easy. But during the bad times, which had come more frequently with each passing year, most of the pennies had disappeared.

She dumped the money out of the tin can and began to count what cash she had. The tiny salary she paid herself covered her basic living expenses, but there had been little left over to save for a rainy day. Now she was twenty-eight, optimism had long since deserted her, and she knew tuppence tossed daily into a tin bank added up to precious little.

She sat down and stared at the tiny pile of money and thought of all the work she'd poured into the business, all the hours, all the hopes. All gone.

She was so tired. She wanted to sleep, to banish the fear that threatened to overwhelm her. "Damn you," she whispered to her dead husband, hoping he could hear her. "Damn you and all your rainbow-chasing dreams to hell."

Pushing aside the papers and the pile of coins, she folded her arms, rested her cheek on her wrist, and fell asleep.

The sound was soft, but Mara awoke with a start. She lifted her head to stare at the door through the dark curtain of her bangs, which had lost their curl hours before and now hung limply in her eyes.

The door was wide open. A man stood in the doorway, and he was watching her. Paralyzed, she stared back at him. Seeing a face of such flawless masculine beauty, she wondered if she were dreaming. The gaslight reflected off his hair, tawny, tousled hair that needed cutting. He stood with one shoulder against the jamb, arms folded across his chest, utterly still. She thought of golden eagles gliding on the wind, moving yet motionless.

No, it was not a dream. In her dark dreams, there would be no such man.

His eyes, the color of sea and sky, looked into her, seemed to perceive and understand everything about her in an instant. He tilted his head slightly to one side. "Why are you sad?"

At the unexpected question she jumped to her feet and pushed back her chair. She felt the knot of her hair coming loose and her hat pin slipping. Her bonnet slid to one side, and she wished she'd remembered to remove it when she'd come in earlier.

She attempted to straighten the mess as she backed away from the stranger, but her efforts only made things worse. An ostrich plume fell awkwardly over one eye and tickled her cheek. "Who are you?"

"Didn't mean to startle you," he said. "Saw your door open. I don't think it shuts properly." He smiled briefly, and in that instant everything in the world shifted, fell into place, and became right. She sucked in her breath. Perhaps he was a dream after all.

He nodded toward the table between them. "Shouldn't leave your money lying about like that. This doesn't seem to be the nicest neighborhood, I'm sorry to say."

Her gaze moved from him to the cash on the table. She stared down at the money and reality returned, making her feel foolish and awkward. She tried to push the feather out of her face. "Thank you for the warning."

She swept the money into her bank. Clutching the tin can to her breast, she gave him a nod of dismissal that bounced her feather back over her eye. She hoped he would take the hint.

He didn't. Instead, he came into the room and circled the table. She stepped back, retreating until her shoulder blades hit the mantel of the fireplace. She glanced down, but the poker was just out of her reach. He came closer, and alarm bells began ringing in her head. He was tall, and strong, and very strange. "Who. . . what are you doing?"

"Your feather is broken." He reached out and gripped the plume that dangled over her eye, then pushed it back, out of her vision. "I don't know much about the latest fashions for ladies," he added in a confidential tone, lowering his head until his perfect face was only inches from hers, "but I don't believe broken feathers are in vogue for bonnets this year."

He moved his hand, brushing the hair out of her eyes with the tips of his fingers, a light touch that made breathing difficult. She remained perfectly still, too terrified to move as he tucked a strand behind her ear.

He took a few steps back, and she began to breathe again. He surveyed his handiwork for a moment, then gave a satisfied nod. "Much better. Now I can see your face. No hair and ostrich tails to get in the way. Have you ever wondered how the ostriches must feel? Do they know their tail feathers are decorating the bonnets of women all over London?"

She didn't know whether to laugh or scream for help. "Who are you?" she asked, ashamed when her haughty demand came out as a helpless squeak.

"I've scared you." His voice held both surprise and regret. "Terribly sorry. Didn't mean to. Allow me to introduce myself. Nathaniel Chase, brilliant inventor and rude terrifier of helpless ladies." He bowed, and the unruly strands of his golden hair caught the light.

"How . . . how do you do," she murmured.

"Fine, thank you." He straightened, shaking back his hair. Again he reminded her of an eagle in flight. "Fair play, ma'am."

She frowned. "Sorry?"

"I've given you my name. What's yours?"

"Mara." She licked her dry lips. "Mara—"

"That explains it then." He nodded sagely. "I see."

"What?"

"Mara means bitter. But I thought perhaps it might be Mariana."

"I beg your pardon?" Trying to follow his meaning was making her dizzy.

"'I am aweary, aweary,'"

She stared at him, wondering if he was a bit touched in the head.

"Don't you know your Tennyson?" he asked.

"Oh, poetry."

He laughed, a sound that was warm and rich and deep, filling her tiny room. "You say that as if it's your daily dose of cod liver oil." With another bow, he said, "It's been a pleasure, Mara Mariana, but I must be off. Opportunities await, and I have work to do." He turned away and looked around. "I had a reason for coming down here," he muttered, raking a hand through his hair and tousling it further. "What was it?" He paused, then snapped his fingers. "Ah! I remember."

He pointed to the open doorway and the wooden crate she had tripped over. "My gears."

She watched him walk out to the landing and lift the box. He gave her a nod of farewell through the doorway.

"The men must have forgotten to bring this up," he said with another of those odd smiles. "Better get that lock fixed," he advised and then disappeared, carrying his box of gears and whistling an aimless melody.

She wondered if perhaps he was a little mad.

2

"I'm sorry, Mrs. Elliot," Percy said. "I never know what to say at a time like this."

Mara looked away from the sympathy in his green eyes. "You don't have to say anything, Percy. I know you had a great fondness for James."

"He was difficult to work for, but he gave me a chance when no one else would. Who else would hire a seventeen-year-old with no formal education, no background, and no experience to be his assistant?" He sighed. "Do you want me to make funeral arrangements?"

"No. Mr. Finch has already done that. There won't be a funeral, just a memorial service. Nine o'clock tomorrow at St. Andrew's Church."

"Is there anything I can do?"

She shook her head. "Not unless you have five thousand pounds tucked away somewhere."

Percy straightened in his chair, astonished. "Five thousand pounds! Whatever for?"

"Joslyn Brothers is calling in our loan. I have three days to pay the balance owed or they take the company."

Percy pulled at his auburn mustache, staring at the floor. After several moments, he looked up at her. "This means we're out of business."

"No it doesn't," she answered, her voice hard. "Not if I can help it."

"What are you going to do?"

She rose and picked up her portfolio. "I'm going to pay Joslyn Brothers a visit. I'll try to persuade them not to call in the loan." She started for the door, but she paused and turned around when Percy spoke again.

"Do you want me to tell the employees?" he asked.

She thought about it for a moment, then she nodded. "Yes, we probably should, but only about James's death. Don't say anything about the loan."

"Of course not. Shouldn't we close down tomorrow?"

"Close down?"

"Most companies do close down on the day of the owner's memorial service. For mourning."

She frowned.

"Mrs. Elliot, forgive me if I'm being impertinent when I say this. I know that you and Mr. Elliot had problems, but he was your husband."

She stiffened. "You *are* being impertinent, Mr. Sandborn."

Percy made no reply. He just looked at her.

She gave an exasperated sigh. "Fine. Close down, make whatever arrangements you think best. I'm going to the bank."

She walked out before Percy could say another word. James Elliot had never been any kind of a husband to her, and she failed to see why she was expected to mourn for him. She would go to the memorial service for the sake of appearances, but she didn't have time to grieve for a man who'd never given the needs of his wife and daughter more than a passing thought.

Portfolio in hand, she left the factory and began the short walk up Houndsditch toward Bishopsgate, joining the throng of delivery carts, cabs, and pedestrians that crowded the streets.

As she walked, she went over all the reasons why Joslyn Brothers should not call in the loan. Elliot's was in much better shape now than when James had departed. He had left her with a pile of debt, almost no sales, and a line of creditors at the door. By planning carefully, watching every penny, and taking no chances, she had turned things around. Surely the bank would see what she had accomplished.

Mr. Abercrombie saw nothing of the kind. He took only a few moments to glance through the financial statements she had brought, then slowly shook his head and set the documents aside. "I'm sorry, Mrs. Elliot, but I'm afraid we will be unable to comply with your request."

"But why?"

"The terms of the loan are very clear." He tugged at his mustache and looked grave. "We must demand that the loan be repaid now."

"But that will break us!" Mara leaned forward in her chair. "We are growing, but we are still a small company."

"My dear lady, times are very uncertain. We can't afford the risk."

"Risk?" Mara's chin lifted slightly at the word. "I assure you, sir, I do not take risks. My business philosophy is most conservative."

"I'm sure it is."

She did not miss the patronizing tone of his voice. "The company is solvent," she went on, fighting to keep her voice confident. "I am a good customer of your bank. I have always made the interest payments on time. You can see by my financial statements that our position has improved tremendously in the last four years. This year, I expect we will make a profit."

She said it with pride, but he was not impressed. "There are other considerations. Your husband is dead, Mrs. Elliot. I sympathize with you, but we cannot allow sentiment to interfere with business decisions."

"I would not dream of bringing sentiment into it, sir. The fact is that if you call the loan now, we will not be able to pay it. Elliot's will be forced into bankruptcy, all our assets will be sold, and you will be fortunate if you can recoup the principal amount."

He said nothing, and she knew she was making no progress with him. She changed her tactics. "Then at least give me time to raise the money."

He leaned back in his chair. "My dear lady, what good will time do you? A few days, a few months—" He shrugged. "What difference will it make?"

"I would have time to find investors willing to capitalize Elliot's."

"Investors?" He stared at her in amazement. "You'll have difficulty finding investors with your present situation."

"The company is a fine investment. If you look at my financial statements again, you will see that—"

"Mrs. Elliot," he interrupted gently, "the fact is that you are a woman. You have little experience in the harsh world of business. It is difficult enough for a man of the world to succeed, much less a lady such as yourself. I doubt you will be lucky enough to find investors who feel differently."

"Lucky?" Mara forced herself not to grind her teeth. "I don't believe in luck, Mr. Abercrombie, and I would have thought that a man of logic and reason such as yourself would not believe in it either."

He stiffened. "The fact remains that your husband is dead."

"James has had nothing to do with the management of Elliot's for some years now. I have been in charge. You know that. I've come in every Monday for the past four years to make deposits, go over our account, and manage our financial affairs."

"Mrs. Elliot, I realize that circumstances forced you to take on some responsibility for the business when your husband went to America. But all this time, he was still within reach of a telegraph if the need arose for serious decisions. Now that he is dead, who will make those decisions?"

"I have been making those decisions for four years now, sir. My husband was a brilliant man in his way, with an uncanny knack for making money, but he also had an uncanny knack for losing it. I assure you, I never telegraphed to him for advice. It was neither necessary nor desirable for me to do so."

The banker was unconvinced. "Nonetheless, your husband owned the company, and he was responsible for it. Now that he is dead, the bank wishes to remove itself from any possible future losses resulting from his death."

"This is ridiculous!" Mara burst out, frustrated by the sheer unfairness of it. "I have been responsible for Elliot's. I have worked very hard to make the company profitable. I will not stand by and watch it all unravel!"

The banker seemed uncomfortable at this display of female emotion. He picked up the documents and handed them to her. "The decision has been made. I am truly sorry if the company is forced into bankruptcy, but this is business."

Mara stared down at the neatly penciled figures of her balance sheet, feeling her options slipping away, but she would not beg. She would not confess that if she lost the company she would have nothing. She could not.

Steeling herself with her pride, she looked at Mr. Abercrombie. "What is the exact balance owed, and how much time do I have to pay it?"

He opened a ledger on his desk. "Principal plus this month's interest comes to five thousand and twenty-five pounds, twelve shillings, and ten. Due by the close of business on Friday, July twelfth."

It was Wednesday morning. Three days. She had three days. Mara rose to her feet. "Fine. Draw up the papers, and be prepared to accept payment in full on Friday, Mr. Abercrombie. You will have your money."

"Mrs. Elliot, I admire your tenacity." He also stood up. "But how will you raise over five thousand pounds in three days?"

Rob a bank. The words hovered on the tip of her tongue, but she didn't think Mr. Abercrombie would appreciate the comment. At the moment, however, robbing a bank didn't seem like a bad idea.

Nathaniel reached for another piece of miniature railroad track and attached it to the preceding one. He pushed the two sections firmly together so that the electric current would pass from one section to the next and the toy train would run smoothly.

Boggs and his son were busy making the alterations to his ceiling, hammering and pounding, but Nathaniel ignored the noise. He continued to put together railroad track, knowing this idea was going to revolutionize the toy train industry.

Grandfather would have liked the idea. He smiled down at the half-completed track on the table, remembering long-ago summer days on the Isle of Wight. The stuttering excitement of a young boy filled with ideas and the encouraging enthusiasm of an old man filled with patience.

It was growing dark. Nathaniel lit the gas lamp on the table and continued building the invention that would determine his future. But his mind was in the past.

Grandfather had believed in him. Heady stuff for a boy who'd never been quite good enough. Not good enough for his own father to listen or give him a chance.

But in his will, Grandfather had given him the chance. Nathaniel had left Cambridge, and at the age of nineteen, he'd finally been given the opportunity to prove himself and had been thrust into the midst of Chase Toys, out of obscurity and into the light for the first time. It was then that his father had first begun to realize that his second son had more in his head than impractical ideas and airy dreams.

Nathaniel fitted the last piece of railroad track into place. It was time to test the train and see if it still worked after being tossed around in transport for the past two weeks.

He reached for the locomotive, but before he could place it on the track, there was a knock on the door. "Come in!"

The door opened to reveal a dark-haired man standing there. "Well, well," the man greeted him with a grin, tugging at the brim of the wool cap he wore. "It's been a long time, my friend."

"Michael!" Nathaniel set down the train and maneuvered his way through the maze of his belongings to the door. He thrust out his hand and the other man shook it warmly. "You got my letter? How are you?"

"Well enough, I suppose, although your letter was a bit of a shock." Michael looked around at the chaos of Nathaniel's flat and started laughing. "Ten years and you haven't changed a bit. What is all this?"

"Sorry about the mess, but I'm moving in, you know." He waved a hand vaguely to the hammering going on above their head. "I've got some workmen remodeling the attic for me."

A loud bang interrupted any reply Michael might have made, and chunks of plaster fell through the hole in the ceiling, forming a cloud of dust as they hit the floor.

Michael took another glance around and caught sight of the train on the table. "What is this?" he asked, stepping over a crate on the floor to get a closer look.

"That is what I asked you to come and see me about," Nathaniel said, coming up to stand beside him.

Michael picked up a piece of railroad track and whistled. "Sectional track?" he asked. "And a figure-eight design? You've made one that works?"

Nathaniel caught the rising excitement in Michael's voice, and he nodded. "Yes. It's taken me three years, but damn it all, it works!"

Michael bent down and studied the track at eye level. "How smooth does she run?"

"Like silk, Michael. Pure silk. But that's not all."

Nathaniel bent down and rummaged in the huge crate beside him, pulling out brightly painted tin miniatures, setting them on the table as he identified them. "Train stations, street lamps, bridges, crossings, town buildings. Michael, I'm talking about complete railway systems!"

Michael picked up one of the prototype train stations to examine it more closely, listening as Nathaniel went on,

"Sectional track makes it possible, and the possibilities are endless."

Michael nodded and looked up, his dark eyes sparkling with excitement. "You market the trains as sets, of course."

"Yes, and sell all the additional accessories by the piece. Can you imagine the profit potential?"

"Tremendous." Michael set down the miniature train station and circled the table to the opposite side. "Let's see her run."

Nathaniel placed the electric locomotive on the track, but before he could attach the dry-cell batteries, Mr. Boggs came up to stand beside him.

"The 'ole to the attic's all done," he told Nathaniel, pulling off his cap to wipe the sweat from his brow. "We put in that ladder you wanted, too."

"Excellent." Nathaniel reached for the wires hooked to the battery and attached them to the track. The motor hummed, but the train didn't move.

Michael grinned at him across the table. "Some invention."

Nathaniel was unperturbed by the teasing. "Do you want me to remind you of all the brilliant ideas you've had that didn't work?"

"Please don't."

The workman interrupted again. "We've swept up the plaster, sir."

"Thank you, Mr. Boggs," Nathaniel murmured. He leaned over the table and studied the locomotive. "It's got to be the motor," he said. "Something's probably been jarred in transit."

"Guv'nor?" Boggs waited a few moments, but Nathaniel continued to stare at his unmoving train, and the workman gave a slight cough. "Well, if that's all, sir, me an' me boy will be goin' now. If you could pay us, sir?"

Nathaniel paid no attention until Michael leaned

over the table and snapped his fingers in front of his face.

"Nathaniel, I believe your workmen would like to get paid."

"Oh." Nathaniel straightened and glanced at Boggs, realizing that the man was still standing beside him. Boggs glanced down at the table, eyeing the train with some skepticism before giving Nathaniel an apologetic smile.

"It's getting late, sir. If you'll just pay us, we'll be on our way."

"Of course." Nathaniel unhooked the batteries from the track. "See if you can figure it out," he told Michael. "I'll be right back."

The other man nodded. "I'll check your motor."

Nathaniel pulled off his spectacles and set them on the table, then crossed the room and looked up at the square hole in his ceiling. He gripped the ladder bolted to the wall and climbed into the attic. By the light of the hurricane lamp the workman had left burning, he took a look around.

Once the rest of his furniture was shipped from San Francisco, he'd have to find another place to store it because even with the attic, he still wouldn't have enough room. But for storing some of the equipment he'd brought with him, this would do nicely. "Perfect!" he shouted down to Boggs. "Now I have plenty of room."

He descended the ladder, lamp in hand, and made his way to his desk. Setting down the lamp, he began to rummage through the papers, books, and other odd items strewn over his desk. "Just what I wanted, Mr. Boggs. You've done a splendid job. You, too, Alfred," he added to Boggs's fourteen-year-old son, who stood silently nearby.

Boggs twisted the cap in his hands and bobbed his head in an almost embarrassed acknowledgment of the praise. "Thank ye, guv'nor."

Nathaniel pushed aside a tinplate carousel and a windup toy dog and continued to delve through the pile on his desk. "Now where did I put it?"

Two books slid off the edge and hit the floor, but Nathaniel paid no heed. He opened drawers one by one, pulling out items as he searched. He knew he'd taken his wallet out of his jacket the day before and put it somewhere near his desk, but he couldn't remember quite where. A white silk cravat, a toy steam engine, and his favorite shaving brush were all tossed aside before he gave an exclamation of triumph.

"There it is!" He pulled out his wallet and began to count out money for Boggs. "I believe two pounds and ten was the fee we agreed on?"

"Yes, sir."

Nathaniel placed the money in the workman's hand. He then tossed the wallet onto a nearby shelf where it landed between the music box with the dancing clowns on top and his beloved Stradivarius violin.

Boggs and his son departed. Nathaniel pulled two bottles of beer and a tin of sweet biscuits from the crate of supplies Mrs. O'Brien had purchased for him. He walked back over to the table with the refreshments and placed a beer on the table beside Michael, who held the toy out to him. "It is the motor. Drive belt slipped off, and I can't quite reach it."

Nathaniel set down his beer and the tin of biscuits and took the locomotive from Michael. Holding it beneath the light of the lamp on the table, he peered at the electric motor inside. He tried to slip the belt back into place, but he couldn't reach it either. "I hate to disassemble it for such a minor problem."

Michael shrugged and took a swallow of beer. "Forget it. Show it to me some other day." He went across the room to the sofa and chairs by the fireplace, pushed a rumpled newspaper off one of the chairs, and sat down. "You haven't changed much, although you've lost your stutter, I noticed."

"Ten years of practice. Without Adrian around, it was easier to conquer it." Nathaniel smiled slightly. "But it still plagues me from time to time."

"What brings you back to England?"

"I'm going to make toys again," he said, following Michael across the room and taking a seat on the sofa.

"What?"

Nathaniel nodded. He set down his beer, grabbed a handful of biscuits, and leaned back. "The train is too good an idea to sell to somebody else. I want to manufacture it myself."

Michael pulled a biscuit from the tin. "In your last letter to me you said your toy company in St. Louis failed," he reminded gently. "Are you sure you want to try again?"

"Yes," Nathaniel answered without hesitation. "I'm buying into the electrical equipment factory right next door. I'm going to make the train."

"Is your brother putting up the money? I can't believe Adrian would agree to back you!"

Nathaniel grinned. "I haven't asked him."

Michael stared at him. "Then where are you going to get the money? I thought you'd lost everything."

"I sold the patents on about half my inventions to raise capital. I'm forming a partnership with the owner of the factory next door. Man named James Elliot. I met him in San Francisco a few months ago. He'd heard about me, and he came to see me. He told me he was interested in making some of my inventions, and he proposed a partnership. That's why I came back to England."

"Adrian isn't involved in this?"

"God, no! Why would I want to be partners with Adrian again? With the hell I went through after Father died, you think I'd ask Adrian for help?"

"Wait!" Michael held up one hand. "Do you mean to tell me you're going into direct competition against your brother?"

Nathaniel laughed. "I'm afraid so."

"He'll be furious when he finds out what you're up to."

"Yes, I know." Nathaniel leaned back in his seat and clasped his hands behind his head, giving Michael a wicked grin. "It'll be good for him."

"I always knew you were crazy."

"Not that crazy. I want you to come and work for me."

"What?" Michael's smile faded. He tugged at his cap and took a deep breath. "Nathaniel, I already have a job."

"Yes, I know." He made a sound of contempt. "Tailoring. You're not a tailor, Michael. You're an engineer. The best damned toy engineer in the business. I need you."

Michael shook his head. "I can't, Nathaniel. I can't risk what I have for some new venture. Not even one of yours."

"Is it because the last time I tried, I went bankrupt?"

"Of course not! I've always believed in your ideas."

"Why then? I'm not asking you to put up any money."

"I'm engaged to be married."

"You are?" Startled, Nathaniel stared at him.

Michael nodded. "Her name is Rebecca Goldman and I work for her father. He's done a lot for me, and he pays me a decent salary. I'm hoping to have enough put by to get married next year. I have a future with Goldman's."

"Do you like being a tailor?"

"Of course not. What does that have to do with it?"

"It has everything to do with it. Michael, listen to me." He leaned forward. "If you don't do this, if you don't try now, then you'll stay a tailor for the rest of your life. You'll get married, you'll have children, and one day you'll wake up an old man, and you'll know you spent your whole life doing something you never wanted to do."

"Nathaniel—"

"Do you think the train will sell?"

"Are you joking? Of course it will." He grinned. "Provided you get the thing working."

"Then what's the problem? I'll pay you ten pounds a week."

Michael laughed, but he didn't sound amused. "You make it tempting."

"That's because it's so much fun."

Michael drew a deep breath and let it out slowly. "It'd be just like the old days at Chase before your father died and Adrian took over."

"Better." Nathaniel took a swallow of beer. "I'll have the controlling interest in this partnership. Fifty-one percent." He paused, then added, "I'm truly sorry Adrian fired you."

"There was nothing you could've done. It's not your fault your brother is a Jew-hater," he said with a hint of bitterness. "Stop apologizing."

"I can't help it. I brought you into Chase. I wish I could have done something to stop him."

"Forget it. How's your new partner feel about making me your engineer?"

"He doesn't care about you being Jewish, if that's

what you mean. When he proposed this deal to me, I knew immediately I wanted you for my engineer. We discussed it, and he agreed. There's no problem."

"When do I get to meet this partner of yours?"

"He's not back in England yet, and there's no word yet on when he'll arrive. I'm meeting with his wife tomorrow to show her the train." Nathaniel took another swallow of beer. "He's been in America for quite some time, and it's my understanding she's in charge until he returns. Converting this factory is going be a lot of work. I'm hoping we can start immediately."

Michael nodded. "It's July. We'll need all the time we can get if we're going to get trains out by the Christmas season."

"We? Are you going to come work for me?"

"I can't. I just can't." Michael looked at Nathaniel and groaned, in an agony of indecision. "I hate being a tailor. And I have to admit, getting back at Adrian would be rather fun."

"Well, then?"

Michael raised his bottle of beer in a gesture of surrender. "All right!" he said, laughing. "I'll do it."

"You won't regret it," Nathaniel promised him.

"I may not live long enough to regret it. Rebecca might kill me."

"If she loves you, she'll stand by you."

"Sure she will. Pigs fly, too." He set down his beer. "If you're going to show that woman the train tomorrow, we'd better get it running."

The two men set to work. They tried using a screwdriver to pull the belt back into place, but that was unsuccessful. "What we need is something with a hook on the end," Michael told him.

Nathaniel set down the train and the two men began to search the flat, looking for a tool that might work.

Half an hour later, they stood in the center of the room, the contents of several crates scattered about their feet.

"I don't believe this," Michael muttered. "The most brilliant inventor I know doesn't have a tool with a hook on the end. What about a buttonhook?"

Nathaniel raked a hand through his hair. He didn't own a buttonhook. Suddenly, an idea struck him, and he snapped his fingers. "Wait here. I'll be right back."

Nathaniel picked up the hurricane lamp from his desk, strode out of the room, and descended the stairs, coming to a halt before the door on the landing. He reached out to knock but hesitated, his hand poised in midair. Her lock was broken, he remembered. He didn't want the door to swing open and embarrass the poor girl. He knocked on the wall beside the door instead.

What was her name? Mara, that was it. Mara with the bitterness in her eyes. He waited a moment, but when his knock received no response, he tried again, a bit louder this time.

He heard a slight sound within and the door opened several inches. A pair of gray eyes peered at him through the opening, eyes that widened at the sight of him.

"Have you a buttonhook?"

"I beg your pardon?" she asked in a husky voice. She shook her head as if she didn't understand. The long braid of her dark hair moved slightly against the white of her gown.

"A buttonhook."

She continued to stare at him in confusion, and he wondered if she had quite taken in his words.

He looked down and saw her bare toes curl beneath the hem of her gown, a gown of white flannel. A nightgown. "I'm sorry," he said contritely, returning his gaze to her face. "Were you asleep?"

"Most people are at this hour." Her voice had lost

its soft, husky note and was now sharp and definitely irritated.

"Is it so very late?" He gave her a smile meant to be charming, but the irritation in her expression did not soften. "I'm afraid I don't often keep track of the time."

"That does not surprise me, sir."

"Terribly sorry, but it's rather important that I get hold of a buttonhook. We're trying to get my train fixed, you see, because I have a very important meeting in the morning, and it could be quite awkward if the train doesn't work. And it won't work unless I can find a buttonhook. And I can't very well go out and purchase a buttonhook, since it's dark out and the shops are bound to be closed now, so I was hoping—"

Her sigh interrupted him. The door began to close, and he was afraid she was going to slam it in his face. But all she did was murmur, "Wait here," before closing the door.

Several moments later, the door opened again and a buttonhook was thrust toward him. "Here."

"Thank you," he said, reaching out to take it from her. "I appreciate . . ." His voice trailed off as he caught sight of the small hand holding out the buttonhook, and in the light of the lamp he held, he saw the scars that marred her skin. Burns.

He took the thin bit of steel from her fingers, and she snatched her hand back, hiding it in the folds of her nightgown.

"Please go."

"Of course." He lifted his gaze again to her face, a proud face, a face of sharply drawn cheekbones and delicately arched brows, a face of soft skin and hard experience. He looked into her eyes and found them as gray and impenetrable as a London fog. "I will return this to you in the morning."

The door closed between them, but Nathaniel remained standing there for a long, thoughtful moment, wondering what had happened to her, wondering what had put scars on her hands and a bitter sadness in her eyes.

Most of all, he wondered what had destroyed the dreams in her heart.

3

The news came as a complete surprise, and Adrian Chase did not like surprises. As a boy, he'd hated unwrapping his Christmas presents because the gifts were always a disappointment. As a man, he hated hearing unexpected news because it was usually unfavorable.

He pushed his breakfast aside and gave his secretary a hard stare across one corner of the huge dining table. "Are you certain?"

The stare made Charles Barrett shift uncomfortably in his chair. "Yes, sir." He pulled a letter from the dispatch case on his lap and handed it to his employer. "This came in the post yesterday afternoon."

"You received this letter yesterday?" Charles nodded, and Adrian's voice softened to a less dangerous level when he added, "Why did you not inform me at the time?"

Charles flushed. "I was unable to locate you."

"Mr. Barrett, I realize that you have been my secretary for only two days. Nonetheless, I expect you to make yourself informed of my schedule."

"Yes, sir."

"After our morning meeting here," Adrian continued, "I play squash racquets at my athletic gymnasium from nine until eleven. I then conduct business at the factory until one. I lunch at my club and attend to appointments in the afternoon. After tea, I can be reached here, unless my social obligations carry over into the evening. When there is important news, you will not wait until our meeting the following morning, but bring it to me immediately."

"I will remember that, sir."

"See that you do. And remember, Mr. Barrett, any information that concerns my brother is important news."

The secretary nodded, and Adrian took the single sheet of paper from his hand. He scanned the few lines written there. As he read, his frown deepened, and his displeasure increased. He folded the letter and leaned back in his chair. "So," Adrian murmured, "my bothersome little brother has disappeared. I don't like it, Barrett."

No reply was expected, and Charles made none. He simply waited.

"Where?" Adrian methodically began to consider possible explanations, but with information as scanty as this, there was no way to tell. Nathaniel's absurd notions might have taken him anywhere. Adrian crumpled the note in his fist and straightened in his chair. There was only one course of action.

"Barrett, I want you to telegraph Foster immediately. I want to know exactly where my brother has gone, and what he's doing. Remind Foster that I pay him very well to keep an eye on Nathaniel, and it's time he earned it."

"Yes, sir." Charles placed the crumpled letter in his case, rose to his feet, and departed.

The servants came to clear away the breakfast dishes, but Adrian waved them out of the room and remained seated. He stared at the cold toast on his plate and wondered what Nathaniel was up to now.

Something troublesome, he was certain. When they were children, Nathaniel had been like a fly buzzing about. Never a serious threat to his own plans, just a bloody inconvenience. But then Grandfather had died, and their father had been forced to give Nathaniel a place in the company. Nathaniel, who couldn't string three complete sentences together without garbling them. Nathaniel, who had no idea how a business ought to be run.

The little bastard had gotten ambitious, though. He'd wormed his way into their grandfather's good graces before Adrian had realized the threat. Then he'd used the same strategy on their father.

Adrian remembered watching in helpless fury as his idiotic little brother became the center of attention at Chase Toys. Everyone at the company had started turning to him for instructions and guidance when their father was unavailable, even though Adrian had been the one trained since childhood to take over the company. It had been torture.

When their father had died, he'd actually left Nathaniel forty-nine percent of Chase Toys, making the two brothers partners in the firm and giving Adrian the shock of his life. Nearly half of what he'd spent his life working for had been stolen from him.

But he'd gotten it back, and he'd sent his little brother packing, ensuring that he would never threaten his position again. When Nathaniel had the gall to start a toy company of his own in St. Louis, he had taken care of that threat, too.

Adrian smiled grimly. Whatever Nathaniel was up to this time, Adrian knew he'd be able to handle it. He'd squelched his little brother's ambitions twice before, and he would again if he had to.

Mara did not sleep well that night. Having been wakened in the night by a man who didn't know the first thing about good manners, she'd been unable to go back to sleep for the longest time. Then, when she'd finally drifted off again, she'd been plagued by dreams of Elliot's on the auction block, with her husband mouthing cheery platitudes and her bizarre new neighbor quoting Tennyson as everything was carted away. She awoke feeling gloomy and cross.

She'd spent all of yesterday afternoon calling on other bankers, hoping she could find one willing to take over the loan, but that had proved futile. A business run by a woman was not, it seemed, a wise investment.

It was so unfair, she thought as she walked to the washstand and began her morning bath. James had been the most irresponsible man, but he'd never had trouble financing even the most ridiculous ventures. She, on the other hand, was extremely responsible, but she couldn't get a simple business loan.

She picked up a towel and dried off, then pulled undergarments out of the armoire and began to dress. She had only two days left, and she was running out of options. Tomorrow, at five o'clock, she had to give the bank five thousand pounds. She had to find an investor. There was no other way.

She thrust her arms into the sleeves of a white shirtwaist and fastened the buttons, then pulled a black skirt out of the armoire. By refusing to swath herself all in black, she knew she was flouting convention, but she didn't care. She had neither the money nor the inclination to buy mourning clothes. This would have to do.

She slipped a length of black ribbon around her neck beneath her collar and tied it into a bow at her throat, then her hands stilled as she became suddenly aware of music. It sounded like the melody of a calliope. She walked to her window and leaned out to look up at the open window above her own. The music was coming from Mr. Chase's rooms.

She pulled back inside, but an even more curious sound had her glancing up at the ceiling. Along with the music, she could now hear a faint, but definite tapping. She shook her head in puzzlement as she sat down on the edge of her bed. Then she reached for her shoes, remembering only after she had put them on that she had no buttonhook.

With a sigh, she bent down and began to button her shoes by hand. It wasn't surprising, she supposed, that he had forgotten his promise to return her buttonhook first thing in the morning. The man couldn't even tell time.

By the time she finished buttoning her shoes, the curious sounds from upstairs had somehow multiplied into a discordant combination of music, tapping, whirring, and clicking. What on earth was going on up there?

She unbraided her hair, brushed it out, and coiled it into her usual simple chignon. She donned her bonnet and reached for a pair of black kid gloves. After pulling them on, she marched upstairs to retrieve her property.

She remembered how he had stood outside her door the night before, rambling on about trains and important meetings. She thought of his rumpled clothes and dreamy blue eyes. As if that man would have important meetings. And what her buttonhook had to do with it all, she couldn't begin to fathom.

The door at the top of the stairs was open, and the strange barrage of sounds coming from within the room increased in volume as she drew closer. She crossed the landing and halted in the doorway. Her eyes widened in astonishment as she stared into the strangest room she had ever seen.

Everything seemed to be moving. She blinked three times, wondering if she were dreaming, but each time she opened her eyes, swirling colors and dancing objects dazzled her, and suddenly she realized what she was seeing.

The room was filled with toys. A clown on a music box danced in time to the melody of a calliope. A puppet on a string winked and waved at her. Drummer boys drummed, carousels turned, and acrobats tumbled.

Toys rested atop stacks of unopened wooden crates, steamer trunks, and furniture. They were scattered across the floor and piled in the corners among countless books, loose papers, and machinery. To her left stood a table where a toy train moved around an elaborate track surrounded by tiny buildings.

A narrow path cut through the clutter from the door to an empty space in the center of the room, where her bizarre neighbor sat cross-legged on the floor. All around him, tops spun, little tin-plated animals scurried to and fro, and trains moved across the floor. A tall wooden statue of an American Indian stood nearby, presiding over the chaos in dignified contemplation.

Toys? She wouldn't have believed it of a grown man,

but she was seeing it with her own eyes. A grown man playing with toys.

In his hands was a little tin-plated dog, and he seemed to be winding a knob in its side. Speechless, she watched as he set the dog on the floor and released it. The animal immediately began moving, wagging its tail as it headed straight toward her. It hit the toe of her shoe and came to a halt, unable to go any farther.

She lifted her gaze from the toy dog to the man seated on the floor. He looked up at her over the gold rims of his spectacles and smiled. "Hullo," he greeted in a voice loud enough to carry over the din.

He pulled off his spectacles and gestured to the dog at her feet. "Terribly sorry," he shouted to her, "but you're in the way. Would you mind moving your foot?"

She frowned in puzzlement, uncertain she had heard correctly. "I beg your pardon?" she called back.

"I want the dog to go out the door, and I'm afraid you're in the way." He turned and set the spectacles on a crate behind him. "So, if you wouldn't mind stepping aside?"

Mara glanced over her shoulder. "But it will go down the stairs."

"Exactly."

She knew it. The man was crazy, nutty as a Christmas fruitcake. She stepped over the dog and turned, watching through the doorway as it crossed the landing, reached the first step, and went tumbling down.

Mr. Chase went past her and down the stairs to retrieve the toy. He came back, holding the tin-plated animal in his hand. "That's the fifth time," he declared as he halted several feet from her. He set the dog on the floor, sending it off in a different direction. "And it's still running. Clockwork mechanisms are usually much more fragile."

She turned her head and watched the dog dubiously for a moment, as it ran between the legs of a large telescope standing nearby and disappeared.

She couldn't think of anything to say. Just how did one talk to a lunatic? She cleared her throat and looked up to find that he had moved closer. He was standing only a foot or two away, watching her, utterly still amid the motion surrounding them.

The morning sun through the windows caught the brown of his hair, turning it to burnished gold and gilding the tips of his thick lashes. His vivid blue eyes held hers with that look of perception she'd seen once before, as if he knew exactly what she was thinking. It was most disconcerting.

"I want my buttonhook," she blurted out.

A frown crossed his handsome face, and he slapped a hand to his forehead. "I forgot to return it to you, didn't I? Terribly sorry."

He moved past her and walked to the desk, navigating his way around the toys still moving across the floor. Then he began to search amid the mess. "It proved to be very useful." He waved a hand vaguely toward the locomotive on the table. "As you can see, my train is working now. Thank you."

"You're welcome," she replied in an ungracious tone, ignoring the warm smile he gave her.

"Meant to return it first thing, but I got distracted." He lifted his head and paused in his search. "Trying to decide which toys are worth making. My meeting, you know. We won't be able to make them all, more's the pity."

"I see." Mara didn't see at all. She felt a bit like Alice in the Lewis Carroll story. She wondered if Mr. Chase owned a rabbit.

He seemed to sense her confusion. A smile lifted the corners of his mouth as he looked at her. "Though this be madness, yet there is method in it." His smile widened at her skeptical expression. "Hamlet," he added and resumed his search.

He looked for several moments more but couldn't seem to find it, a fact which did not surprise Mara at all. He turned around, facing the bookshelf beside the window and began to rummage through the books and toys piled there.

"Ah, here it is!" he exclaimed, pulling the tool off one of the shelves. "I knew I'd put it over here somewhere."

Just then something out the window caught his attention. He stepped closer and looked down into the alley below. Before she could even begin to wonder what he was watching with such fascination, he turned back around and walked past her, thrusting the buttonhook into her hand as he headed for the door. "Thank you again," he said absently. "I have to go out for a moment, but I'll be back. You're welcome to stay if you like."

He walked out of the room, leaving Mara standing there alone, dumbfounded by his abrupt exit. She walked to the window and looked down. She saw nothing but the empty alley below.

"Nutty as a fruitcake," she muttered. She took one more glance around the untidy room before following him out the door, but he had disappeared. She went down the stairs to her own flat, wondering again who would agree to have a meeting with a man who was touched in the head.

She put her buttonhook back in the drawer where it belonged, then made her usual breakfast of tea and toast. As she ate, she wondered if whoever was meeting with her strange neighbor had any idea what he was getting into.

*   *   *

When Nathaniel reached the alley, it was empty. The boys were gone. Leaning his back against the brick wall of Mrs. O'Brien's lodging house, he closed his eyes. "Damn."

He'd seen them through the window, half a dozen of them, surrounding a younger, much smaller boy, and he'd known instantly what was happening.

Laughter rang in his ears, taunting, childish laughter from long ago. His eighth birthday.

"G . . . g . . . give it b . . . b . . . back! It's m . . . mine." He could see himself watching in frustration and rage as a group of older boys, his brother among them, played catch with his birthday gift. They tossed the wooden locomotive from hand to hand, keeping it just out of his reach.

"M . . . mine," Adrian had mimicked him, making all the other boys laugh. They had eventually tired of tormenting him. Adrian had smashed the toy against a rock, and the boys had wandered off. Nathaniel could still remember picking up the broken pieces of his birthday present.

Opening his eyes, he pushed away thoughts of his past. He walked to the other end of the alley and glanced up and down the street, but he could find no trace of the child whom he'd seen the other boys tease so mercilessly.

He left the alley and returned upstairs to find that Mara had gone. He wasn't surprised. From her manner he could tell that she thought him rather bizarre, but he had long ago ceased to care what other people thought of him.

He looked down at the toys on the floor, their motion stilled now. Unbuttoning the cuffs of his shirt, he rolled up his sleeves and put thoughts of his melancholy neighbor and the tormented little boy out of his mind. He still had work to do if wanted to be ready for his meeting with Mrs. Elliot.

*   *   *

But it seemed that all his work had been for naught. Three hours later, Nathaniel stood in front of Elliot Electrical Motors and stared in disbelief at the neatly lettered sign tacked to the locked front door.

"With the utmost sadness, we announce the death of our founder, James Samuel Elliot," he read aloud. "In memory, Elliot Electrical will be closed for this 11th day of July 1889. Business will resume July 12. Direct all inquiries to Mr. Henry Finch, Solicitor, Bloomsbury. A service will be held at nine o'clock this morning, St. Andrew's Church, Houndsditch."

Nine o'clock. It was certain to be over by now. Nathaniel stared at the sign, thinking with sorrow of the man he'd met in San Francisco.

James had seen the potential in Nathaniel's ideas at the point in his life when Nathaniel himself had doubted them most. He'd been hiding from the world ever since his toy company in St. Louis had gone bankrupt, working on inventions and selling them to others, convinced all his dreams were lost to him, when James had first come to see him.

James had believed in him and had brought him out of the dark hole of despair he'd fallen into, a debt he would now never have the chance to repay. James had convinced him to hold on to his dream, to try once more to achieve it. Now, staring at the sign and the black wreath that hung below it, Nathaniel felt the doubts and the despair return, the frustration of dreams once again out of his grasp.

What the hell was he going to do now? There was nothing in writing. The two men had formed a partnership based on nothing more than a gentlemen's agreement and a handshake. No one at Elliot's seemed to know who he was or why he was there. Nathaniel wasn't sure what his legal position was in all this, but he figured it wasn't a very strong one.

He stared at the sign. There was only one way to find out. It was time to pay a visit to James's solicitor.

4

Mara was bone-weary. She had gone to the memorial service with Mr. Finch and Percy that morning, expecting them to be the only ones there. But several dozen people had attended, many of them employees of Elliot's.

When it was over, they had crowded around her to express their sympathy and tell her their stories of what James Elliot had done for them. Mara couldn't fathom how a man who never stayed in one place long enough to make friends could have so many.

After the service, she'd spent the rest of the day meeting with potential investors. But her efforts had been in vain. Men with money to invest were not enthusiastic about having a female partner.

As twilight descended, she trudged home through the narrow, twisted streets of Whitechapel, tired, discouraged, and even frightened. She had one day left, and she was out of options. The bank would take the company, and she would have nothing but the twelve pounds and six in her little tin bank.

Mara passed an abandoned warehouse, and she paused to glance at the boarded-up windows and the "For Sale" sign on the door, fully aware that Elliot's would soon look much the same. A cackle of laughter caused her to glance down, and she saw a thin, disheveled figure huddled amid the trash in the shadowy doorway. She froze, unable to tear her gaze away from the empty, hopeless stare of the old woman sitting there.

"'ave ye tuppence for me, dearie?"

Mara's heart twisted with compassion. She fumbled in her pocket and pulled out a sixpence, more than the woman had asked for, enough for a night's lodging. She stepped forward and thrust the coin into the gnarled hand reaching up to her. "Get yourself a room, ma'am."

"Room?" The woman clutched the coin to her breast and shook her head fretfully. "No, no, I'm going t'feed the pigeons." She laughed again. "Tuppence for the pigeons, dearie."

Mara shivered and quickly walked away, but the vision haunted her all the way home. *Tuppence for the bank, Mara. Tuppence for the pigeons, dearie.* Tuppence was never enough. Her future had never looked more bleak.

She arrived at her lodging house. By the light of the street lamp, she could see the gray kitten she'd first noticed two days before. It was sitting on the front stoop. It hissed at her as she approached.

"Scat!" she ordered, waving a hand to urge the kitten away. It jumped back, but it did not run. Instead, it backed up into a corner by the door and watched as she mounted the steps and stepped inside her lodging house.

She closed the door behind her and climbed the stairs to her room, knowing it was time she faced facts. She was going to lose the company. The bankers were not going to change their minds, she was not going to find investors. No guardian angel was going to appear and save her from poverty.

She reached the landing and turned toward her room, then halted in surprise at the sight before her. Her neighbor from upstairs was kneeling in front of her door, a screwdriver in his hand. Beside him stood her solicitor, Mr. Finch, holding a lamp to light the dim landing.

"Use your free hand to hold the latch in place while I insert the screws," the former instructed, and Mara watched in astonishment as the dignified Mr. Finch knelt on the floor beside Mr. Chase. The two men remained there for several moments, then rose to their feet.

Mr. Chase must have sensed her presence for he suddenly turned and glanced in her direction. Looking at her over the rims of his spectacles, he smiled. "We've fixed it," he announced proudly and stepped back so that she could see the shiny new brass handle that now graced her door.

"You should have strong locks if you insist upon living in this area of town, my dear," Finch chided her as he crossed the landing to hand her a key.

Mara took it from him automatically. She couldn't think of a thing to say. She glanced from one man to the other, completely baffled.

"We've been waiting for you," Mr. Chase said. "Thought we'd pass the time putting a new latch on your door. Haversham's Hardware is just up the street, you know."

"Thank you." Mara shook her head, still trying to sort things out. "You've been waiting for me?"

"Mr. Chase came to see me today," Finch told her. He glanced at the other man. "Perhaps we should go upstairs?"

"Excellent idea." Mr. Chase lifted his spectacles to place them atop his head, then took the lamp from Finch, turned, and started up the stairs.

Mr. Finch held out his arm to her. "Mr. Chase and I have been discussing a business proposal," he explained. "Given your situation with the bank, it might be of interest to you."

Her problems with the bank aside, Mara couldn't fathom what sort of business proposal her bizarre neighbor might have that could possibly interest her, but she put her arm through the solicitor's, and they followed Mr. Chase.

When Mara stepped through the door into his rooms, she noticed that many of the crates had disappeared, but the steamer trunks were still where they had been that morning, and his belongings were still scattered everywhere. She was relieved to note that none of his toys were whirring or spinning.

Glancing at Mr. Chase, she wondered how anyone could live in such disarray. His eyes were amused as they met hers, as if he were fully aware of her disapproval and didn't care a whit. Gesturing to the sofa and chairs to Mara's right, he added, "Shall we sit down?"

He removed papers, various toys, and other gadgets from the leather sofa, clearing space for his guests to sit. He turned to the fireplace and dumped the armful of items he'd gathered into the empty coal bin. "I'd offer you tea, but I'm afraid I've none here. As you can see, I'm still moving in."

Mara took a seat on the leather sofa and privately thought it wouldn't matter how long Mr. Chase lived in these rooms. They would never be tidy. Mr. Finch sat

beside her and Mr. Chase took the chair directly opposite. He placed his spectacles on the low mahogany table
that lay between them, then looked at her. Silent, he
studied her for a long moment.

Mara tapped her foot against the floor, uncomfortable
with the scrutiny. Why did he have to stare at her as if he
wanted to read what was in her soul? "Perhaps you
should tell me why we're here," she suggested with a
hint of impatience. "You have a business proposal that
might interest me?"

"I was very sorry to hear about your husband,"
Nathaniel said unexpectedly. "I knew him, you see."

"What?" Mara was startled as much by the change of
subject as by the surprising news that he'd known
James. Not so surprising, she amended to herself. Her
husband had known many strange people.

He nodded, and one unruly lock of hair fell over his
forehead. He brushed it back with an impatient gesture
and went on, "I didn't know you were his wife, of
course, until I went to see Mr. Finch. I explained to him
why I was here in London, and he suggested that we
come and see you. Of course, I had an appointment
with you—although I didn't know it was you—for
eleven o'clock this morning, but when I got there
everything was closed, and I realized James was dead,
and I went to see Mr. Finch. That's what it said on the
sign, you know." He paused for breath. "So, here we
are, you see."

Mara didn't see at all. She felt hopelessly fogged,
but she concluded that nothing this man said ever
made any sense anyway. She decided it might be best
to start over. "You said you knew my husband?"

Mr. Chase nodded and looked over her head, staring
into space for several moments without speaking. "'He
was a man, take him for all and all,'" he murmured,

breaking the silence. "'I shall not look upon his like again.'" He glanced at her. "Hamlet. Shakespeare, you know."

Mara spoke to forestall any more quotations from Shakespeare. "Where did you meet?" she asked, praying Mr. Chase would eventually say something important.

"We met in San Francisco several months ago. I'd been living there for some time, and James came to see me. He'd heard about me and was interested in seeing some of my inventions." He paused and gave her a quizzical glance. "You did know I was an inventor, didn't you?"

"Yes, yes," she said, wondering if he was ever going to get to the point. "You told me. Go on."

"Well, James was very excited about my ideas. He wanted to manufacture some of them, and we decided to form a partnership. Pool our resources. We arranged to meet in London around the tenth of July. And, so, here I am."

Mara wanted to scream. "What exactly is your proposal, Mr. Chase?"

"Mara—"

"Mrs. Elliot, if you please," she said.

Her emphasis on propriety seemed to amuse him. A slow smile lifted the corners of his mouth and crinkled the corners of his eyes. "Mrs. Elliot," he said in a voice so low and intimate he might just as well have used her Christian name, "it seems only right that we carry on with the plan. I propose that we form a partnership."

"A partnership? You and I?" Mara nearly laughed aloud. Her gaze traveled down the length of him, noting his untidy hair and the wrinkles in his white shirt. "You must be joking."

"I never joke about my work."

"Neither do I," she assured him. "The answer is no."

"Mara, there's no reason to be hasty," Mr. Finch interjected, speaking for the first time. "Perhaps you should at least listen."

"Really, Mr. Finch! I don't think—"

"As I said earlier, Mr. Chase may have a solution to your problem," the solicitor reminded her gently. "You have very few options, my dear."

The solicitor was right, although Mara didn't like being reminded of the dire situation in front of Mr. Chase. "Very well," she said to the man across the table. "I'm listening."

He leaned forward. "It's quite simple, really. I wish to buy a portion of Elliot Electrical."

Mara could scarcely believe that this man had enough money to solve her problem, but she refrained from saying so. She lifted one brow and asked the vital question. "How large a portion, and how much are you willing to pay?"

"I'll pay off Elliot's debt to Joslyn Brothers—it comes to approximately five thousand pounds, I believe—in exchange for fifty-one percent of the company."

"Fifty-one percent!" Mara straightened with a jerk. "Absolutely not."

He smiled. "I believe the company's net worth is less than ten thousand pounds. Therefore, my offer is a fair one. You won't get a better deal from anyone else, and your time is running out. The bank intends to foreclose on the loan tomorrow, do they not?"

She turned to give Mr. Finch a hard, accusing stare.

The solicitor gave her a helpless shrug in response. "I knew Mr. Chase was serious about investing," he said. "A potential investor has the right to know what the situation is."

She could have killed Finch for taking away any

power she might have had to bargain, but she decided to try anyway. She turned back to Mr. Chase and took a deep breath. "Forty-nine."

She watched his expression harden into stubborn lines. For the first time, she wondered if there might not be a shrewd intelligence behind those baby blue eyes. When he spoke, his voice was low and quietly firm. "If I'm going to bail this company out of the mess it's in with five thousand pounds of my money, I must have the controlling interest."

"Mess?" The word caused her spine to stiffen.

"Mess, Mrs. Elliot." He slanted a look at her from beneath his lashes, a look that dared her to contradict. "Fifty-one percent."

Her lips pressed together, and there was a long moment of silence as their gazes locked in combat. All her instincts told her this man had absolutely no business sense, that he was, in fact, crazy. But she knew she had no options, and the man sitting across from her knew it, too.

Mr. Finch gave a slight cough, breaking the silence. "I took the liberty of drawing up a partnership agreement." He reached into the dispatch case beside him and pulled out a document.

Mara looked from one man to the other, feeling as if she had been outmanned, outgunned, and definitely out-maneuvered. Here was a way to save the company, but it was hardly the ideal solution. She wanted to know more.

"Why would you want to buy only fifty-one percent?" she asked. "If you know about the foreclosure, you must also know that the bank will sell the company. You could probably buy the whole lot for not much more than what you're intending to pay now."

"True." He leaned back and stretched out his long legs, casually putting his feet on the table as if it were a footstool. "But it seems only right and just that you be a part of all this. James and I had an agreement, and although he is dead, I owe him a debt of gratitude."

"I don't want anyone's gratitude, sir."

He held up a hand to forestall any further protests from her. "There is more to it than that. I need you, Mrs. Elliot. Mr. Finch informs me that you are quite experienced in financial matters. I need that sort of expertise."

Mara stared at him skeptically for a moment. Every other potential investor she'd spoken with held the opposite point of view, and she found it hard to believe that he was any different. But she could see no trace of deception in the eyes that gazed back at her.

"What is your decision?"

Mara bit her lip, hating the idea of giving up control. She didn't want anyone else to be in charge. Especially him. Indecision gnawed at her.

He was a very odd man.

She had no choice.

He was a poetic fool.

She had no choice.

Her mind spun in desperate circles, looking for any other solution, but she could think of none. Owning forty-nine percent of a company was better than losing it all, she supposed. She sighed, feeling a headache coming on as she gave in to the inevitable. "Where do I sign?"

Mr. Finch handed her the document. As she read it carefully, the solicitor pulled a bottle of ink and a pen from the case and placed them on the table before her. She signed the agreement in her neat, copperplate handwriting beside Mr. Chase's scrawling, unreadable signature, and her insides twisted with dread. She was handing over control of Elliot's to a man she knew nothing about, a man who was very odd, to say the least. The company was safe from the bank, but Mara had the feeling it was in just as much danger from the man seated across from her.

She set the pen on the table, blew on the document to dry the ink, and handed the paper back to Mr. Finch. "What happens now?" she asked.

Mr. Chase reached for the bank book that lay on the table and opened it. "Tomorrow, I'll want to take a complete tour of the factory," he said, picking up the pen. "What is the exact balance owed to Joslyn Brothers?"

"Five thousand twenty five pounds, twelve shillings, and ten pence," she answered. As she said the words, a dull ache began in her heart.

He wrote out a bank draft and handed it to the solicitor. "I've added an extra two hundred pounds to be deposited in Elliot's account. You'll see that everything is handled?"

Mr. Finch took the slip of paper from his hand. "Of course."

"Good. You'll investigate that other matter as well?"

When Finch nodded, Mr. Chase set aside the bank book, and turned back to her. "I'll also want to go over operating procedures with you, Mrs. Elliot."

Mara was too upset to wonder what "other matter" Finch was investigating for Mr. Chase. She rose to her feet.

"We start at eight o'clock," she told her new partner, wanting to escape. Now that this partnership was a reality, the ache in her heart was almost unbearable, and she wanted desperately to leave before his perceptive eyes could see it. "We'll meet in my office."

"Excellent. We can begin modifying production procedures right away."

"Modifying production procedures?" Mara frowned

down at him. "Our system of production doesn't need modification. It works very well as it is."

"I'm sure it does," he answered, "but it won't work at all once we've made changes to the product line. When I was there, I noticed—"

"Wait!" Alarmed, Mara held up one gloved hand to halt his flow of words. "What do you mean? What changes to our product line?"

Mr. Chase lowered his feet to the floor and rose. "Let me show you."

He came around to the sofa and took her by the elbow, pulling her toward the table near the door. As she watched in bewilderment, he fastened a wire to the track of the toy train. The locomotive began to move, gathering speed as it pulled away from the miniature station.

He straightened and walked around to the other side of the table, watching the train move along the track. "See how it takes the curves? Rather marvelous, isn't it?"

Mara folded her arms beneath her breasts, uninterested in his toys. "What changes do you want to make in our product line?"

"You and I are embarking on a grand adventure, Mrs. Elliot." His eyes sparkled with the excitement of a boy as they met hers across the table. "We are going to make dreams come true."

She shook her head impatiently. Did the man always have to speak in riddles? "I don't understand what you're talking about."

"Toys, Mrs. Elliot. We are going to make toys."

Mara stared at him, stupefied. She looked down at the locomotive moving around the miniature track and swallowed hard as the sick feeling of dread returned to settle in her stomach like a stone. She had just signed

over control of Elliot's to a madman. She groaned and
pressed a gloved hand to her aching head. Elliot's was
doomed.

5

Percy looked worried. Mara studied his troubled face, and she couldn't help the tiny, secret satisfaction she felt at his lack of enthusiasm.

"Toys?" he repeated.

She nodded, and he groaned as he fell into the chair opposite her desk.

"I'm afraid so. The man wants to completely change our manufacturing to toys. Trains, mostly."

"But, Mrs. Elliot, we don't know anything about manufacturing toys."

"I know. But Mr. Chase is determined to do this."

"Does he know anything about making toys?"

She thought about the train and all the other gadgets in his flat. "I think so," she answered doubtfully.

Percy straightened in his chair, struck by a sudden realization. "Mr. Chase? He's the man who came to see Mr. Elliot. I made an appointment for you to meet with him. Remember? Yesterday, eleven o'clock."

Mara realized what Mr. Chase had been rambling on about with all his talk of important meetings. She'd been the important meeting he'd mentioned.

"Why didn't you tell me who he really was?"

Percy's question startled her out of her reverie and she gave him a blank look. "What do you mean?"

He gave his mustache another tug. "Chase Toy Company. Owned by Adrian Chase, the Viscount Leyland, if I'm not mistaken. Chase Toys is the largest toy maker in England. Surely you've heard of it."

Mara, who knew little about toys and less about titles, shook her head.

"Chase Toy Company," Percy went on. "Nathaniel Chase. They must be related somehow."

"He's related to a viscount?" Mara thought of his rumpled clothes and disheveled hair. She could hardly credit it.

"If I recall correctly," Percy went on, "the viscount had a brother who ran off to America. It must be at least ten years ago, now, but I don't remember his name. It could have been Nathaniel." He added, "Of course, I might be wrong. It might just be a coincidence."

"I don't care about his background," she said with an impatient shake of her head. "He arranged this meeting to discuss making toys, but I plan to explain to him that what he wants to do just isn't possible."

Percy glanced at the clock. "If he ever gets here. He's late."

Mara wasn't surprised. But as the minutes went by, and Mr. Chase still did not arrive, she began to wonder if something serious had delayed him. He'd probably wandered into the street and walked in front of an omnibus.

When the clock chimed nine, she stopped dictating correspondence to Percy and sent the secretary in search of him. "Find out if he sent word that he was going to be detained," she said. "If not, he lives next door at Mrs. O'Brien's. Find him."

"Yes, ma'am."

Percy departed, and Mara went back to work.

It was only a few minutes before the door opened again and Percy entered her office with the startling pronouncement, "He's already here."

"What?" Mara rose to her feet. "Where?"

"I don't know, but I'm told he's been here for over half an hour, walking around the factory, introducing himself to the employees."

Mara tossed down her pencil. She strode out of the room, past Percy's desk, and into the corridor. "Of all the idiotic things to do," she muttered as she walked down the long hallway. "Call a meeting for eight o'clock and not even bother to let us know he's arrived."

She paused at the entrance to the production floor and scanned the room, then glanced up to the mezzanine. There was no mistaking the tall form standing by the worktables. She started up the stairs. "Keeping us waiting while he introduces himself to the employees. Presumptuous fellow. Couldn't he have waited?"

When she reached the top of the stairs, she came to a halt and glanced down the rows of tables, noticing that the women who were supposed to be assembling parts into motors were not doing so. Instead, they were watching Mr. Chase.

His tawny hair caught the sunlight coming through the windows as he leaned over the table beside Emma Logan, watching her work. He said something to her and smiled. Mara imagined there was a faint intake of feminine breath at the sight of that smile, although she couldn't actually hear any such thing over the roar of machinery below.

Immune to the devastating effects of male charm, Mara strode forward, ready to give him a piece of her mind. She was scowling.

Nathaniel wondered if Mara Elliot ever smiled. He doubted it. He watched her approach, and he noticed that as she came toward him all the women at the tables instantly resumed their work with industrious zeal. Their smiles disappeared, and their laughter faded away.

She came to a halt by the table and placed her hands on her hips. "Mr. Chase, when you demand a meeting for eight o'clock, you might at least have the courtesy to be there for it."

He smiled at her. "Good morning, Mrs. Elliot."

It didn't work. Her scowl deepened, bringing her raven brows together in a sharp line above her narrowed eyes, eyes which were as dark and turbulent as the thunderclouds of a summer storm. "It is not a good morning, sir, and I refuse to pretend that it is."

She lifted one gloved hand and grasped the pendant watch that lay against the tucks of her pristine white shirtwaist. Turning it in her hand, she checked the time. "It is now quarter past nine. Do you wish to start work, or would you prefer to fritter away the entire morning gossiping?"

Nathaniel straightened, glancing at the man by the stairs, recognizing him as the secretary he had met several days earlier. He looked at the women who had again stopped work to watch. A glance below told him the men were also watching. Most of them couldn't hear what was said, but they understood what was happening and were wondering what their new boss would do.

"Mrs. Elliot," he began, "why don't we—"

"Those who work here are expected to arrive on time, sir. Even you."

He stared into her determined, angry eyes, and knew that she was challenging his authority, trying to establish control. He couldn't really blame her. He was once in her position, and he'd done the same. Nonetheless, he couldn't allow it. He tried again. "Mrs. Elliot—"

"Your tardiness must not become a habit," she interrupted him a second time. "I must insist that you be punctual."

Nathaniel didn't like to humiliate anyone, especially a woman. He found that charm was usually more effective than force. But she really hadn't left him any choice. If the employees saw him back down to her, he would never earn their respect. He had to make it clear in front of everyone that he was the boss. He pulled a snowy white handkerchief out of his pocket.

"Mr. Chase," she went on, "I realize that you have very little concern for time, but this is a factory. We have a schedule, we have quotas to meet."

He gave reason one last try. "Yes, I know, but—"

"I cannot permit you to set this kind of example. If I do, there will be nothing but problems. And as for your presumptuous behavior . . . "

He reached out with the handkerchief the moment she paused for breath, stuffing the center between her teeth and tying the ends behind her head, effectively cutting off her lecture. "You're quite right, Mrs. Elliot. It wouldn't do for us to set a bad example. It wouldn't do at all."

He smiled at her, ignoring the murderous look in her eyes. Amid the laughter that rose above the puff of steam engines, she whirled around and walked away, her hands reaching up to untie the knot of his handkerchief. She tore it from her lips and strode past Percy, then disappeared down the stairs.

Nathaniel followed her as far as the stairs and halted

before the man standing there. He held out his hand. "I'm Mrs. Elliot's new partner."

The other man continued to stare at him and said nothing.

Nathaniel glanced at the stairs leading to the next floor. "I'd like to see the rest of the factory. What's up there?"

"The first floor is used for storage. The second floor is empty."

Nathaniel looked around. "I've seen all there is to see on the ground floor." He gestured to the stairs. "Lead on."

Percy hesitated only a moment before he answered. "Of course."

The two men went up to the first floor, which consisted of one huge room. Nathaniel took a glance around, noting that there were plenty of tables and chairs. Packing crates and pieces of equipment that were no longer needed lined the walls. He continued up the stairs, and Percy followed.

The second floor was also one huge room. Columns rose to the high ceiling, supporting the flat roof, and a row of windows let in the light. A sink and faucet stood in the far corner, there was a view of the Thames in the distance, and stairs at the other end went up to the roof. He could have his office and laboratory here. He could even live here. It would be convenient, and he'd have plenty of room when the rest of his things arrived.

He faced the other man. "Is there any management staff employed here?"

There was a long pause before Percy answered. "No, sir."

"Not even a foreman?"

"No, sir."

Nathaniel sighed. "Percy, you don't have to call me sir. Who supervises production?"

"Mrs. Elliot handles that."

Before Nathaniel could ask any more questions, Percy asked one of his own. "Are you planning to turn Elliot Electrical into a toy company?"

"Yes."

"I see." Percy opened his mouth as if to ask another question, but closed it again without speaking.

"Percy, you may not believe this, but I know what I'm doing. I intend to make this company the most successful toy company in England. To do that, I need hardworking, honest people who aren't afraid to speak their minds. Whatever you want to ask me, just ask."

"Yes, sir. I was wondering—" He broke off, took a deep breath, and rushed on, "Perhaps you would tell me what you expect of me, sir."

"Well, I don't expect you to always agree with me. I'd be highly suspicious if you did. I don't expect you to say 'yes, sir,' and 'no, sir,' and, 'whatever you say, sir.' I don't expect you to work long hours just to impress me, but I expect you to do your best. Does that make it clear?"

"Yes, s—" He swallowed. "Yes, Mr. Chase."

"Laying down the law already?" a voice asked from the doorway.

Both men turned as Michael entered the room.

Nathaniel laughed. "You're late."

"I don't believe this. You lecturing me on punctuality." Michael looked around. "Not much of an office."

"Not yet." Nathaniel turned to the secretary. "Percy, this is Michael Lowenstein. I've hired him as my chief engineer. Michael, my secretary, Percy Sandborn."

Michael tugged at his cap. "Pleasure to meet you." He looked at Nathaniel. "You going to show me around this place?"

"Not yet. We're meeting with my new partner this morning." He turned to the secretary. "Percy, downstairs a gentleman named Boggs is waiting with some of my things. Instruct him to bring them up here. Tell Mrs. Elliot that we're ready to begin our meeting. We'll have it here."

Percy nodded and left.

Michael waited until the secretary had left the room. "I witnessed your little tête-à-tête with Mrs. Elliot. Your tact and diplomacy never cease to amaze me."

"Thanks." He sighed and raked a hand through his hair. "I'm afraid I'm running into some resistance from her."

"Does it matter? It's her husband you have to work with."

"Not anymore."

"What do you mean?"

Nathaniel told him about James's death and the deal he'd made with Mara.

Michael expressed surprise and sorrow at the news, and then commented, "A beautiful female partner. I should be so lucky."

"I don't feel lucky at the moment." Nathaniel frowned. "They laughed at her. I don't like to embarrass people in front of others."

"I know, but what else could you have done?"

Nathaniel thought about it. "Nothing," he admitted. "I couldn't let her call me on the carpet in front of everyone as if I were a recalcitrant schoolboy." He sighed and turned away, walking to one of the windows. "I want us to work together, but I have the feeling it's going to be difficult. Bad partnerships. My special gift."

He thought of all the fights he'd had with Adrian after their father's death, pointless arguments over company policy. It had been inevitable, he supposed, given that their father had made them partners. He and his father had worked side by side for a year while Adrian was finishing at Cambridge, and he'd known that they had reached an understanding of sorts, but he'd never expected to be given nearly half the company.

It hadn't mattered. Adrian had been given the controlling interest. For two years, Nathaniel had tried. He'd tried to work with his brother, he'd tried to compromise, but with Adrian, there had been no room for compromise.

For two years, he'd been forced to stand aside, helpless, watching as Adrian made shoddy products and shady deals, firing many of the talented people Nathaniel had brought into the company, including Michael. He could still remember countless nights of pacing across the floor of Mai Lin's rooms in Limehouse, pouring out his frustrations as she'd listened with all the placid decorum of her Chinese heritage, countless hours of losing himself in her arms, turning frustration into passion as she held him with all the sweet warmth a mistress could give.

But Mai Lin was gone, Adrian had won, and Nathaniel was still reaching for dreams.

He pushed his memories and regrets away. Adrian was just a competitor now, and that was all. He'd asked Finch to make inquiries into all the other toy train manufacturers, including Adrian, so that he could deal with the future, but the past was dead and gone.

He turned away from the window. "So, did you tell your fiancée?"

"Yes."

"How did she take it?"

"Better than I expected. Her father was furious. My future in-laws are not happy with me just now." He sighed. "I don't know why I'm doing this."

Nathaniel grinned at him. "Because you have wisdom beyond your years, Michael. Let's get to work."

*   *   *

Mara never gave in to fits of temper. She prided herself on her ability to deal with any difficulty in cool, practical fashion. This partnership was no different from any other difficult situation, she reminded herself as she strode down the hallway to her office. She would be calm and logical, she would not give in to emotion.

She entered her office and slammed the door.

This partnership was a farce. Mara twisted his linen handkerchief around her fists, wishing he were standing in front of her now so she could wrap the piece of linen around his neck and choke that smile from his face.

The laughter of the workers still rang in her ears. It had taken four years of great effort for her to gain their tentative respect, and Mr. Chase had destroyed that respect in less than a minute. By taking him on as a partner she had saved her company, but what had that accomplished? She herself was no better off.

Buffeted about for eight years at one man's whim, suffering the consequences of one man's fancies. She'd fought so hard to get away from that, but now she found herself there again. It was a bitter pill to swallow.

The knock on her office door broke into Mara's thoughts. Dropping the handkerchief on the desk, she whirled around to find Percy in the doorway.

"Mrs. Elliot? Mr. Chase sent me down to tell you he's ready to begin our meeting. He's waiting for us up on the second floor."

"The second floor? Why does he want this meeting all the way up there?"

"I don't know, ma'am. But that's what he said."

Percy departed and Mara reached for the company's latest financial reports, knowing Mr. Chase would want to see them, but her hand paused over the handkerchief that lay on her desk. Now he was waiting for her, was he?

"Let him wait," she muttered, and circled her desk to

sit down. She pulled out a sharp pencil and a fresh sheet of paper, then began to list all the reasons why making toys was impossible.

Thirty minutes later, she read over her list and felt more in control of the situation. Once she had presented her reasons, he would see that it was much more feasible for Elliot's to remain as it was. Mr. Chase would have to put this silly notion of toy making aside.

With a satisfied nod, she rose to her feet, tucked her pencil behind her ear, and carried the stack of reports upstairs, fully prepared to make her arguments in a calm, reasonable fashion.

But when she entered the room, all her rational arguments flew right out of her head. Mr. Chase and a dark-haired man she'd never seen before were sitting on the floor, surrounded by pieces of metal that they were putting together to form a miniature railroad track, looking like a pair of schoolboys with a set of building blocks. Percy sat close by, taking notes. Various toys lay on the floor, including Mr. Chase's train.

"This sectional track you've designed fits together extremely well, Nathaniel." The stranger's enthusiastic voice carried across the room to her. "Percy, we'll need to determine the amount of tin and wood for each set."

"Of course." Percy jotted down a few words in the notebook on his lap. Mara hugged the pile of papers to her breast. Rather than wait for her, as she'd expected, they'd just started the meeting without her. She watched them for a moment, feeling very much like an outsider in the company she used to control.

Taking a deep breath, she entered the room, and all three men rose to their feet as she approached.

"Sorry I'm late," she said, careful to keep her voice expressionless.

"I don't believe we've met." The dark-haired man stepped forward, tipping his cap, but not removing it. "You must be Mrs. Elliot. I'm Michael Lowenstein. Your new engineer."

Mara gave him a blank look before glancing over at Mr. Chase. "I see," she murmured. "Gentlemen, will you excuse us, please? I'd like to speak privately with Mr. Chase."

"Oh, er, yes," Percy stammered and started for the door. Michael Lowenstein followed.

She faced Mr. Chase, expecting to see laughter in his eyes, but she was surprised to find no hint of mockery there. He was watching her impassively, and she wondered what he was thinking.

He glanced past her to the doorway. "Michael, when do you think you can have a materials and parts list ready?"

"I'll have it to you by Sunday," the engineer answered. "I'll be downstairs looking over your equipment if you need me."

Percy added, "I'll have that list of toy retailers to you by this afternoon. I'll also have a key to the building cut for you."

Nathaniel nodded. "Do we have a safe?"

"There's one in my office," Mara said. "Why?"

He gestured to the train. "I want to start locking up the train at night, along with the track, the accessories, and the design specifications. The toy business is very competitive, and I don't want my train to suddenly disappear. Michael, I want you to be responsible for locking up the train."

He glanced at Percy. "Let's not discuss this with anyone else. Once the train is in stores, it won't matter, but until then I want to keep this as quiet as possible."

The two men left the room, and Nathaniel turned

back to Mara. "You missed the meeting," he said, but there was no censure in his voice.

"Unlike some, I had work to do."

"Mmm, I see." He flashed her that mercurial smile. "Planning various ways to murder me without getting caught, I imagine."

His outrageous comment was so close to the truth, Mara couldn't help the answering smile that tugged at her mouth. "You might say that."

"Well, the lady has a sense of humor. I was beginning to wonder."

Her smile disappeared instantly. "Not all people find life as amusing as you do, Mr. Chase."

He held up his hands in a placating gesture. "I was only teasing you, Mara. Don't stiffen up and get all prickly again."

She didn't relax. "Mrs. Elliot, if you please, sir."

He knew she was angry at what he'd done, and that she thought he was bizarre, even crazy. But Mara was his partner, and he didn't want to begin their partnership with hostility. "I'm sorry about what happened earlier. We've gotten off to rather a bad start, it seems. Can we begin again?"

She studied him for a long moment, and he expected her to reject his offer of peace. But finally, she nodded. "Very well."

Only two little words, but Nathaniel sensed it had cost her a great deal to say them. He decided to change the subject. "What are those?" he asked, gesturing to the stack of papers in her arms.

She walked across the room, careful to step around the pieces of metal and wood on the floor, and came to a halt before him. She removed the top sheet, then held the stack out to him. "These are Elliot's financial statements for the past six months. You'll want to go over them, of course."

He shook his head and waved them aside. "I don't need to see them."

"You don't want to look over our financial statements?"

"I trust your judgment and your ability to keep accurate records. Mr. Finch spoke very highly of your financial expertise. I don't have that ability myself, and balance sheets and income statements are Greek to me."

"Don't you have questions about our financial situation?"

"Mr. Finch answered all my questions. Besides, aren't there a few things you want to discuss with me?"

"Definitely. For a start, don't you think you might have consulted with me before hiring an engineer?"

"I'd already discussed the decision with James, and I had already hired Michael when I learned James was dead."

"We don't need an engineer."

"Yes, we do. I'm not a bad engineer myself, but I can't do it alone."

"What are we paying this engineer we don't need and can't afford?"

"Ten pounds a week."

"What? That's outrageous!"

"Michael's the best toy engineer there is. He's worth every penny."

"Toys again." She looked down at the papers in her hands. "You still plan to go through with this crazy idea of making us a toy company?"

"It isn't crazy, and yes, I do."

"I can't believe you're serious. The costs would be tremendously high. If you're familiar with our finances, you know we can't afford it. The new equipment alone would break us."

"No, it won't. We'll start making toy trains first.

We can make the motors here and the bodies of the trains without purchasing any new equipment. Any parts we can't make here with equipment we have, we'll subcontract out."

"Subcontracting costs the earth!"

"But we'll have no overhead."

"The cost per piece will still be outrageously high," she argued. "How can we make any profit?"

"You are in charge of financial matters, Mrs. Elliot. I suggest you do a cost analysis or whatever you call it." He pointed to the train set on the floor. "Figure out the cost to make each piece and a list of the contractors who will provide quality parts at the lowest prices. Make sure they give us thirty days' credit, because we'll need the time delay. Any questions?"

"Why are you so set on doing this?" she asked. "What is wrong with making engines and dynamos, as we have always done?"

"I didn't buy fifty-one percent of this company to build dynamos. I bought it to build toys." He jabbed one finger toward the train. "My toys."

"If ordinary motors and dynamos are too dull for you, Mr. Chase, perhaps you should have bought into a different company. Elliot's can't afford what you're proposing!"

Nathaniel raked a hand through his hair, frustrated by her refusal to consider possibilities. Skepticism and doubt—God, he was so tired of that. He was tired of words like can't and mustn't and won't. He hated those words.

"We'll make the changes gradually," he explained, but he had the feeling he was talking to a marble statue. "At the same time, we'll phase out most of what we make now, until we are making only the motors for our own products. I plan to make us England's finest toy maker."

"Big dreams, big ideas," she scoffed. "But equipment isn't the only cost involved in something like this. Where are we going to get the money to develop and manufacture these new products? Are you going to provide it?"

"No."

"No? Why not? You're from a wealthy family, aren't you?"

He lifted his head sharply. "Who told you that?"

"Percy. He said your family owns Chase Toy Company."

His lips tightened into a thin line. "I don't have access to that money. My elder brother owns Chase Toys, and I hardly think it likely that Adrian would give me the money to go into competition against him."

Mara stared at him in astonishment. "That's what this is about? You're going into competition against your own brother? In heaven's name, why?"

He glanced again at the train, thinking of all the reasons. His grandfather's legacy, the need to prove himself. But only one reason mattered. His dream. "Making toys, toys I invented, has always been the only thing I've ever wanted to do. My brother had nothing to do with it."

"So if you want to build the toys you've invented, why not do that at Chase Toys? Why start your own company?"

"My brother never did like to share, even when we were children."

"I see." She was silent for a moment, then she returned to her original question. "How do you plan to finance all these inventions you want to make?"

"Simple. We'll take out a loan from the bank."

"What?" Mara stepped back, shaking her head. "Oh, no. We will not."

"Why not? Businesses often raise capital that way."

"It's too risky."

"If you want to accomplish anything in life, you have to take risks."

"No!" she countered. "You accomplish things in life by hard work, persistence, and concentrated effort. Not by going off half-cocked, borrowing money for crazy schemes that won't work."

"How do you know they won't work until you try them?"

She yanked her pencil from behind her ear and stepped forward, tilting her chin to look up at him. "I have no intention of trying anything that puts my company in jeopardy!"

"Your company?"

"Yes, Mr. Chase, my company. While my husband went waltzing off to America looking for adventures, I'm the one who stayed here and kept everything from falling apart," she said, and began to pace angrily in front of Nathaniel. "I did the work. James may have started this company, but I'm the one who kept him from bankrupting it." She came to a halt and glared at him. "I've earned the right to call it mine."

"I didn't know that." He studied her face, beginning to see what had given her the bitter eyes and hard edges.

"Well, now you know. It's easy for you to talk about taking risks," she said as she resumed her agitated steps. "There are a thousand ways your idea can go wrong. If your scheme doesn't work and the company goes bankrupt, I'll be in the street and so will all of the people who work here."

She paused again. "But I don't suppose that matters to you," she added with scorn, pointing at him with her pencil. "You can always go back to the Chase family mansion in Mayfair or the country estate in Devon or wherever it is the rich aristocrats live. Most of us aren't so fortunate."

"I told you, I don't have access to the Chase fortune. Even if I wanted to go back to the family mansion, I can't. I burned that bridge long ago. If this venture proves unsuccessful, I'll be in the street right along with you. Paying off your loan took nearly every cent I had."

"Why are you doing this?" she cried. "Why invest all you have and jeopardize all I have on a venture that's risky at best? Elliot's is solvent. Why can't you just leave it be?"

"Solvent is a far cry from successful," he pointed out. "Besides, your husband and I planned this together. It was his dream as well as mine to make Elliot's a toy company."

As he watched her expression harden he realized that was the wrong thing to say. "You think that will persuade me to go along with this harebrained scheme?" Her hand clenched into a fist around her pencil. "My husband's dreams were as inconstant as the weather and just as unpredictable. Every dream James ever had was the miracle that was going to make us wealthy and happy."

She took a deep breath. "But every time he realized there would be work involved in any of his schemes, the shine wore off. He'd pack his bags and head for the next rainbow in search of the pot of gold, leaving me to clean up the mess he left behind. Once I'd done that, of course, I was expected to join him. Mr. Chase, my husband dragged me all over the world. I've lived in so many places, I couldn't list them all. Africa, India, Hong Kong, Egypt, anywhere James thought that rainbow might be."

Silence fell between them. In her cloudy gray eyes, he saw the shadows of pain and disillusionment—the dark side of her husband's rainbow. He suddenly found himself wishing he could take those shadows away.

Her pencil snapped in her hand, and the sound

echoed in the quiet, empty room, breaking the silence. "Don't tell me about my husband's dreams, Mr. Chase," she said bitterly. "I know all about them."

"You don't know about *my* dreams," he answered. "I'm not looking for the pot of gold at the end of the rainbow, and a little hard work isn't going to make me run away. I liked your husband, but I'm not like him."

"Yes, you are! You come here with your big ideas, with no thought to the havoc you'll create and the mess you'll leave behind when you get tired of it. You're just like him." She threw down the broken pieces of her pencil. "Another rainbow-chasing dreamer," she said and turned away, heading for the door.

"And what's wrong with being a dreamer?" he called to her. "Don't you have any dreams, Mara?"

She came to a halt in the doorway. Slowly, she turned her head to look at him over her shoulder. "No," she said quietly. "Not anymore."

She was gone before he could ask what her dreams might have been. He looked down at the locomotive on the floor and decided that perhaps he could give Mara Elliot a new dream to believe in. His dream.

6

The books didn't balance. Mara added up the column of numbers again and came up with yet another total. Frustrated, she set down her pencil and leaned back in her chair. It was no use. She just wasn't concentrating.

She glanced at the clock. Half past seven, and she'd only gotten through one tenth of her day's paperwork. She picked up her pencil.

Don't you have any dreams, Mara?

She'd had her dreams once. She'd dreamed that James would stop dragging her and their daughter all over the world and settle down. When she'd realized that dream was just a fantasy, she'd formed another.

She had dreamed of her own home, a home with blue shutters and window boxes of red geraniums, a paid-for home that nobody could take away, with a huge kitchen and a full larder so her daughter would never go hungry. But that dream, too, had turned to ashes, leaving her with scars much deeper than the ones on her hands.

Husbands left, homes burned down, and children died, and it was just too painful to begin again.

So she had dreamed of running her own business, controlling her own life and her own destiny. That dream, too, had failed to come true. She stared down at the gloved hand that held the pencil. What had dreams ever gotten her? Nothing at all.

She began to add the long column of numbers, counting aloud, hoping that might help. "Sixty-four. Carry the six. Six . . . ten . . . nineteen . . . one-hundred-ninety-four pounds. That isn't right," she muttered. "How did I get that?"

Don't you have any dreams, Mara?

She groaned and lowered her forehead to the desk.

"Having a problem?"

She lifted her head. Nathaniel Chase was standing in the doorway, holding a cardboard box in his hands and smiling at her. She refused to smile back. He was the reason she couldn't concentrate. "I don't balance. I've added these numbers a dozen times and I get a different total each time." She sighed, too tired to wonder why he'd come to her office, too tired to care what havoc he was going to create next.

"Maybe you need to take a break." Nathaniel moved into the room and placed the box in front of her.

"What is that?"

"Dinner." He lifted the lid and tossed it aside. "I thought you might be hungry."

She leaned forward and stared at the sandwiches, glasses, and bottles nestled inside the box and realized she hadn't eaten since early that morning. The sight of the food made her suddenly ravenous, but she couldn't eat in front of him. She never ate in front of anyone. "Where did you get this?"

"Mrs. O'Brien made the sandwiches. I often obtain

meals from her. I had Percy pick up the beverages at Somerville's Cafe."

"Mrs. O'Brien!" Mara made a sound of vexation. "She probably gouged you shamelessly on the price. How much?"

"Two shillings." He grinned at her frown of disapproval.

"Highway robbery. You shouldn't have paid more than one."

"I'll remember that next time," he said, smothering what sounded suspiciously like a laugh. He pulled out two bottles. "Sarsaparilla or lemonade?"

A beverage she could accept. "Lemonade, please," she answered and watched as he pulled a corkscrew out of his pocket. He uncorked the two bottles, then poured the lemonade into a glass and handed the glass to her. She took a swallow, savoring the sweet-tart taste for a moment before she set the glass on her desk.

He began to rummage inside the box. "I didn't know what you'd like, so I had her make several different kinds of sandwiches. I've got roast beef, tomato and cucumber, and chicken. She put some sour pickles in here, too."

Mara stared up at him, unable to think of a polite way to refuse his offer to share supper with her, even as the mention of chicken and roast beef made her insides twist with hunger.

He noted her expression. "I thought," he said as he pulled sandwiches out of the box, "this might be a peace offering. What kind would you like?"

"Thank you, but I'm not hungry," she said stiffly, clasping her gloved hands tightly together in her lap.

He set the empty box aside. Keeping one foot on the floor, he sat on the edge of her desk and studied her for a moment. Not wanting his perceptive eyes to see through her lie, she lowered her gaze and wished he would go away.

"You must be hungry," he contradicted her softly. "I know you've been busy working. I'll bet you haven't eaten a thing all day." Reaching forward, he pushed one of the sandwiches closer to her.

The scent of freshly baked bread made her mouth water. She pushed the food away almost desperately. "No, really, I'm not hungry. I . . . I'm too busy to eat anyway."

He reached out, and the tips of his fingers brushed beneath her chin as he lifted her face to look into her eyes. "I'm fairly certain that ladies always remove their gloves when they eat," he said in a gentle voice, "but if you choose to commit a serious breach of etiquette, I won't tell anyone."

He'd guessed her predicament. Of course. He'd seen her hands once before. Mortified, Mara pulled her chin from his grasp and looked away from the compassion in his eyes. She didn't want any man's pity.

He picked up another of the sandwiches, took a bite, and glanced at her. "Mmm. Delicious. Rare roast beef, fresh bread, plenty of mustard. Are you certain you won't have one?"

Mara stared at the sandwich in his hands and wavered, good manners and pride wrestling with hunger. Then, before she could stop herself, she reached for the sandwich and took a bite. It tasted so good, she almost groaned. She felt him watching her and looked up.

"Good, aren't they?" Without waiting for a reply, he turned his attention to the open ledger on the desk. "What are you working on?"

"August budget," she answered, grateful for the change of subject. "Halfway through the month, I do a budget for the following month. Once that's done, I can order materials and do a production schedule for the employees."

Nathaniel nodded and waved a hand in the air as he swallowed the bite of roast beef. "Eating and talking about employees reminds me of something. I have an idea."

Mara wasn't certain she liked the sound of that. "What?"

He grinned down at her, amused by the wariness in her voice. "Don't worry, Mara," he said. "This isn't anything revolutionary. I just wondered about the first floor—you know, the one we use for storage. We don't really need it for that." He licked a dab of mustard from his finger and went on, "What about letting people use that floor for their lunch break?"

She didn't bother to correct him on the proper use of her name. Instead, she considered his suggestion. "That's a good idea," she admitted.

"You don't have to sound so surprised," he said, laughing. "I do occasionally have them."

His laughter was infectious, and Mara found herself enjoying the sound of it. "The tables and chairs we can leave up there," she said, "but what about the other stuff? We could move it to the second floor, I suppose."

"No, we'll leave it. There's enough room. I want to use the second floor as my office." He looked at her. "That is, if you have no objection?"

She thought it over. "Why should I object? We don't use it for anything else. But it's awfully large for an office, isn't it?"

"I want my laboratory up there as well. I have a lot of equipment. I was thinking that perhaps you might want to move your office up there, too."

Mara froze, the sandwich poised halfway to her lips.

The second floor was too far from an exit and too far above the ground to jump. If there were a fire, she'd be trapped up there. "No."

"Wait. Hear me out."

"I will not have my office up there," she said firmly. "I like my office just where it is."

"But if your office is down here and mine is up there, it will make it very hard for us to work together." His eyes held a teasing gleam as he looked down at her. "You'd have no idea what I'm doing. I could get into all sorts of trouble if you're not up there to keep an eye on me."

"Why can't your office be down here? There's another empty room across the hall."

"That tiny cubbyhole? No, thank you."

"I'm not moving my office," she repeated.

As he studied her rigid expression, she hastily invented an excuse.

"That room upstairs is so far away from things down here. What if I'm needed on the production floor?"

He considered her words for a moment, then he asked a totally unexpected question. "Do you enjoy supervising the employees?"

"What do you mean?"

"Exactly what I said. Do you enjoy doing it?"

She stared at him in bewilderment. "What difference does it make whether or not I enjoy it? I have to do it."

"Why?"

"If I don't, who will?"

"Michael," he answered and picked up another sandwich. "He's perfectly capable, and he's been a foreman before. I think we ought to let him do it."

Mara's sandwich suddenly tasted like cardboard, and she pushed it aside. He'd already taken everything else away from her. Control of the company, respect of the employees. Why not take away her responsibilities as well? All her defenses came up. "Why? Because I wouldn't be a good supervisor after that stunt you pulled this morning? Did you enjoy making a fool of me?"

"No." Nathaniel set down his sandwich and turned to face her, resting his forearm on his knee. "I didn't intend to humiliate you. But it was my first day in charge, and you were dressing me down in front of everyone." He lifted a hand to halt her protest. "Yes, you were. This morning has nothing to do with my suggestion anyway. I just think it would be a good idea."

"And what would I do all day?" she asked. "Sip tea and eat crumpets?"

He ignored the sarcasm. "I feel this idea has some advantages."

"What about Saturdays? Mr. Lowenstein is Jewish, and this factory is open Saturdays until noon. Who'll act as supervisor when he isn't here?"

"I will. Or you will. What difference does it make?" He sighed, seeing the stubborn set of her jaw. "Mara, I said I was sorry about this morning. I won't say it again. Do we have to fight about everything?"

She didn't want to fight. One day of battling with him had worn her out. Besides, she couldn't possibly win. "What are the advantages?"

"Right now, you spend most of your day handling problems on the floor. As it is, you don't even get started on the books until after six o'clock. If we made Michael the supervisor, you'd be able to spend more time on the financial end of things. You might even be able to go home at a decent hour."

Home? To her tiny flat with its cracked plaster and rickety furniture? She didn't want to go home at a decent hour. There was nothing to do there but watch the clock tick.

She said nothing, and he went on, "You aren't able

to do any future planning. You aren't able to go out and see what's going on, see what competitors are doing, or call on customers. The owners of a business shouldn't have to spend all their time worrying about routine operations."

She swallowed hard, not wanting to consider that he might be right.

"Why are we even discussing this?" she asked as she rose to her feet. She closed the ledger and shoved it aside, then walked around the desk and headed for the door, wanting only to get away. She grabbed her bonnet from its hook by the door. "If I say no, you'll put Mr. Lowenstein in charge anyway." Then she walked out of the office.

Nathaniel slid off the desk and followed her.

At the front door, she whirled around to face him. "Why are you following me home?"

"I live there, too. Remember?"

With an exasperated sigh, she turned and walked out of the building, with him still right behind her. She locked the door and walked quickly toward the lodging house, trying to ignore him, but he took the curb side and matched her hurried steps with his long, easy stride. When he spoke again, she began to realize Nathaniel Chase was not a man easily ignored.

"I have another request."

She halted on the sidewalk and looked up at him. The light of the street lamp caught his unruly hair, emphasizing the rakish, wind-blown look of him.

"What do you want?"

"It's what I don't want." He shoved his hands in the pockets of his trousers and looked down at her, a smile playing around the corners of his mouth. "I don't want you walking home alone after dark."

"Why not? I do it every day."

He glanced around. "As I reminded you when we first met, this is not a very nice neighborhood. It's not safe at night."

She could hardly believe he was concerned for her well-being after his callous treatment earlier in the day, but something in his voice told her that he was. Mara couldn't recall the last time a man, any man, had been concerned about her. A tiny flicker of warmth spread through her, making her feel flustered and a little breathless. "It's only just next door."

"I don't care. From now on, if you're going to work late, let me know and I'll walk you home."

"I work late every night."

"Then I'll walk you home every night."

The man was invading her entire life. What she did and how she did it. Where she went and how she got there. Was it really concern, or was it just another way to dictate to her? Doubts crept in and defenses came up again. "You needn't bother. I can take care of myself."

"Really?" He studied her for a long moment, with those vivid eyes, so intense, so perceptive. "I wonder."

"Why do you always look at me like that?" she asked, uncomfortable with the scrutiny, wanting to change the subject.

He continued to study her, his eyes midnight blue in the dim light. "Like what?"

"Like that. You don't just look. You stare."

He stepped closer to her. "Does it make you nervous?"

She took a step back, then another. He followed until her back hit the brick wall of the factory. A wild shot of panic raced through her as his arms came up, trapping her against the wall.

"Does it make you nervous?" he repeated, leaning even closer, his breath warmer against her cheek than the sultry summer air.

She ran her tongue over her suddenly dry lips, staring into his eyes, watching the direction of his gaze change, drop lower, to her mouth. Her heart began to pound like a trip-hammer. "Stop it," she muttered, cognizant of sudden danger. The realization made her weak and dizzy. "You've made your point."

He immediately straightened and lowered his arms to his sides, freeing her. "Good."

She stepped around him, trying to regain control of her rapid breathing as she walked hurriedly to the lodging house. She could hear his footsteps behind her as he followed her inside and up the stairs.

At the door of her flat, he paused beside her, waiting as she unlocked the door and stepped inside. In the doorway, she whirled around to face him. "Why does it matter to you what I do and when I go home?" she demanded.

"It matters," he said quietly. "There are many wonderful, extraordinary things in this world, Mara. But there are some ugly and dangerous things, too, things we can't always handle alone."

She stepped into her flat, watching as he turned away and went up the stairs. Just before she closed the door, she heard his voice float down to her. "It helps to have friends."

Charles didn't wait for the cab to come to a complete stop. In his agitation, he jumped down while it was still rolling and thrust a pound note into the hand of the driver. Not bothering to retrieve his change, he raced for the front steps of the new and quite luxurious Mayfair mansion, circling around the other carriages that crowded the forecourt. He ascended the steps and yanked the bell pull.

Cursing slow-moving servants, Charles straightened his tie and brushed at his damp clothing, trying to regain some semblance of order as he waited.

When the door opened, the butler took in his disheveled appearance and wet clothes with one raised eyebrow. "May I help you, Mr. Barrett?"

Charles didn't waste time on explanations. "Where is Lord Leyland?"

Lovett frowned in disapproval at the abrupt question. "My lord is entertaining guests this evening. They are presently at dinner."

Charles hesitated, uncertain how to proceed. But the viscount had told him that he wanted to be informed of important news immediately. Taking a deep breath, he pulled off his hat and made a decision. "Interrupt him."

"I cannot, sir!" The butler stared at him in horror. "This is Viscount Leyland's engagement dinner. Perhaps, afterward—"

"This is important." Charles stepped around the other man.

Lovett sighed and gestured to the open doors at Charles's right. "Very well. You may wait in here."

Charles nodded and turned to enter the parlor. He paced across the carpet as he waited for his employer, wishing he could banish the horrifying scene he'd witnessed from his mind.

It seemed like an eternity before Charles heard the sound of footsteps on the polished parquet floor of the foyer. He jumped to his feet as Adrian Chase entered the parlor.

"Mr. Barrett, I trust that the news you bring warrants this intrusion?"

Charles swallowed hard and met the cold blue eyes of his employer. "I think so, sir. There's been an accident."

"Indeed?" Adrian brushed a speck of lint from his black evening suit. "I'm listening."

"A boiler explosion at the factory an hour ago. Sir, a man was killed."

"I see." Adrian walked to the sideboard and poured himself a glass of port. "Any damage?"

"Sir?"

"Was there any damage to the factory?" Adrian repeated with a hint of impatience, turning away from the sideboard to face his assistant.

"The boiler was half-full and the water immediately extinguished the fire," Charles answered slowly, unable to believe a man could face the news of another man's death with such indifference. "There's some water damage, I imagine, but all in all, we were very lucky."

"That's all?" Adrian's handsome face twisted with scorn. "You interrupted my engagement dinner to tell me this? Mr. Barrett, exactly what do you expect me to do about it at this moment?"

Charles stared at him in astonishment. "I was under the impression that important news should be brought to you immediately, my lord. I thought you would want to see the damage. Talk to the man's family. I don't know."

"You said the fire was put out before it caused any significant damage. So, what is there for me to see or do that cannot wait until tomorrow?" Adrian took a sip of port.

Charles wished his employer would offer him a glass. He needed it. "A man was killed."

Adrian sighed. "That's unfortunate, but occasionally these things do happen, I'm afraid. Who was he, by the way?"

"Robson. Samuel Robson."

"A pity, but I'm sure we can find another foreman as skilled as Robson."

Charles closed his eyes briefly and again saw Samuel lying lifeless on the floor, his body burned beyond recognition.

"We'll need to replace the boiler, I assume?"

Charles heard the words of his employer and opened his eyes. "Yes," he answered in a choked whisper. "The boiler will have to be replaced."

"Contact Lloyd's tomorrow. Our insurance should cover a new one."

"My lord, the boilers are very old. All of them ought to be replaced. Another one could go at any time."

"I doubt it." Adrian downed the last swallow of port in his glass and set the crystal goblet aside.

"It's unsafe!"

"You worry too much, Mr. Barrett. I plan to replace them next year. In the meantime, we will make do with the ones we have. That will be all."

Charles pressed his lips together and walked out of the room. Insurance would cover the damage to the factory, but Charles doubted Mrs. Robson would find any comfort in that.

7

During the next two weeks, Mara tried to avoid Nathaniel Chase and continue with business as usual as if he wasn't even there. To her surprise, he didn't make Michael the supervisor, but let her remain in charge. Nonetheless, when she tried to circumvent his decisions, she found herself blocked at every turn. The workers made it clear that they knew Mr. Chase was the boss and that when his decisions conflicted with hers, it was his orders that had to be followed.

After four years of being in control, that control was now gone, and it made her feel lost, afraid, and defensive. The more she tightened her grip, the more she saw control of the company slipping away.

She never ran into Nathaniel on her way to work, for he was always late, seldom coming in before nine. But he followed her home every night and when he tried to discuss changes with her during the short walk, she ignored him with the cool words, "Do what you like. You will anyway."

Nathaniel watched her enter her flat and shut the door in his face after repeating that statement for the third time in three minutes, and he sighed with frustration. He didn't want this. He wanted to make this partnership work. He knew she felt defensive and afraid of the changes, but there had to be a way to get past her defenses.

He went up to his flat and played the violin, trying to find a solution, a way to make peace as he let a Bach concerto relax him. When he finally set the violin aside, he had an idea. He just hoped it was the right one.

The next evening, after everyone had gone home and the factory was quiet, he went to her office. He knocked on her door, then opened it. "May I come in? I want to talk with you."

Mara set her pencil aside. "About what?"

He stepped into her office and shut the door behind him. She noticed he had a flat, paper-wrapped package in his hand.

"What's that?"

He leaned his back against the door, and studied her for a long moment without replying. "It's a present for you," he finally said and walked to her desk. He placed it before her.

She studied the package, wrapped in tissue paper and tied with blue ribbons. "For me?"

He sat down in the opposite chair. "For you."

She frowned suspiciously, wondering what he was up to. Memories flitted through her mind of James giving her gifts, as if frivolous silk dresses she never wore and bottles of cologne she didn't like could make up for abandonment and months alone, as if they could magically wash away pain and neglect, as if they could turn her warm and soft in bed when she'd long ago ceased to find pleasure there. *Be nice to me,* he'd coax in the darkness. She closed her eyes to blot it out.

When she opened them, Nathaniel Chase was watching her.

"Why?" she asked in a choked voice. "Why are you giving me a present?"

He shrugged. "It's a Christmas present."

"It's July," she pointed out.

He smiled at her, that irresistible smile. "Well, at least I'm not late, for once."

She tried, she tried hard, to resist that smile. Biting her lip to stop her answering one, she pushed the package toward him. "I don't think it would be appropriate."

His smile widened, and he leaned forward to push the package back. "Perhaps not, but it's practical."

Curious, she reached out and fingered the satin ribbon, letting it slide across the leather of her glove.

"Open it," he urged.

She hesitated, but curiosity got the better of her. She untied the bow, rolled the ribbon, and set it aside. Then she began to unwrap the package, careful not to tear the paper.

"Don't be so slow," he urged, watching her. "Just rip it open."

"But if I'm careful, the paper can be used again."

He reached out, putting his hand over hers, forcing her to stop and look at him. "Mara, half the fun of giving someone a gift is watching them open it, watching them excitedly tear the paper off. You're missing the point."

"Oh," she murmured. When he leaned back in his chair, she hesitated a moment, then began ripping away the paper, and she had to admit it did make getting a gift more exciting. She cast aside the shredded paper. "Is that better?" she asked, opening the box.

"Much."

She looked down into the box and frowned in puzzlement at what lay within. She lifted the odd item, studying its rectangular ebony frame, gold filigree trim, and jade beads, at a loss. "What is it?"

"It's an abacus. I thought it might help you with your work."

"I've heard of them." She ran one finger across the beads, listening to them click. "But I don't know how to use one."

"I'll teach you. You'll understand how to use it in no time at all, and it'll make things much easier for you."

She ran one finger along the gold trim. "It's very kind of you," she murmured. "Thank you, but your present's much too dear. I can't accept it."

"Mara, I've had that abacus for years and I've never had the need to use it. You already know how I feel about accounts and balance sheets. If it would make your work easier, it makes sense for you to have it."

She looked at him again, and found herself unable to refuse. "All right, if you insist. Thank you." She set the abacus back in the box. "But, if we are celebrating Christmas early, I should have a gift for you."

"You do."

His swift answer gave her pause. She looked up at him. "What?"

"All I want is for you to be nice to me."

She froze, her hands tightening around the box. *Be nice to me.* Everything in her turned to frigid stillness. She shoved the box across the desk toward him. "Of all the low, dishonorable, ungentlemanly ideas," she choked, rising to her feet, "that has to be the lowest. If you think you can give me gifts and obtain unspeakable favors of that sort—"

"What?" He stared at her for a moment in astonishment as he listened to her angry words. Then as he understood, he felt an answering anger rising within him. "Is that what you think?"

She slammed the lid back on the box, then grabbed her reticule. "I think you are an unforgivable cad."

Nathaniel watched her walk to the door, and his own anger erupted. He followed, and when she jerked open the door, he reached over her and slammed it shut again. She yanked on the latch, but with his weight against it, she couldn't move it an inch.

Forced to face him, she turned around and lifted her chin. "Let me go."

He grabbed her around the waist and turned with her in his hands, lifting her as easily as if she were a bunch of flowers. In three short strides, he set her unceremoniously on top of the desk.

"Listen to me, Mrs. Elliot, and listen carefully, because this may be the last time I ever speak to you." Nathaniel drew a deep breath, hating her for making him lose his temper, hating himself for letting her. "When I said nice, that is exactly what I meant. Nice, in the ordinary, commonplace definition of the term. Nice. Polite, decent, fair. That's all."

"Oh." She stared up at him, comprehension dawning in her expression. "I didn't realize . . . "

"No, of course you didn't," he said through clenched teeth. "How could you when you look at the world with such bitter eyes, when you mistrust everyone's motives and hurl your accusations and believe the worst possible things about everyone you meet."

He placed one hand on the desk beside her hip and reached for the box behind her with the other, the movement bringing him so close that his thighs brushed her knees. He grabbed the abacus, then straightened, holding the gift between them.

"I gave you this for two simple reasons. One, I wanted to let you know that I'm trying to make this partnership work, hoping you would find it within yourself to do the same. And two, I wanted to give you something that might make your job easier."

She ducked her head, unable to meet his eyes. "I . . . it seems I misunderstood you."

"You're damned right you did. You've also made me lose my temper, something no one has been able to do for a very long time."

There was nothing she could say. Shame heated her cheeks.

"Just the same," he went on, "I don't want you to lose any sleep worrying about my dishonorable intentions, so let me clarify this and put your mind at ease. If I intended to make you my mistress, I'd certainly have deemed you worth more than this," he said, dropping the abacus in her lap. "I've given my mistresses far more lavish gifts, I assure you. Furthermore, should I choose to seek a woman with whom to spend a pleasurable evening, it certainly wouldn't be you. I doubt pleasure of any sort lies within your experience."

With that, he turned away and left her there, slamming the door behind him. Mara lifted the abacus in her hands and hugged it to her chest, feeling miserable and ashamed. She had misjudged him terribly, and she knew of no way to rectify her mistake.

She slid off the desk and placed the abacus on her blotter. She then left her office, and walked down the long hallway to the exit, thinking about what he'd said. The dishonorable intentions she'd assumed had never even occurred to him. She quickened her steps, trying not to think about the tiny little part of her deep down inside that wondered why.

When she left the building, he was waiting to walk

her home, and that made her feel even worse than before, especially since he obviously meant what he'd said. He didn't speak to her, not a single word.

Apologies did not come easily to Mara, but she knew she owed one to Nathaniel Chase. The following morning, she waited until she knew he'd arrived at the factory, then she paid a visit to Mrs. O'Brien. The landlady willingly provided tenants with meals, provided they were willing to pay the exorbitant prices she charged. Normally, Mara would never dream of purchasing a meal from her, but today, she intended to do exactly that. Negotiating with the landlady took a quarter hour, but Mara eventually got an acceptable price.

She carried the tray of scones and tea through the factory and up the stairs to Nathaniel's new office, wondering what she was going to say. A simple, succinct apology would be best, and she hoped he wouldn't be too smug about it. If he gloated as if he'd won a victory, she'd die of embarrassment. And if he repeated another of James's favorite phrases, such as "I knew you'd come to your senses," she'd dump the tea over his head and apologies could go hang.

She reached the mezzanine and continued up the stairs, thinking about his suggestion to move her office. He'd only been teasing, but she took his words to heart. She did want to keep an eye on him, and she couldn't do it with two floors between them. He was determined to have his office up here. Perhaps she should move hers, too, though the thought made her feel slightly ill.

She reached the top of the stairs and paused in the doorway. Most of Nathaniel's equipment had already been brought over from Mrs. O'Brien's and had been stacked at one end of the room. A few tables and chairs had been brought up from the storeroom below. She'd expected to find him alone, but he was not. A workman was standing beside him in the center of the huge room, and he was giving the man instructions.

"Mr. Boggs, I need a worktable and some storage shelves back here. Also, I'll need you to make me some partitions. Half a dozen of them."

The workman pulled off his cap and scratched his head. "Partitions?"

"Yes, you know, partitions." He held his arms wide and made motions in the air as he explained. "You just make a standing frame out of wood and stretch fabric tight across it. About five feet high by about five feet wide. You use them to divide a room so that you don't have to build walls, and you can move them around and rearrange them to suit. Do you see?"

As she watched Nathaniel, Mara sensed again the energy that seemed to emanate from him. Every move he made, every word he said, was quick and sure and confident. She wondered briefly if he ever felt uncertain about anything.

As if he sensed her presence, he suddenly turned and caught sight of her standing in the doorway. He beckoned her forward, and she approached, setting the tray on a nearby table. "Mrs. Elliot, this is Mr. Boggs. He'll be doing some carpentry for me up here over the next week or so. Mr. Boggs, my partner, Mrs. Elliot."

"Ma'am." The workman bobbed his head in her direction and turned back to Nathaniel. "I'll be gettin' started this afternoon," he said. "Will there be anything else, guv'nor?"

Nathaniel shook his head. "No, I think that's about all for now."

The workman started to walk away, and Nathaniel's

words came back to her. *I could get into all sorts of trouble.* Mara bit her lip and reconsidered her decision again.

"Mr. Boggs, wait," she cried impulsively. When Boggs paused and turned to look at her, she took a steadying breath, and pushed aside her misgivings. "I was wondering . . . could you have this room painted?"

She glanced at Nathaniel, who was watching her in some surprise. She ignored the searching look he gave her.

"Certainly. What color?"

She glanced around at the peeling green paint on the walls. "A nice neutral color. Off-white perhaps. Once your remodeling and painting are done, please have my things moved up here as well."

"I'll put the first coat on tomorrow." The workman nodded and took his leave. Mara watched him go, hoping she was doing the right thing.

"What brought about this change of heart?"

"I plan to keep an eye on you," she answered firmly. "I want the side with the windows."

"Done," he agreed and gestured to the tray on the table. "What's this?"

Suddenly she felt almost shy. She took a deep breath and looked up at him. "I . . . umm . . . had Mrs. O'Brien make a pot of tea and some scones. This is . . . umm . . . I thought about what you said . . . about being nice, you know. . . decent, honest, fair, and all that . . . and I . . . I thought perhaps, if you weren't terribly busy . . . if . . . um . . . you'd . . . tea is very nice in the mornings . . ." She took a deep breath amid the tangle of words. "I'm terribly sorry!"

The smile started at the corners of his eyes, moving slowly across his features, and Mara's agony of embarrassment faded away. Looking up at him, seeing that smile, she once again felt that odd reassurance, that feeling that everything in the world had come aright. It was a heady feeling. Heavens, Nathaniel Chase was a handsome man.

"I accept your apology," he said, "and a very nice one it is, too. I love scones and cream." He pulled two chairs closer to the table, and when she sat down, he pushed hers in for her before taking the one opposite.

He watched as she began to pour tea, remembering how vexed she'd been when he'd told her how much he'd paid for the sandwiches that first day. "Mrs. O'Brien, hmm?" he teased.

"She wanted to charge me a shilling." Mara paused and looked over the teapot at him. "Can you imagine? A shilling for one pot of tea and four scones. But I managed to negotiate a much fairer price. I gave her sixpence plus tuppence for the cream."

She sounded so pleased with herself, he laughed. "I'm glad. Perhaps we can have tea and scones more often then."

"Sugar?"

"Yes, a bit. Lemon, please, not milk."

She fixed his tea as he'd requested, then poured a cup for herself, adding nothing to it, and leaned back in her chair.

"Aside from the awful paint, what do you think of our office?" he asked.

She looked around. "I think we need more furniture."

"I've had the rest of my furniture shipped from San Francisco. It should arrive in a few weeks. We can put some of it in here." He paused, knowing this was the time to suggest his plan. "Actually, I thought I'd move in here."

"What?" Startled, she set her cup down in its saucer. "Here?"

"I like to be free to work anytime, and it would be

convenient to be able to sleep here. You said yourself it's way too big for an office. Half the room could be my flat, and half could be our office."

"Oh, no." She shook her head. "We couldn't possibly."

"Why not?"

He watched the blush color her cheeks. The feminine reaction was so unexpected, he stared in astonishment. Somehow, her face lost its hard edge in that blush, softened, became suddenly beautiful. His throat went dry.

"It wouldn't be proper." She pulled her lower lip between her teeth, and the pink in her cheeks deepened.

He was staring, and he forced himself to say something. "Mr. Boggs could build a wall between the two rooms."

"People would . . ." Her voice faltered, and she ducked her head to hide her expression. Embarrassed, she shifted in the chair. "People would talk."

He didn't point out to her that people were going to talk anyway. He knew gossiping tongues would be wagging soon, if they weren't already. He stared at the raven-colored crown of her hair, imagined it loose around her shoulders, and he knew what they would be saying. It wouldn't be too far removed from the assumptions she'd made the night before about his intentions, and he knew she would be the one to suffer for it. "I hadn't thought of that," he finally said. "You're right, of course."

She gave him a tentative smile, then reached for one of the scones in the basket between them and the jam pot. As she spread jam on her scone, he studied her. He'd been too angry last night at having his gift thrown back in his face to consider what she'd thought he had proposed, but looking at her in the wash of morning light streaming through the windows, with the flush of pink in her cheeks, he considered it now, and suddenly he found it a rather pleasant notion, all in all.

She looked up and a tiny frown appeared between her brows. "What are you smiling about?"

He hastily assumed a serious expression, but he wondered what she'd do if he answered her question. Slap his face, probably. "Nothing," he said and reached for a scone. "Do you want any cream?" he asked, and when she shook her head, he slathered a generous portion on the pastry before him.

"Wherever did you get that thing?"

He looked up, licking a dab of cream from his thumb. "What?"

She pointed to the statue of the Indian he'd brought over from his flat. "Oh, that. I picked it up in Kansas City."

"Why?"

He shrugged. "I liked it, I bought it. Simple as that."

"Oh. I thought there might be some significance to it."

"Well, in a way, there is, at least for me. When I went to America, I didn't know what I wanted to do. I traveled quite a bit, and I tried to pick up something from every city I visited. I found the statue in front of a general store in Kansas City, and the proprietor agreed to sell it to me."

"So, when you kept traveling, you just carted that thing with you?"

He grinned. "Not very practical, I admit. But I could afford to travel with all my excess baggage, so why should it matter?"

She pulled another scone from the basket. "And the abacus?"

"Chinatown. In San Francisco."

"You don't have a need for it, yet you learned to use it. Why?"

"I just like to know how things work. Curiosity, I

suppose. Do you still want me to teach you how to use it?"

She set down the scone and looked up at him, her gray eyes wide with a sudden vulnerability. "I've done nothing but fight with you since you came here. Why should you care about making my job easier?"

"I told you before, things happen that we can't always handle by ourselves. Sometimes, we need a little help."

She bit her lip and looked away. "What you said about me was true," she confessed. "I'm not very good at asking for help, and I don't trust people." Then, so softly that he barely heard her words, she added, "I didn't used to be that way."

As if she suddenly regretted speaking so frankly, she abruptly lifted her pendant watch to check the time. With a vexed exclamation, she rose to her feet. "I'd better go down. It's nearly ten."

He watched her head for the door. "Mara?"

She stopped and glanced back at him.

"Don't be afraid to ask for my help if you need it," he said quietly. "You can trust me. Think about that."

8

Mara thought about it. She thought about it a great deal the following morning as she stared at the brawny wall of Calvin Styles's chest. Just now, if Nathaniel were there, she'd ask for his help without hesitation. "I gave you an order, Mr. Styles," she said through clenched teeth.

The man folded his arms across his chest, unimpressed. "So?"

Mara lifted her gaze from the man's sweat-stained shirt to his face. She pointed in the direction of the crates stacked against the wall by the open door leading from the warehouse into the alley. "You will load these motors onto those delivery carts, and you will do it now."

"I don't take orders off no skirts."

Styles took a step forward, closing the short distance between them, and Mara swallowed hard. She could feel the eyes of the other men watching her. "Very well, then." She took a deep breath. "You're fired."

"You can't fire me," he sneered, lowering his head until his face was only inches from hers. "You're not the boss no more, Miss 'igh 'n' Mighty."

His hot breath fanned her cheek, and the smell of onions made her want to retch. She could see the hostility in his eyes, and she felt sudden danger. Fear danced along her spine, but she had never backed down to an insubordinate employee before, and she wasn't about to start now.

"Is there a problem here?"

She turned her head to see Nathaniel striding toward them, the crowd of men falling back to let him through. She felt Styles step away, and she nearly sagged with relief as Nathaniel reached her side.

He glanced at the man, then at her. "What is going on, Mrs. Elliot?"

"I gave Mr. Styles an order to load those crates onto the delivery carts, but he doesn't seem inclined to do it." She met Nathaniel's eyes. "He says he doesn't have to follow my orders anymore, so I fired him."

He glanced at the man again. "You fired him? But he's still here."

"He refuses to leave."

She held her breath, wondering if Nathaniel was going to countermand her decision. But he merely lifted his brows as if surprised. "You are the supervisor," he said, loud enough for all the men to hear his words clearly. "Doesn't he realize he has to follow your orders?"

Mara stared at him. "Apparently not," she murmured.

She watched him turn to Styles and jerk one thumb toward the door. "You heard Mrs. Elliot. Get out."

"What?" The man glanced from Mara to Nathaniel and back again. "I'm still supposed to take orders off this piece o' fluff?" He pointed at Mara, jabbing one finger into her shoulder and pushing her. She stumbled backward.

Nathaniel's fist slammed into the man's belly before Mara even regained her footing. Styles's body jerked in response, and Nathaniel's other fist caught him on the jaw, snapping his head to the side and sending him crashing to the floor.

He looked down at the man who rolled onto his back with a groan. "No, Mr. Styles," he said calmly. "You don't have to take orders from anyone here. You're fired. You can pick up your wages on Monday."

Styles struggled to his feet and lifted his clenched fist as if to strike back. Out of the corner of her eye, she saw Nathaniel move ever so slightly as if preparing to defend himself against the blow. For a long, tense moment, everyone in the room remained silent and motionless, waiting to see if Styles would try to take a swing at the other man, but he didn't. He touched a hand to his swollen jaw and glared at Nathaniel. "You'll be sorry for that, mate."

With that, he staggered to the door and left.

Nathaniel placed his hands on his hips and turned his gaze to the other men who were watching the scene in silent amazement. "Is there any other man here who doesn't want to load these crates?"

Mara wrapped the rag more securely around the pieces of ice she'd chipped from the block in Mrs. O'Brien's icebox and climbed the last flight of stairs to Nathaniel's office. He hadn't shown any sign of pain after the blow he'd dealt Styles, but Mara had immediately gone for ice. She'd never hit anyone in her life, but she imagined it must hurt.

Once again she considered Nathaniel's suggestion to let Michael take over as supervisor. Part of her still rebelled at the idea of handing over control to someone else, but she didn't want a repetition of this morning's events. She had thought she'd gained the respect of the men and that it was Nathaniel who had taken it away, but perhaps she'd only been fooling herself.

When she entered the office, she saw him at the far end of the huge room, bent over a table littered with bits of metal, building some newfangled contraption. She glanced around the room. "I see Boggs has put on the first coat of paint."

Nathaniel looked up and watched her cross the room toward him. "This morning," he answered and gestured to the walls. "Be careful not to touch. Paint's still wet."

She halted beside him and looked down at the bits of tin and wood on the table. "What are you building? More railroad track?"

"This? I'm trying to design an even smoother track," he answered as he continued putting pieces together. "I'm not satisfied with the figure eight. I think it could be better. It's all a matter of geometry." He launched into an explanation of planes, angles, and curves. After a sentence or two she was lost, but she listened anyway, liking the sound of his voice.

She watched as he put the pieces of track together, studying his hands. She noticed people's hands, perhaps because she always kept her own hidden within the protection of gloves. The sleeves of his shirt were rolled to the elbow, and she could see the muscles of his forearms flex, could see how the brown hairs glinted gold in the light, could see the strength and sureness in his hands as he worked. She thought about that night in her office when they'd eaten sandwiches, when his fingers had brushed beneath her chin. A warmth hit her in the stomach and shimmered outward like the ripples on a pond, wider and wider.

"What's that?"

His question broke into her thoughts, making her realize he was no longer talking about geometry.

"What?" Blankly, she looked up and watched him nod to the bundle in her hand. "Oh. Ice," she answered and cleared her throat, suddenly feeling foolish, realizing she'd forgotten all about it. "I thought perhaps . . . umm . . . your hand might hurt."

She thrust it toward him. "Take it. My fingers are going numb."

He laughed and accepted the melting gift.

"How is your hand?" she asked.

He clenched and unclenched his right fist. "A bit sore," he admitted, pressing the ice over his knuckles. "This will help. Thank you."

She cleared her throat and lifted her head, but she still did not look at him. "I . . . umm . . . I thought you said you never lose your temper."

"You think I lost my temper with Styles?"

"You did hit him."

"I didn't think he was in the mood to discuss the situation amicably, and I felt a punch or two would do him a world of good. I was angry, yes, but if I'd really lost my temper, I'd have thrown him through the window."

"You didn't throw me through the window."

He grinned. "No, but the thought did occur to me."

Suddenly, both of them were laughing. He looked at her, startled by her smile and the way it softened her features, blurring the hard edges until only the beauty remained. He realized he'd never heard her truly laugh before. Slowly, their laughter faded into silence.

"I'm sorry Styles pushed you," he said quietly.

"Yes, well, these things happen." She made a restless

movement, shifting her weight from one foot to the other, and her black skirt swayed with the motion. "I should be going. I have work to do."

Despite her words, she made no move to leave, and Nathaniel sensed there was something else she wanted to say. He waited.

She drew a deep breath. "Mr. Chase, you were right," she finally said. "It makes much better sense for Michael to be the supervisor."

The admission had been a difficult one for her to make, but Nathaniel felt no sense of triumph. "Mara, that man did what he did because he thought he could get away with it, a conclusion he probably came to after that incident with the handkerchief. What happened this morning was my fault."

"This isn't the first time something like this has happened. I try to maintain an air of authority, but it can be difficult." She clasped her hands behind her back and ducked her head, looking suddenly shy. "Thank you for coming to my aid. And thank you for supporting me in front of them."

He knew she hadn't expected his help, and he knew she would never have asked for it. "Mara, we're partners. I'll always back you up in front of others, even when I don't agree with you. All I ask is that you do the same for me. That's what a partnership is all about."

"I wouldn't know. I've never had a partner."

Nathaniel had, and he knew what a misery partnership could be. Voices invaded his mind, furious raised voices from long ago.

"This would never have happened if you d . . . didn't work them so hard. Children, for God's sake!" He could see himself at twenty-two years of age, standing in Adrian's office, leaning over the desk, shaking with fury. *"Fourteen, sixteen hours a day, d . . . doing things you*

c . . . couldn't pay a g . . . grown man to do. No wonder they fell."

Adrian had been so logical, so callous. *"Their families need the money. If their mothers don't care, why should I?"*

He'd shouted, he'd raged, but to no avail. Adrian hadn't given a damn. *"I remind you, little brother, that I'm in charge here."*

True enough. Adrian had been in charge, and two eleven-year-old boys had paid the price. One had stumbled on a scaffold, too tired at the end of a sixteen-hour day to watch his step, and the other had tried to catch him. Both of them had fallen sixty feet and died. Adrian had coldly suggested that if Nathaniel didn't like the way things were run, he could always sell his share and leave. Nathaniel had, and had caught the first boat to America, leaving Adrian to slowly destroy the Chase Toys empire alone, leaving Mai Lin behind when she refused to accompany him, leaving behind everything he'd ever wanted.

"Does the ice help?"

He heard Mara's voice and the memory shattered. "Yes," he answered and tossed the sodden rag onto a chair. "How is that cost analysis coming?"

She bit her lip and turned away, walking across the room to study the train on the table. "I haven't started it yet. I've been busy."

He stared at her rigid back, feeling her resistance coming up again. He knew she was stalling, hoping to change his mind about the trains. "Mara, I've had a partner before, and I can tell you from experience that trust and faith is required for any partnership to succeed."

"Trust?" She choked out the question. "You use words like trust and faith and partnership, but that's all they are. Words."

"No." He strode over to stand beside her. "They're more than that."

"Are they?" she asked, staring down at the train set. "I told you that I didn't want to make trains, that I didn't want to take that kind of risk, and what was your answer?" Before he could respond, she went on, "You basically said that's a shame, but we're going to make trains anyway." She gave a humorless laugh. "So much for partnership."

She started to turn away, but he put a hand on her shoulder to stop her. "Mara, if I hadn't come along, you would have certainly lost the business."

"Perhaps, but that isn't the point." She shook off the hand on her shoulder. "When I signed that agreement, I didn't know what you intended to do. You could have told me, but you didn't. You waited until after I'd signed the papers. You knew I would never agree to your plans if I'd known."

He felt a flash of guilt. That was true. He hadn't told her the whole truth because he'd seen the doubts in her eyes. He'd been certain that he could banish her doubts later, but now he wasn't so certain. "I know if I'd told you, you might have refused," he admitted, "but what would that have gotten you? You would still have lost the business."

She lifted her chin. "It seems I've lost it anyway."

She brushed past him and ran for the door. He didn't try to stop her. He could see the fear in her, but there was nothing he could do about that. He could not stop now. This time, he was going to fight for what he wanted. He was determined that nothing was going to get in the way of his dream. Not even the sad gray eyes of Mara Elliot. This time, he was going to win.

"You haven't lost anything, Mara," he told the empty doorway. "We're going to succeed. I know it, and before I'm finished, you'll know it, too."

*   *   *

The following afternoon, Nathaniel began his campaign to convince Mara Elliot that making trains was a good idea. He found her in her office, working, of course. "Good afternoon," he said, pausing in the doorway.

She spared a glance at him before returning her attention to the ledgers spread across her desk. Undeterred, he crossed the room and leaned over her desk to repeat his greeting. "Good afternoon."

She did not look up. "Good afternoon," she answered politely.

"What are you working on?" he asked, refusing to be ignored.

"Payroll. It's Friday afternoon, and I have to get figures ready so that Monday I can pay the employees."

He watched her add a column of figures and waited until she had entered the total at the bottom of the page before he spoke again. "Mara, I want you to stop working on payroll and put your ledgers away for the rest of the day. I need your help with something else."

That got her attention. She looked up at him. "But I have to make sure the figures are correct before I go to the bank Monday morning."

"You can do that later." He circled her desk and closed her ledger. "Right now, you're coming with me."

She tried to open the ledger again, but he grabbed it. When she jumped to her feet and tried to reach for the book, he held it out of reach.

"I don't have time for this nonsense. I have work to do."

"No, you don't." He tossed the ledger on her desk and gently dragged her by the arm, away from her paperwork. "You are taking the afternoon off."

"What?" Astonished, she stared up at him. "I can't do that."

"Of course you can. We own this company. We don't

have to be here all the time. That's one of the reasons why we made Michael the supervisor, remember? This particular afternoon, we aren't going stay locked up in the factory. I have something very important to do, and you are coming with me."

She made a grab for her reticule as he ushered her toward the door. "Where are we going?"

He stopped and reached to the hook beside the door for her straw bonnet. "Outside is a cab waiting to take us to the West End," he informed her, setting the hat on her head.

"The West End? What for?"

"We are going shopping." He studied her face beneath the hat brim, then pushed the bonnet to a rakish tilt and tied the ribbons beneath her chin. He gave a satisfied nod. "Much better. That way, it complements your face."

She ignored that comment and obstinately pushed her hat back to a properly dignified angle. From her reticule she took out her hat pin and secured the hat in place before he could make any other attempts to change it. "I don't have time to go shopping. Besides, there isn't anything I need."

"It's necessary that both of us go on this particular shopping trip."

"But—"

He reached out and pressed a finger to her lips, silencing her protest. The tip of his finger felt warm against her mouth, and she smelled the clean, spicy fragrance of soap. "Do me a favor," he said. "For once, don't argue with me. Just trust me and come along."

Again he gripped her elbow and walked out of the room with her in tow. They went down the long hallway and across the production floor, pausing long enough to tell Michael they would be out for the rest of the afternoon. Nathaniel's grip on her arm did not relax until they were outside of the building, where he let her go and pointed to the cab waiting in the street.

"This is silly," she mumbled as the cab rolled down Holborn toward Oxford Street. "Why do you need me to go shopping with you?"

"Because I value your opinion. Just wait. We'll be there soon."

When the cab pulled up in front of Harrod's department store, Nathaniel jumped down and held out his hand to help her down. Then he turned to the driver and instructed him to wait.

"What are you buying?" she asked.

He shook his head and started toward the entrance doors. "Nothing."

She sighed and followed him. "I don't understand why you always talk in riddles."

"Don't you like riddles, Mara?"

She didn't answer that. "I thought you said we were going shopping."

"We are. I believe it's called window shopping."

When they entered the huge building, Nathaniel passed by the grocery, haberdashery, and dress materials, making for the stairs to the upper floors. She followed, more puzzled than ever.

A few moments later, she found herself following him into the toy department on the first floor. She came to a halt. "You want to look at toys?"

He grinned and leaned down to whisper in her ear, "It's called studying the competition. Let's have a look around, shall we?"

Waving the sales clerks aside, he proceeded to walk amid the tables and shelves of brightly painted toys. Mara followed, wondering why on earth he'd brought her along. She knew nothing about toys. He went straight to the trains located at the far end of the room.

Mara paused beside him. She watched as he pulled his spectacles from his jacket pocket and put them on. Then he lifted a locomotive in his hands, staring intently at the solid brass construction. "A dribbler," he commented. "Good design, very high quality, but damned expensive to make."

"Why is it called a dribbler?"

"It's steam powered. When the train moves across the floor, it leaves dribbles of water all over the place. An unfortunate problem with steam," he added, setting the locomotive back down.

He picked up another. "Well, well, well," he said to himself. "Adrian, your trains are pitiful."

"This is one of your brother's trains?" She frowned. "It looks all right. What's wrong with it?"

"Everything. This train has the same design my grandfather used. It's outdated." He ran one finger along the top of the boiler. "He's using very cheap tin, and the riveting is poor. He's covered it with pretty paint, but this thing will fall apart in a matter of weeks."

He set the train back down and studied a few more of the locomotives made by Chase Toy Company, finding none of them to be of high quality. After examining them herself, Mara agreed. "Using such poor materials doesn't make sense," she said. "It never pays off in the long run."

Nathaniel smiled grimly. "Adrian is relying on the Chase reputation, but he's never cared much for quality. Someday, it will catch up with him. I intend to be there when it does."

His expression suddenly hardened. It was so unexpected, and so unlike him, Mara suddenly felt cold.

"Why are you so determined to compete with your brother?" she asked.

Nathaniel's hands tightened around the toy train, and she watched as the ruthlessness faded away. "Making toys has always been my dream. Adrian makes toys, too. Competition is inevitable."

He set down the toy and moved a few steps to the right, but Mara remained where she was, staring after him, shaken by the determination she'd seen in his eyes.

"Ah," he said, "now we're seeing some interesting ones."

He looked over at her and smiled. It was that special smile, the one meant to reassure, to charm and cajole. The darkness she'd seen only a moment before was gone, and Mara wondered if she had only imagined it.

He studied these locomotives appreciatively. "The Germans know how to make trains. Look at the detail. And the quality is outstanding. I'll wager that ten years from now, the Germans will be our toughest competition."

Mara doubted they'd be in business to compete with the Germans ten years from now, but she refrained from saying so. She followed him silently as he made a thorough examination of every train in the toy department.

When he was finished, he pulled off his spectacles and put them back in his pocket. "Now that we've seen what everyone else is offering, tell me something. What is it about our train that makes it so different from all of these?"

Mara glanced back at the toys. "I don't know much about trains."

"Use your eyes. Open your mind, Mara."

She looked up at him. He was watching her, clearly waiting for an answer. She sighed, and started to shake her head. "I don't know," she said, "they all look—" Then an idea struck her. "None of these are electric."

He nodded. "That's part of it. What else?"

She studied the trains. "None of them have tracks." She turned to look at him. "They all appear to run on the floor."

"Exactly. Which means?"

She visualized Nathaniel's elaborate train. "Which means that they don't have stations, and bridges, and all the other fancy things."

"If you were a child, which train would you rather play with?" he asked as he headed for the stairs.

"Wait," she called, quickening her steps to catch up with him as possibilities began to take shape in her mind. "The other day when Michael and Percy were with you, I saw those pieces of track all over the floor," she said. "Michael said those pieces of tin were sections that fit together."

"Um-hmm," he confirmed. "Why do you suppose I designed it that way?"

"So that children could put the track together any way they wanted it." The full potential of the concept suddenly hit her, and she came to an abrupt halt on the bottom step. "So that children could create their own miniature railways!"

"Yes!" He stopped at the foot of the stairs and turned, spanning her waist with his hands and lifting her off the bottom step with a shout of laughter. He whirled her around in the air. "Yes, yes, yes!"

She gripped his wide shoulders to steady herself, and her answering laughter rang out as he spun her around. Bolts of fabric on display passed her in a blur of color, making her dizzy. She focused her gaze on his face, and everything else receded. In that moment, something stirred within her, a feeling she thought she'd lost a long time ago. Hope.

The room slowly stopped spinning. She felt herself sliding down the length of his body until her feet hit the floor. An awareness emerged in her as she could feel the muscles of his shoulders beneath her fingers, his strong hands on her waist, the rise and fall of his chest beneath her forearms. It rushed through her, then ebbed away, leaving her with nothing but the chill of her own fear.

Everything came into focus again, making her realize they were practically embracing in the dress materials department of Harrod's. She took a hasty step back and turned away, only to find three stout matrons and several sales clerks staring at them in horror.

Heat suffused her cheeks, and she stepped around Nathaniel, heading for the exit doors. He followed and fell in step beside her, but she could not look at him. She walked outside and started for the waiting cab, but Nathaniel's hand on her arm stopped her.

"Mara, now that you understand what I'm trying to do—"

"I want to go back," she said stiffly and pulled her arm from his grasp. "I still have work to finish."

He expelled his breath with a sigh. "All right."

Neither of them said much on the way back. Nathaniel made several attempts at conversation, but she kept her gaze fixed on the window and replied in unencouraging monosyllables. She didn't even look at him.

She was embarrassed, he knew, but there was more to it than that. She was afraid. He could see fear in the thin line of her lips, the hands clasped so tightly together in her lap, the rigid set of her shoulders.

For a moment, she'd gotten excited about the idea of making trains. But the instant she'd realized it, doubt had taken over and she'd withdrawn again. Mara Elliot was a woman who could switch from cool logic to deep insecurity and back again all in the space of two heartbeats, and there were times when Nathaniel had no idea how to deal with her. This was one of those times.

Let her retreat back into her shell if she wanted to, he finally decided. But he was not going to let her stay there.

9

Mara had a routine that never varied. Sunday morning, she did what she always did on Sunday mornings. She went to the baths, taking a fresh towel, a change of clothes, and the one luxury she allowed herself—lilac-scented soap. She also took her bundle of laundry with her to do while she was there.

Afterward, she took her clean laundry home and hung it to dry on a line she stretched across her room, then she went to early Sunday service. She was in her office by ten o'clock.

The neat stacks of ledgers and papers on her desk today depressed her. Because of her trip to Harrod's with Nathaniel Friday afternoon, she had been forced to spend most of Saturday doing payroll, which had put her an entire day behind schedule. One look at the desk told her how far behind she was. She hated that.

With a sigh, she sat down behind her desk and reached

for the first item on the stack of papers to her left. She scanned it and frowned in bewilderment as her gaze ran down the list. Thirty brass wheels, one-inch diameter, with flanges. Four of same, one-and-one-half-inch diameter. Four sheets tin . . .

The parts list for the trains. She flipped through the thick stack of papers, finally coming to the design specifications. Michael had been busy. She looked closer. No, the nearly unreadable notes beside the diagrams were not in the same handwriting. *Only Nathaniel could have such horrible penmanship,* she thought, remembering the sloppy signature she'd seen on their partnership agreement.

Thoughts of that document caused her frown to deepen, and Mara shoved the list aside. She'd get to the trains some other time. She needed to begin working on a budget for September now.

A tiny prick of conscience told her Nathaniel expected the trains to be included in her budget, but she pushed it aside. The increased costs would mean going to the bank for a loan, a possibility she refused to contemplate.

Just the thought of borrowing money scared her. She'd seen James borrow money so many times, then run off when the money was due. She was still amazed at how skilled her husband had been with the glib talk that somehow convinced businessmen to invest in him. But glib talk didn't pay the bills, a fact Mara knew only too well. From the time she married him, Mara had been the one forced to deal with the creditors every time James left town. She would not go through that again. Not for Nathaniel Chase. Not for anyone.

Several hours later, when the budget was finally finished, trains were not on it. Mara set the ledger aside, and reached for the sales reports.

"I thought I might find you here."

Startled, she jumped in her chair, looking up at the tall figure standing in the doorway. "What are you doing here?"

Nathaniel leaned one shoulder against the doorjamb. "Looking for you."

Dismayed, she stared at him. Could the man give her no peace? "Why?"

"Mara, it's a gorgeous day. It isn't raining, for once, and the weather is fine. Why have you locked yourself away in this stuffy little room that doesn't even have a window?"

She gestured to the ledgers piled on her desk. "It's your fault. If you hadn't dragged me off to Harrod's, I wouldn't be so far behind."

He shook his head. "Don't blame this on me. I know for a fact you work on Sundays anyway. Although why you do is beyond my ken."

"The work has to get done somehow. And Sundays are always quiet and peaceful." She frowned at him. "At least, they have been until now."

He laughed. "'Gather ye rosebuds while ye may. Old time is still a-flying.'" He crossed the room and moved around her desk until he stood behind her chair. Then he reached over her shoulder and took the pencil away from her. "And that same flower that smiles today, tomorrow may be dying."

"What are you doing?"

"Robert Herrick," he added and pulled her to her feet. "C'mon."

"I can't take another afternoon off," she protested, unmoved by poetic encouragement.

She tried to remove her elbow from his grasp, but he refused to relinquish his hold. "Why not?" he countered. "You got the payroll done yesterday, didn't you?"

"Yes, but—"

"Good. Then there's nothing that can't wait until Monday. Come along."

"Where are we going?" she asked as he guided her toward the door.

"We are going to have some fun." And he refused to say more.

Thirty minutes later, she found herself in Hyde Park, standing by the Serpentine and staring doubtfully at the rowboat that bobbed gently on the water of the lake. "You want to go boating?"

"Can you think of anything better to do on a Sunday afternoon in midsummer?" he asked, handing money over to the boat handler.

Her expression grew frantic. She could think of many better things to do. "Nathaniel, I don't want to get in that boat."

"Why?"

"I can't swim."

He smiled down at her. "We're not going swimming." He studied her panicked expression and added gently, "It's all right, Mara. I wouldn't let you drown."

"Somehow, that thought doesn't comfort me!"

"It should. I happen to be an excellent swimmer." He took her elbow and guided her into the boat.

"I don't think I like this," she murmured, gripping the sides of the boat as she carefully sat down.

He sat in the rower's seat and gripped the oars, then gave the man on the dock a nod to untie the moorings. "You've traveled all over the world, yet you're afraid to punt around the Serpentine?"

"That was different," she answered. "Those were big, safe steamships."

The man on the dock sent the boat away with a shove of his boot and within moments, the boat was gliding across the lake.

Nathaniel waited until they were well into the center of the lake before he broached the subject on his mind. "Tell me something," he said, lifting the oars out of the water, "Why are you so opposed to making trains?"

"What?" She stared at him, startled by the abrupt question. "You want to talk about your trains now?"

"Yes."

A tiny frown appeared between her brows. He could tell that she thought him out of his mind. "Here?"

"Yes, here. I think this is the perfect place to discuss the matter." He nodded to the water around them. "Out here, you can't avoid the subject or run away."

He studied her face, watching the mask steal over her features, wiping away all expression. It angered him, that ability to freeze to an unresponsive chunk of ice and shut him out when she didn't like the conversation. He yanked the oars out of their locks and placed them across the boat.

She cast an almost desperate glance at the water surrounding them. "I want to go back," she declared, squirming on the seat and rocking the boat.

"No. We are going to talk about this. Right here, right now."

"There's nothing to talk about."

"Oh, yes, there is." He gave her a level stare. "Why don't you want to make trains?"

"I want to go back," she repeated, refusing to answer his question.

"Not until we get this business settled once and for all. Tell me why."

"I already did. It's too risky."

"And I told you, some risks are worth taking." He watched her jaw set. "Damn it, you are the most stubborn woman I've ever met. You're so worried about not failing, you never think about succeeding. Haven't you ever taken a risk, Mara? Haven't you ever wanted anything so badly, you were willing to gamble all you had to make it happen?"

"No." She swallowed hard. "That would be foolish."

"So you hide in your little office on Sunday afternoons and save your pennies in a little tin can and worry about all the things that might happen, but that never do. Don't you want more from life than that?"

"Maybe I expect less from life than you do."

"Not enough from life and too much from yourself."

"I don't know what you mean."

"You've made it clear you hate having a partner, and I thought it was because of me." Nathaniel leaned forward, resting his forearms on the oars between them. "But that's not it, is it? You hate the idea of a partner because you want to control everything, do everything. All by yourself."

"As usual, I don't know what you're talking about."

"Don't you? If you rely only on yourself, you'll never be disappointed. If you don't trust anyone, you don't have to worry that they might fail you. You can always have things your way. You don't have to make concessions."

"Don't talk to me about concessions, sir!" Anger flared in her eyes as her icy composure splintered apart. "I spent eight years making concessions. Giving in, yielding to whatever whim happened to take my husband's fancy, allowing him to drag us all over the world."

"Us?"

Mara drew a deep, steadying breath. "We had a daughter, Helen. I knew picking up and moving every other year wasn't good for her. She needed stability. Four years ago, when she was seven, I decided I'd had enough. We were living here in London and James had started Elliot's, but we'd been here less than a year before he was packing to leave again."

Her words came out in a rush, pouring out the anger and pain as if she could no longer contain them. "I asked him to stay for Helen's sake, but he said that's why he was going, to make a future for her. I asked him to stay for my sake, but he patted me on the shoulder and said I'd be just fine until he could send for us. I asked, I pleaded." Her voice broke. "I begged."

She glared at Nathaniel, her face twisted with pain. "I begged him, do you understand?" she cried. "I begged him not to leave. Do you know what his reaction was?"

She didn't wait for an answer. She took a deep breath, and went on, "He took out a loan of five thousand pounds, putting up Elliot's as collateral, and sailed off for America anyway. He gave me half the money before he left. Wasn't that generous of him? I used it to pay all the other debts he left behind. The money was gone in less than a month."

She wrapped her arms around her ribs, fighting to regain her precious control. "It didn't matter much. A few days after James left, Helen died."

"How?"

Her expression hardened once again to an unreadable mask, but he saw the pain in her crystal gray eyes.

"How did she die, Mara?"

Her lower lip trembled. She caught it between her teeth and didn't answer.

"Fire?" he asked gently.

"Yes." She turned her head away with the stiffness of a marionette. "And I had nothing," she added, staring across the water, "nothing but a business that was nearly bankrupt and a wastrel husband who didn't even bother to send a letter until six months after her funeral."

Nathaniel heard the raw, ragged edge in her voice, and he knew he had touched the core of her wounded and bitter heart. He'd known the moment he'd met James that the man was brilliant and irresponsible, charming and deceitful. But that hadn't mattered to him at the time. All that had mattered was that James had given him his chance, one more chance to achieve what he'd always wanted.

Yet, it seemed that James had also been a man with a callous disregard for the needs of his family. A selfish man who fed on a dream until he got bored, who had left his wife to grieve alone for the loss of their daughter. "What did you do?"

"What could I do? I took over the business."

"Hmm." Thoughtfully, he studied her. "That seems a bit risky to me."

"It would only have been a risk if there had been something to lose."

"But there was, Mara," he said softly. "You risked failure."

"Only because I had no other choice."

"Of course you had a choice. Plenty of choices, in fact. You could have sold the business, and possibly gained a small profit from it. You could have gone to work in a shop. You could have scraped together the money to return to South Africa. Yet, you did none of those things. Why?"

She kept her face turned away from him and didn't answer.

"Could it be that you had your own dream?" As he spoke the words aloud, he began to realize how true they were. "That's it, isn't it? Your dream was to be independent and run your own business. You wanted it so badly, you—"

"Yes, yes, all right!" she cried, turning her head to face him again. Her chin lifted defiantly. "Yes, I wanted it. Yes, I took a risk. I admit it. Does that satisfy you?"

"Not by half."

"What do you want from me?"

"I already told you. Acceptance, a bit of trust. Compromise."

"And what about what I want?" she fired back. "Why is it that when you and I talk about partnership and compromise, I'm always the one giving up something? What about you?"

"Name one thing I haven't been willing to compromise on."

"This business with the toys comes to mind."

He shook his head. "You don't want compromise. You're afraid to take the risks, and you want me to give in to your fear. I won't do that."

She turned her face away again, and he reached out. Grasping her chin, he forced her to look at him. "Like it or not, Mara, the fact is that I invested five thousand pounds in this company—and saved your bacon, I might add—for one reason. I want to make toys. But I'm willing to minimize the risks you fear by making the transition gradually. That's compromise."

"And what about the loan?" she countered, jerking her chin out of his grip. "You insist on borrowing money, despite my opposition to the idea."

"It's true I want to take out a loan to finance the venture, but I'm willing to discuss other options with you, if you have any."

"There aren't any other options. You call that compromising?"

"All right! Let's settle this once and for all. Forget compromise, since that obviously isn't working. I propose a wager."

"A wager?" She eyed him with suspicion.

"Exactly. Do that cost analysis. If you can prove to me that there is no profit in the trains, we won't do it. We'll continue to do just what Elliot's has always done. But if it proves to have profit potential, then you'll stop fighting me, and we'll work together to make it happen."

"I don't make wagers."

"Why doesn't that surprise me? But think about this for a minute, don't reject it out of hand. To quote your own words, there's only a risk if there's something to lose. You have nothing to lose and everything to gain."

She said nothing as she weighed all the pros and cons carefully. Finally she nodded. "All right."

"I expect you to be fair," he warned, lifting one oar and locking it into place. "I expect you to make every effort to find good prices on parts and reasonable bids. I'll talk to toy retailers and determine a price for the trains. Then we'll sit down and compare notes and see where we are." He looked at her as he replaced the other oar in the lock and seized the grips. "Agreed?"

"Agreed, but it'll never work. You're going to lose."

His smile was supremely confident as he began rowing back toward the shore. "We'll see."

But when she wasn't looking at him, he looked up toward heaven and murmured a silent prayer for luck.

Mara could not sleep. She kept changing her position, rolling onto one side, then the other, then onto her back. It made no difference. She punched her pillow and straightened her sheets. It still made no difference.

What if Nathaniel turned out to be right? What if there were just enough profit margin in his trains to justify his plans? Mara had no illusions that they might be able to make the trains a successful venture. It was too silly, really. Those trains would cost the earth to make, and who would buy them?

She rolled onto her back again. A thin shaft of moonlight through her window illuminated the white ceiling, and she wondered if counting the cracks in the plaster were as good as counting sheep. She stared up at the ceiling, and her thoughts continued to spin in useless, fearful circles.

So many things could go wrong. If they made the trains, they'd need a loan. If they took out a loan and the trains didn't sell, they'd be bankrupt. She'd lose everything. The enormity of the risks engulfed her.

She hadn't had any choice, she reminded herself. As Nathaniel had pointed out, she'd had nothing to lose by making that wager with him, but she'd had something to gain. Consoled by that thought, Mara rolled onto her side and closed her eyes, trying to force herself to fall asleep.

Two cats meowed and hissed, indicating a fight. Boot heels tapped the pavement of the street, floating down the alley and through her open window, and she knew the local policeman was strolling past. Another sound, a new and unexpected one, pierced the night, and Mara sat up in bed. What was that?

She listened, and the sound came again, then another, then another. Musical notes. A violin. Him again. It had to be him.

She tossed back the sheet and walked to the window. Thrusting her head through the opening, she looked up. Sure enough, the sounds of a melody drifted down to her. The man was actually playing the violin. She pulled back and fumbled for her pendant watch that lay on the washstand. She held it up to the moonlight and groaned. It was after two o'clock.

Mara would have closed the window, but the room would become unbearably stuffy if she did. She walked back over to the bed and crawled between the sheets, waiting with growing irritation for the music to stop. But it continued on, a soft and delicate melody.

Why, why, was he playing that thing at this hour? She groaned again and pulled the sheet over her head. It didn't help. She would never be able to go to sleep now. Once again she tossed back the sheet.

Rising from the bed, she slipped into her wrapper, unlocked her door, and marched upstairs, one hand on the stair rail guiding her through the darkness. She halted in front of his door and knocked. The music stopped, and she quickly thrust her hands into the pockets of her wrap to hide them as she waited for the door to open.

When it did, Mara opened her mouth to tell him exactly what she thought of his prowess with the violin, but the words stuck in her throat. Light spilled from the doorway over his bare shoulders and gave his skin the tawny smoothness of polished leather. He was wearing nothing but a pair of trousers. She stared straight into the solid wall of his naked chest and couldn't think of a thing to say.

What on earth was the matter with her? She was no innocent miss. She'd been a married woman. She'd lived in places where men went around nearly naked. Reminding herself of those facts, she forced her gaze to his face.

"Mara? What is it?"

His voice intruded on her wayward thoughts and succeeded in renewing her irritation. "Mr. Chase, it is two o'clock in the morning," she informed him with a sigh. Nodding to the instrument and bow in his hands, she asked, "Do you have to play that thing at this hour?"

"I couldn't sleep," he answered. "Playing music relaxes me."

"They have nerve tonics for that sort of thing, don't they?"

"I don't know how to play a nerve tonic," he answered, a smile tipping the corners of his mouth.

Mara was not amused. "Now I can't sleep either. Thanks to you."

"Mara, music is the oldest sedative of all. It is a natural nerve tonic, and Brahms's *Lullaby* is particularly soothing. If you would just listen to the music and relax, you would be asleep in a few minutes."

"I doubt it."

He didn't reply but just smiled at her. With another sigh, she turned away and went back downstairs. She should have known better than to waste her time. When she reached her room, she could once again hear the strains of a melody floating down from upstairs.

She scowled at the ceiling. He really was the most impossible person. She tossed aside her wrapper and crawled back into bed, knowing it was futile to bother. He was going to keep her up all night, and that was all there was to it. Natural nerve tonic, indeed. She rolled over on her side, plumped up her pillow, and once again reminded herself the man was mad as a hatter.

She closed her eyes. Still resenting him for keeping her awake, Mara drifted off to sleep to the poignant notes of Brahms's *Lullaby*.

10

When Mara left her flat the next morning, she found Nathaniel coming down the stairs from his own rooms, and she had to resist the temptation to scurry back inside and wait for him to pass by.

"Good morning," he said, pausing on the landing beside her. "Did you sleep well?"

Mara frowned up at him. "Is that question supposed to be amusing?"

His blue eyes told her he thought so. "'Music has charms to soothe a savage beast, to soften rocks, or bend a knotted oak,'" he quoted. "William Congreve. Didn't you find Brahms soothing?"

She would have died rather than admit she'd actually fallen asleep to the languid melody floating through her window. "Not at two o'clock in the morning," she answered as she locked her door.

He laughed, not the least bit perturbed by her disapproval. "Do you mind if we walk together?"

Mara did mind, but she could think of no polite way to say so. Day or night, she couldn't seem to get away from him. She gave a brief nod, thrust her latchkey in her pocket, and continued on down the stairs. He followed, falling in step beside her as they walked out of the lodging house.

"I think—" he began.

She groaned and came to a halt on the stoop. Turning to face him, she held up one hand. "Please, don't. Don't think. Your thinking has the unfortunate tendency to wreak havoc in my life."

"I think it's going to rain today." He looked down at her innocently, but she thought she detected a tiny smile lurking at the corners of his mouth. Praying for patience, she moved to start down the front steps, but she found the kitten in her path.

"You again?" Mara urged the kitten to move aside with a gentle nudge of her boot. The kitten meowed, but it didn't hiss at her. It also didn't move out of the way. She stepped around it. "Do you really think it'll rain today?" she asked Nathaniel with an anxious glance at the sky.

Her query received no answer, and she turned back around to find Nathaniel kneeling on the steps, talking to the kitten. He held out one hand, and the kitten backed away from him, hissing.

"Careful," Mara cautioned him. "It'll scratch you."

"Perhaps," he conceded, but moved his hand a bit closer. "Hullo, little one," he murmured to the cat. "Cautious, aren't you?"

The kitten backed up, tail in the air, and hissed again. Nathaniel rose to his feet and joined Mara on the sidewalk. "Poor thing. It's got a cut on its ear. It's probably been in a fight."

"It lives in the alley behind the factory, I think. I see it almost every day."

They had taken only a few steps when Nathaniel glanced back over his shoulder. "He's following us."

"What?" Mara saw the kitten was indeed following them, keeping a cautious distance. It meowed at her, and she halted.

Nathaniel leaned closer to her. "I think he likes you."

"Don't be ridiculous. It's an alley cat, not a pet." She waved a hand at the cat. "Shoo. Go on."

The kitten sat back on its haunches and stared at her.

"He's awfully young," Nathaniel said. "Maybe he thinks you're Mama."

She shot him a rueful glance and once again resumed walking. The kitten continued to follow. When they reached the factory, the cat tried to follow them inside, but Mara quickly closed the door.

"Let him in," Nathaniel urged. "He won't hurt anything."

"And have it underfoot, getting in everybody's way?" She shook her head. "No, leave it outside."

"It could be useful, having a cat in here. I saw a mouse the other day."

She stared at him. "I've never seen a mouse in this building."

He shrugged. "I saw one upstairs. It makes sense to have a cat around. Besides, the poor thing is starving. Put yourself in his place. Wouldn't it be frightening to be a baby cat in a savage world of alley toms without your mama there to protect you? Think of what the little fellow's going through. He's probably lonely and scared and needs a friend."

He was teasing her again. Mara sighed and opened the door to find the kitten sitting there. "Oh, all right," she mumbled. "Come on in." She opened the door a bit wider and the kitten scampered inside.

"It'll just get in the way," she told Nathaniel, watching the animal pounce on a scrap of paper that lay on the floor.

"True."

"If anybody tries to pet it, it'll scratch."

"True."

She looked at him, then back at the kitten, and sighed. "I'll pick up some milk later," she said and walked away, wondering why on earth she should care that a hissing alley cat might be lonely.

That evening, Nathaniel went to the little cubbyhole Mara called an office to walk her home. She was seated at her desk, papers and ledgers in neat stacks all around her.

"Are you ready to go?"

She shook her head and held up one hand, running the pencil in her other hand down the column of numbers before her as he leaned one shoulder against the doorjamb and waited. "Thirty-eight, forty-seven, fifty-seven, sixty-two pounds," she counted and wrote the final number in her ledger. "I still have about an hour's worth of work to do," she said.

"Started gathering information from subcontractors, have you?"

She nodded. "I intend to be thorough."

"I never doubted it for a second." He came into the room and took the chair opposite her desk. He watched her for a moment as she added up another column of figures. When she'd written the total at the bottom of the page, he said, "Would you like me to teach you how to use that abacus? It truly would make what you're doing easier."

She glanced at the abacus that lay on one corner of her desk, lifted it in her hands to study it for a moment, then looked over at him again. "Yes, I would. If—" She hesitated. "If you wouldn't mind?"

"If I minded, I wouldn't have offered." He stood and circled her desk, dragging his chair with him so that he could sit beside her. He reached for the abacus and placed it flat on the desk, with the rods strung with beads in a vertical position like the bars of a prison cell.

"Notice how this crossbar divides the top part from the bottom?" When she nodded, he went on, "There are nine rods, and each rod is strung with seven beads, two in the top section, five in the bottom. The Chinese call the top half heaven and the bottom half earth."

She gave him a skeptical look. "Heaven and earth?"

"The Chinese are a very poetic people." He began pushing beads around until all the beads in heaven were flush with the top of the frame and the beads in earth were flush with the bottom. "The first thing you have to do is set the beads so that your abacus is at zero, like this."

She leaned a bit closer to study the abacus, and her shoulder brushed his. He could smell the lilac fragrance of her hair, and he savored it, like the warmth of a spring day after a long, lonely winter. He turned his head to look at her as she studied the abacus. The profile of her face was somehow both sharp and delicate, her parted lips soft above her stubborn chin, her ivory skin smooth over the plane of her cheek. Involuntarily, he leaned even closer to her.

"Does each bead represent a different number?"

Her question penetrated his mind slowly, and he swallowed hard, fighting to clear his senses of the scent of lilacs and the warmth that radiated from her body so close to his.

"No," he answered, forcing his attention back to the matter at hand. "The beads in heaven are worth five and the beads in earth are worth one. Each rod represents the position of a multiple of ten, with the first column on the right being ones, the second column tens, the third column hundreds, and so on." He reached toward the rod of beads on the far right and pushed one bead down from the top and one bead up from the bottom until both hit the crossbar. "Five and one. That means the number six. If I do the same thing in the next row as well, then I have sixty-six. Do you see?"

She nodded. "That's seems simple enough. But how do I add a column of numbers together?"

"We have sixty-six here. If I want to add, say, thirteen to that number, I add three to the first column by pushing up three more beads, and I push up one bead in the second column to represent ten. I now have the sum of seventy-nine."

"This is simple!" she exclaimed, surprised. "Let me try it."

"All right." He gave her two numbers to add, and she immediately ran into difficulties.

"I have to carry the number to the next column. How do I do that?"

He showed her how to carry over, and within minutes she was adding numbers well into the thousands. "I can't believe how easy this is."

She sat back in her chair and looked over at him. "Can I subtract?"

He nodded. "You can also multiply and divide, although that's a bit more complicated."

"Show me."

He did, and an hour later she was totaling numbers in her ledger twice as fast as she would have done with her pencil, easily dividing them into pounds, shillings, and pence.

He sat back and watched her, smiling. She worked so

hard, and she took everything so seriously. He was going to have to teach his partner that work, while important, wasn't everything.

"You're pushing those beads around like a Chinese silk merchant in the marketplace," he commented as she entered another total in her ledger. He leaned forward and studied her for a moment. "Maybe you should start wearing your hair in a braid down your back."

"I can't believe how easy this abacus is to use. It will help me a great deal. Thank you."

He leaned a bit closer. "Now that I've proven myself useful, aren't you glad I'm your partner? Don't think about it. Just say yes."

"Yes."

"What a nice thing to say."

She smiled suddenly, a wide, genuine, spontaneous smile. He watched the change come over her, like the sun coming out from behind a cloud.

"You have a lovely smile," he said quietly. "I wish I saw it more often."

Her expression changed, her smile disappeared, and it was as if a wall had suddenly come up between them. "It's late," she mumbled and rose to her feet. "I should be going."

He walked her home. When they reached her flat, she thanked him again for the abacus, and she bid him good night, but she didn't smile. The sun had gone back behind a cloud, and he wondered when it would come out again. He hoped it would be soon.

Nathaniel spent all the following day up in his office. He had a new idea and whenever he had a new idea, he became obsessed, spending hours, days, even weeks, trying to make it work. This idea was no exception.

He stared down at the diagrams he'd drawn. There had to be a way. Steam trains were commonplace, but if he could figure out how to keep the steam train from leaving water on the floor, he'd be a step ahead of every competitor. He thought he'd had the answer, but now he wasn't so sure.

Footsteps pounded on the stairs, sounding like a marauding herd of cattle, and Nathaniel turned his head as Boggs entered the room, a bag slung over one shoulder, a ladder under his arm, and a can of paint in his other hand. He was followed by four young children, each of whom also carried a can of paint, except the youngest, whose arms were full of paint-spattered sheets.

"Afternoon, guv'nor. I've come to put on the second coat." He set down his burdens and jerked one thumb toward the youngsters, who lined up in a row beside him. "I 'ad to bring 'em along. Me missus told me so. I 'ope ye don't mind. They'll be quiet as lambs, I promise ye."

Nathaniel doubted that. His gaze traveled down the row of angelic faces and back again. "Are all of them yours?"

Boggs gave a heavy sigh and pulled at his cap. "Them and four more."

Nathaniel grinned. "Eight? How do you keep track of them all?"

"It ain't easy, guv'nor, that it ain't. Ain't easy feeding 'em either."

"It must be hard on your wife, too."

Boggs shook his head and reached for the ladder. "Oh, no, sir. Not me wife. The missus an' me weren't never married proper."

"What?" Nathaniel stared at the workman and began to laugh. "Eight children and you're not even married?"

"Never got 'round to it," Boggs confessed blithely. "But got eight little ones just the same." He gestured toward the children. "You met me Alfred the other day. 'e's me oldest." He pointed to each child in turn. "Davy, ten. Millie, nine. Jane, eight. And Cyrus, 'e's six."

Nathaniel nodded to the children, who set down their burdens and stood in line like towheaded toy soldiers until Boggs herded them toward one end of the room. "Now you sit over 'ere an' stay put," he ordered.

As if it was a signal, they all began to talk at once.

"Father, what's that?"

"Can we play with the toys?"

"That's an Indian, ain't it?"

Boggs roared, "I want it quiet!" and they immediately fell silent.

"That's better. An' no fightin' or spittin'," he added as he walked away.

"Yes, sir," they chorused. They obeyed—for about thirty seconds.

Nathaniel heard the first punch and the wail that followed. He turned around in time to see sweet-looking little Millie grab her brother Davy by the hair. The other two jumped in, and the four of them began rolling around like cats in a sack.

Boggs dropped the sheet he was spreading over Nathaniel's train set and strode over to the children to break up the melee. "I said no fightin'," he shouted, pulling Davy and Millie apart. "Didn't I say that?"

"But Father, Davy pulled my hair!" Millie wailed.

"You pulled mine first!"

"Did not!"

"Did too!"

"I've 'ad enough!" Boggs said. He shoved each child into a different corner of the room and then glanced at Nathaniel. "Sorry, guv'nor. Take my advice, sir. Never 'ave children."

Nathaniel smothered a laugh. "I'll keep that in mind, Mr. Boggs."

He returned his attention to the diagram before him, but it wasn't long before the Boggs children started shouting at one another from their corners, and everything seemed to deteriorate from there. Nathaniel gave up on the intricacies of improving the toy steam train and watched in sympathetic amusement as Boggs again stopped working to establish peace.

"I'm sorry, sir, that I am," Boggs told him, disentangling Cyrus's arms and legs from Jane's. "Would've left 'em at 'ome, but me missus 'ad a cleanin' job, and she couldn't take 'em along."

"It's all right," Nathaniel assured him. "They're just bored. Perhaps they need something fun to do." They weren't the only ones, he decided, looking down at his diagrams, at the idea that just wasn't working. He crossed the room, pulled down a crate from the top of one stack, and took it to the children. "They might find some things in here to play with."

"Oh, no, sir," Boggs said. "Not yer toys. They might break 'em."

Be careful with that toy, Nathaniel. His father's irritated voice came back to him. *You might break it.*

"Toys are meant to be played with, Mr. Boggs," he answered and opened the box.

When Mara went upstairs later that morning, she found Nathaniel on the floor, surrounded by children and toys. Mr. Boggs was perched on a ladder several feet from her, putting a second coat of white paint on the walls and oblivious to the noise and rambunctious play going on across the room.

She returned her attention to the group on the floor. Nathaniel had set up a makeshift platform about two feet off the floor and was demonstrating some of his windups for the children, deliberately sending the toys over the edge to crash on the floor below and making the children laugh.

Mara frowned, disturbed by the sight of children in the factory. She didn't like it. She didn't like it at all.

"'ullo, ma'am," Boggs said.

She glanced up at the workman on the ladder. "What is going on here?"

He turned slightly and waved his paintbrush in the direction of the group on the floor. "'e says it's research."

"Research?" Her frown deepened. "Research for what?"

"I don't know, ma'am. But that's what 'e said."

She walked down the length of the room, watching as Nathaniel rose up on his knees to place another toy on the platform. The draft through the open windows ruffled his hair, and he shook his head impatiently to keep the wayward strands out of his eyes, then he released the toy. It raced across the piece of wood, went over the edge, and hit the floor.

The children clapped their hands, screaming with laughter, and a roar began in Mara's ears. Fear shimmered through her, and she came to an abrupt halt. She couldn't seem to breathe. The room was suddenly hot.

Nathaniel reached down to retrieve the toy and noticed her standing several feet away. A frown of puzzlement knit his brow. "Mara?"

She swallowed hard. "What are these children doing in here?"

He opened his mouth to answer, but suddenly the oldest boy hurled himself at Nathaniel with a war whoop. The other children followed suit, tackling him with joyous enthusiasm.

"Wait! Wait!" he cried before he went down, laughing, buried beneath the children. "Enough!" he shouted.

Struggling to a sitting position amid the tangle of arms and legs, he looked up at her again. "These children belong to Mr. Boggs. He brought them along with him today."

"They have to leave. Children aren't allowed in the factory."

"Why not?"

"We have equipment and machines." Her voice shook. "It's too dangerous."

"There isn't any machinery up here, Mara," he pointed out. "They're perfectly safe."

She looked down at her trembling hands. Children weren't safe anywhere. "I want them out of here. Now!"

There was an urgent edge to her voice, and she knew he heard it. He pushed the children gently aside and stood up. "Mara, what's wrong?"

"Now!" she repeated.

"All right." He turned away.

She fixed her gaze on a seam in the wood floor, listening as Nathaniel and Mr. Boggs led the children out of the room and down the stairs. She let out her breath in a rush of relief at the sudden silence, but it didn't last.

The screams of a child ripped through her memory. Not screams of laughter, but of pain. The fire roared in her ears and she clamped her trembling hands over her ears to stop the sounds. She closed her eyes, fighting until the screams died away.

11

When Nathaniel returned upstairs, he didn't know what he expected to find. He'd seen the flash of panic in her eyes at the sight of the children, and it bothered him. There was so much fear in her.

He found her standing by one of the windows, lost in thought. He walked over to her, the sound of his footsteps echoing in the empty room.

"They're gone," he said quietly. "Boggs took them home."

She gave a brief nod and turned away from the window. "I hope it's clear I don't want children in here again. It's not safe."

"Boggs and I wouldn't have allowed them to remain if we thought there was any danger. They're just as safe here as they would be at home or at school or anywhere else."

"At home or at school, they are not my concern," she

answered. "But here, in this building, they are. I don't want them here."

"It's going to be hard keeping them away. This is a toy factory."

"Not yet."

Her determined tone made him want to smile. "Don't you ever give up?"

She didn't answer that, and he went on, "I think it's a good idea to let children play with the toys we plan to make. It's a good way to test how well they'll hold up. And it's a good way to see if our toys will be popular."

"We have all sorts of hazardous equipment. They might get hurt."

"Yes, they might. The odds are lousy, since the equipment is downstairs and we're up here, but they might. I might fall down those stairs and break my neck. You might step in front of a runaway carriage. The building might even get struck by lightning, split in half, and fall on Mrs. O'Brien."

"Don't make fun of me!"

He looked down into her pain-twisted face and wished he could make the pain go away. "I'm not," he said gently. "It's just my way of dealing with you when I don't know what else to say. Exactly what is it you think might happen to them?"

She pulled a piece of paper out of her pocket and handed it to him. It was a clipping from *The Times*. "I thought you might want to see this. I've had it for a few days, but I keep forgetting to give it to you."

With that, she left the room, closing the door behind her.

He glanced down at the torn sheet from a two-week-old newspaper. It was a small item, only a few lines, but Nathaniel found it very interesting. It reported that an explosion had occurred at Chase Toy Company, killing one man and injuring several others. Fire had broken out, but the flames had been extinguished before any further damage had been done. A faulty boiler was presumed to be the cause of the accident.

Nathaniel read the item a second time. Adrian had always been too cheap to buy new equipment. They were probably still using the same boilers Father had purchased when he'd converted everything to steam, and that had been at least thirty years ago.

How many times had he and Adrian argued about those damned boilers? Two? Three? A dozen? It hadn't made any difference. Buying new equipment might mean the footmen could no longer wear gold trim on their livery. Cheap tin and bright paint for his trains, but real silk for his cravat. Old equipment that should have been scrapped years ago, but a luxurious new mansion in Mayfair. With Adrian, it was all show, no substance.

He shoved the scrap of paper into his pocket and dismissed Adrian from his mind. He stared at the toys on the floor and thought about Mara instead.

She was afraid to have children around. The sight of a small, scar-covered hand holding out a buttonhook came before his eyes. Her daughter had died in a fire, and explosions caused fires. He wanted to ask Mara about it, but he had the feeling she would never tell him any more than she already had.

During the next two weeks, Mara spent every free hour she had gathering information. She spoke with subcontractors and negotiated bids. She became an expert with the abacus, totaling costs with lightning speed and entering the sums in a ledger. She pored over the engineering specifications, until she knew as much about the trains as Michael did. She'd given her word she would be fair, and she intended to honor it. Besides, there was no reason to cheat. The numbers would speak for themselves, proving her case once and for all.

Although she was very busy, Mara found time twice each day to feed the kitten with milk she bought from Mrs. O'Brien. The little cat wouldn't let anyone pet him, including her, but he became a nuisance, following her, playing with her skirt, curling around her feet while she worked. She nearly stepped on the little fellow a few times, but she didn't have the heart to scold him.

Nathaniel was also very busy. He came in every morning long enough to check on Boggs's progress with the remodeling of the office and for Michael to tell him everything was running smoothly, then he disappeared for most of the day, taking his train set with him in a special case built for that purpose. He came to her office every night to walk her home, waiting for her if she still had work to do, but he never asked about her reaction to the children in the factory, and she was relieved. She had no intention of explaining her reasons to him.

Mara knew that he spent his days calling on merchants, and she wondered if he were having any success. She doubted it would matter. Her figures were confirming what she'd suspected all along. The cost to manufacture each train was very high, and she doubted he'd find merchants willing to pay such a price.

Two weeks after they'd made their bet, she copied all her notes and figures into a final report. When Nathaniel walked her home that night, she told him she was prepared to go over figures with him whenever he was ready. He didn't set a time, but merely said that he would let her know when he was ready.

The following afternoon, she returned from an errand

to find a note from him on her desk. She unfolded the paper, and a puzzled frown knit her brows as she scanned the scrawling lines.

Seven o'clock is the hour of our fate
When numbers tell the truth, so don't be late.
Seek out the toys and you will find
The way to have a meeting of minds.

It was a riddle. Mara read the note again, and an unwilling smile tugged at the corners of her mouth. Didn't the man ever do anything in the ordinary way? He wanted to meet at seven o'clock. That much was obvious. Seeking out the toys must mean that the meeting was to be upstairs, since he kept all his toys up there.

She folded the note and set it aside, then checked her watch. It was just past six. She fed the kitten, went over her arithmetic one last time, gathered all her information, and at precisely seven o'clock went upstairs to meet with Nathaniel, her little friend tagging behind her.

But when she arrived, her partner was nowhere to be seen. She hadn't been up here in over two weeks, and she was astonished at the changes that had taken place. The painting had been done, and gaslight wall sconces had been installed. The partitions he'd ordered from Mr. Boggs were finished and blocked off most of the huge room from her view. Although she couldn't see beyond the makeshift walls, the part of the room in which she stood had been transformed into an office.

To her left stood Nathaniel's huge desk, piled with papers. In the center of the office, a table and chairs had been set up, and behind them, a doorway between two partitions led into the other part of the room. The wooden Indian stood beside the doorway like a sentry.

To her right, there was only empty space, with a placard on a stand that read in carefully printed letters, "Mara's Office." Behind the sign was a door, and she wondered why on earth Nathaniel would have a door put in that would lead into empty space. Confused and curious, she walked past the sign and opened the door.

A steel platform jutted out at her feet, surrounded by a rail. Steel stairs led down, zigzagging back and forth to the alley below. A fire escape.

Mara dropped her portfolio and let out a choked sound. She pressed her hands to her cheeks, and the sting of tears pricked her eyes as she sank down, the steel solid and cool beneath her knees. She had no idea how long she remained there, holding back tears and trying to accept the fact that Nathaniel had done something like this. He'd done it for her.

"Not the usual gift a man gives a lady," said a low voice behind her, "so I'm hoping it doesn't cast aspersions on my character."

She turned her head to find Nathaniel standing in the doorway. The light behind him kept his face in shadows, making his expression unreadable. Mara opened her mouth to thank him, but the only sound that came from her throat was a choked sob.

"You're welcome," he said and knelt beside her. "You know, crying women always make me feel like an idiot. If you'd rather have a handkerchief or a bottle of cologne—"

"I don't wear cologne." She sniffed. "And I'm not crying. I never cry."

"Of course not. Maybe you have something in your eye."

"Why did you do this?"

He shifted, leaning back against the brick wall and stretching out his long legs on the steel platform. "It's a bribe. I'm trying to butter you up in case your numbers are better than mine."

She smothered her laugh, but not before he heard it. "It won't work," she told him.

"I didn't think so, but it was worth a try."

"Don't be flippant, Mr. Chase." She turned on her knees to face him but immediately ducked her head. "It was a very nice thing to do," she said shyly.

He looked at her bent head. It always seemed to catch her by surprise when he did something for her, and he found himself wondering why. He wanted to ask her more about her life before they met, he wanted to know about her daughter and fires, but if he asked, she'd probably freeze up and get all starchy and their tentative truce would be lost. He didn't want to lose it.

He cleared his throat. "Yes, well, it's not quite finished. Boggs still has to install a door on the first floor. We won't have access to it from the mezzanine, so I've also asked him to put a ladder on the opposite side from the stairs. That way, if there's a fire, everyone, no matter where they are, can get out. Why haven't you put a fire escape in before now?"

"We weren't using this part of the building. Given that, I couldn't justify the expense."

Putting in a fire escape hadn't cost that much, but he'd seen enough information about the company to know the cost would have come dear. There had been almost no cash in the bank account. Nathaniel might not know a lot about balance sheets and income statements, but he knew when a company was barely surviving. They'd probably had to scrounge just to make the weekly payroll. She'd carried a difficult burden for a long time.

He thought about James and tried to understand why he'd left his wife and daughter here on their own. No man worth his salt would do such a thing. But then, Nathaniel was beginning to think James hadn't been much of a man.

"Penny."

He glanced up at her. "What?"

"Penny. For your thoughts."

He leaned his head back against the wall and stared between the rails at the flickering lights being lit across the city. "They aren't worth a brass farthing. I was thinking about James."

"Oh." Silence fell between them again, and it was a long time before she spoke. "Mr. Chase, I know that you agreed to go into partnership with my husband, but how much did you really know about him?"

"Not much."

"Did you know that he was . . ." She hesitated a moment, then she asked, "Did you know that he was not always honest in his business dealings?"

"I didn't know for certain, but I suspected it, yes. At the time, it didn't matter to me. What did matter to me was that he was excited about my ideas, he believed in them. He said he owned a company we could modify to make my inventions. I verified that information, of course, and insisted on having the controlling interest. I deemed those precautions to be enough, knowing that as long as I held the controlling interest and kept an eye on him, everything would be fine. And, despite my suspicions, I liked him."

She changed her position to sit beside him. "Yes, everybody liked James. He had charm, and you couldn't help responding to it. There was a time when I adored him." She sighed. "There was a time when I loved him."

"But love wears thin, I imagine, when the money runs out."

She shook her head. "It wasn't the money."

He saw her lower lip quiver. She caught it between her teeth and fell silent. He waited, sensing she wanted to say more.

"Mr. Chase, I know you think I'm cheeseparing and hard—" She stopped and raised a hand to halt his protest. "My father was a miner in South Africa, working the diamond mines for pitiful wages. I was the oldest child in a family of eight, and we were very poor. I married James when I was sixteen, and it wasn't only because I loved him. I wanted to escape. Can you understand that?"

Nathaniel knew all about wanting to escape. "Yes."

"James gave me dreams. Hopes. But his biggest dream was to get rich. I didn't care. Whether you believe it or not, money was never that important to me. I didn't care if we ever got rich. I just wanted us to be a family. I wanted a home and a husband who stayed around longer than a few months at a time. But James had wanderlust. Whenever we moved to join him, things were wonderfully fine for a while. He would talk about how, this time, things were going to work out. This time, he'd found his true calling. But . . . "

"But it never lasted," Nathaniel finished for her.

"No. He would begin to get irritable and start going for long walks, hours at a time. Then he'd disappear for days. Pretty soon, he'd be packing, talking excitedly about some newfangled notion. Archaeology in Egypt, or sheep ranching in the Argentine."

"That must have been hard on you." He took a deep breath and broached the forbidden subject. "What about your daughter?"

Mara sat up. "I think it's starting to rain. We should go in."

She rose to her feet, picked up her portfolio, and went back inside. He followed her, closing the door behind him. He asked no more questions, but it hadn't escaped his notice that no rain was falling.

He walked over to his desk and began rummaging

among his papers. "What do you think?" he asked, waving a hand about the room as he searched.

"My side's a bit bare," she said. "Does this mean I have no responsibilities whatsoever?"

"I'm sorry about that," he said, sounding genuinely contrite. "Boggs would have moved your things up, but you weren't here and we didn't know where—" He paused and looked at her, noticing the hint of a smile on her lips. "Mara, I do believe you're teasing me."

"Perhaps I am," she admitted. She watched him rummaging through the things on his desk. "What are you looking for?"

"I'm sure it's here somewhere," he muttered. She doubted he'd even heard her question.

While he searched for whatever he'd misplaced, she decided to take a peek at his laboratory. She crossed the office and stepped between the partitions. A worktable had been set up to the right, and bits of machinery lay scattered all over it.

Mr. Boggs had built shelves behind the worktable, but they didn't seem to help keep things tidy. It was a mess. She was unable to fathom how Nathaniel could get any work done at all amid such chaos. She'd go mad if it were her.

"Here we are. I think this is it." She stepped out of the laboratory to see him lift a sheaf of papers from the desk and hold it at arm's length to study it for a moment. Then he nodded. "Yes, this is it."

"What?"

He set his notes on the table and pulled out a chair for her. "Shall we get started?"

Mara sat in the chair and allowed him to push it in for her. She placed her portfolio on the table, pulled out a pencil, and waited for Nathaniel to sit down, but he didn't. He frowned, patting the pockets of his waistcoat. "Where did I put them?"

She immediately realized what he was searching for. "Your spectacles are on your worktable. I saw them."

"Ah!" he exclaimed, "that's where I left them. I remember now." He disappeared into the laboratory to retrieve his spectacles and Mara took that opportunity to glance at the papers he'd put on the table, but she had no time to satisfy her curiosity.

"No peeking, Mara," he told her, looking at her over the partition.

Guiltily, she glanced away as he returned to sit opposite her across the table. He put on his spectacles. "All right, what have you got?"

She placed the first sheet of her report in front of him. "This is a list of all the parts we can make here, and what it will cost." She began pointing with her pencil as she went down the columns of the report. "We can make the motors and the bodies of the trains here. To do that, we'll need—"

"Mara, wait." He grabbed the pointed end of her pencil to stop its progress down the sheet. He looked at her over the rims of his spectacles. "I know you went to a lot of trouble to get this information, but you can give me the details later," he said. "For now, just give me the final figures. What will it cost to make the train set, including the locomotive, the tender, a figure-eight track, and two batteries?"

"Oh." Mara withdrew her pencil and began thumbing through the papers before her. "You don't want to see how I got my numbers?"

"Not unless you cheated."

"I did not cheat," she informed him loftily. "I was scrupulously fair."

"We'll see." He waited for her to locate the sheet with her totals and set it before him. She pointed to the figure at the bottom of the page with her pencil, and Nathaniel looked down at the number. He smothered a jubilant shout only with great effort. Fighting to keep his expression as properly serious as hers, he lifted his head. "I see."

"It's very high, I know," she said, and he could have sworn there was a hint—just a little hint—of regret in her voice. "But I was fair. That's about as accurate a figure as we can get."

"I understand." He reached for his notes, and pulled out the sales commitment from Harrod's. "This is Charles Harrod's order for five hundred of our trains, to be delivered by Friday, November 27." He placed it in front of her and pointed to the number at the bottom. "That's his purchase price."

"Three pounds!" Mara looked up at him, her eyes wide. "He's willing to buy them for three pounds each? But that would mean a profit of seventeen shillings apiece!"

Nathaniel couldn't help it. Her astonishment at the high profit margin was so obvious, he gave her a wide smile, aware that he probably looked as satisfied as the cat with the cream. "I'd guessed about fifteen, myself."

"You mean you already knew what the result of my cost analysis would be? You made that wager with me, knowing the outcome."

He heard the accusation in her voice. "I told you, I guessed. I didn't know for certain. Would you have been satisfied with one of my guesses?"

"No," she admitted bluntly. "But how could you make such a guess? There are so many factors that go into something like this."

He leaned forward and murmured, "Maybe I know what I'm doing."

Mara stared at him. Ever since she'd met this man, she'd thought him a bit touched. A man who reached for things way beyond his grasp, who dreamed about things that couldn't possibly happen. And yet, perhaps she'd misjudged him. He was odd, he was different, he seemed oblivious to convention, but he had an unerring way of knowing the truth. "Maybe you do."

His smile widened into a grin, and he began to chuckle. The sound rumbled from deep inside him until he could no longer seem to contain it. He threw back his head and laughed aloud, a lusty combination of joy and triumph.

Mara watched him, trying to maintain a stern demeanor, but it was futile. His exhilaration was infectious, and she found herself laughing with him.

They just might be able to make this happen. Crazy visions danced through her mind. Green-painted trains with brass wheels proudly displayed in shop windows. Enough money in the bank to pay the bills. A white house with blue shutters and window boxes of red geraniums. Her house.

She was building castles on clouds, higher and higher. But what would happen if she fell? How many times had she sat at a table in some remote corner of the world, building castles of dreams with James? Dozens. Hundreds. Where were all those castles now?

Their laughter slowly faded away. Her castles crumbled and her clouds disintegrated and she was back in a factory in Whitechapel. She looked down again at the order from Harrod's. "This is on consignment," she said flatly.

"Of course it is," he answered, surprised. "That's standard practice with a new product from a new company. You know that as well as I do."

She stared down at the order, not meeting his eyes. "If people don't buy the trains, he can return them. Then what do we do?"

"The trains will sell."

He sounded so confident. She knew confidence wasn't enough. But they'd had a bet, and he had won. "It's getting late. I should go."

She heard his heavy sigh, and she knew her sudden withdrawal somehow disappointed him. He pushed back his chair. "Of course."

She gathered her notes and put them back in her portfolio, then stood up, disentangling the kitten from beneath her feet.

As they went downstairs, Nathaniel noticed the kitten following them. "I think you've made a friend," he said. "Have you come up with a name for him yet?"

"I didn't think it would become a pet."

He grinned. "You're feeding him. What did you expect?"

They left the kitten in the factory. But instead of turning toward the lodging house, he took her arm and turned in the opposite direction. She had no choice but to accompany him. "Where are we going?"

Before she'd even finished asking the question, Nathaniel came to a halt before the coster's cart on the corner. "Hullo, Henry," Nathaniel greeted the old man leaning against the street lamp behind the cart.

"Evenin', guv'nor." The coster nodded in Mara's direction. "Ma'am."

Nathaniel pointed inside the cart. "How are the peaches?"

"A treat, guv'nor," the coster pronounced, but in the melancholy tone an undertaker might have used. "Sweet as sugar, but not too ripe."

Nathaniel selected one from the basket inside the cart and glanced at her. "What would you like?" he asked.

Mara looked up at him and opened her mouth to refuse. But Nathaniel took a bite of the peach, and gave a low sound of appreciation. She swallowed hard, watching him slowly lick peach juice from his lower lip with the tip of his tongue, and a sudden pang that was not hunger at all hit her in the belly. She caught her breath and stared at him.

"Delicious," he said and took another bite, rubbing a trickle of juice from his chin with the back of his hand. His voice jarred her out of her embarrassing reverie.

"I'll have one," she said abruptly and plucked a peach from the basket. She bit into her peach and waited as Nathaniel paid the man.

"I've brought that ointment I promised you, Henry," Nathaniel said. Reaching into the pocket of his jacket, he pulled out a tiny jar and handed it to the coster, along with tuppence to pay for the peaches.

The man took the offered jar, and Mara suddenly noticed the lower half of the man's left leg was gone, replaced by a wooden peg. "It's not too bad this evenin'," Henry said. "But it's been achin' for days now."

"I'm sorry to hear that." Nathaniel took another bite of his peach. "But the ointment should help."

"I do appreciate it, thank ye."

"No trouble," Nathaniel assured him. He turned away with a nod, and Mara fell in step beside him. Slowly they walked back to Mrs. O'Brien's, eating their peaches in silence. Mara thought about the old man on the corner, and she wondered if anybody else had ever offered him something to help ease the pain in his leg. Probably not.

"Algernon."

Mara paused in the act of taking another bite and glanced up at Nathaniel, bewildered. "What?"

"For the cat," he said. "Don't you think that's a good name for a cat?"

"I was thinking of something simple," she replied and bit into her peach. "Like George."

He sighed. "No imagination," he murmured and

tossed his peach pit behind him as they started up the steps of the lodging house. "If I had to come up with the dullest name imaginable, George is what I would choose."

She gave him an unamused glance, tossed aside the pit of her own peach, and entered the lodging house. When they reached her room, she unlocked the door and slipped inside, then turned to face him. "I guess you win," she said, finally making the admission of defeat, and closed the door.

Leaning her back against it, she waited for him to leave, but instead she heard his low reply through the door.

"No, Mara, we both win. If you don't see that, you see nothing at all. We both win."

She closed her eyes, listening to the sound of his footsteps as he ascended the stairs to his own room. "I hope so, Nathaniel," she whispered the words like a prayer. "I hope so."

12

Adrian slammed the ball with his racquet, sending it flying over the net. The ball sailed past his opponent, hit the wall of the squash court, and bounced out of reach before Baron Severn could return the volley.

"Point and match, Severn," Adrian declared, out of breath but smiling with satisfaction as he ducked under the net for the customary handshake.

"I never thought you'd do it, Leyland," the baron told him as they turned to walk off the court together. "You were so far behind."

"I don't like to lose." Adrian caught sight of his secretary standing by the doors and glanced at Severn. "Go on. I'll meet you at White's later."

The Baron nodded and went through the doors leading into the changing area of the club, leaving Adrian alone with his secretary.

"Yes, Mr. Barrett?"

Charles handed him a telegram. "This arrived from

San Francisco, my lord. It came in late last night, and they delivered it this morning."

Adrian shifted his squash racquet to his left hand and took the slip of paper. He scanned the telegram from Foster, smothering an exclamation of frustrated surprise. "London," he muttered. "He actually had the gall to come back here."

Crumpling the telegram in his hand, Adrian looked at Charles. "I want my brother found, Mr. Barrett. Employ more detectives, do whatever needs to be done. I want to know what he's doing, where he's living, everything."

"Yes, sir." Charles gave a nod and departed, but Adrian did not. He remained on the court for several more minutes, wondering why Nathaniel was in London. Ten years after he'd managed to rid himself of his little brother, Nathaniel was back. Adrian didn't like it. He didn't like it at all.

Mara rested the box in her arms against one hip, tilted her head to one side, and studied her desk. "No," she said, "Turn it the other way."

Boggs and his son lifted her desk and turned it around so that it faced the room rather than the window. She nodded. "Much better. Mr. Boggs, please bring up my bookshelf and place it over here. Also, move all my ledgers up here and place them in the bookshelf."

Boggs nodded. "Very good, ma'am."

He and his son departed to carry out her instructions. Mara set the box on her desk and moved her chair behind it. She sat down and began removing items from the box, placing them back on her desk in the exact places they had been an hour before.

As she worked, Mara couldn't help glancing over her shoulder from time to time to verify that there was indeed a door behind her. A silly thing to do. She'd already gone up and down that fire escape twice this morning to reassure herself that it was as sturdy as it looked. It was.

She turned back to her desk and reached for her pencil case, but her hand stilled as she stared at the desk directly opposite her own.

Was he right? Or was he just crazy? Doubt nagged at her. The man had a way about him, that was certain. He could charm birds out of trees with that smile of his. He could twist all her ideas around until she didn't know where she was. He could make her believe things that all her experience told her weren't true. She was afraid to believe him. But, suddenly, desperately, she wanted to. And what scared her the most was that his crazy ideas were actually beginning to make sense.

She hadn't seen him at all this morning, and she wondered what he was doing at this moment. His laughter from the night before echoed through her mind, and she wished she could be as jubilant as he. She wished he would come up those stairs with all his brash confidence and talk nonsense and smile that smile that told her everything would be fine. She wished . . .

"Mrs. Elliot?"

Mara glanced up to find Percy standing in the doorway, and the sight of him reminded her there was work to be done. She firmly pushed all her wistful thoughts to the back of her mind and reprimanded herself. Daydreaming was a wasteful and foolish pastime. "Yes, Percy, what is it?"

"Mr. Chase sent me to find you. He and Michael need you downstairs."

"Why?" She rose and crossed the room to follow the secretary. "Is there a problem?"

"I don't think so," Percy replied as they started for the

stairs. "They're discussing some changes they want to make for production. I think they want your opinion."

She followed him down the stairs, moving aside for Boggs and his son carrying her bookcase.

Michael and Nathaniel were standing in Mara's old office, leaning over a table, the only piece of furniture that remained. "I won't do it, Michael," Nathaniel was saying as she paused in the doorway. "You know how I feel about giving speeches."

"The employees need to be told what we're doing."

"I agree," Nathaniel said, studying the diagram on the table. "But you're the supervisor now. You tell them."

Michael sighed. "It would be better coming from you."

"I won't do it," Nathaniel repeated. Mara was watching him, and she saw his jaw tighten stubbornly. For a moment, she thought there was a hint of apprehension in his handsome profile. It was so unlike Nathaniel, who never seemed worried about anything.

He glanced up at that moment and saw her over the rims of his spectacles. The flash of apprehension she'd seen disappeared instantly.

"Good morning," he greeted her.

There it was. That smile. But it didn't give her the assurance she craved. Instead, it did strange things to her insides, making her feel more nervous than before. She drew a deep breath. "Good morning. Percy said you wanted to see me?"

He nodded. "We're discussing some ideas. Tell us what you think."

Mara had the feeling whatever they wanted to discuss with her had nothing to do with Nathaniel giving speeches to the employees.

"Michael and I have been talking about putting assembly back here," Nathaniel told her, pointing to the diagram on the table. "We can put Michael's and Percy's offices up on the mezzanine and put assembly down here."

She stared down at the diagram he'd drawn of the ground floor and watched his hand move across the paper, scarcely hearing what he said. He had fine hands. Strong hands. She remembered the feel of them on her waist.

Her face grew warm, and she kept her head lowered. She forced herself to focus on what he was saying. By the time he finished his explanations, she had pushed her wayward thoughts firmly aside. "It has some advantages, but we'll have to tear out these walls," she said, pointing to the drawing of the room in which they were standing. Her hand brushed his, and through the leather of her glove, she could almost feel the warmth of his skin. She jerked her hand back.

"That's not a problem," Michael interjected. "Only two of the walls along this corridor are bearing walls. We can take the rest of them out."

"If we move assembly down here, we'll have completed trains on the ground floor already," Nathaniel added. "It makes it so much easier. We can take them through the door at the end of this corridor straight into the warehouse without having to carry them down the stairs from the mezzanine."

Mara nodded, knowing it made sense. But she couldn't help asking, "How are we going to pay for all the additional remodeling?"

She looked at Nathaniel, watching as he straightened away from the table and removed his spectacles. "Michael," he said, placing the spectacles on the table, "would you go and talk with Mr. Boggs? I believe he is on the first floor putting in a door for the fire escape." Nathaniel folded the diagram and handed it to the other man. "Have him give you an estimate."

Michael took the diagram and departed, leaving them alone. Mara felt his gaze on her and reluctantly lifted her head to look at him. "It's going to be so costly," she said.

"Mara, you know we're going to have to get that loan from the bank."

She sighed and turned away. "You know how I feel about borrowing money."

"Yes." He stepped forward to stand beside her. "There are other ways to raise capital, but a loan makes the most sense."

Mara felt the panic rising in her. "If it doesn't work, if the trains don't sell and we can't pay back the loan, I would lose all that I have."

There was a long pause. His hand came up to touch her shoulder, and she felt him turn her to face him. "Are you planning to renege on our wager?" he asked, his voice low.

There was a hint of accusation in it, and she stiffened. "No. We had an agreement, and I will abide by it." But she ducked her head and the confession slipped from her. "I'm scared."

His hand tightened on her shoulder. "This is going to work. The trains will sell."

"How can you be so certain?"

"I won't let it be any other way," he said simply.

Mara looked into his eyes, and she believed him.

That afternoon, while Nathaniel was at a meeting with Whiteley's Department Stores, his things arrived from America. Mara was upstairs, still putting her new office in order, when Percy came up to tell her.

"What should we do with them?" he asked.

"Tell the workmen to take them to his flat at Mrs. O'Brien's, of course." Mara turned to put another ledger in the bookshelf behind her, but turned around again when Percy spoke.

"I'm not certain that will work," the secretary told her.

"Why not?"

"Well, he has quite a bit. Seven carts full behind the warehouse."

"Seven!" Mara followed Percy downstairs and through the warehouse to find seven wagons piled high with furniture and crates lined up, completely filling the narrow alley. "Heavens, all that will never fit in his flat."

She sighed. "We'll have to put his things here in the warehouse for now. We certainly can't leave them in the alley, and there's no room anywhere else. But when we start making trains, they'll be in the way."

"We could find a storage facility for lease."

Mara thought about that for a moment, then nodded. "Very well. But it will be at Mr. Chase's personal expense, not the company's, since it's his furniture."

Percy departed to find storage space for lease. Mara beckoned the workmen to begin unloading. At her direction, they started bringing in crates and furnishings in a steady stream. Mara watched as box after box was stacked against the far wall of the warehouse. How had one man managed to accumulate so much, she wondered, watching two men carry a pair of burgundy leather armchairs past her, followed by a rosewood bureau and cabinet. An armoire came next, then two matching tables, and a huge bathtub with a mahogany surround. And a bed.

It was a massive thing, truly decadent, with a carved headboard and footboard of mahogany, and a mattress thicker than any she'd ever seen. She stared at the pieces of the bed as they were marched past. His words about his mistresses came back to her, and the idea of him in that bed with some fancy woman sent a bolt of violent jealousy through her, a feeling beyond all logic and reason. His mistresses were his own business, she told herself, and she had no right to be jealous. But she was, and it angered her.

She whirled around and stalked out of the warehouse, but visions of him in that bed with a beautiful mistress haunted her for the rest of the day, making her cranky and irritable.

When the factory closed down for the day, she had a meeting with Michael. He asked her when she would be finished with the train budget, saying Nathaniel needed it to get the loan from the bank, and she nearly bit his head off with her defensive answer. Michael beat a hasty retreat and went home for the day, leaving her feeling ashamed, bereft, and out of control.

Mara marched upstairs, turned on the gaslights, and sharpened her pencil. They might have to get a loan, but she decided it was up to her to make sure it was the smallest possible amount. She began working on a budget for the production of trains.

A loud wail followed by the sound of impatient scratching interrupted her work, and she glanced over her shoulder at the door to the fire escape. Algernon wanted in and was obviously unhappy with the closed door.

"All right, all right," she grumbled and tossed down her pencil. She shoved back her chair and went to open the door. The kitten was sitting on the fire escape.

"I don't see how Nathaniel thinks you'll be able to catch mice in the factory if you're always out," she told the animal as he sauntered past her into the room.

Algernon responded to her criticism of his mouse-catching abilities with an uninterested yawn and began to meander around the room. Mara closed the door and sat back down. The moment she was seated, he walked beneath the desk and burrowed under the hem of her skirt.

Mara felt him curl into a ball around her feet. He was a smart cat, that was certain. It hadn't taken him more than a day to figure out the fire escape led right to the door of her office—although she still couldn't understand why the silly thing had such a fondness for her. She bent her head and resumed her work.

"Mara? Are you up here?"

She heard Nathaniel's voice calling her name and rose to look over the partition as he descended the stairs from the roof. "Hullo," she greeted him in surprise as she watched him cross the room and enter the office. "I didn't know you were back yet. How did the meeting go?"

"Whiteley's has agreed to purchase three hundred trains for Christmas."

"Three?" Mara did some quick arithmetic. "Harrod's has ordered five. That's eight hundred."

"No, actually we're at twelve hundred. I have orders from several of the smaller stores, too."

She started to ask which ones, but he gave an impatient shake of his head and beckoned to her with one hand. "Let's talk about that later. Come up on the roof. You have to see this."

She didn't move. "See what?"

He grinned at her. "Why do you always have to question everything? Just trust me and come along. It's marvelous."

She had to disentangle the cat from her feet before she could follow him. A few weeks ago she would have insisted that he explain what he was about before going anywhere with him, but experience had taught her that with Nathaniel Chase, it was usually a waste of breath.

"Your things arrived, and we put them in the warehouse," she said, following him across the laboratory. "We didn't know where else to put them."

"Yes, I know," he answered and grabbed her hand, pulling her toward the roof. "C'mon."

When they reached the top of the stairs, she emerged to find herself engulfed in blackness. Below, gaslights flickered on street corners, enabling her barely to detect the shadowy form of his telescope set up at one end of the flat roof. "I don't know what you expect me to see. It's pitch-black out here."

He stepped up behind her. "Look up."

"Up?" Mara tilted her head back. Thousands of stars glittered in the night sky. "I don't see anything."

"Just watch."

"I don't—" She paused as a flash of light directly above caught her attention. "I saw a falling star," she said doubtfully.

He leaned closer and shook his head. A tendril of his hair caught the breeze and brushed her upturned cheek. "Not a star. It's a meteor shower."

His arm came over her shoulder as he pointed. "Look, there goes another one. Isn't it amazing?"

He stepped back and grabbed her hand. "You can see it much better through the telescope. Come over here."

She allowed him to lead her over to the piece of machinery as tall as herself. He showed her what to do, and she leaned forward, closing one eye as she peered into the lens with the other. She saw nothing at first, but suddenly there was a flash that reminded her of the fireworks she'd once seen in Hong Kong, and she watched in fascination as three meteors seemed to fall from a central point and left their trails of light behind them in the shape of a three-branched star. "Oh, my," she breathed. "It's lovely!"

"It'll probably last an hour or two," he told her, "but

most of the meteors will fall during the next few minutes."

She straightened when she felt him step up behind her. He lifted his arms on either side of her to tip the telescope slightly higher, and she tensed, feeling the warmth of him behind her. Her breath caught as she waited for him to step back, but he didn't move. Instead, his arms remained where they were, encircling her without touching her, and she felt a sudden desire to lean back against him, feel the strength of him.

She didn't. Instead, she remained perfectly still, afraid to move closer, yet unwilling to move away. Seconds went by, days, lifetimes, before he lowered his arms and stepped back.

She peered into the telescope again and tried to focus on what was happening in the skies above, but her senses seemed aware of nothing but him. She knew the exact moment when he moved away, she felt it, regretted it.

After a few moments of pretending vast interest in the telescope, she turned away from it and scanned the roof, looking for Nathaniel. Accustomed to the darkness now, she found him almost immediately, and the unexpected sight of him lying stretched out on the roof staring up at the sky brought a smile to her lips. He really was the most eccentric man.

He turned his head slightly at her approach. "The telescope is good, but this is the best way to watch," he told her.

She was certain that lying on a roof, looking at stars with a man beside her was most improper. But she didn't care. She sank down to the slate surface, and stretched out next to him. They watched the meteors in silence for quite some time, and Mara wondered if Nathaniel was thinking about the phenomenon going on over their heads.

Nathaniel was not thinking about meteors. He was thinking about raven hair and reluctant smiles and the scent of lilac soap. He could smell it now, that fragrance, drifting to him on the breeze. He thought about small scarred hands and bitter gray eyes, about shadows of fear and the dark side of rainbows. She was so close. He could touch her. He wished he could heal her.

"Why did you tell Michael you wouldn't speak to the employees?"

Her soft question was like a physical blow. It sent him reeling, stumbling back through time, to agonizing childhood days at Harrow. "I don't like giving speeches," he answered shortly, hoping that was the end of it.

"Why? Does it bother you?"

Bother him? Did that describe it? He closed his eyes, shutting out the shower of light above him, the lilac scent of the woman beside him, seeing nothing but a boy standing in front of his schoolmates, stumbling his way through the tongue-twisting agony of Milton. A boy who knew, despite the laughter, that *Paradise Lost* was not a comedy. "I just don't like it."

He sat up. "The meteor shower is over," he said and rose to his feet. "I'd better walk you home."

He held out his hand to help her up. As they went inside, Mara paused to glance back up at the night sky and saw another meteor fall.

Billy Styles lay on his back in the alley, trying to catch his breath. He could hear the footsteps of the other boys as they ran away. He sat up, then tried to stand, but his short legs felt like two licorice whips and his head was spinning. He fell back down on the cobblestones and sat there for a few minutes until the dizziness passed. He sniffed and wiped one puny fist beneath his nose. By the light of the street lamp at the end of the alley, he saw the sticky dark smear of blood on his hand.

He didn't have a handkerchief, so he settled for his sleeve, pressing the back of his wrist to his nose until the bleeding stopped.

It wasn't fair, he thought, tears of frustration and shame stinging his eyes. It just wasn't fair. He hated Jimmy Parks, the big bully, and his friends, too. He could still hear their taunts ringing in his ears, and he could still feel Jimmy's fist slamming into his stomach.

He tried again to stand, but when he did, the dizziness came back, and he doubled over, tossing up the apples he'd stolen from a coster's cart an hour before. He retched until his belly was empty and the spasms stopped.

Then he dragged himself home to the tiny room he shared with his father on Old Castle Street, holding a hand to his bleeding nose and blinking back the babyish tears that still threatened to fall. His head hurt, his ribs hurt, everything hurt.

If Billy's father had been home, he would have given his son a hard whack and told him to stop crying and not to be such a baby, to be a man and learn how to fight.

But Billy's father wasn't home. The tiny flat was empty. When his mum was alive, she'd been there to hug him and wipe away the blood and tell him that it didn't matter when the other boys made fun of the mark on his face because she loved him no matter what. When she'd been there, when he could bury his head against her breast and hug her tight, it hadn't been so bad that the other boys made fun of him and called him names and beat him up.

But now there was no one there to wipe the smudges of blood from his nose. There was no one to mend the tears in his shirt. There was no one to comfort the scared, lonely eight-year-old boy. His father was in the pub, and his mother was dead. Billy Styles crawled into his cot and pulled the dirty wool blanket up over his head. He tried to tell himself not to be a baby. He didn't cry, but he hugged his pillow very, very tight, wishing it were his mum.

13

It would have been so easy. Mara paused on the corner and bought a Cornish pasty from the coster. Preoccupied with her thoughts, she didn't even grumble at the high price. Gloves on, she nibbled the meat pie as she walked down Whitechapel High Street, heading back toward Elliot's. Her thoughts returned again to that night on the roof a week before.

Yes, it would have been easy to lean back against Nathaniel, easy and tempting. Even the memory of it brought a blush to her cheeks. He had done nothing improper, but she had wanted him to. She had wanted him to hold her. She had wanted to lean back against him, feel his strength. She wanted to rely on him, trust him, and that was the most frightening thing of all.

Mara could not recall a time in her life when she'd had that luxury. She'd never had another person to depend upon. It seemed to be her role in life that others should depend upon her. She had never minded that before, preferring to be in control of things. But that night had been different. That night, she'd imagined for a brief moment that she could give him what he kept asking for. Her trust. Just imagining it had brought an incredible rush of relief. She wasn't alone anymore. She had a partner. For the first time, she was beginning to see the advantages in that, but it still frightened her.

Mara popped the last bite of her lunch into her mouth, brushed the crumbs from her gloves, and turned down her street. Her meeting with Halston Tin had gone well. When she had researched suppliers, their bid had been the lowest, lower even than Chesterfield's, and this morning they had promised her that they'd be able to supply all the tin she and Nathaniel required. They had assured her that thirty-day-credit terms were not a problem, and the deal had been made.

As she opened the front door of the factory, she realized she didn't hear the roar of operating machinery. She entered the production floor and saw Michael up on a table, surrounded by men. Glancing up, she noticed the women leaning against the rail, looking down on the scene and listening to Michael talk. She could see Nathaniel's tall form quite close to the table.

Mara came to a halt at the edge of the crowd. Michael was telling the employees their plans to build trains and explaining some of the assembly-line changes they had discussed the week before.

He finished his explanations, thanked everyone, declared the meeting over, and jumped down from the table. She watched as Nathaniel clapped him on the back with a pleased nod, before they were engulfed by the men around them. Suddenly, a roar of laughter ran through the crowd, and Mara saw Nathaniel being lifted by several of the men.

Michael tried to stop them, but to no avail. The men

clearly wanted their new boss to speak. She could see Nathaniel struggling in protest, but the men refused to let him go, and he was forced up onto the table. He rose to his feet and said something under his breath. She couldn't catch what it was, but those standing closest to him erupted again into laughter.

She moved through the crowd, drawing closer. She watched as Nathaniel looked around him, and she listened as the room grew silent. He drew a deep breath and raked a hand through his unruly hair. He opened his mouth to speak, closed it again, and glanced around with an almost desperate air.

He was scared. The realization hit her, and Mara came to an abrupt halt several feet away, staring up at him in disbelief. He'd said he didn't like giving speeches, but this was more than dislike. This was fear. She could hardly believe it, and yet, there was no mistaking his sudden panic. It was as if all his brash confidence had chosen this moment to desert him. He looked suddenly and completely vulnerable.

"I . . . umm . . . really didn't want t . . . to do this," he said, stumbling over his words as if they were the most difficult ones he'd ever had to say. He cleared his throat, and glanced around again. She had the feeling that if he were not surrounded by men, he'd jump down from the table and flee like a startled animal.

I'll always back you up in front of others. That's what partnership is all about.

Mara didn't know what had caused this sudden panic in him, and she didn't care. She had no idea what she could do, but she had to do something. She pushed her way through the crowd of men, edging around them until she was directly in Nathaniel's line of vision.

"As M . . . Michael's already told you, we're making a g . . . great many ch . . . changes around here," Nathaniel went on, struggling valiantly, but she could tell he was sinking deeper into the mire of his own words. She lifted her hand, waving until she caught his attention. She met his eyes, and the misery in their depths twisted her heart. She lifted her hands, pointing to her own eyes with her fingers, and she mouthed the words, "Look at me, Nathaniel. Look at me."

She nodded encouragingly, keeping his attention focused on her, hoping he understood. For a few breathless seconds, they looked at each other, and then she saw him give her a slow nod in return. He focused his gaze on her as if she were a lifeline, took another deep breath, and began to speak.

"I . . . umm . . . I told Michael that he sh . . . sh . . . should tell you what we're d . . . doing. I d . . . didn't plan to give a damn speech."

There was a fresh outburst of laughter. She smiled and gave him another nod of encouragement as he waited for the laughter to subside.

"I guess the first thing we should talk about is what I'm d . . . doing here," he continued. "M . . . many of you knew James Elliot, but what most of you don't know is that I knew him, too."

He spoke slowly, enunciating every word with care, still looking at her. "James and I decided to form a partnership making toys. I c . . . came to London so that together we could turn Elliot's into a toy company."

Murmurs of surprise rippled through the crowd at this news, but Mara didn't take her eyes off Nathaniel. She held her breath, watching him watch her, listening as he went on, "James is dead, God rest his soul, but what he and I set out to do is still very much alive. Mrs. Elliot inherited this company from her husband, and she and I have formed a new partnership. As M . . . Michael's already explained, we will be changing Elliot's manufacturing to toys over the next few months. We're going to start with toy trains, and gradually build from there, until we're also making boats and tops and games and all sorts of other things."

His words came faster now, and he wasn't stumbling over them, but he still kept his gaze fixed on Mara as if she were the only person in the room. "If we're going to do this, we're going to need the help of each and every one of you. Mrs. Elliot and I will be demanding all your cooperation and a lot of hard work, and some pretty long hours as we get closer to Christmas. Now, if I were in your shoes, I'd be asking myself what's in it for me."

The crowd stirred a bit at those words, almost guiltily, as if that's exactly what they'd been thinking. Nathaniel took a deep, steadying breath. "You people know your own jobs better than anyone else does," he said. "If you see ways we can do things better, I want you to speak up. If you have a problem or a complaint, tell us about it, and tell us how you think we can solve it. You won't lose your job or get into trouble. In fact, I'll pay you for it."

More murmurs ran through the crowd. Nathaniel waited for them to subside. "If you bring me an idea that will save us money, I'll pay you a pound. I wish I could tell you I'm doing this out of the goodness of my generous heart, but I'd be lying. I'm not that generous."

The confession was made with a rueful smile that seemed natural and easy, but Mara knew it was not. She took her eyes from him long enough for a quick glance around and was relieved to discover the faces in the crowd smiling back at him.

"I'm willing to do this for one simple reason," Nathaniel continued. "Your ideas can save us money. Your ideas will mean more money for the company and will help us to be successful, so it's only fair that those ideas also mean more money in your pockets."

Murmurs of approval greeted that statement, and Nathaniel seemed aware of it, for he tore his gaze from hers and lifted his head to look at the crowd for the first time.

"Michael is now your supervisor, but you can also bring your suggestions to me or to Mrs. Elliot. There's a great deal of work ahead, and it isn't going to be easy. But we can do it, if we all work together."

He jumped down from the table, and a round of cheers went up. He walked toward Mara, receiving approving slaps on the back from the men as he shouldered his way through the crowd. When he reached her, he grasped her hands in his before she could think of anything to say. "Thank you."

"You don't have to thank me," she answered and smiled at him. "Partners, remember?"

He didn't smile back. He just looked down at her, and there was gratitude in his eyes, gratitude and promises and something more. "I stuttered when I was a boy."

Her hands tightened around his. "I know."

"I won't fail you."

"I know that, too."

His smile came then, slowly, and a strange sensation began in her midsection, a tremble of breathless excitement and anticipation, as if she had just jumped off a cliff. And just this once, for just this moment, she wished she could fly without thinking about what would happen when she hit the ground.

Nathaniel studied the pieces of machinery spread out before him on the worktable, forcing himself to concentrate on his latest idea. He was still trying to design a steam train that didn't leave trails of water all over the floor, but his thoughts kept straying from that task.

In his mind, he kept reliving the events of the preceding afternoon. He kept seeing the sea of faces, the rough workmen looking up at him, waiting for him to say something. He kept feeling the knot of sickening fear twist in his guts. He kept hearing his own stuttering words.

One face had been clear amid the blur. A face with the raven brows and mournful eyes of Shakespeare's sonnets. Bow-shaped lips forming the whispered words that had saved him. If Mara hadn't been there, he'd have jumped down from that table and run. Just like the scared little boy of twenty years ago.

They were truly partners now. She had seen him foundering and had come to his aid, and he would never be able to tell her how much that meant to him.

She could have simply allowed him to drown in his own stuttering words. But she hadn't. She could have thwarted his plans, the plans she'd fought so hard against. But she hadn't.

Perhaps she was beginning to believe in what they were doing. There had been trust in the hands that had tightened around his. He knew how difficult it was for Mara to trust anyone. And she was trusting him with the only thing she had. Elliot's. He would not fail her.

A sound on the stairs caused Nathaniel to lift his head. Over the partition separating his laboratory from the office, he saw her walk through the door with a tray of tea and scones in her hands. The kitten followed her like a shadow.

Her gaze lifted to his as she walked toward him. "Good morning," she said with a smile. "This is a change. You're here early."

"So are you."

"I always come in early." She set the tray on the table. "I'm working on a proposal for us to take to the bank."

Her tacit agreement to seek a loan from the bank surprised Nathaniel. He watched as she clasped her hands behind her back. The schoolgirl gesture made him want to smile. She always did that when she was nervous or embarrassed.

"I . . . umm . . . assumed they'd want to know how we're going to spend the money. And I thought it would be prudent for us to present them with a proposed budget."

"Very prudent," he answered gravely.

"It will also give us an estimate of how much money we'll need to borrow. I want to get it done, but there's no time during the day, so I've been coming in a bit earlier than usual."

He left the laboratory, moving through the makeshift doorway into the office. He watched Mara sit down at the table, and he came up behind her to push in her chair. As he moved around to the opposite chair, he saw the kitten dive beneath the table, and he paused, bending down to take a look. He could see the kitten batting at the hem of Mara's skirt. "I believe our little alley cat has actually become a pet," he said as he straightened and took the chair across the table from her. "Have you named him yet?"

"I decided your suggestion was a good one," she admitted. "I've named him Algernon. But he isn't a pet, he's a nuisance."

Nathaniel leaned back in his chair. "A nuisance, is he?"

She nodded. "Oh, yes, he's always getting underfoot. He still won't let me pet him though."

"He will. He has to learn to trust you first." He paused and met her eyes. "It's odd how they're like people that way, isn't it?"

He could see that she didn't miss the reference to herself, but she didn't reply. She began to pour tea.

"Tea and scones again?" he asked, watching her.

"When I looked out my window this morning, I saw the lights on, and I knew you were up here. I thought it would be a nice idea."

"It is," he agreed. "I think we should do this every morning."

She fixed his tea the way he liked it and handed him a cup and saucer. "We could use this as a sort of morning meeting," she suggested, "to talk about the business."

He hadn't suggested it for that reason. He'd suggested it because he liked the idea of starting his day this way. But he didn't say so. Instead, he took a scone from the basket. "If we're going to have tea every morning, I should probably be the one to bring it, since I come in later than you. And," he added, reaching for the tiny pot of cream, "I can make sure that we have enough cream. You never bring enough."

She frowned at the generous dollop of cream he spooned onto his scone as she reached for the jam pot. "Cream's expensive. You shouldn't be so extravagant."

He grinned at her. "Mara, I think everyone is entitled to choose their luxuries. I like plenty of cream on my scones. You like lilac soap, and that's expensive, too."

She gasped. "How do you know that?" she asked, setting down the jam pot. Her cheeks suffused with color.

He loved watching her blush. It did magical things to her face, it allowed him to see beyond her defenses, and it brought out all the softness she tried so hard to hide. "I know the scent of lilacs when I smell it," he said. "And you don't wear cologne. You told me that."

The realization that he knew such an intimate thing about her unnerved her, but if he told her what he was thinking at this moment, it would shock her. He was thinking of how the scent of lilacs clung to her skin and her hair, of how she would look sitting in a tub with her leg drawn up and the way she would rub that soap over her skin. If he kept thinking like this, he'd go insane.

"It . . . it isn't proper to talk of such things," she said and took a bite of her scone, still blushing.

It wasn't proper to think about them either, but that didn't stop him. He smiled, watching her.

"What are you smiling about?" she demanded.

"You have jam on your chin."

She lifted her hand to wipe it away, but he was already reaching out his own hand. He scooped the tiny strawberry dab onto his thumb. Their eyes met, and he saw hers widen as he slowly pulled his hand back and licked the jam from his thumb.

He could hear her breath coming in small whispers between her parted lips, and he knew he was going to get up, walk around the table, and kiss her.

Footsteps sounded on the stairs. Mara made a flustered, almost panicky movement of her hand and tried her best to look casual as Emma Logan paused in the doorway. Nathaniel rose to his feet, taking a deep, steadying breath, glad of the distraction, aware that if Emma had been a moment later, the gossip would have spread like wildfire.

"Emma!" he greeted the woman with a smile. "Good morning."

She bent her knees for a casual curtsy. "Mr. Chase," she answered, and bobbed her blond head in Mara's direction. "Ma'am," she murmured politely before returning her gaze to Nathaniel's. "I 'ope I'm not interruptin'."

"Not at all," he assured her and gestured to the table. "Mrs. Elliot and I were just having our morning meeting over a pot of tea. Would you like to join us?"

Her eyes widened. "Oh, no, sir. Thank ye, but I wouldn't want t'disturb yer meetin'."

"It's quite all right." Nathaniel stepped forward, took her arm, and led her to the table, pulling out a chair for her. She sat down and seemed quite unnerved when he pushed it in for her.

"Would you care for tea?" Nathaniel asked. He took his own cup and went into the laboratory to dump the dregs from it and rinse it out in the sink, then brought it to Emma before returning to his own chair. He reached for the teapot and poured a cup for her.

"Are you quite comfortable?" he asked. "Would you care for a scone?"

He held the basket out to her and she smiled at him. "Thank ye, sir," she said, taking the pastry from the basket and accepting the jam pot he handed to her.

"Sugar?" he asked. "Not that you would need any," he added, "already being as sweet as you are."

Mara choked on her tea, but the other two didn't seem to notice.

"Thank ye, sir," Emma breathed, smiling as if he'd offered her heaven instead of tea. "Three lumps, if you please."

"Of course." Nathaniel dropped three lumps of sugar into the cup. "Would you like lemon or milk?"

"Oh, a bit of milk would be lovely, sir."

After adding milk to her tea, Nathaniel handed her the cup, asked about the health of her children, and made several more polite inquiries as to her comfort. She basked in the glow of his attention like a cat in a sunny window. Mara watched, wondering when the girl was going to start purring. Privately, she found his solicitous manner excessive, and more than a bit irritating. But she said nothing.

Finally, when Mara began to wonder if Emma was going to spend the entire morning in their office, Nathaniel asked, "What brings you up here, Emma?"

She set down her teacup and lowered her gaze. "Well, sir, I was thinking about what you said yesterday, about bringin' ye our ideas."

He nodded encouragingly. "And you have an idea that might help us?"

She lifted her gaze to his and took a deep breath. "I was thinkin' we'll be needin' tin to make these trains of yers. Well, sir, I worked in a foundry, an' I know tin gets pressed into sheets. Mr. Lowenstein said we'd be cutting tin and shapin' it t'fit, but those sheets won't be just the right size, will they, sir? An' there'll be scrap, won't there, sir?"

"Yes. There's always scrap metal."

"Well, sir, me boys—I got three boys, one gel—me boys, they goes 'round the neighborhood collectin' scrap, so's I know scrap tin be worth a penny a pound. The men what cut the tin could toss the scrap into barrels as they's workin', sir, an' we could sell it so's it wouldn't go t'waste."

"That's a very good idea," Nathaniel said. "It wouldn't take any trouble at all. Very clever, Emma!"

She wriggled in her chair, looking flustered and pleased by the praise. Mara thought the whole thing extremely silly, especially since they were already planning to sell the scrap metal.

Nathaniel rose and crossed to Mara's desk. He pulled open the drawer where she kept the petty cash and took out a pound note. Closing the drawer, he returned to the table and placed the note in her hand. "Thank you."

She took the note and rose to her feet, looking up at him with adoration and gratitude. "Thank ye, sir," she breathed, rubbing the note between her fingers. "Oh, thank ye."

He took her arm and walked her to the door. "You're quite welcome, Emma. You've earned it. And may I say, I'm very glad a clever girl like you is working for us."

Mara rolled her eyes, wondering how much more of this she could take.

Emma blushed and tucked the note in her pocket. "I'm glad t'be workin' for ye, sir. Yer a right fine gentleman, an' it's not just me what thinks so. Everybody else does, too. We'll do our best for ye."

With that, she finally departed, much to Mara's relief.

"Charming girl," Nathaniel said as he sat back down.

"Indeed," Mara said dryly. "Very charming."

Something in her tone caught his attention, and he gave her a questioning glance.

"For heaven's sake," Mara said, "why did you do that? I can understand this plan of yours to pay people extra for ideas that save us money, but Emma's idea was one we already had. Did you have to pay her for it?"

"There are times when we all need a bit of help, Mara. Emma needed the money." He lifted the last scone from the basket and held it up inquiringly. She shook her head and he broke it apart for himself. Spooning the last dabs of cream onto the scone, he said, "Her husband's a drunk, and she finally tossed him out. Now, she's got four children to support on her own."

"What does that have to do with us?" Mara asked, telling herself not to be taken in by a hard-luck story. "Are we now the local toy factory *and* charity?"

"When he left, it was payday. He took all her money, and he didn't even leave her enough to pay the rent. She was in desperate straits. If she didn't pay, she was going to be thrown out in the street and her children right along with her."

Mara sighed and took a sip of tea. "I didn't know that."

"Well, these people work for you, too. Perhaps there are some things you should find out about." He lifted the teapot and smiled at her. "More tea?"

*   *   *

Mara did find out. That evening, she asked Michael about Emma's situation, and the engineer confirmed what Nathaniel had said, reassuring her that Emma now had the money to pay her rent, at least for the next few weeks.

Emma's situation bothered her, bringing back painful memories of her own marriage. James had not been a drinking man, but he'd found plenty of other ways to spend their money, and Mara could remember several occasions when she'd been as destitute as Emma, with a daughter of her own and no money to feed her. But, unlike Emma, her husband wouldn't have been found in the local pub. No, James had usually been on a ship bound for some faraway port with creditors dogging his heels. And hers. There had been times when an extra pound could have made all the difference.

She spent several hours with Michael, going over the supplies list. Afterward, she went upstairs and found Nathaniel sitting at the table, a pencil in his hand and a huge diagram spread out before him.

He glanced up as she entered the office, but immediately bent his head again over his work. Mara came up beside him and leaned over the table, studying the diagram he was working on.

"What are you doing?" she asked, watching him scribble notes in the margin.

"I'm working on improving the design of our steam train." He made another notation in the margin. "Children don't care, of course, but I find it very irritating that steam trains leave puddles of water all over the place. It's sloppy. I'm trying to figure out a way to prevent it."

She began to laugh. He paused in the act of jotting down another idea on the diagram and stared at her over the gold rims of his spectacles. He enjoyed the sound of her laughter but wondered at its cause. "What are you laughing about?"

"You," she confessed with a wide smile. Eyes dancing with amusement, she pulled out the opposite chair and sat down. "The man who is always late, the man whose office is a disorganized maze, the man who's always losing his spectacles, is concerned because his steam train has the untidy habit of dribbling water on the floor."

She was teasing him, and he liked it. "I may be disorganized, but I'm never sloppy about my work, I'll have you know," he informed her with mock sternness. "I hate the idea of selling a train that dribbles."

"Why do you have such a passion for toy trains?" she asked, watching him scribble another notation on the paper before him. "Is it just because you grew up around the toy business?"

"That's part of it, but I think it comes mostly from just plain stubbornness." He hesitated, and she thought he wasn't going to elaborate, but after a moment, he set his pencil down and said in a low voice, "When I was a boy, my father refused to allow me to participate in any facet of Chase Toys. My elder brother was being groomed to take over the reins, but my father refused to consider giving me any similar preparation. He thought it unnecessary, since he never planned to give me any responsibility in the company when I grew up."

"Why not?"

Nathaniel pulled off his spectacles and set them on the table, then leaned back in his chair to gaze thoughtfully up at the ceiling. "My mother died in childbirth when I was born, and although my father never said anything about it to me directly, I always had the feeling he blamed me for that. And I was a disappointment to him when I was growing up. I was small, and often sick. I caught every illness that came along, and I had asthma. I couldn't play games and sports like other boys."

He paused and picked up the pencil, rolling it thoughtfully between his palms. "There was also my stutter. My father really didn't have the patience to listen to me. I did very poorly with my studies because my tutors didn't have any more patience with it than my father did, and I was so ashamed, I didn't even learn to read until I was almost ten. In short, my father thought I was an idiot."

The confession was made with a smile, but Mara didn't miss the slight flash of hurt that the smile was intended to mask. She thought of his terror when he'd stood on that table in front of the men. "The other children teased you," she murmured, feeling compassion for the boy Nathaniel had been.

"Oh, yes." He said the words with a resigned sigh, then shrugged and tossed down the pencil. "I outgrew the asthma and the other childhood ailments. It took years, but I finally conquered my stutter, although it does return to plague me at the most inconvenient times."

"When you're forced to give a speech?"

"It reminds me of days at boarding school, standing up in front of the class reciting compositions, hearing the other children laugh." He shook his head impatiently, as if warding off painful memories. "As for the trains, well, I don't know myself how that really came about. I just found myself one day taking apart one of my trains—it was just a pull train—and studying the parts to see how it worked. I guess I was about five years old."

He smiled ruefully at her across the table. "My nanny told my father what I was doing, and he was so angry. He thought I was destroying it. I tried to explain, but he

got impatient, and he ordered me never to do it again."
He paused, then added, "But I couldn't stop. I had this
insatiable curiosity. I just had to know how things
worked. I think I took apart every toy I ever got after
that. I studied them and put them back together. I even
figured out ways of improving them. But I had to do it
all secretly, or I'd get into trouble. I had these fantasies
that someday I'd show my father my ideas, prove to him
I wasn't the idiot he thought I was."

Mara made no reply, but she studied Nathaniel's
thoughtful expression and realized how hard it would be
for someone with his creativity, with his innovative
mind, to be forced to hide it as if it were something to be
ashamed of. "What was your first invention?"

He laughed. "A train, of course. I built a tiny steam
engine and modified one of my pull trains so that it
could be powered by steam. I was twelve years old.
Steam-powered toy trains were just beginning to come
out, but Chase Toys hadn't come up with one yet. It was
Christmastime, and my grandfather was visiting. He
caught me building it."

His laughter faded, but his smile lingered as he went
on, "My grandfather asked what I was doing, and I knew
there was no way I could lie about it. I told him, but I
was certain he'd tell Father and I'd get into trouble
again. I made him promise not to give away my secret."

Mara tilted her head, studying him. "Your grandfather
was very important to you, wasn't he?"

"My grandfather was the first person who listened to
me. He was the first person who didn't get impatient or
try to finish my sentences for me. After that Christmas, I
spent every summer at his home on the Isle of Wight
until he died when I was eighteen. We came up with
dozens of toy ideas. He taught me how to fish. We took
walks around the island and talked. He cared about me.

He gave me a chance when no one else would. When he died, I lost my dearest friend."

The ache of loneliness in his voice touched her deeply. She, too, had known loneliness, always moving from place to place, never having a home, never seeing her husband for more than a few months out of the year. She looked at Nathaniel across the table, and she realized that they had something in common. Impulsively, she reached out and placed her hand over his.

He gave her a surprised look, and she realized what she had done. She started to pull her hand back, but he caught it in his and held it there, entwining her fingers with his, refusing to let her withdraw her tentative offer of friendship.

They remained that way for a long time, saying nothing, thinking a great deal, as the clock on the wall ticked away the minutes. And, in that brief moment of companionable silence, Mara realized that Nathaniel was right. Sometimes, everybody needed a little help, even if it was only a comforting hand and the knowledge that there was someone else in the world who cared.

14

Over the next several days, Mara and Nathaniel saw little of each other. Michael was ill, and Nathaniel spent his time on the production floor, acting as supervisor while Mara worked on the business proposal for the bank.

Mara tried to concentrate on her work, but she found her thoughts continually returning to that night in their office, to the man who had invaded her life and turned it topsy-turvy.

Nathaniel. When she had reached out and touched his hand that night, she'd done it without thinking. She had tried to pull back, but he hadn't let her. He must have enjoyed the casual intimacy of those brief moments, too.

Despite her lack of concentration, Mara managed to finish the proposal for the bank by Friday afternoon, and she went down to the mezzanine and scanned the production floor below to let him know it was finished.

She caught sight of him almost immediately. He was

leaning against a table, talking to several of the men. His waistcoat was off, and his white shirt was darkened with sweat from the heat of steam engines. He said something to the men, and he smiled when they laughed in response. Mara found herself smiling, too. For several moments, she continued to watch him, feeling again his strong fingers entwined with hers, feeling again the blessed relief of knowing that she wasn't all alone.

She'd been alone for so long. For those few moments, the ache of it had lessened, and life had seemed just a bit easier. The moment had passed, of course. She'd finally withdrawn her hand, and their contact had been broken, leaving her alone again, with all her fears, with all her doubts.

Mara felt someone step up beside her and she jumped, startled out of her reverie. Emma Logan stood beside her, leaning over the rail. She, too, was watching Nathaniel. "'e's a peach, ma'am, that 'e is."

Heavens, Mara thought, looking at the other woman. When she looked at Nathaniel, did her own face wear that worshipful expression? More sharply than she'd intended, she said, "Don't you have work to do, Emma?"

"Yes, ma'am," she murmured and turned away, looking abashed.

"Emma?"

The girl turned back inquiringly. "Ma'am?"

"I'm sorry," Mara said. "I didn't mean to snap at you."

Emma's eyes widened as if that were the last thing she'd expected Mara to say. The girl gave her a tentative smile. "It's all right, ma'am."

Mara glanced back down at the scene below and sighed. She'd come down for a reason, and now she couldn't even remember what it was. What on earth was the matter with her?

A movement out of the corner of her eye caught her

attention, and she saw Mr. Finch standing by the doors, waving to her. She beckoned him to come up, but as the solicitor crossed the room, he paused beside Nathaniel and the two men spoke for a moment, then walked together toward the stairs.

Mara met them at the top. "Mr. Finch," she greeted, keeping her gaze on the solicitor. "What are you doing here?"

"Good morning. Mara, my dear, James's things arrived from San Francisco. I thought you might want to go through them." He studied her dismayed expression and added, "If you'd rather not, you don't have to. I can—"

"No," she interrupted, "I'll do it. Where are they?"

He pointed to the production floor below. Mara glanced down and saw a steamer trunk beside the front doors. "I'll have it taken upstairs."

"I'll find Boggs and have him bring it up," Nathaniel offered. "Why don't you show Finch our office?"

He turned and went back down. Mara gestured to the stairs. "Shall we?"

The solicitor nodded, glancing down at the production floor one more time before following her. "Quite a few changes going on around here. When did you move your office?"

"A few days ago," she answered over her shoulder as she began to climb the stairs. "We're also doing some remodeling."

"Yes, I noticed some men downstairs demolishing that hallway."

"It's going to be much more efficient when we're finished, but I've heard nothing but complaints about it. Everyone hates the dust and the mess."

Finch followed her to the third floor and came to a halt in the doorway. "My goodness, this is a definite improvement."

She glanced around. "It is rather nice," she admitted.

Finch glanced toward her desk, noting its neat, organized appearance. He then looked at Nathaniel's side and laughed. "I can tell which side belongs to you," he said.

She followed his gaze to the disorderly pile of papers strewn across Nathaniel's huge desk and sighed. "His laboratory's the same way. He won't let me touch a thing," she said. "He says he likes it this way."

"And I do." Nathaniel's voice caused both of them to turn toward the door as he entered the room. "If she straightened my things, I'd never be able to find them again. I have my own way of organizing my things."

The other man laughed. "Yes, I know. I've seen your flat."

"Would you like tea?" Mara asked. "I can have Percy—"

"No, no," he refused, shaking his head. "Thank you, but I can't. I have another appointment." He looked at Nathaniel. "There have been quite a few changes around here. Walk me down and show me what you've been up to."

Nathaniel met the solicitor's eyes, and a look of understanding passed between them. "Certainly."

Finch turned to Mara. "If you need anything, my dear, let me know."

"I will," she murmured. "Come for a longer visit next time."

"Of course," he answered, and the two men walked out. A vague sense of disquiet came over her. It had been evident they wanted to talk privately, and Mara wondered what they had to discuss that did not involve her.

A sound in the doorway caused her to look up. Boggs stood there with the steamer trunk on his broad back, gripping the stout rope that was wrapped around the trunk. "Where d'you want it, ma'am?"

She pointed to the center of the room. "Just leave it there, please."

The workman lowered his burden to the ground and pulled the key to the trunk from his pocket. Dropping the key on top of the trunk, he departed.

Speculations about the secretive behavior of Nathaniel and Finch fled from her mind as she stared down at the steamer trunk on the floor. She'd expected her husband's things to arrive eventually, but she hadn't expected the emotions that overcame her at the sight of that familiar old trunk.

Mara walked slowly over to the trunk and knelt down. But she didn't open it. She stared at it for a long time, thinking about the past. The sight of this old steamer trunk had always meant hello or good-bye. Separation or reunion. She took the key and turned it in the lock, then lifted the lid.

She pulled out items one by one. There were several shirts and well-cut suits. His shaving kit. The gold cuff links she had given him during one of the good times. A sketch of Helen that she'd done when the child was five. The wedding ring he'd always worn. Her letters to him tied with silk ribbon.

She went through the letters, but the last one she'd written, the one telling him never to return, wasn't there. He'd thrown that letter away and forgotten it. Just like James to ignore what he didn't want to face.

Mara set aside the sketch of Helen. She would donate the rest of his things to St. Andrew's. It was foolish to give away the ring and the cuff links, but although she couldn't bear to keep them, she couldn't bear to sell them either. She bent back over the trunk, but only one item remained.

It was a box tied with string, and she knew it was a gift for her. As if a present could wash away all the hurts and make everything right. She pulled out the box and put all the other things back in the trunk, then stared down at the box for a long moment.

He must have bought it after he'd met Nathaniel, after he'd made plans to come back to England. With his incredibly self-centered optimism, he'd assumed that when he came back, she'd forgive and forget. For abandoning her, perhaps she could have forgiven him, because she knew that came partly from her own inadequacy—her love had never been enough to make him stay. But she couldn't forgive him for abandoning Helen. For that there was no forgiveness.

Mara fetched a pair of scissors, cut the string tied around the box, and lifted the lid. She pulled the gift out of the box and stared at the gown of blue silk in her hands. A ball gown.

The absurdity of it struck her and she began to laugh. Bitter, humorless laughter. James had often talked about how, when they were rich, they would go to balls and dance the waltz and drink champagne from crystal goblets, about how he'd buy her a ball gown of blue silk.

Before she could stop it, the laughter changed, dissolved into tears. Mara buried her face in the soft blue silk of a gown she would never wear, and she cried for the first time in four years. She cried for her own shattered dreams. She cried for her daughter, who would never grow to womanhood. She cried for all the lost love and all the lost chances. Most of all, she cried for James, who had never been able to live within the prison of reality.

Nathaniel waited until they were outside the building. He leaned one shoulder against the brick wall of Elliot's and faced the other man.

"I assume you want to know about your brother's company first?" the solicitor asked.

"You've found out something?"

"Nothing definite, but plenty of rumor."

Nathaniel was, in some ways, a traditional man. He liked his dessert last. "Tell me about the other major competitors first."

Finch pulled a small notebook from his jacket pocket and scanned the notes written there. He gave Nathaniel an overview of the primary competitors for the toy train market. Bassett-Locke was doing well, but their selection was limited. Ives, the American company, didn't make models popular with the British market. And Issmayer, although they appeared to have invented a sectional train track, wasn't doing anything with it.

"As for your brother," Finch went on, "it seems he's having problems."

"I'm listening."

"Union troubles, for one thing," Finch said. "You heard about the explosion at Chase Toys?"

"I did. Faulty boiler, the paper said."

"That was true, apparently. The unionists have organized at Chase, and there is a great deal of pressure on your brother to improve conditions at his factory. Rumor has it that conditions at Chase Toys are hazardous, the hours are exceptionally long, and the wages he pays are pitifully low."

"I'm not surprised," Nathaniel said, staring across the alley at the brick wall of Mrs. O'Brien's. "But I'd have thought even Adrian would come up with the cash to improve things once the unions got to him."

"He might not be able to."

Nathaniel turned his head sharply. "Financial problems, too?"

Finch nodded. "Again, this is merely gossip, but it seems he might be close to queer street. Sales have been falling over the past few years."

"I've seen some of the products Chase has been putting out," Nathaniel commented. "No innovation, nothing new. I've been keeping up on things—I've seen their catalogs. The last new product he had was that mechanical bank, and that was one of my inventions from years ago. Besides, the quality of his toys is poor. It's no wonder his sales are falling."

"Well, that's true enough, but there's more to it than that."

Nathaniel glanced at him, and the solicitor went on, "It appears that your brother has borrowed immense sums of money during the last few years. Nearly everything he has is mortgaged." Finch shook his head. "I don't understand it."

"I do. I know my brother very well. He probably didn't use the money he borrowed to make improvements or develop new products. I saw the new mansion in Mayfair. Quite impressive. I'd say it must have cost him a pretty penny."

Nathaniel leaned back against the wall. "You see, Adrian's greedy. He doesn't want to give up anything, even to save his business. Appearance is everything, if you know what I mean. He'd have to be on his knees in the gutter before he'd admit he can't afford silk cravats and lavish parties. Perhaps not even then."

"He does like to live well," Finch agreed. "He has an extensive household staff, a home in Mayfair, an estate in Devon, a villa at Brighton, an impressive art collection, membership in several clubs. . . ."

Nathaniel nodded. "Exactly. The problem is that he's gotten himself into a downward spiral. Sales keep falling, revenue declines until suddenly he's losing money instead of making it. So he cuts his costs by using poor quality materials and sales fall even further."

"But what caused this downward spiral? When you

sold your share to him and went to America, Chase was doing very well. Ten years later, it's nearly insolvent. What happened?"

"Adrian never had any ability to manage the company. I told you, he's greedy and impatient. He wants instant profit, and he's never reinvested those profits back in the business." Another thought struck him. "If Adrian's in trouble and his creditors called in his loans, he'd be ruined."

Finch shook his head. "That isn't likely to happen. He's engaged to be married. Wealthy American heiress with a substantial fortune."

"Honoria Montrose. Yes, I know."

"If Adrian is really in trouble, his creditors will be waiting to see what happens. If he marries Honoria Montrose as planned, his problems will be solved. If the marriage is called off for any reason, his creditors will probably come after him like attacking sharks."

"If Adrian's in such trouble, she'd be bound to know about it."

Finch shrugged. "No doubt her solicitors would have investigated him, but she may have ignored their advice. It's reported to be a love match."

Nathaniel's sound of contempt clearly indicated what he thought of that. "Adrian has charm, I suppose," he conceded. "But I can guarantee you he doesn't love her. He loves her money. If she lost it all tomorrow, it makes my head spin to think how quickly he'd call off their engagement."

"Perhaps, but Honoria Montrose is no fool. Adrian may be marrying her for her money, but she's probably marrying him for the title. It's seems to be quite the thing these days for wealthy American women to marry titled, impoverished Englishmen."

"Have you learned anything else?"

"Yes."

Nathaniel turned to look at him. "What?"

"Why didn't you tell me that you started a toy company in St. Louis and that it failed?"

Nathaniel sighed. He didn't want to discuss his past defeats. "I don't like to talk about it."

"I believe you had a hard time getting suppliers to provide materials on credit, and you didn't have the cash to pay for them up front, so your output was low. You also had problems getting supplies delivered on time."

Nathaniel shot him a wry glance. "I don't need a summation, thank you. I remember perfectly well what happened. And I don't recall asking you to investigate me."

"And then, you went bankrupt," Finch went on, ignoring Nathaniel's words.

Nathaniel scowled at the solicitor, but Finch did not back down. He simply stared back at him, waiting, his gaze mildly curious.

Nathaniel closed his eyes. "Yes, I went bankrupt. I just didn't have the desire to start over." He paused, then added, "Until I met James."

"I understand," Finch replied. "James had the ability to make people believe in themselves, to believe that anything they wanted was achievable. You have that ability as well, my friend."

Nathaniel shook his head and opened his eyes. "Please don't make any comparisons between James and myself. I would never abandon my wife and daughter."

Finch sighed. "Well, James was never what you'd call responsible. He loved his family as far as he was capable, but he resented being tied down to anything for long. He was the sort of man who probably never should have married at all." He paused, looking at Nathaniel and asked, "Are you planning to tell Mara about your failed business?"

He couldn't. It would serve no purpose, and it would endanger the tentative trust he'd gained from her. "No."

"Don't you think she has the right to know? She is your partner."

"Mara doesn't have anything to do with it. It's in the past. It's over." He straightened away from the wall. "Why rake it all up again? All it would do is make her worry, and she has enough to worry about."

"It will worry her a great deal more if she learns about this from someone else."

"Are you planning to be that someone?"

"No. I was hoping you would tell her yourself." He studied Nathaniel's set expression and sighed. "I know you feel you should protect her, but the truth has a way of coming out whether we like it or not. How do you think she'll feel when she learns you've kept this from her?"

Nathaniel didn't answer. He turned away and started down the alley toward the door into the factory, but he paused and glanced over his shoulder when Finch spoke again.

"Nathaniel, you're not only dealing with your own future, you're dealing with hers, too. Remember that. Don't hurt her."

"I don't intend to."

Finch gave a slight cough. "Yes, well, you know what the road to hell is paved with."

Nathaniel walked through the door and slammed it shut behind him. Yes, he knew, better than anyone.

When Nathaniel entered the office, all thoughts of his brother vanished from his mind. Mara was kneeling on the floor in front of her husband's steamer trunk, her face buried in the folds of a blue dress. He heard her muffled sobs, and he came to an abrupt halt in the doorway.

"Mara?"

She straightened with a jerk, and he could see her struggle to regain control. She averted her head, wiping away tears with a hasty swipe of her hand.

She rose and tried to walk past him, but he stepped in front of her and put his hands on her shoulders. He bent his head to look into her face. "Mara, what is it? What's wrong?"

"Nothing," she said, but her tearstained cheeks made her a liar.

He glanced over her shoulder at the clothes that lay in neat piles within the trunk, the items she had set aside, and the empty cardboard box. His gaze moved to the frothy garment of silk and lace in her hands before he looked again at her downcast face. "What is that?" he asked gently.

"It's a gift from James," she said in a low, tight little voice. "A ball gown. He was always giving me silly, useless gifts. I assume he intended to bring it with him when he came back."

Nathaniel lifted one hand from her shoulder and tilted her chin upward. "It's a very pretty dress."

Her lip quivered, a muscle worked in the line of her jaw, and her eyes darkened to the tumultuous color of storm clouds. "It's a useless dress. A useless dress from a useless man who hadn't the sense God gave a rabbit. Where would I ever wear a dress like this?" she demanded, her voice quavering with the effort of controlling her emotions. "It probably cost the earth. Why couldn't he have just brought the money? That I could have made use of."

Nathaniel's thumb caressed her trembling chin, a touch he wished could soothe the hurt that lay beneath her anger. "He had dreams for you. Dreams of the life he wanted to give you."

"Dreams. Fantasies. Promises. What good are they?" Mara stepped back, holding up the dress between them like a wall. "What good is this?"

"You might wear it someday."

She bundled the dress into one hand and gestured to their surroundings. "Oh, of course. I go to balls all the time. Invitations pour in every day, the maid brings them with my morning tea. Haven't you noticed?"

Her face puckered, her chin lowered, and the dress slid to the floor by her side. "I don't even know how to dance," she whispered as another tear fell from her eye and glistened on her cheek. "James always promised to teach me." She stared down at the dress on the floor and added, "He never did."

She stepped around him and ran out of the room. Nathaniel didn't try to stop her. He bent down and lifted the delicate dress from the floor, fingering the silken folds. He wished he could teach Mara to dance; he wished he could make her laugh again and wash away all her pain. Most of all, he wished he could make her realize that dreams were what made life worth living.

15

Adrian froze, *the cup of tea* raised halfway to his lips, and stared at the small man seated in the opposite chair of his study. "He's what?"

"He's bought into an electrical equipment company in Whitechapel," the other man replied. "It seems the company was in serious trouble and about to go bankrupt. Your brother purchased fifty-one percent of it."

"Electrical equipment?" Adrian frowned. "How odd. You're certain?"

Owen Rutherford, private detective, stiffened in his chair, clearly affronted.

"Sorry, I'm just surprised, Mr. Rutherford. I would have expected my brother to be involved in another toy company."

The detective relaxed slightly. He pulled a sheaf of papers from the dispatch case on his lap and scanned his notes. "Definitely not a toy company. Elliot Electrical

Motors manufactures dynamos, searchlights, and other electrical equipment. No toys at all."

Adrian took another sip of tea. "Fifty-one percent," he murmured. "Who owns the other forty-nine percent?"

"A widow. Mrs. Mara Elliot."

"A woman?" Adrian's lip curled with contempt. Only Nathaniel would find himself saddled with a female partner, and it probably didn't even bother him.

"It seems the woman's husband—a Mr. James Elliot—owned the business. Something of a rake, by all accounts, with no money and plenty of debt. He died recently, and the bank holding the loan against the company foreclosed. Your brother purchased fifty-one percent for about five thousand pounds, paying off the loan against the company. He also moved into a lodging house next door."

Adrian's frown deepened. "Where did he get five thousand pounds?"

"It seems that he sold patents on several inventions to raise the capital." Owen turned a page on his lap and once again scanned his notes. "There would have been enough to cover the loan, but not much more."

Adrian sat back, resting his head against the leather upholstery of his chair, and was silent for several moments. "Why?" he asked himself the question aloud. "Why would Nathaniel invest everything in an electrical equipment company? It isn't like him at all."

"His toy company failed. Maybe he decided to try something different."

"No." Adrian knew Nathaniel would never choose to make dynamos for a living. "Toys are his obsession. This makes no sense."

Owen coughed. "Well, Lord Leyland, your brother seems to have a reputation for being rather odd."

Adrian was dissatisfied. He knew his brother too well

to be fooled by appearances. Nathaniel might be bizarre, but he wasn't stupid. Adrian knew that better than anyone. He refused to underestimate his brother. He'd done that once before, and it had nearly cost him half of Chase Toys. "There's more to this than eccentricity, Mr. Rutherford. Find out everything you can about what he's up to."

"Yes, my lord."

"Nathaniel's planning something. I can feel it, and I want to know what it is."

The detective put his notes back into his case and closed the lid. Then he departed, closing the study door behind him and leaving Adrian to his tea and private speculations.

What were Nathaniel's real intentions? Perhaps he had some new invention and was planning to manufacture it. But what? Adrian's hand tightened around his cup. Nathaniel. Always cropping up like a bad penny, making things difficult. Ever since they were children.

"Whitechapel," he muttered. It was just like his brother to have an address in the East End, to live in a lodging house like a common dustman. Nathaniel had never cared about his reputation, his station in life, or what people thought of him.

Adrian swallowed the last drop of tea and set the delicate Dresden cup and saucer aside. It was time to pay his little brother a visit.

Mara walked, with no conscious thought of her direction. She simply moved one foot in front of the other, her strides carrying her farther and farther away from the factory, away from the man who thought wishes came true.

Her husband had always believed the same thing.

Mara tried to recall a single promise kept, a single wish come true, a single dream realized, and she could think of none. James had never stayed around long enough to keep his promises, only long enough to make her believe them.

How long would Nathaniel stay before the dream lost its fascination, before a new and brighter dream lured him away?

A picture of him formed in her mind, a picture of eyes like the sea and hair like the sun. She recalled his words about trust and partnership, and the feel of her hand in his. She thought of that night on the roof, of how tempted she'd been to lean against him, rely on his strength and confidence.

Mara came to a halt on the sidewalk, staring straight ahead but seeing nothing as the realization hit her. She was doing it again, listening to dreams and promises and believing them. She was being taken in by beguiling talk and charming smiles. She was a fool.

She glanced around. Shadows of twilight darkened the narrow street. A gust of wind stirred the rubbish nestled against soot-covered brick buildings and whipped the ragged skirts of the two girls playing on the sidewalk. This was Whitechapel, for heaven's sake. The streets weren't paved with gold and opportunity had never knocked on these doors.

It was getting late, and Mara knew she shouldn't be wandering the neighborhood after dark. She had to go back. Reluctantly, she turned around, retracing her steps, trying not to think about what would happen when Nathaniel's dream became tarnished and he went off to seek a brighter one. She didn't want to think about being alone again.

* * *

Nathaniel stared out the window, watching the street and waiting for Mara, growing more worried as time went by and she did not return. He'd let her go this afternoon, knowing how upset she was, but now he wished he hadn't.

He knew she hadn't gone home. He'd paid Mrs. O'Brien half a crown to let him know if she returned to the lodging house. Night had fallen, and he had no idea where she was.

When he turned away from the window, the glimmer of silk under the gaslight caught his eye. He walked over and lifted the dress from the floor. For a few moments, his fingertips traced the watermarks of tears, then he laid the dress neatly in the trunk atop James's other belongings, closed the lid, and pushed the trunk into an out-of-the-way corner.

Mara had lived with years of broken promises. Nathaniel knew he couldn't fulfill all the promises James had made to her, but he could fulfill at least one. He looked at the stacks of crates against the wall and wondered which one contained his gramophone. Rolling up his sleeves, he set to work. When he was done, he went back to the lodging house, changed his shirt, and left a note for Mara with Mrs. O'Brien. Then he went back to the factory and waited.

By the time Mara arrived home, it was dark. She stepped into the dim interior of the lodging house and started for the stairs, but she'd only taken two steps before Mrs. O'Brien's shadow fell across the wall and banister.

"Mrs. Elliot?"

Mara turned to her landlady. The woman was standing in the doorway to her parlor, the light from within outlining her silhouette. "Yes?"

She stepped forward, holding out a folded sheet of paper sealed with wax. "Mr. Chase asked me to give this to ye."

Mara took the note and broke the seal, turning away as Mrs. O'Brien leaned forward, obviously hoping for a peek. Mara unfolded the note and held it up to the light from the parlor.

> *Where toys are made and dreams come true,*
> *A friend stands by and waits for you.*
> *Promises were broken, and so you wept.*
> *But promises made are sometimes kept.*

Mara smiled. Another riddle. He was obviously waiting for her in the factory, but what was he up to?

"Thank you, Mrs. O'Brien," Mara said over one shoulder as she turned and left the lodging house.

She walked back to the factory, feeling a mixture of curiosity and anticipation as she wondered what Nathaniel was planning. She quickened her steps as she entered the building and ascended the stairs, but when she walked into the office, her steps faltered at the sight of him.

Nathaniel had moved the table and chairs to one side of the room, and he was bent over the table, tinkering with a wooden box of some sort. He looked up at the sound of her footsteps. "You got my note?"

"Yes, I did. Mrs. O'Brien gave it to me," she answered in a rush, out of breath and trying not to sound it. "But I don't understand what it means." Feeling awkward, she glanced away and added, "I'm not very good at riddles."

"You don't have to be. It's enough that you came." He bent back over the table, turned a handle on the side of the wooden box, and music suddenly began to play, issuing from a sort of horn on the opposite side. It was the lilting melody of a Strauss waltz.

Mara stared at the contraption with a mixture of skepticism and awe. "What is it?"

Straightening, he began to walk toward her. "It's a gramophone. An invention of Mr. Edison. He sent it to me about a year ago."

"How does it do that?"

"I'll explain it some other time."

There was something intense and purposeful in his eyes as he came to a halt in front of her, and Mara's breath caught as she gazed up at him. When he reached for her hand, she jumped. "What are you doing?"

His fingers closed around hers, tightening when she tried to yank her hand away. Gently he pulled her further into the room. "I am going to teach you how to dance."

"What?" She tried unsuccessfully to extricate her hand from his grasp as he led her toward the empty space he had made in the center of the room. "No, really, that's quite nice of you, but—"

"Every woman should know how to dance." He turned to face her with only a hand's breadth between them.

Mara licked her dry lips and stared at his white shirt-front and remembered the tautness of muscle and skin beneath it. "I don't think so."

"Yes." He lifted her hand in his, and put his other hand on her waist.

She pulled back at the light touch, resisting the impulse to twist away from it, to run. She made a fluttering motion with her free hand, and he answered her unspoken question.

"My shoulder."

Her hand came to rest there, lightly, her palm fitted against the dent of his shoulder, her fingers curving over the top, black kid against white linen. "This is silly," she mumbled.

"No, it isn't. You are going to learn the waltz. Now, pay attention, and I'll show you how it's done. Follow me." He began to move his feet in time to the lilting melody, pulling her with him, showing her the steps. "The easiest way is to count in your head as you go," he told her. "Like this. One-two-three, one-two-three."

Mara watched his feet and followed with awkward, stilted movements, trying to concentrate on the steps of the dance rather than the man. But he was so close. She could feel the warmth of his fingers through layers of fabric, through walls of defense. Too close.

She stumbled, tripping over her own feet, and she felt his hands tighten to steady her as they stopped moving.

"Mara, don't look at the floor. Look at me."

"I'll step on your feet."

"They've been stepped on before. Look at me."

She lifted her gaze as far as his chin and saw the hint of a smile above it, a lingering, teasing twist of the lips. Was he laughing at her?

Challenged, she looked higher and saw the humor in the crinkles at the corners of his eyes.

"That's better." His smile widened and he began moving again, pulling her with him in the steps of the waltz. She kept her gaze locked with his, but she only made it through three steps before she stumbled again. He came to a halt and sighed.

"This is not going to work if you don't allow me to lead," he told her.

She stirred restlessly in his hold. "I don't understand."

"It's very simple. I lead you where I want you to go, and you follow."

Mara didn't like that notion at all. She looked down at his black boots. "I'm not any good at this," she said, shaking her head and pulling free of him as the music ended. She clasped her hands behind her back. "I appreciate what you're trying to do. Really, I do, but this isn't going to work. I can't dance."

She waited, but he continued to stand before her, and finally she looked at him. His smile was gone, and he was studying her with that thoughtful, perceptive look.

"I have an idea." He lifted his hand, palm facing her. "Don't move."

She watched him disappear into the other part of the room and heard the sound of him rummaging about, obviously looking for something. Wildly, she wondered if she should just leave, but before she made up her mind, he reappeared with a length of white silk in his hand.

A cravat? She frowned suspiciously. What was he up to? With Nathaniel, it could be anything. There was no way to predict what crazy ideas would enter his head. She watched, her curiosity keeping her there when all her instincts told her to run.

He walked to the table and again turned the handle on the gramophone. A moment later, the waltz began again, and he returned to stand before her. "If you're going to follow my lead, you're going to have to let me guide you."

"I told you, I'm not any good at this. Let's just forget it, shall we?"

There was a hint of desperation in her voice, and she knew he heard it.

He shook his head. "Oh, no. You're going to learn how to do this. I'm going to lead, and you're going to follow, and we are going to waltz."

He lifted the cravat in his hands. Too late, she realized what he intended. The silk came around her eyes, blinding her to everything but the wall of white before her, and she began to panic as she felt him knot the length of silk behind her head. "No, I can't."

*I*f you
have a passion
for great
historical
romance,
here's an offer
you'll love...

4 FREE NOVELS

SEE INSIDE.

Introducing
The Timeless Romance

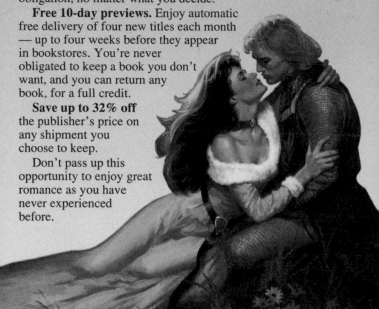

Passion rising from the ashes of the Civil War...

Love blossoming against the harsh landscape of the primitive Australian outback...

Romance melting the cold walls of an 18th-century English castle —— and the heart of the handsome Earl who lives there...

Since the beginning of time, great love has held the power to change the course of history. And in Harper Monogram historical novels, you can experience that power again and again.

Free introductory offer. To introduce you to this exclusive new service, we'd like to send you the four newest Harper Monogram titles absolutely free. They're yours to keep without obligation, no matter what you decide.

Free 10-day previews. Enjoy automatic free delivery of four new titles each month — up to four weeks before they appear in bookstores. You're never obligated to keep a book you don't want, and you can return any book, for a full credit.

Save up to 32% off the publisher's price on any shipment you choose to keep.

Don't pass up this opportunity to enjoy great romance as you have never experienced before.

Reader Service.

Yes! I want to join the Timeless Romance Reader Service. Please send me my 4 FREE HarperMonogram historical romances. Then each month send me 4 new historical romances to preview without obligation for 10 days. I'll pay the low subscription price of $4.00 for every book I choose to keep--a total savings of at least $2.00 each month--and home delivery is free! I understand that I may return any title within 10 days and receive a full credit. I may cancel this subscription at any time without obligation by simply writing "Canceled" on any invoice and mailing it to Timeless Romance. There is no minimum number of books to purchase.

NAME

ADDRESS

CITY   STATE   ZIP

TELEPHONE

SIGNATURE

(If under 18, parent or guardian must sign. Program, price, terms, and conditions subject to cancellation and change. Orders subject to acceptance by HarperMonogram.)

"Yes, you can."

"I don't want to." She reached up to pull the cravat away, but his hands captured hers, and she felt the panic wash over her in waves. "I don't want to do this!"

His voice was low against her ear. "You'll be fine. We're just going to waltz. I'll take you where you're supposed to go."

"Nathaniel?"

"Yes?"

"What if I don't like where you're taking me?" she asked in a whisper.

His hands tightened around hers, and she knew he understood what she meant. "You'll just have to trust me," he said.

He released one of her hands, lifted the other in his, and began the waltz. She had no choice now.

Her free hand reached for the solid reassurance of his shoulder as he whirled her around. "Count," he said softly. "One-two-three."

She focused on that, repeating the numbers in her head as he moved her through the steps. He gave her no opportunity to be tentative, and without sight to guide her, she began to find the rhythm of the dance in him.

She stopped counting and clung to him, the only solid thing in a world that was spinning, her movements following his by instinct alone. The music receded until all she could hear was her own heartbeat. The tension left her until all she could feel was the strength and reassurance emanating from him.

When the music ended, he brought her to a stop. Exhilaration flooded through her. "I did it!" she cried. "Nathaniel, I really did it."

He laughed. "Yes, you did. And very well, too."

His hands released her, moving to the back of her

head to untie the cravat. When he let it slip down her nose to rest beneath her chin, she smiled.

"Thank you. I'm ever so grateful."

She felt the wisp of silk slide against her throat, and she realized his hands were still behind her head, his wrists resting on her shoulders. She would have pulled away then, but she felt his thumb caress the side of her neck, and she couldn't seem to move. She couldn't seem to breathe.

His fingers slid into the knot of her hair, pulling gently to lift her face. He bent his head slowly, ever so slowly, until his lips brushed hers, feather light and warm. "As a very strong-minded woman once said to me," he murmured against her mouth, "I don't want your gratitude."

The light grazing of his lips sent an involuntary shiver through her.

He had the ability to turn her upside down and inside out. He took away all her safe ideas and replaced them with dangerous new ones. He guessed her private secrets and tore down her protective walls. It was so easy. Easy because she let him.

Mara was lost in the sensation of his mouth against hers, her open eyes watching his close, watching his thick gold lashes sweep downward to rest against his skin. She felt him pull her lower lip between both of his, and he brushed his tongue back and forth over it, teasing and tasting, savoring her like a comfit. In that moment, something hard and tight deep within her unclenched, yielded. Her mouth opened.

His response was immediate. His tongue entered her mouth, and she realized that was what he'd been waiting for, that silent yielding. His hands tangled in her hair as he pulled her closer and deepened the kiss. The knot loosened, sending her hair and her defenses tumbling down.

She lifted her hands to grasp at something that wasn't him, but as it had been when she'd danced blindfolded in his arms, he was the only thing solid to hang on to. Her fists opened and closed on the air, helpless. She couldn't pull him closer, but she couldn't push him away.

Nathaniel broke the kiss, pulling back to look into her face. He was breathing hard, and she realized that she was, too, her breath coming out in little whispers between her parted lips, mingling with the hiss of the gramophone.

Her body tingled and her pulse beat frantically. She stared up at him in shock and wonder. So long . . . it had been so long . . . oh, heavens. She couldn't think.

He was smiling, looking down at her. It was a smile unlike any other before, a smile of infinite tenderness. His hands slid from beneath the heavy curtain of her hair to cup her face, and his thumbs swept back and forth across her cheekbones.

His head lowered a fraction, and she knew he was going to kiss her again. A tremor ran through her, a tremor of sudden panic, and she stepped back with a little gasp. He drew a deep breath and let her pull away.

He tugged the cravat gently from her throat and pushed back a wisp of her hair that had fallen over one shoulder, then his hands fell away, leaving her free. Alone.

She didn't want to be alone. She wanted to lean into him, feel his strength and gentleness again, hold on to him and keep him there. But she didn't. She couldn't. Something inside her held her back, the insecurity, the knowledge that she couldn't really hold him, not for long.

He lowered his gaze to the cravat in his hands and rubbed the silk between his fingers. "I think I had better take you home."

His voice sounded harsh, something she'd never heard before. Mara bit her lip and ducked her head, feeling relieved, disappointed, and quite inadequate all at once. She nodded, looking at the floor. "All right."

She heard him breathe a heavy sigh as he turned away. He walked her back to the lodging house, but neither of them spoke. When they reached her door, she unlocked it, hesitated with one hand on the latch, and looked up at him. "Nathaniel, I—"

"It's late," he interrupted her, pushing the door open. "I'll see you tomorrow."

He turned away, but instead of starting up the stairs to his own rooms, he went back down.

"Where are you going?" she asked.

"I'm going for a walk," he replied over his shoulder without looking at her. "A *long* walk."

She watched him descend the staircase and disappear. A walk at this hour? She shook her head, stepped inside her room, and shut the door. He really was the most unpredictable man.

16

It was twenty past eight. Nathaniel was often late, Mara reminded herself. He usually didn't come in until after nine. She knew she should be working, not watching the clock and waiting for him to come breezing in with their tea. There was a note on her desk from Michael, asking if she would meet with him this morning to go over next week's production schedule, but she didn't move to respond to it.

The proposal for the bank was finished. She could check it for errors one more time before she gave it to Nathaniel. She pulled the document out of the stack of completed work on the left side of her desk and began to read it.

Why had he kissed her? Afraid to ponder such a question, Mara continued to read the report in her hands. Ledgers and reports and numbers were tangible things, understandable. Men, however, were an unfathomable mystery. After twelve years of marriage, she hadn't understood James at all, and she knew that Nathaniel Chase was a much deeper, much more complicated man than James had ever been.

Did he think she was pretty? She wasn't, she knew that, not anymore. She looked in the mirror, and she saw the hardness in herself. But last night had been different. She had been different.

Mara came to the end of the proposal, and she realized that she had read the entire thing without paying any attention to it. She gave up and went to place the document on Nathaniel's desk, perching it atop the untidy pile of papers already there so that he would see it when he came in.

She started to turn away, but the sight of his jacket slung carelessly over the back of his chair caught her attention. She smiled, remembering it had been there the night before. He'd forgotten to take it with him.

She lifted the jacket from the chair and turned away, thinking she'd hang it on one of the brass hooks Boggs had installed beside the door, but she took only two steps before she paused. Holding it in her hands, she breathed in the clean, spicy scent of him, and the night before came back to her in all its hot confusion.

"Why did you kiss me?" she whispered and rubbed her cheek against the soft black wool before pressing her lips to it. She felt again the heat of his mouth, the touch of his thumbs caressing her neck, and the shivers along her spine. She felt it all again, and she indulged in a luxury she hadn't allowed herself for a long time. "I wish . . . "

What she wished was never voiced aloud. The sound of footsteps on the stairs brought her out of her daydream with a jerk, and she quickly hung the jacket on one of the hooks. When Nathaniel entered the office carrying the tea tray, she was seated at her desk, an open ledger before her and a pencil in her hand, hoping she looked as if she'd been hard at work all morning.

She made the mistake of glancing at him, and her facade of composure nearly deserted her. One dance, one kiss, and everything was different. She couldn't look at his hands without remembering the feel of them in her hair. She couldn't look at the straps of the braces he wore without remembering the solid strength of his shoulder beneath her hand. She couldn't look at his cravat without remembering the feel of silk against her throat.

She couldn't look at his mouth without remembering how it had felt when he'd kissed her.

She didn't want to be alone. She didn't want to keep carrying all the burdens by herself, yet she was a coward: she was afraid to trust. A bittersweet longing filled her as she looked at him. *I wish . . .*

"Good morning." He walked in and set the tray on the table. His expression gave her no clue as to what he might be thinking.

She looked away. "Good morning." Feeling the need to say something, anything, she asked, "Did you enjoy your walk last night?"

He didn't answer.

He was watching her, and when she looked up, his eyes met hers across the room. "No." He gestured to the table. "Shall we?"

She joined him, feeling puzzled, apprehensive, curious. But he said nothing more about his walk. She sat down, and he took the opposite chair.

"I thought you'd want to read the proposal before we go to the bank," she said, pouring their tea. "It's on your desk."

"Good," he answered. "I've got an appointment with Arthur Gamage this morning, and other appointments this afternoon, so I'll read it later. Just give me the gist of it, would you?"

She handed him his cup of tea. "We need three thousand pounds."

Nathaniel pulled a scone from the basket and looked at her. "That gives us enough money to produce the trains for orders we already have?" When she nodded, he asked, "What about any additional orders we might get?"

"We've got orders for twelve hundred now. We shouldn't commit ourselves to more until we know how well they will sell."

"If my meeting with Gamage goes well, we'll have more orders today."

"But all our orders are on consignment. If people don't buy the trains, the retailers can return the unsold product and demand a refund. Then we'll have thousands of unsalable trains, a huge loan, and no way to pay it back."

He took a sip of tea. "Mara, we discussed this before. Taking orders on consignment is standard practice with a new company and a new product. But Charles Harrod and William Whiteley were confident that the trains would sell. They didn't get where they are by being wrong about what people will buy."

He heard her sigh and looked at her across the table. "We'll need to grab as much business as we can and establish ourselves. Once other toy makers see what we're doing, they're going to be racing to come up with their own version. By next spring, every toy maker in Britain will have a train very similar to mine."

"But your train is patented, isn't it?" She slowly spread jam on one half of her scone.

"Of course, both here and in America. But a patent only protects you against a competitor coming out with the exact same product. All other toy companies have to do is make a few minor modifications, and they can sell virtually the same train we do. We have to establish ourselves as the leader right from the start."

"How much—" She paused and put down the knife, then cleared her throat. "How much do you think we'll need, then?"

"I expect we'll be able to more than double our sales before the Christmas season begins. So we'll need at least eight thousand, I'd say. Plus another two thousand for contingencies."

"Ten thousand pounds? That's the company's entire net worth. They'll never loan us that much."

"Of course they will. I am the brother of a viscount after all. I can get credit on my family name."

Mara began to panic. She slid back her chair and jumped to her feet. "No, we can't."

He stood up and circled the table. "Yes, we can."

"Ten thousand pounds." She moaned, feeling sick, and buried her face in her hands. "Ten thousand pounds."

He halted beside her. "Everything is going to be fine," he said softly and pulled her hands away from her face. He released her wrists and put his hands on her shoulders, turning her to face him, but she kept her head lowered. She looked so vulnerable, so lost and uncertain. He wanted to give her the security she craved, he wanted to promise her that nothing would go wrong, but he could not. "I know you're worried," he said, his hands moving in soothing circles over her shoulders, "but this is an all or nothing proposition. Our main concern will be to get those trains made and delivered by November 27. The biggest mistake we can make is underestimating our expenses."

She lifted her head. "Why can't we just borrow the three thousand for now?" she whispered. "We can always ask for more money later, if we need it."

He shook his head. "No, I don't want to do that.

We're in a position of strength right now. We have an innovative product, the means to produce it, and no other debt on our books. If any problems come up, and we have to ask for more money, we'll lose our bargaining power with the bank. They might even begin to question our solvency, and they could deny us additional funds."

"You sound as if you expect problems to occur," she murmured miserably.

"Mara, I know you like to plan for every possible contingency, but unanticipated problems always come up," he said. "I want to be prepared to deal with them. That's all."

He gave her his reassuring smile. She wasn't reassured.

"Please don't," she whispered. "Don't ask me to sign my name to a debt of ten thousand pounds. I can't."

His smile faded, and she saw a glimmer of steel come into his blue eyes. His mouth tightened and he let his hands fall away from her shoulders. She thought for a moment he was going to argue with her, but instead, he turned away. Going over to his desk, he picked up the proposal she'd written and brought it to her. "I've got to go. Let's talk about this when I get back."

She nodded and took the document from his hand, then watched as he headed for the door.

After pulling the black jacket from its hook, he walked over to the table by his desk and picked up the carrying case that held his train set. He started out the door, but paused and looked back at her.

She met his eyes, not bothering to hide how she felt. But he said nothing more and turned away, leaving her there alone. Mara looked down at the bank proposal in her hands, and she had the feeling she was going to find herself ten thousand pounds in debt whether she liked it or not.

She set the proposal on her desk, placing it neatly in

the center of her blotter, and went downstairs to meet with Michael about next week's production schedule, trying to put thoughts of Nathaniel aside. She'd thought a kiss had changed everything, but she'd been wrong. A kiss changed nothing at all.

Hell. Nathaniel listened to the steady clip of horses' hooves as the cab carried him through Cheapside, but all he heard was the pleading in Mara's voice. He stared at the shops and open markets he passed, but all he saw was the fear in Mara's face.

He was becoming far too susceptible to wide eyes and warm lips and whispered fears. Knowing it would be foolish to borrow less than they needed, he'd almost given in to her request anyway. All because of a kiss. *Hell.*

They were in business together, he reminded himself. He would do well to remember that from now on. There was no place in a business partnership for romance and courtship. No place for waltzes and soft kisses. No place for desire and sweet oblivion. He should never have kissed her. But the truth was that he hadn't been able to stop himself.

All night, the lilac scent of her had haunted him. Even now, he could still smell it. He could still feel the silky tangle of her hair and taste the sweetness of her lips. He could still feel the sensation of drowning in her.

Thinking about the night before, reliving it, brought all his desire rushing back in a flood, and Nathaniel took a deep breath. He leaned back in his seat and closed his eyes, wishing he could close his heart.

He hadn't expected that. He hadn't expected to lose himself in her. It had taken every bit of willpower he possessed to stop it when he had. One more kiss, and he'd have agreed to anything she wanted.

If he could not keep some distance between them, he would begin giving in to her fears, and the only thing he'd ever wanted would be in jeopardy. All because he didn't want to see bitterness and hurt in her eyes.

He knew he shouldn't kiss her again. But he was sure that given half a chance, he would. *Hell.*

That afternoon, Mara left the factory and walked back to the lodging house to get milk for Algernon. Bottle in hand, she returned to the factory and started up the stairs to her office, but Percy's voice stopped her on the mezzanine.

"Mrs. Elliot?"

She went over to Percy's desk. He and Michael had both moved their desks up here, and assembly had been moved downstairs, even though the remodeling was not quite finished. "If I hear any more complaints about the noise and the dust, I'm going to scream," she told him. "Boggs will be finished in a few more days."

Percy shook his head. "That isn't it. There's a gentleman upstairs waiting to see you. He asked to see Mr. Chase, but I told him Mr. Chase was out and asked if he would wish to speak with you. He said he would, and I took him up to your office." Percy lowered his voice and added, "It's Viscount Leyland."

"What?" Mara glanced at the stairs. "Nathaniel's brother?"

Percy nodded. "I know he's a competitor, but Mr. Chase took his train with him, so I thought it would be all right to let the viscount wait upstairs."

Mara frowned, feeling uneasy. She remembered the ruthless determination she'd seen in Nathaniel's eyes that day in Harrod's when he'd talked about competing with his brother. The viscount must be an odious man.

But when Mara entered the office, she found that handsomeness and charm must be Chase family traits, for Adrian Chase possessed both in abundance. He was standing by her desk, looking out of the window, when she walked in, and he turned at the sound of her footsteps.

His resemblance to Nathaniel was clear in other ways as well. He was nearly as tall and nearly as handsome, with the same sky-blue eyes and tawny hair. But there were also definite differences. His hair was trimmed to the fashionable short length. His boots were polished. His cravat was properly tied and fastened with a jeweled stickpin. In fact, the viscount dressed with all the luxurious neatness of a vain and wealthy man who had a valet.

She walked toward him, feeling like a butterfly on a pin beneath his assessing gaze. "Lord Leyland," she said.

"You must be Mrs. Elliot." His gaze perused her slowly, appreciatively.

She glanced down, realizing she still had the bottle of milk in her hand. She stepped closer to her desk and set down the bottle, feeling uncomfortable and flustered. Adrian Chase wasn't what she'd expected.

"A cat?" he inquired, still smiling.

"Umm . . . yes. My secretary informs me that you're here to see your brother. Mr. Chase is out, I'm afraid. He won't return for some time."

"I'd like to wait for him, if you don't mind. I haven't seen him in ten years, so I'm sure you can understand I'm eager to renew ties, now that I've learned of his return to England."

"Certainly." She gestured to the chair opposite her desk, not pointing out that Nathaniel obviously had a different view of the matter. "Please sit down."

He moved to the chair but did not take it. Instead

he waited, good manners dictating that she should sit first.

She circled her desk and sat down. Then he followed suit.

"I heard that Nathaniel had invested in a new business and now had a partner," he said, settling back in his chair. "I must confess, I didn't expect her to be beautiful. Tell me about yourself, Mrs. Elliot."

His words made her even more uncomfortable. She lowered her gaze to the desk, unable to think of anything to say.

Suddenly she frowned. She kept her papers in meticulous order, and she knew perfectly well that she had placed the bank proposal in the center of her desk so that she could work on it when she returned. Now, it was just a bit to the left, offending her sense of symmetry. She would never have left it like that. Someone had picked it up, read it, and put it back.

Waves of anger swept through her, and she discarded any notions of making polite small talk with Viscount Leyland. Her first conclusion had been correct. An odious man. No wonder Nathaniel disliked him so.

She looked at him, frantically wondering what she'd written in the proposal about the trains. "My lord, I really believe that there is only one thing I need to tell you." She rose to her feet, and her smile vanished. "Get out of my office."

He didn't move. He simply stared at her like a cat toying with a mouse, as if he knew perfectly well what she had realized and didn't care. He smiled. "My dear lady, I'm Viscount Leyland. I leave when I please."

Mara went rigid at the arrogant words. "Not in this factory, sir," she said through clenched teeth. "I've got thirty-eight Cockney workmen downstairs who don't give a fig who you are, *Lord Leyland.* Now get out or I'll have them come up here and escort you out."

He shrugged, but his smile remained. "Don't bother, Mrs. Elliot. I think I can find my own way."

"See that you do, sir."

He rose. "Good luck making your dynamos or whatever it is that you manufacture here. I wish you all the best. I certainly hope Nathaniel has better luck with you as a partner than he did on his own. Poor fellow."

Mara had the feeling she was about to be snared, but she took the bait just the same. "What do you mean?"

Adrian's brows rose in surprise. "He didn't tell you? It really was the most unfortunate thing." He shook his head and sighed. "He invested all he had starting his own toy company in America. It failed, of course."

She couldn't keep the surprise out of her expression, and Adrian saw it. He gave her a pitying smile. "My dear, Nathaniel is rather . . . odd, as I'm sure you already know. He tends to take very big risks, and they don't usually pay off, I'm sorry to say. His boyish eagerness often gets in the way of his judgment."

She began to shake, and she quickly thrust her hands in the pockets of her skirt, balling them into fists. With all the discipline she could muster, Mara wiped all expression from her face. "I appreciate the information," she said, relieved that her voice was steady. "Good day, sir."

He departed. Mara sank back down in her chair, listening to his footsteps on the stairs fade away as his words about Nathaniel echoed in her mind. *His own toy company in America . . . failed, of course.*

She thought of all the times Nathaniel had asked for her trust. All the times he had stressed the importance of partnership and discussion. But somehow, in all their discussions, he'd forgotten to mention that he'd had a toy company before, a toy company that had failed. She'd been right all along. Trust and partnership were just words. They didn't mean anything.

Nathaniel knew something was wrong the moment he returned. When he walked into the office, Mara was sitting at her desk, but she wasn't working. She wasn't scribbling in one of her ledgers, or adding up numbers on her abacus, or calculating profit and loss. She didn't even glance at him when he entered the room, and she didn't say a word. It was as if she hadn't even heard him come in. There was a bottle of milk on the desk, and Algernon was sitting on the floor, staring up at it and meowing, but she didn't seem to hear that either. Her face was pale and weary, reminding him of the first time he'd seen her, looking like the tragic Mariana of Tennyson's poem.

"Mara?" He set down the train set on the table by his desk and walked over to her, not liking the way she sat so still, staring straight ahead. "What's wrong?"

She finally looked at him. "Why didn't you tell me?"

"Tell you what?" He frowned at the vague question as he faced her across the desk.

"You had a toy company in America," she said, her voice a flat monotone. "It failed."

He sucked in a sharp breath, then let it out slowly. "How did you find out about that?"

"It's true, then."

"Yes." He saw the disappointment and the doubts in her eyes, and it hurt. It cut into him like a knife, laying open all the doubts he had about himself and his abilities, exposing all the wounds he'd hoped time would heal. A lifetime of doubts. He turned away. "It's true."

"Why didn't you tell me about it?"

He raked a hand through his hair. "What would have been the point?" he asked over one shoulder. "It's in the past, it's over. I don't like to talk about it."

"You could have at least told me."

"Could I have?" He turned around sharply to face her again. "I've spent the past six weeks trying to gain your cooperation and your support. What was I supposed to do? Do you really think I'd tell you all about my previous failures? That would really inspire your trust, now, wouldn't it?"

"It certainly doesn't inspire my trust when I hear about your failures from a third party!" Mara burst out, reacting to his sarcasm with a spark of her own anger.

"What third party?" he asked, bracing his hands on the edge of her desk as he looked down at her.

"Viscount Leyland paid us a little visit today."

"Adrian?" Nathaniel straightened with an abrupt movement. He hadn't expected that. Not yet. He'd hoped to have at least another month before Adrian discovered where he was and what he was doing. He needed that competitive edge. A combination of dismay and frustration and past hurts fused into a cold feeling of dread. "He was here?"

"Yes. He said he wanted to see you, renew family ties."

He made a choked, humorless sound at the irony of it. "Family ties? And you believed that rot?"

"I didn't let him in!" She waved a hand toward the door. "I went next door to get milk for Algernon. He arrived while I was gone, and Percy told him he could wait in our office. When I came in, he was already up here. I told him you were out, but he asked if he could wait for you. What was I supposed to do—say no?"

"And my failed business just happened to come up during your conversation. I see."

"He told me about it, yes." Mara's hands came together, twisted round each other in agitation. "You should have told me."

"My past is my own business," he shot back, feeling defensive. "It has nothing to do with you or with what we're doing now."

"No?" She glared at him across the desk. "I thought it had something to do with that trust you keep talking about. Couldn't you have trusted me?" Before he could answer, she went on, "I had the right to know."

"Why? So that you could weigh the evidence, condemn me, and execute me before I'd even had a chance to prove myself?"

"I wouldn't have done that."

"Oh, yes, you would. You've been doing it ever since we met. You're doing it now. Criticizing, judging, drawing conclusions."

"That's not true," she protested.

"Isn't it? I can just imagine what would have gone through your mind if I'd told you. His business failed? Well, then, off with his head." He ran one finger across his throat.

She winced at the ruthless gesture. "How did it happen?"

"What difference does it make?"

She swallowed hard. "People tend to make the same mistakes over and over. I don't want to see what happened before happen again."

"And you think it will?" He saw her answer in her eyes. "Go ahead and judge me. I took some risks, I made some mistakes, my business failed. But then, you wouldn't understand that, would you? You sit inside your suit of armor, finding fault and feeling superior, watching the rest of us muddle through life, secure in the knowledge that you never make mistakes." He sighed wearily. "No, you never fail, Mara. You never fail because you never try."

She jerked her head back as if he'd slapped her. Shaken, she watched him turn away and disappear into his laboratory. Then she heard his footsteps on the stairs and knew he was going up to the roof.

Was that really how he saw her? Critical and judgmental, superior and fault-finding? She bit down on her trembling lip, feeling hurt. If she had a suit of armor, it wasn't helping her now.

A month ago, she wouldn't have cared what he thought. No, she'd have dismissed his words as the idiotic notions of a crazy man.

A plaintive meow caught her attention, and Mara glanced down. Algernon was sitting by her chair, and she realized she still hadn't fed him. She went into the laboratory and took down his bowl from the shelf above the sink. After filling it with milk, she set it on the floor beside her desk and watched as the kitten pounced on his late lunch.

"We're quite a pair, aren't we?" she murmured. "Hissing alley cats, both of us."

She didn't want to be a hissing alley cat. She sat down and rested her elbows on the desk and her chin on her clasped hands. Last night, she hadn't been like that. She closed her eyes, remembering how it had felt to trust and to yield. It had felt magical and marvelous and right. And very scary.

Algernon finished his milk and walked over to her. He rubbed his head against her leg as if demanding attention. Startled, she looked down at him. He'd never done that before.

Tentatively, she bent down and reached out her hand, moving slowly, until it touched the kitten's neck. Immediately, Algernon lifted his head, pushing into her palm, and he began to purr.

They remained there for a long time, and Mara realized that one could only earn trust if one reached out for it. She decided it was time to try.

17

Nathaniel sat on the roof, staring between the stone columns of the parapet, watching the sunset. He knew he should probably go in and get some work done, but he didn't move.

Adrian knew where he was. He hadn't expected his brother to discover his whereabouts so quickly, and it wouldn't take Adrian long to learn what he was doing. If Adrian managed to copy the train before Nathaniel had the chance to establish himself, he knew he'd never be able to compete with Chase.

Given half a chance, Adrian would steal his invention and claim it as his own. Nathaniel knew he couldn't give his brother that chance, but he couldn't succeed without Mara's help. They needed each other.

Six weeks. It had taken him six weeks to earn her trust, but Adrian had destroyed that trust in a matter of seconds with a few well-chosen words. The trust he'd gained from her was fragile indeed if it disintegrated so easily.

No, he couldn't lay the blame on Adrian. He should have told Mara the truth. He had lashed out at her in anger when he was the one at fault.

He heard the door open and the tap of her boot heels on the slate. He stared straight ahead, waiting, as she walked over and sat down beside him.

"I'm sorry," he said without looking at her. "I should have told you."

"It doesn't matter."

"Yes, it does. I—"

"Nathaniel," she interrupted, "it doesn't matter. We all have failures in our past." She paused, then added softly, "Even me."

He slanted a sideways glance at her, but she wasn't looking at him. She was staring at the sunset. "I wonder what failures are in your past," he mused, only realizing when she glanced at him that he had spoken aloud.

"Many." She plucked at her skirt, and added softly, "I wasn't a very good wife, for one."

He watched the evening breeze catch a tendril of dark hair that had come loose from her chignon. The fading sunlight made it look the color of mahogany.

"Why do you say that?"

She brushed back the wisp of hair and turned to stare at the sunset. "Do you remember the day you gave me the abacus?"

"Of course."

"'Be nice to me,' you said. James used to say that, too, and when you said that, I assumed you meant what he always did when he said it to me."

There was a blush in her cheeks, from the crimson sunset or private shame, he couldn't tell. "I see."

"At first, I told myself that he had to leave in order to

make a life for us. But over a long period of time, I began to realize it wasn't for us. It was for himself. And I began to turn away from him, I became very cold, very unloving. That, of course, drove us further apart. There came a point when I could no longer forgive him for leaving, or forgive myself for driving him away."

"Mara, it wouldn't have mattered. He would have left anyway." He reached out and touched her shoulder, but she did not look at him.

"I tried to tell myself that, but during our marriage, I said so many bitter, terrible things to him. Sometimes, I feel as if I have this demon lurking inside me, this dark and cruel creature that drives me on, that I cannot exorcise from my soul." She looked at him with those crystal gray eyes. "Nathaniel, you have no idea how cruel I can be."

He studied her face and saw only a woman abandoned and afraid. "I don't see cruelty in you."

"It's there, Nathaniel. The failure of my marriage wasn't all James's fault. It was mine as well."

"I think you're giving James far more credit than he deserves. He was a louse. Anyone would become bitter."

She shook her head. "I knew what he was like when I married him. But I was only sixteen, I was so young. After marriage, I just expected him to change, and I blamed him when he couldn't. He was what he was. I ended up hating him for being the man I had fallen in love with."

She wrapped her arms around her bent knees, hugging herself as if trying to hold in all her feelings. "We were living in a rented house off Hanbury Street when James left for America. It was a nice house, but we had to move right after he left. I couldn't afford the rent. I had no money, because I'd already used the money he'd given me to pay off his other debts."

"The money he'd borrowed against Elliot's," Nathaniel said. "Yes, I remember you telling me about that."

She didn't look at him; he didn't know if she even heard him. She was staring at some distant point on the horizon. "We took a room in a cheap little lodging house in Brick Lane. I don't know how the fire started. I woke up, I could hear Helen screaming, and everything was on fire."

Nathaniel listened, knowing she was reliving it all as she spoke.

"It was too high to jump and there was no way to climb down. When the floor fell in, we went with it. Helen became trapped beneath the timbers. The smoke was so thick, I couldn't breathe. I couldn't even see. I didn't notice that the wood was smoldering, I just started grabbing pieces, clawing through them, trying to dig her out. I don't know when the screaming stopped. I just kept pulling away the wood. Some men came in and grabbed me, dragged me out of the house. They kept shouting that she was dead, over and over, and they wouldn't let me go back in."

Mara turned and looked at him, tears streaming down her face, catching the last rays of the sun. "They gave me morphine. They bandaged my hands. When James wrote to me and told me where he was, I wrote back. I told him Helen was dead, and I told him it was all his fault, that if he hadn't abandoned us, Helen wouldn't have died. I called him a murderer, and I told him never to come back." She made a choked sound. "As usual, he didn't listen. He was planning to come back, wasn't he? Four years later, and he thought he could waltz right back into my life again, with a gift under his arm and a promise on his lips."

Nathaniel reached out and grabbed her hand, held it tight. There was nothing he could say. He wished he could take her pain away, absorb it into himself, but he could not. So, he just held her hand in his and they sat in silence, watching as twilight faded into night. It was a long time before she spoke again. "Nathaniel?"

"Hmm?"

She pulled her hand from his. "Your brother saw the bank proposal. He read it before I came up."

Nathaniel wasn't surprised. "How do you know? Did you see him?"

"No, but I keep the things on my desk in a certain order. When I came back from Mrs. O'Brien's, the proposal was not where I'd left it. I'm sure he read it while he was waiting."

Nathaniel raked a hand through his hair. "If he read the proposal, he knows about the train."

"There was nothing about the trains in my proposal."

He frowned, perplexed, and she went on, "I had decided that it would make for a more effective presentation if you were to demonstrate the train for the bankers instead. So I took out all the explanations. Viscount Leyland knows we're planning to make trains, yes, but that's all he knows."

"You didn't mention the sectional track or the accessories?"

"No."

Nathaniel thought about it for a few moments. "Adrian will realize that we're making electric trains, since this is an electrical equipment company, but without knowing the concept, he won't be able to copy us. That gives us some time." He paused, then said, "Today's Saturday. We'll go to the bank Monday."

"All right."

Her acquiescence surprised him. "How much do we borrow?" he asked.

"I suppose three thousand is out of the question?"

"I think so."

"Four?"

He smiled at her attempt to negotiate. "Eight."

"Five."

"Seven," he said firmly, hoping for six.

She groaned, pressing her forehead to her bent knees. When she spoke, her voice was so muffled he barely heard her. "Done," she whispered.

She sounded so miserable, he didn't know whether to laugh or wrap his arms around her. He did neither. "I need you, Mara. If we're going to succeed, we have to work together. You have to trust me."

She nodded from the depths of her skirt. "I trust you. I don't have any other choice." She lifted her head to look at him in the moonlight. The wind once again lifted the loose wisp of her hair and it caught at the corner of her mouth. "But I'm still worried. You must think I'm foolish."

"No," he answered in a very gentle voice. He reached out his hand and pulled the tendril of hair from her lips. "I think you're very brave."

He might believe she was brave, but Mara knew it wasn't true. She wasn't brave at all. She was terrified.

They went to the bank Monday afternoon. After ten minutes in Milton Abercrombie's office, Mara couldn't decide whether she was relieved or irritated. Six weeks before, when she'd come to the banker asking for a mere extension to an existing loan, she'd been turned down flat, without a moment's consideration. The banker hadn't even listened to her.

But Nathaniel was having no such difficulty. If, at first, Mr. Abercrombie had not been quite deferential enough to the Honorable Nathaniel Chase, the drop of

Viscount Leyland's name had corrected any misunderstanding regarding Nathaniel's station in life and his position in society. Mr. Abercrombie had then become quite solicitous, causing Nathaniel to give Mara a wink, clearly indicating that although he thought his brother beneath contempt, he wasn't above using the title to get his own way.

Mara studied the two men as they leaned over the desk in the banker's office, as they watched a little tin train circle round and round on a little tin track. She listened to them rhapsodize over the unique features and the power of electricity as they waited for the loan papers to be drawn up.

She sat, gloved hands folded over the proposal in her lap, a proposal the banker had barely glanced at before giving Nathaniel his full attention. She watched and waited until finally a clerk brought in the loan papers. Nathaniel unhooked the batteries, and the train rolled to a stop.

The clerk gave the loan papers to Nathaniel, and he immediately handed them to Mara. She read the document carefully. The terms were fair, and she nodded, handing it back to him. He scanned it, took the pen, and scratched his name in the appropriate place.

When she took the pen and paper back from him, her eyes met his for only a moment before she looked away. She dipped the pen in the inkwell, took several deep breaths, and signed her name next to his.

It was done. A few minutes later, Mara and Nathaniel left the bank, with an additional seven thousand pounds in their account and the heartfelt blessings of Joslyn Brothers, Limited.

"Viscount Leyland's brother, indeed!" She sniffed. "Close friend of Lord Barrington." She rolled her eyes. "Of all the rubbish."

"I am a close friend of Lord Barrington." He glanced up and down the street before tucking her arm through his and guiding her across. "We went through a year at Cambridge together. Of course, I haven't seen him in a dozen years, but what's a little time between old friends?"

She laughed as they began walking back to Elliot's. "Now that we have the money, what's our next step?" she asked.

"We need to meet with Michael and decide on quotas, then we can start making the train engines. He'll need to hire the tinsmiths and start ordering parts. We'll also need to decide which products to phase out of production."

She nodded in agreement. "We can't just add the trains to what we already manufacture or we'll never be able to handle the overload."

They discussed options as they walked. Mara was surprised that they agreed on many ideas, but the ones they didn't agree on were hotly debated.

"Searchlights are one of our highest profit items," she said as they passed Mrs. O'Brien's. "Why should that be the first product we abandon?"

"It's also the one that takes the most time to make. "I don't—"

He stopped abruptly and released her arm. Taking a step backward, he looked down the alley between Mrs. O'Brien's and the factory.

"What is it?" she asked, also stepping back to see what he was looking at. In the center of the alley, two boys were fighting. One was on top, punching the other, as the boys around them shouted encouragement. She hadn't even heard them. They had seemed like part of the ordinary street noise to her, but for some reason they had caught Nathaniel's attention.

"Stay here," he said, pushing her away from the entrance. He turned back, and started down the alley. Mara peeked around the corner and watched.

Nathaniel brought two fingers to his mouth, and the sharp sound of his whistle echoed in the narrow corridor. "What's going on here?"

The boys instantly scattered, escaping at the opposite end, leaving their victim lying on the ground, sobbing. The sound of frustration and rage—and shame. Nathaniel recognized it and quickened his stride.

He knew this was the same boy he'd seen being teased weeks before. Although his hair was dirty, it was carrot red and not many children had hair of that bright shade. The child's nose was bleeding, and Nathaniel pulled his handkerchief from his pocket as he knelt down beside him, trying not to grimace at the smell that emanated from the boy. "Well, now, what's this?"

The child struggled to sit up, pressing a hand to his nose. "Leave me alone!"

He turned away, but not before Nathaniel saw the birthmark, a dark splotch on the boy's left cheek, and he understood what was happening. He understood all too well. Children could sometimes be so cruel.

"My name is Nathaniel." He held out the handkerchief. "Take it."

The boy snatched the piece of linen and held it to his nose, managing to cover the mark on his cheek at the same time. A small cut at his hairline had left a thin line of blood, already beginning to dry, down his forehead. Over the edge of the handkerchief, his blue eyes, bright with unshed tears, glared at Nathaniel. "Go away."

Nathaniel didn't move. "Are you all right? Let me see."

He reached out, intending to have a look at the boy's

nose, but the child jerked his head away and scrambled backward. "No! Leave me alone."

"Your nose might be broken," Nathaniel said, moving closer as the boy retreated. When the child tried to rise, he caught him by the shoulders.

"Let me go!" the boy shouted. He kicked and struggled against the hold, still trying to shield his face with the handkerchief.

Nathaniel simply waited. After a few moments, the boy gave up the struggle, and Nathaniel examined the damage. "No, it's not broken," he announced. "Just bloody."

He gently pressed the handkerchief back over the boy's nostrils. "Hold it there. The bleeding will stop in a minute or two."

The boy obeyed, his outraged sobs quieting to hiccups.

Nathaniel heard footsteps and turned his head as Mara approached.

"Is he all right?" she asked, dropping to her knees beside him.

"He seems to be," Nathaniel answered and turned his attention back to the boy. "This is Mrs. Elliot. Anything hurt? Your ribs, maybe?"

"Everything hurts," the boy mumbled, his words muffled by the linen.

"I'm just going to have a look, all right?" Nathaniel quickly ran his hand over the child's ribs, noting that the white shirt he wore was ragged and filthy. One sleeve was stained with blood, and Nathaniel realized he must have scraped an elbow. "You're pretty tough," he said. "Nothing broken."

He glanced at Mara. "He's got some cuts and they ought to be washed. I've got iodine and bandages. Let's take him to my flat."

She nodded and rose to her feet. "Certainly."

"No!" the boy protested. "I ain't goin' nowhere with you."

Nathaniel stood up and held out his hand, ignoring the boy's protest. "C'mon," he said.

"No." He glared at them over the bloody handkerchief.

Nathaniel placed his hands on his hips. "Young man, you've got a lot to learn about fighting. The first rule is don't fight with somebody who's five times your size. You've got some cuts and we need to clean them. So, if you don't get up and come with me, I'll just lift you up and carry you."

The boy didn't answer, and he didn't move, but when Nathaniel started to make good his threat, he scrambled to his feet. "All right, all right, I'm comin'," he grumbled, his words muffled by the handkerchief. "I'm comin'."

Nathaniel gripped him firmly by the shoulder and marched him toward Mrs. O'Brien's as Mara followed.

When they reached his flat, Nathaniel grabbed the boy around the waist and lifted him up onto a table. "Let's get you cleaned up," he said.

Mara's gazed traveled up and down the child, and she wished they could do more than wash his cuts. The boy smelled frightful, and she wanted to drag him to the nearest bathhouse.

Nathaniel disappeared into the other room, and returned with a pitcher of water and a basin. "Keep an eye on him," Nathaniel instructed her as he set both pitcher and basin on the table. "I'll find the iodine and bandages."

Mara stepped up to the table and reached for the pitcher as Nathaniel turned away. She cast a dubious glance at the boy as she poured water into the basin, but he sat without moving, his legs dangling over the edge of the table, still holding the bloodstained handkerchief to his nose, staring down at the holes in his ragged knickers.

Helen had been only a bit younger than this boy when she died. Not wanting to think about that, she struggled for something to say. It had been so long since she'd been around children.

"What's your name?" she finally asked him.

"Billy Styles."

"Styles?" she repeated as Nathaniel stepped up beside her and placed a bottle of iodine, a roll of linen bandages, and a couple of clean rags on the table. "Is Calvin Styles your father?" she asked.

He nodded. "That's me dad."

Nathaniel frowned but made no comment. Taking off his jacket, he tossed it aside and began to roll up his sleeves. "All right, Billy. Let's take care of those cuts."

The boy shook his head violently from side to side as Nathaniel reached for the handkerchief. Mara watched as he gently began to pry the bloody scrap of linen from Billy's fingers and spoke to the child.

"You know, when I was a boy, I used to get beat up all the time. The other boys made fun of me, you see. I talked funny."

Billy lifted his head and loosened his grip as a frown of skepticism knit his brows. "You did not."

"Did, too. I stuttered." Nathaniel set down the handkerchief and reached for the rag. He dipped it in the basin of water, and wrung it out. "St . . . st . . . stuttered all the t . . . t . . . time. They used to laugh at me and make fun of me and then I'd get mad, and they would beat me up."

Lifting Billy's chin, he gently began wiping away the dried blood from the boy's face. Mara saw the boy flinch, and she noticed Nathaniel quickly started talking again as he cleaned the cut.

"One time, when I was a few years older than you, I came home with a bloody nose just like yours. It was summertime, and I was staying with my grandfather. My clothes were all torn and bloody, too, just like yours, and I thought sure I was going to get into trouble for fighting, but I didn't."

Nathaniel dropped the rag in the water and lifted the boy's elbow. Unbuttoning the cuff, he pushed the sleeve up the boy's arm and examined the scrape. "Grandfather didn't shout at me or anything. He just cleaned me up, and he asked me what happened."

Mara stood beside him and watched his hands, noticing the gentleness in them as he cleaned the boy's scraped elbow even as she recalled the force with which he'd rammed a fist into the belly of the boy's father.

"Well, I told him how they always made fun of me and how they were always trying to fight with me. I always ended up losing the fights and getting beat up because I wasn't as big as they were. I was stuttering so badly, I'm surprised Grandfather understood what I was saying, but he did. And he didn't laugh at me either. Do you know what he did?"

Billy shook his head, staring up at Nathaniel and listening intently. Mara picked up the bottle of iodine and a clean rag. She saturated a corner of the rag with the orange liquid, enjoying the sound of Nathaniel's voice as he told the story.

"Grandfather took me down to see Mr. Donovan, the blacksmith." Finished wiping away the blood, he dropped the used rag in the basin of water, and Mara handed him the one soaked with iodine. "Now, I only went to Grandfather's in the summertime, but even I knew Mr. Donovan was the best boxer around. He could beat anybody. He was tough. Do you know how tough he was?"

Again Billy shook his head.

"He was so tough . . ." Nathaniel pressed the iodine-stained rag to Billy's elbow and the boy was so entranced by his story, he hardly reacted to the sting. "He was so tough," Nathaniel went on, "that five years later, when he died, the shoemaker used his hide to make boots."

Billy burst out laughing, and Mara smiled. She reached for the roll of bandages and cut off a length to wrap around his elbow, listening as Billy asked, "How come yer grandfather took you to see 'im?"

"So Mr. Donovan could teach me how to fight," Nathaniel replied and began to apply iodine to the cut on Billy's forehead. "When I went back to school that autumn, one of the other boys tried to beat me up, but I won the fight. I never got beat up again."

"Really?"

"Really."

"I wish I knew 'ow t'fight."

The boy's wistful words impelled Mara to speak. "Fighting isn't always the answer," she said, giving Nathaniel a frown. "Usually it's best just to walk away."

"What if ye can't?"

Mara wrapped the bandage around the boy's elbow and did not reply. She opened her mouth to ask for Nathaniel's help, but he was already cutting several narrow strips of linen from the roll. He leaned closer to assist her. She held the bandage in place, and he began securing it with the linen strips.

They were silent, but it was a companionable silence, and Mara realized it was one of those rare moments when they were not arguing about something. They were working together, their own interests set aside for those of a small boy, and there was an incredible feeling of rightness about it.

But the moment was brief. Mara felt the pang of regret when Nathaniel tied the last strip to secure the bandage in place and stepped back.

She rolled down Billy's sleeve and buttoned the cuff. "You'd better have your mother wash that shirt tonight," she told the boy, "so the blood will come out."

"Don't 'ave a mum," Billy said. "Just me dad."

She looked into Billy's face for a moment, then she glanced at Nathaniel. She could see her own concern for the boy reflected in his eyes, but both of them knew there was nothing they could do.

Nathaniel put his hands on the boy's waist. "C'mon," he said, "we'd better take you home. It's getting dark."

Billy's face fell. "I don't want t'go 'ome."

Nathaniel hesitated for a second, then he swung the child down from the table and took his hand. "It's late. Your father will be worried about you."

Billy's blue eyes turned suddenly cynical and much older than his eight years. "'e's in the pub by now. Probably won't be 'ome until midnight."

Mara saw the muscle tighten in Nathaniel's jaw and the flash of anger in his eyes. But he said nothing about Billy's father. Instead, he asked, "Are you hungry? Why don't we get you some dinner?"

He led the boy out of the flat and Mara followed. A few moments later, they were downstairs in Mrs. O'Brien's kitchen.

"Mr. Chase," the landlady greeted, beaming at him. "A pleasure to see ye." She bobbed her head perfunctorily in Mara's direction. "Mrs. Elliot."

Her coolness where Mara was concerned did not escape Nathaniel. He shot her a teasing grin. Mara knew perfectly well that it was her refusal to pay the landlady's exorbitant prices for tea and sandwiches that caused the cool greeting, and she was not amused.

Nathaniel turned back to Mrs. O'Brien. Gesturing to the boy, he said, "Billy here needs a bite of dinner, and we were hoping you might be willing to make one of your delicious meals for us."

The landlady's smile widened. "Why, certainly." She glanced at the child, who stepped back, his cheek pressed to Nathaniel's hip, hiding his birthmark. "Why ye be the Styles boy," she said in surprise.

The boy's nervousness was plain, and Nathaniel spoke again. "What about some of your shepherd's pie?"

Thirty minutes later, Billy was seated in Mrs. O'Brien's tiny dining room, devouring his third helping of shepherd's pie. Hunger had overcome his wariness after only a few bites. Mara watched him with an aching heart, knowing from her own childhood what it was like to go hungry.

Billy finally pushed back his plate with a sigh of contentment.

"All finished?" Nathaniel asked. The boy nodded and slid down from the chair. "Thank ye, ma'am," he said to Mrs. O'Brien as she took his plate away.

Mara led him toward the door as Nathaniel paid the landlady and followed. The three of them left the lodging house. It was dark, but by the light of the street lamp, she could see the downcast expression on the boy's face. She sighed, feeling helpless and frustrated, wishing there was something more they could do for him. "Where do you live?"

Billy pressed his lips together, refusing to answer. He looked so miserable, her heart ached with pity. The thought of this boy having to go home to a father like Calvin Styles made her sick. She knelt beside him and pointed to the top floor of Elliot's. "See that? That's where we work."

"Me dad used t'work there."

Mara glanced at Nathaniel again, then back down at the boy. "It's a toy factory. Come by tomorrow and we'll show you some of the toys, all right?"

He nodded and sniffed. "All right."

"But," she went on, "if you're going to do that, you have to get some sleep. So we've got to get you tucked into bed. Where do you live?"

Billy lowered his chin to his chest. "Old Castle Street," he mumbled.

She rose and met Nathaniel's eyes over the boy's head. He was smiling at her. "I had to say something," she murmured as the three of them began walking the two blocks to Old Castle Street.

His smile widened. "Of course."

"We have a fire escape now," she added, knowing she was rationalizing the breaking of her own rule. "It's much safer."

"Yes, it is."

"Tomorrow, I want you to examine all the equipment."

"I already did, two weeks ago. But, it wouldn't hurt to do it again."

Satisfied, she took Billy's hand, and she was grateful that Nathaniel didn't comment on her change of heart.

"You're certain your father won't be home?" she asked Billy as they turned down Old Castle Street.

"Not until the pubs close. Sometimes, 'e don't come 'ome at all."

Shocked, Mara looked at Nathaniel. She saw his lips tighten slightly, but he said nothing.

The tenement where Billy lived was filthy. By the moonlight shining through a window by the door,

Mara saw the shadowy form of a rat scurry along the wall. Her grip on the boy's hand tightened as she pressed her other hand to her nose, but the smell of dried grease, urine, and filth was impossible to escape.

"This way," Billy said and started up the dark stairs, pulling her with him. Nathaniel followed them up the stairs to the third level, where Billy entered a room at the end of a dark corridor.

They followed him inside. She heard the flare of a match, and glanced over at Nathaniel as he held the lighted match high. Seeing a candle on the table, she handed it to him and soon the tiny room was lit by the feeble flame. The room contained only a table and two cots and was as filthy as the rest of the lodging house. Mara's stomach wrenched with nausea and dismay.

She pulled back the blanket from the cot and noted sadly that there were no sheets beneath. Billy crawled into the cot, and she pulled the blanket up to his chin. "There," she said, "tucked in all safe and sound."

It was a lie, and in the dim candlelight, Billy's eyes told her so.

"You come and see us tomorrow," she whispered, her voice clogged with compassion. "Promise?"

"Yes, ma'am." He swallowed and a tear slipped from his eye.

He hastily brushed it away, but not before Mara saw it. She pressed her lips to the mark on his cheek. "Good night, Billy."

"'Night, ma'am. 'Night, Nathaniel."

"Sleep tight," Nathaniel said, giving the boy's shoulder a squeeze before turning away.

She and Nathaniel left the building and started home. Neither of them spoke. The rank smell of the tannery pervaded the neighborhood, but both of them breathed deeply of the night air just the same, trying to escape the stench of the lodging house on Old Castle Street.

18

Mara and Nathaniel met with Michael the next morning after tea. Quotas were assigned. Michael agreed to place their first order for parts, hire the additional staff, and arrange for a company insignia and sign. Nathaniel would continue getting orders for trains, while it would be Mara's job to oversee finances.

Nathaniel and Mara promised Michael a final decision on which train accessories to put in production. Percy said he'd have Nathaniel's things moved out of the warehouse and put in storage immediately. Then the meeting was adjourned.

Billy Styles came to visit that afternoon. Nathaniel took him around the factory and showed him all the equipment, stressing what was safe and what was not. At the same time, he kept his promise to Mara, and checked all the machinery again, but everything was in perfect condition.

Nathaniel showed Billy their office, and Mara watched, glad that he explained the fire escape to the child. He then showed Billy the train, and Mara went back to work. But she paused often, lifting her head to watch as Billy asked Nathaniel question after question.

"Bloody smashin'!" the boy pronounced as the train came to a stop. Nathaniel then took Billy into the other room to show him the laboratory, and Mara watched them go, feeling both gratified and relieved.

Although she didn't approve of the language he used, his positive endorsement of the toy reassured her. If Billy's opinion was any indication, the trains were sure to do very well indeed.

"What's that?" Billy's voice floated to her over the top of the partition as he asked his favorite question, and Mara smiled, again lifting her head from her work to listen.

"These are the parts of a steam engine just like the ones downstairs, only smaller," Nathaniel's voice answered. "You see? Here's the cylinder and the piston."

"What are ye goin' to do with 'em?"

"I'm going to put them together."

"Can I 'elp?"

"You can be my assistant. See this little wheel here? That's called a gear. If you'll hold it in place, I can fasten the screw."

"Like that?"

"Just like that."

Mara couldn't resist taking a peek. She crossed the room and stepped around the partition to watch. Nathaniel had placed a stool in front of his worktable and Billy was standing on it. Their backs to her, man and boy worked side by side, and she was able to enjoy the sight unobserved.

She listened as Nathaniel continued to give instructions. His "assistant" complied with eagerness, and Mara knew a situation of clear and obvious hero worship was developing right before her eyes.

But it wasn't just Billy who responded to Nathaniel that way. Everyone at Elliot's felt the same. Perhaps it was because people could sense that Nathaniel truly believed in their abilities, or perhaps it was the compliments that seemed to come from his lips so easily. And yet, it was more than that. There was some indefinable quality of leadership about him that inspired people, gave them hope and confidence, made them work harder than they had ever worked before, just to get a smile from him and a word of praise.

Mara studied Nathaniel's back, her gaze following the Y-shape of his braces along the contours of his body, from his wide shoulders to his narrow waist, and she thought again of the night he had taught her to dance, when he'd led her blindfolded through the steps of the waltz, when he had forced her to rely on him for guidance, made her relinquish control and put her trust in him. She closed her eyes and savored again the feel of his hands at her neck, the warmth of his mouth on hers. The shock and wonder of a kiss that left her breathless. The magical intimacy of a smile that filled her with the ache of longing. He had left her wanting to risk all she had for one more kiss, one more smile.

"Now what?"

Billy's voice intruded on her reverie. Mara opened her eyes and came to her senses, realizing she'd been standing here daydreaming like a schoolgirl. Intent on their task, neither Nathaniel nor his pint-sized assistant had noticed her presence, and for that, Mara was grateful.

"Now we have to put the engine inside a train," Nathaniel explained. "When we light the wick, it makes the water boil and the steam from the water makes the train go."

"Show me, please," Billy pleaded. "I 'elped make it. I want to see it go."

Mara stepped forward, pushing aside memories of a waltz and a kiss. They turned their heads at the sound of her footsteps. "Not tonight, Billy," she said. "It's getting late."

"But I want to see the train go around."

Nathaniel put a hand on the boy's shoulder. "Mrs. Elliot's right. It'll be dark soon. We'd best get you home."

Billy's face showed his disappointment, but he didn't argue. He jumped down from the stool. "Can I come back tomorrow?"

Nathaniel shot Mara an inquiring glance, clearly asking her to make the decision.

She thought it over. She knew Nathaniel had checked all the equipment and had assured her that Billy understood what was safe. She still had misgivings, but she looked down into Billy's hopeful eyes, and she couldn't say no. "All right," she agreed, but added firmly, "after school."

"Can't I come in the mornin'? I don't go to school."

Mara frowned with concern, meeting Nathaniel's eyes over the boy's head. "Why not? Haven't you ever gone to school?" she asked Billy.

"I used to go, when me mum was around. She made me. But I don't go no more, since she died. So I can come in the mornin', can't I?"

"Billy, you should be in school," she said gently. "You can come here afterward."

Billy's chin jutted out stubbornly. "I don't like school, an' me dad says I don't need it anyway."

"But—" Mara started to protest, but she caught sight of Nathaniel shaking his head at her, silently asking her not to argue with the boy, and she complied.

Nathaniel hunkered down to Billy's eye level and smoothed back the tousled red hair that fell over his eyes. "Mrs. Elliot and I have to work in the morning. If we don't get our work done, we won't be able to make any trains. So, you have to come in the afternoon."

"I want to 'elp. Can't I make trains, too?"

"Of course you can, but there's all sorts of other stuff we have to do that you can't help with until we show you how. So you come in the afternoon, and I'll show you some of the things you can do to help, all right?"

"All right."

He ruffled the boy's hair. "C'mon, Scrapper. Let's take you home."

He grabbed the boy around the waist and slung him over one shoulder. Billy laughed and wrapped his fingers around the back strap of Nathaniel's braces to hang on. He looked up, grinning at Mara as Nathaniel carried him out of the laboratory.

She followed, smiling as she watched them head for the door.

"'Night, ma'am," Billy called, releasing his grip on Nathaniel's braces with one hand to wave at her as he was carried out of the room. "See you tomorrow."

"Good night, Billy."

She watched them go. Billy's wariness the day of their first meeting was gone, and Mara marveled at the change one afternoon with Nathaniel had made in the boy's life. It was a miraculous thing indeed.

But then, Nathaniel had a way about him, a way of making miracles happen. She thought again of the night they had waltzed, the kiss they had shared. Oh, yes. He had a very special way about him.

Adrian knew Joslyn Brothers had granted Nathaniel his loan the previous afternoon. Owen Rutherford had given him the news only a few hours before. He settled back in his seat, the music of the opera below scarcely penetrating his thoughts.

He could have prevented the loan, of course, but he had chosen to wait, preferring to allow his little brother to get himself well and truly in debt, knowing that would be the most effective way to destroy him in the end. Adrian knew that if he had prevented the loan, Nathaniel would simply have gone to another bank.

Nothing Nathaniel had done thus far surprised him. He did find it interesting, however, that Nathaniel had borrowed seven thousand pounds when the proposal he'd seen on the young woman's desk had requested three.

He stared down at the stage below with unseeing eyes. He found Mara Elliot much more interesting than *Carmen* at the moment.

Their conversation had been brief, but he had learned a great deal about her nonetheless. The proposal on her desk told him she was conservative, which meant she wasn't necessarily willing to go along with Nathaniel's reckless schemes. She was shrewd, an appalling quality in a woman, but then, Adrian wasn't interested in bedding her. Her shrewdness might be a problem.

She wasn't beautiful, but there was a haunting quality about her that probably appealed to Nathaniel's misplaced sense of the romantic. She blushed at compliments, which meant she wasn't used to receiving them and indicated that she wasn't as cold as she liked to appear. If Nathaniel cared about the woman at all, she might be useful.

Carmen's lover was dying. Adrian glanced down at the scene below, then to the woman beside him. Honoria was totally engrossed in the opera, unaware that Adrian was not. He observed the tear that glistened on one of her pudgy cheeks, and he rolled his eyes. Americans were so ridiculously sentimental, Honoria especially so. He returned his attention to more important matters.

His first suspicion had been correct. Nathaniel was planning to build toy trains again. It had been bad enough when Nathaniel had dared to declare himself a rival from thousands of miles away, and he had easily taken care of that. But now Nathaniel had the gall to try it here in England, right under his nose. His brother had even hired back that Jewish engineer to help him. Adrian intended to destroy those plans before they reached fruition.

He began to consider possibilities. This time, there was another factor that might provide him with an additional advantage. Mara Elliot. She just might prove to be Nathaniel's most vulnerable point.

There was also the loan. Adrian nodded to himself. Yes, there were many ways to smash Nathaniel's ambitions. By the time he was done, his little brother wouldn't have a brass farthing, and he'd go running off once again with his tail between his legs, defeated. It was going to be so easy.

Adrian knew the first step was to change banks. Tomorrow, he would have all his accounts transferred to Joslyn Brothers. Then he would find out who Nathaniel's suppliers were and what credit terms they offered. With a little luck and a little money in the right hands, those terms would be changed.

"We're going to spread ourselves too thin." Mara looked up from the notes she was scribbling and glared across the table at her partner as a crack of thunder sounded outside.

Nathaniel shook his head. "We have to have some accessories available for sale immediately, or what's the point?"

"Some, yes, but seventeen different items is a bit excessive, don't you think?" She studied his set expression and sighed. "All right, all right, we'll keep the two bridges, but we don't need to offer three stations!"

"Done," he agreed promptly. "We'll offer two. But I want all four types of passenger car."

Mara groaned and set down her pencil. They had been at this for over three hours. The numbers were running together, and all the ideas he was tossing out at her, one after another, were making her dizzy. She rested her forehead on one hand and began to rub the tense muscles in her neck with the other, listening as the heavy rain began to drum against the roof.

"Headache?"

She nodded. "Yes, and it's your fault," she grumbled. "You gave it to me."

He pushed back his chair. "Then it's up to me to get rid of it," he said and moved to stand behind her. He placed his hands on her shoulders.

She stiffened, and all her muscles tensed even more. "What are you doing?"

"Relax," he ordered and brushed his thumbs across the muscles beneath her neck.

She could feel the warmth of his touch through the white linen of her shirtwaist, and she realized he actually intended to massage her neck.

She leaned forward and shrugged her shoulders in discouragement, hoping he would move away. "No, really, this isn't necessary," she protested, feeling a hot blush creep up her cheeks at the familiar feel of his touch and memories of two nights before.

He paid no attention, of course. "Why do you always have to argue with me?" he asked, the tips of his fingers caressing her collarbone, sliding the linen back and forth across her skin.

She wriggled uncomfortably in her chair, wishing she could escape. But she was trapped by the table in front of her, the arms of her chair, and the man behind her. "I don't always argue with you."

"Yes, you do. All the time."

"I do not."

"Stop fidgeting," he ordered, unperturbed by her struggles. His hands tightened on her shoulders, and his thumbs suddenly pressed hard into the muscles below the nape of her neck.

An excruciating pain shot through her, and she cried out. "That hurts!"

"I'm not surprised." His thumbs pressed even harder, moving in slow circles. "You're a bundle of knots. It's no wonder your head aches."

Mara gritted her teeth against the pain, but after a few minutes, the tenseness in her muscles eased, the pain dissolved, and a warm, pleasurable sensation began to take its place. Her eyes fluttered shut as she listened to the soothing sound of the rain on the roof and enjoyed the comforting feel of Nathaniel's fingers massaging her neck. A groan escaped her.

"Feeling better?"

Mara nodded and made a tiny affirmative sound, so relaxed by the magic touch of his fingers she couldn't speak.

He slid one hand around her neck, and before she realized what he intended, he untied the ribbon at her throat and unfastened the top button of her shirtwaist. Dazed, she felt his hand slide beneath her collar and around to span the back of her neck, caressing gently, bare skin to bare skin.

She felt another shot of pain as he began to massage the tiny muscles on either side of her neck, but she was more relaxed now, and it didn't seem so bad. In fact, it began to feel quite nice. She let out her breath on a contented sigh.

Nathaniel heard the sound, somewhere past the pounding of his heart and the roar in his ears and the desire clogging his senses. This had not been one of his best ideas, and he cursed his own impulsiveness. He could see only two inches of ivory skin, tinged with pink, between the dark upsweep of her hair and the white linen of her collar, but he could feel all the softness of it beneath his fingers. Reluctantly, he pulled his hand back, away from the heat of her skin to the safer territory of her shoulders.

But he found that to be no help, for now he had to fight the temptation to bend his head and kiss the skin he had caressed, to breathe in the scent of lilacs, to take down her hair and bury his face in its dark softness.

Desperately, he reminded himself of all the things he'd been raised to believe in, things like honor and propriety. He reminded himself of his own resolution to keep his distance from her for both their sakes. His hands stilled. Despite his resolutions, he slowly lowered his head.

The sound of hurried footsteps pounding on steel stairs caused Nathaniel to straighten abruptly. He and Mara both turned toward the door leading onto the fire escape as an impatient knocking began and Billy's voice called, "Nathaniel? Are ye in there?"

Not knowing whether he was relieved or irritated, Nathaniel lifted his hands from Mara's shoulders and walked to the door. Lifting the latch, he opened the door to find Billy standing on the fire escape, coatless and drenched.

"What are you doing here?" he asked.

"It's quicker to come up this way," Billy answered. "Otherwise, I'd have to go all the way around to the front door."

"That's not what I meant," Nathaniel said. He pulled

the boy inside and shut the door. "I took you home hours ago."

"I couldn't sleep. The thunder kept wakin' me up."

"You weren't scared, were you?"

"No. It was just noisy."

Mara rose and crossed the room. "You should be in bed, young man," she admonished him. She checked her pendant watch, and her frown deepened. "Heavens, it's after midnight. The pubs are closed. Does your father know you're out so late?"

Billy stared up at her. "'e ain't 'ome yet. What good's it do to stay in bed when ye can't sleep?" His blue eyes widened with deliberate innocence. "If ye ain't glad t'see me, I'll go 'ome," he said woefully.

Mara glanced at Nathaniel and saw a smile tilt the corners of his mouth.

He saw her frown and hastily assumed a serious expression. "Of course we're glad to see you, Billy. But Mrs. Elliot is right. It's not good for you to be out this late, especially in the rain. You're soaking wet."

"It's not so bad, Nathaniel." Billy shook himself from side to side like a shaggy dog, sending droplets of water in all directions. "I'll dry. Can I play with the trains now?"

Mara and Nathaniel exchanged glances, and Mara shook her head. "No, Billy, it's long past your bedtime. Nathaniel is going to take you home."

"But I don't want to go 'ome." Billy kicked at the puddle of water forming at his feet. "I don't like it there."

Mara felt the boy's mournful voice tug at her heart, but she couldn't let him stay. "I know you don't," she said gently. "But your father will be worried about you if he comes home and you aren't there."

"'e don't care." The contempt in Billy's voice was plain.

She forced herself to remain firm. "Billy, you have to go home."

He folded his arms across his chest stubbornly. "I don't want to."

"Not another word." She mirrored his stance and spoke to him in the same tone of voice she normally reserved for recalcitrant workmen. "You are going to march home right now, young man."

"But—"

"Now."

Nathaniel put a hand on the boy's shoulder to halt any further protests and leaned down. Loud enough for Mara to hear, he whispered, "Billy, I've learned when a woman talks like that, it's best not to argue. You can't win."

Billy turned his head, his eyes meeting Nathaniel's. "Me mum used to talk like that when she made me eat peas," he said quietly.

Nathaniel nodded and gave Mara a teasing glance. "Then you know what I mean."

"Yes, sir."

Mara frowned at the pair of them and pointed a finger to the door, doing her best to look stern. "Out."

"Yes, ma'am." Nathaniel straightened and offered Billy his hand.

Billy took it. "Yes, ma'am," he echoed meekly and walked with Nathaniel to the door. Nathaniel opened it, and they stepped out onto the fire escape.

Nathaniel paused long enough to glance back at her. "Wait here, and I'll walk you home. Don't walk back by yourself."

"All right." Following him as far as the door, she whispered, "If his father is home, it could mean trouble. Don't go inside with him."

He grinned at her. "Worried about me?"

She was, but she had no intention of admitting such a thing. "I'm worried about Billy."

"Oh," he said, sounding almost disappointed.

She watched as he descended the stairs of the fire escape, Billy in tow. The rain had stopped, and the moon had come out from behind a cloud to light their way. Hand in hand, the tall man and the small boy walked down the alley toward the street.

"Nathaniel?"

Billy's voice floated back to her in the quiet of evening. "Yes?"

"When Mrs. Elliot talks to me like that, does that mean she likes me?"

"Yes, Billy, I think it does."

"I'm glad."

Mara smiled. "So am I, Billy," she confessed softly and shut the door. Leaning against it, she gave a sigh of pure contentment and reached up to rub her hand against the back of her neck. She closed her eyes and savored again the magic touch of Nathaniel's fingers.

A wonderful thing, massage. Her headache was gone, and Mara didn't think she'd ever felt this good in her life.

19

During the weeks that followed, Mara spent many hours on the production floor with Nathaniel, helping to perfect their system. Raw materials and train parts would begin arriving around the middle of October, and Nathaniel insisted that he needed her help to get things ready.

Neither of them mentioned the night in the office when he had massaged away her headache, but Mara often found the memory of it steal over her without warning. If she watched him talking with the workmen, sometimes a gesture of his hand would remind her of how he'd touched her. If she saw him tug at his collar as he worked, she would recall how he had loosened the ribbon at her throat. The sweetness of it would all come rushing back, and an unbidden wish to have him touch her again would whisper, *If only . . .*

Whenever she caught herself spinning romantic daydreams, the stark, horrible fear that she was falling in love with him inevitably hit her like a splash of icy water, followed by panic and vehement denial.

She didn't need him, she told herself firmly. She didn't need anyone. She didn't love him. He was a dreamy fool with the mind of an engineer and the soul of a poet. He was brilliant. He was crazy. He was absurd.

Her husband's whimsical dreams had brought her nothing but heartache, she reminded herself time and again. But as the days passed, she found herself becoming more and more caught up in Nathaniel's dreams of toys and trains, and the painful memories of James and all his broken promises grew dimmer and became harder to cling to.

Billy became a familiar sight around the factory, and Mara was glad because the boy provided any number of distractions for her wayward thoughts. He ran errands for her, and he helped with what he proudly called "research" by playing with various toys and giving Nathaniel and Mara his honest opinion.

When the boy realized that the people in the factory didn't laugh at the sight of his birthmark or make fun of him the way other children did, he quickly lost his wary fear of strangers, and the workers became accustomed to the sight of the pint-sized shadow tagging behind Nathaniel. Whenever they walked through the assembly section, the women would look up from their work and exchange smiles as they listened to Nathaniel answer Billy's never-ending supply of questions.

Mara became accustomed to Billy's presence, but his refusal to go to school weighed heavy on her mind. She worried about the boy more than she had a right to, perhaps because it was easier to think about the welfare of the child than about her own bewildering feelings. Besides, one simple fact continually brought Billy's situation to the forefront of her mind. He smelled.

Saturday afternoon found her alone with the boy. The factory had closed for the weekend, and Nathaniel was out calling on toy merchants. Mara looked up from her work and watched the boy as he experimented with Nathaniel's latest idea: a coil of wire that somehow flipped end over end, moving across the floor. Nathaniel had explained how it worked, enthusiastically rambling on about the laws of physics and concepts of propulsion until her head started spinning, at which point she had given up trying to understand and had simply accepted the fact that a coil of wire could move all by itself.

Billy was sitting cross-legged on the floor of the office, completely absorbed in the toy. His clothes—the same knee-breeches and dingy white shirt he always wore—were ragged and dirty, and he constantly scratched himself. Mara refused to speculate on what tiny creatures might have made Billy their home, but she decided it was time to do something about it.

But when she broached the subject to Billy, he balked. "What? Get in water and wet meself all over? Not me." With that declaration, he raced out of the office as if demons were after him.

Mara watched him run away and sighed. The boy needed a good scrubbing, and she intended to make sure he got one. But Billy guessed her intentions and didn't return that day.

Undeterred, she began her campaign the following morning. After visiting the baths herself, she went to Cheapside and did some shopping. Then she went in search of Nathaniel and found him in his laboratory. She greeted him by thrusting a stack of new clothes into his arms.

"Hullo," he said, looking at her over the pile. "What's this?"

"New clothes for Billy," she said, adding two clean

towels to the pile. "It's nearly afternoon and he'll be here any minute. You are going to take him to the baths."

"I am?"

"Yes," she said firmly and placed a small crock of soft lye soap atop the towels. "He smells to high heaven, and I can't stand it any longer. It's obvious his father won't take him. So you're going to do it."

"But I've already taken a bath today. Besides, aren't we meeting with Michael this afternoon?"

She added a can of kerosene to the stack. "It won't hurt you to take another bath. I'll meet with Michael and let you know what we discussed."

He looked down into her determined face and knew she was serious, but he felt compelled to point out the obvious. "He won't like it."

"Too bad."

"Why don't you take him?"

"Nathaniel, that boy worships you. He'd go with you much more easily than he would me."

He acknowledged the truth of that with a sigh. "All right," he agreed reluctantly and glanced at the items in his arms. "Kerosene?"

"For the lice."

"Lice?" Nathaniel started to change his mind.

She nodded. "Lice, fleas, and whatever else he's got. You'll have to scrub him with it. Then use the soap."

"I understand."

Quick and eager footsteps on the stairs told them Billy had arrived.

"Make sure he gets behind his ears," she added last-minute instructions in a whisper. "And for heaven's sake, keep him away from gas jets."

"Yes, ma'am." He shifted the bundle in his arms to raise one hand in a mock salute before stepping around her and leaving the laboratory.

*   *   *

Two hours later, Mara was seated at her desk, discussing the final production schedule and product line with Michael, when the voice of a very impatient eight-year-old intruded on their meeting.

"Ma'am, ma'am!"

She looked toward the doorway as Billy ran into the room. He raced for her desk, skidding to a halt beside her chair. "What ye think?"

"Well, now," she murmured, pretending puzzlement. "Who's this?"

"It's me, Billy." He pointed a finger to his chest.

"Billy Styles?" She shook her head. "No, it can't be. Billy Styles doesn't wear clean white shirts and smell nice like soap."

Billy squared his shoulders proudly. "'e does now."

She leaned forward, studying him more closely. His hair was still damp, but it was clean. The clothes she'd bought fit him quite well, with a bit of room to grow. Even his boots had been polished. She smiled. "Billy Styles, as I live and breathe. It is you."

"Nathaniel took me t'the baths. 'e poured that kero . . . kero . . . "

"Kerosene?"

He nodded. "All over me. An' scrubbed me with it." He made a face. "It makes yer 'ead sting." His words came tumbling out as he explained. "An' then 'e threw me in the tub full o'water and scrubbed me with the soap. I didn't like it at first, ma'am, but then it wasn't so bad. Nathaniel 'elped me comb me 'air an' gave me these new clothes. 'e said you bought 'em an' I like 'em so much. Thank ye, ma'am," he ended breathlessly.

She laughed. "You're welcome, Billy. You'll take good care of them won't you?"

"Yes, ma'am."

She brushed back a lock of his long hair, curling it to a perfect swirl on his brow. "You look very handsome."

"I do?"

"Yes," she said and grasped his smaller hands in hers. Squeezing them, she repeated, "Very handsome, indeed."

She looked over the boy's head and smiled at Nathaniel, who was standing in the doorway, watching them. His hair was also damp, tousled, and beginning to curl at the collar of his white shirt.

"Both of you," she added and watched Nathaniel's smile widen at the compliment.

Realizing what she'd said, Mara released Billy's hands and turned her head away, only to find Michael's surprised gaze fixed on her. She felt herself blushing and didn't know where to look.

Billy gave her sleeve a tug. "I've got t'go, ma'am. Nathaniel an' me 'ave to go shopping."

"Shopping?" She glanced up as Nathaniel approached the desk, and she noticed the smile still lingering at the corners of his mouth. "Why are you going shopping?"

Nathaniel leaned down and murmured over the boy's head, "You forgot to buy him underwear."

A choked sound from the opposite side of the desk told her Michael was trying not to laugh. Mara felt her blush deepening. "Oh."

His gaze held hers with an expression somewhere between a tease and a caress as he straightened. "Want to come with us?"

She shook her head. "I've still got some work to do here."

"It's a Sunday afternoon," he reminded her and took Billy's hand. "Don't work too hard."

"'Bye, ma'am," Billy called back with a wave as he and Nathaniel headed for the door. "'Bye, Michael."

They left and she looked over at Michael, noticing the amusement in his eyes. "Don't say a word, Michael Lowenstein. Not a word."

"I won't." His smile faded and a thoughtful expression took its place. "Billy Styles?" he asked. "Isn't his father—"

"Calvin Styles is his father, yes."

"I didn't know that." Michael frowned. "I don't mind having the boy around, Mara," he said, leaning back in his chair. "But do you think it's wise?"

"Probably not," she admitted and lifted her hands in a gesture of frustration. "What else can we do? The boy is starving, not just for food, but for some attention and care. We can't just stand by and do nothing."

Michael studied her across the desk. "You've changed," he said quietly.

The change of subject caught her by surprise. "What?"

He nodded. "Yes, you have. In the three months I've known you, you've changed a great deal. Don't misunderstand me, but you're not as hard as you were when we first met."

She thought about it for a moment. "I suppose I have changed," she admitted. "I feel different. I feel . . ." She paused, trying to think of the right word. "I feel hopeful."

"Nathaniel does bring out that sort of feeling in people; he inspires them. When he was at Chase, there wasn't a person there who didn't think he walked on water. It's hard to resist his enthusiasm, and he can be very persuasive when he chooses. Believe me, I know."

Mara knew it, too. "You once worked for him, didn't you?"

"Yes. Nathaniel hired me when he was chief engineer under his father. But when Gordon Chase died, Adrian took over and fired me."

"Why?"

"I'm Jewish. Adrian doesn't like Jews."

"Couldn't Nathaniel stop him?"

"I'm afraid not." Michael rose. "If we're finished here, I think I'll go on home. See you tomorrow?"

She nodded, watching as Michael left, and she thought about what he had said. His words were nearly identical to what she had been thinking a few weeks before. There was a different sort of feeling in the air since Nathaniel had come, a sense of camaraderie, a spirit of hope and cooperation.

She'd thought herself immune; she'd tried so hard to remain indifferent, but she had failed. Despite her resistance, Nathaniel had shown her that there was more to life than simply existing. Life was riddles to solve and surprise gifts to savor, poetry and music to hear, meteor showers to watch and toys to play with, stray kittens and children to be helped.

Her smile faded. She could no longer imagine life without those things. She could not imagine life without Nathaniel. Like it or not, she was beginning to need him; she was beginning to depend on him. And that was what scared her the most.

Adrian glared at the three men seated at the opposite end of the conference table. "These sales figures are pathetic," he said, tossing down the report in his hands. "I thought I made myself perfectly clear three months ago, gentlemen. Sales were supposed to go up this quarter, not down."

The men exchanged glances. One of them coughed nervously, then spoke. "Lord Leyland, the fact is that our sales representatives are still receiving complaints from customers about our products. Many are becoming concerned that our toys fall apart too easily. Charles Harrod himself—"

"That is ridiculous," Adrian interrupted. "These are toys. Children play with them, they fall apart. Parents are supposed to buy new ones."

"But they aren't buying ours," Mr. McGann pointed out. "The perception is that our quality is poor, and our toys aren't worth what we charge. I recommend we either improve quality or lower our prices."

"Both of those solutions cost me money. Therefore, they are unacceptable. If perception is the problem, then our sales representatives need to change that perception. That is what they get paid for."

"You can't make a silk purse out of a sow's ear," McGann answered tartly.

Adrian slammed his palms on the table and rose. "That will be enough, Mr. McGann. If you can't motivate your salesmen to do their job, I will hire a manager who will, and you will be seeking other employment. Is that clear?"

McGann also rose to his feet, and the other two men followed suit. "Perfectly," the sales manager replied and walked out of the conference room, followed by the production supervisor and the chief engineer.

"Idiots," Adrian muttered, sinking back into his chair. "I am surrounded by idiots."

McGann and the others didn't understand his difficulties, and Adrian had no intention of enlightening them. He knew perfectly well that he was cutting corners, but until he married Honoria in April, there was nothing else he could do. He could worry about improving quality when he had the money to do so. Until then, his staff would have to make do with the resources available.

Charles Barrett appeared in the doorway, breaking into his speculations. "Sir, Mr. Rutherford is here for his meeting with you."

"Ah, yes. I'll meet with him here. Show him in."

The secretary nodded and departed. A few moments later, he reappeared with Owen Rutherford behind him. He showed the detective to the place vacated by McGann and withdrew, leaving the other two men alone.

"Do you have any new information?" Adrian asked as the door closed.

"A few interesting items," the detective replied, settling himself in his chair and opening his dispatch case. "You asked me to find out if your brother is experiencing any labor difficulties. I have been investigating the matter, and I must say that does not appear to be the case."

"No difficulties at all?" Adrian found that hard to believe. Employees were always whining about low pay and long hours and unfair treatment.

"There was one incident." Owen pulled out his notes and flipped through them until he found the item he wanted. "Yes, here it is. Mr. Chase fired a man for insubordination shortly after he bought into the company, a man by the name of Calvin Styles. It seems Mrs. Elliot gave the man an order, and he refused to obey her. He pushed her, and your brother intervened, striking Mr. Styles. He then fired him. The man made a few threats before he left, but nothing else seems to have come of it. That's the only thing I've been able to find that even remotely resembles a labor problem."

He looked up from the notes. "Your brother seems to be well liked by everyone who works there. I heard many compliments about his abilities."

Adrian didn't want to hear about Nathaniel's abilities. However, he found the information about Calvin Styles very valuable. Resting his elbows on the table, he clasped his hands together and rubbed one knuckle against his upper lip, lost in thought. Yes, he decided, this Styles fellow could prove to be a valuable pawn in the game. "Anything else?" he asked the detective. "What about his trains?"

"They are planning to manufacture an electric train, just as you suspected," Owen answered. "I heard a great deal of talk about tracks and accessories and things."

"Tracks and accessories?" Adrian lowered his hands and leaned forward. "What do you mean? Sectional track?"

"I don't really know, sir. I'm afraid what I've been told is pretty vague at this point. I'll be able to tell you more once they begin manufacturing this train."

"What about his suppliers? Have you learned who he's buying from?"

"Yes, sir." The detective turned a page of his notes and began to read a list of names. "For tin, Halston's. For brass, Conklin's Brass Works. Since it is an electric train, I assumed batteries were involved, so I spoke with battery manufacturers as well. Harvey & Peak is supplying those."

Owen paused for breath, and Adrian took the opportunity to interrupt. "That's fine, Mr. Rutherford," he said and rose to his feet, indicating the meeting was at an end. "Leave me the list, if you please."

The detective placed the list of suppliers on the table, then also stood up. "I'll let you know when I have more information."

"Do that. I want to know details about that train of his. Do some more investigating, talk to people, learn everything you can."

The detective nodded. "It shouldn't be difficult. It's amazing what people will tell a perfect stranger after they've had a few pints in the pub."

Adrian gave him a hard stare. "I don't need to remind you to be discreet, do I, Mr. Rutherford?"

"I am always discreet, sir." With that, the detective departed.

Billy was proud of his new clothes. When he walked up Whitechapel High Street toward the factory the following afternoon, he couldn't help swaggering a little. He'd never had a set of brand-new clothes before, and he planned to take good care of them, just as he'd promised Mrs. Elliot.

After Nathaniel took him home the night before, he had carefully folded them just the way his mum used to make him, and placed them under his cot along with his boots and socks. He had crawled into bed in his new underwear and stared up at the ceiling after Nathaniel had gone. As usual, his father hadn't come home until the pubs closed. By then, Billy had been fast asleep, exhausted after his exciting day with Nathaniel.

They had gone to Cheapside and purchased his underwear, just as they'd told Mrs. Elliot they were going to do, then Nathaniel had found a wool jacket and cap to match the trousers she had bought him. When they finished shopping, Nathaniel had purchased meat pies and a sack of cherries from a coster, and they'd sat on the docks, spitting out cherry pits and seeing who could spit them farthest as they watched the ships go up and down the river.

Then they'd gone to Lincoln's Inn Fields and watched the men play football. Nathaniel had gotten dragged into the game. He'd scored a goal and they'd celebrated with ice cream. Yesterday had been a smashing good day.

Billy grinned, thinking about it. He turned down the alley by the factory, but came to a halt at the sight of the three boys playing marbles beside the fire escape. His cheerful mood evaporated, and he wondered if he ought to go in by the front doors, when the other boys caught sight of him.

"Well, what we got 'ere?" Jimmy Parks jumped to his feet and pulled the cigarette out of his mouth, then came toward him, followed by Davy Boggs and Hal Seaford. "Look at this, lads. Billy Styles all fancied up."

Billy took a wary step back, but he couldn't make a run for it now. That would be cowardly. He stood his ground as Jimmy halted in front of him.

Tossing down the cigarette, Jimmy looked him up and down. "Spotty Face 'as some new clothes," he said to the other two boys. "Gettin' above 'imself, don't ye think?"

Davy put a hand on Jimmy's arm. "Leave 'im be."

"Sod off, Boggs." Jimmy pushed away the hand on his arm and pointed to the cap on Billy's head. "That looks like me cap what I lost the other day." His eyes challenged Billy. "I think 'e stole it."

"I did not." Billy pulled the cap further down on his head and tried to go around the older boy, but Jimmy stepped in front of him, blocking his path.

"I want me cap."

"It ain't yers." Billy felt the sickening familiar knot of fear in his guts. He tried again to walk past, but once again the older boy stepped in front of him. "Leave me alone."

Jimmy laughed and glanced at the other two boys. "Did ye 'ear that? 'e's givin' orders now."

"Gettin' bossy, ain't 'e?" Hal chimed in, but he kept his distance.

Jimmy snatched the cap from Billy's head and gave him a shove, sending him stumbling backward. "Seaford's right. Ye gots t'be taken down a peg."

Billy recovered his balance and tried to grab his cap. "It's mine."

"Is not." Jimmy stepped aside, easily avoiding Billy.

He settled the cap on his head. "See, it is me cap. Fits me perfect."

It didn't. It was too small for Jimmy, and all of them knew it, but Billy also knew it didn't matter. What Jimmy wanted, Jimmy took. Billy reached for it again. "Give it back!"

Jimmy ducked to the side, avoiding his grab. He jabbed one fist into Billy's stomach, causing him to double over and brought his other fist down on his neck, driving him to his knees. Then Jimmy settled the too-small cap atop his head as best he could, turned, and walked away, whistling.

Billy lifted his head and watched him go, misery and anger bubbling up inside him. The sight of the cap Nathaniel had bought him on Jimmy Parks's head was too much to bear. With a cry of outrage, he jumped up and threw himself at the other boy. He tackled Jimmy and sent both of them sprawling. The cap went flying. Davy and Hal scrambled to get out of the way.

"Get off me, ye bloody bastard!" Jimmy cried, struggling to turn onto his back beneath the weight of the other boy.

"It's me cap!" Billy shouted and pummeled Jimmy with his fists. "Ye can't 'ave it."

Jimmy succeeded in turning onto his back. He grabbed Billy and rolled so that he was on top, then began punching the smaller boy in the face, the ribs, and the belly, anywhere he could reach.

Billy howled and cursed, struggling as best he could, but he was no match for the larger boy. Jimmy gave him one last punch in the stomach, then jumped to his feet. Breathing hard, he scowled down at Billy. "It's me cap, Spotty Face, an' yer lucky I ain't goin' to kill ye for tryin' t'steal it."

He gave Billy a final kick in the ribs, snatched the cap

from the ground, and walked over to the fire escape to grab his set of marbles. Hal followed.

Davy hesitated, staring down at Billy.

"C'mon, Boggs," Jimmy shouted. "Let's go."

Davy muttered a curse and turned away, leaving Billy Styles sprawled on the cobblestones, sobbing and alone.

20

Billy did not come to the factory that afternoon. It was the first day in over a month that the boy had not visited them, and when one o'clock came and he still had not put in an appearance, Mara became concerned.

She set aside the budget she was working on and went in search of Nathaniel, hoping the boy was with him. She found him on the mezzanine, leaning over the rail, looking down at the production floor. She paused, studying him for a moment. She saw him nod and lift one hand in a beckoning gesture, and she knew he was giving instructions to the men below.

His waistcoat was off, and the sunlight from the windows behind him caught his shirt as he raised his arm to gesture to the men, giving her a translucent glimpse of his lean torso beneath the white linen. She caught her breath, remembering how he had looked with no shirt at all, remembering the smooth skin and the sculptured muscles that lay beneath his shirt, and she involuntarily stretched out one hand as if to touch him.

"Leave it there!" he shouted, jarring Mara out of her reverie, and she suddenly felt foolish. She walked over to him, reminding herself of her reason for coming down here.

He gave a thumbs-up sign to the men below as she came up to stand beside him, and she glanced down to see Michael mirror the gesture. "You're moving some of the equipment," she remarked in surprise, watching as the men grasped the heavy ropes that dangled from pulleys on the ceiling beam and began securing hooks to one of the steam engines.

"We thought it might be better to have the soldering done on the other side of the boilers," he explained, "so we have to move the steam engines a bit closer to the mezzanine."

She watched as the men used the winches to raise the engine off the ground, and she nodded in agreement as they swung the engine into place and lowered it again. "That will work much better." She looked up at him again. "Nathaniel, have you seen Billy?"

He gave her a surprised glance. "He's not with you?"

"No. I was hoping he was with you."

Nathaniel shook his head. "I haven't seen him at all today."

"He's been here every day by quarter past twelve," she pointed out. "It's after one o'clock and he hasn't arrived yet."

"It's after one?" He noticed the worried frown between her brows. "Michael asked me for some help with this, and I didn't realize the time. Give me a minute, and I'll go see if I can find him."

"Thank you. I may be worrying about nothing. He's probably out playing with his friends or something like that."

Nathaniel doubted it. Billy was so much like he had been at that age, and he would have bet the boy didn't make friends easily. But he didn't voice his thoughts aloud. "Probably."

A short time later, after walking to Billy's tenement and not finding him there, Nathaniel began searching the nearby streets, but without success. He started back, looking down each alley he passed, but it was in the alley right next to Elliot's where he finally found the boy.

Billy was sitting on the bottom step of the fire escape, his legs dangling over the edge. He heard Nathaniel approach and lifted his head. Nathaniel came closer and saw the dark purple shadow beneath Billy's eye that blended into the birthmark on his cheek. He also saw the cut on his lip.

"What happened?" he asked, noting that Billy's brand-new clothes were covered with dirt, and one sleeve of his shirt was torn.

"What ye think?" The boy's eyes were filled with pain and frustration.

"Mmm." Nathaniel looked down at him, knowing there was nothing he could say to make the boy feel any better. So he didn't try to comfort him. He just stepped closer. "Move over."

Billy scooted a bit to the left, and Nathaniel climbed the short ladder of the fire escape to sit beside him on the bottom step.

Out of the corner of his eye, he watched Billy and waited. It wasn't long before the boy brought up the subject.

"Why are they so mean?" he asked.

"I don't know," Nathaniel answered truthfully. He was over two decades older than the child beside him, but he still hadn't figured out the answer to that question, and it was one he'd asked himself hundreds of times.

"Jimmy took me new cap," Billy said. "It didn't even fit 'im, but 'e wanted it, so he took it." He slammed one small fist against the steel step. "'e called me names and 'it me. I tried to stop 'im, but I couldn't."

Nathaniel listened as Billy poured out the story in stilted sentences. He heard the frustration and the shame in Billy's voice, recognized it as the same voice of another boy a long time ago. The boy he had been.

"I broke me word," Billy went on in a choked voice. "I promised Mrs. Elliot I'd take care o'me new clothes an' I didn't."

"I think she'll understand. I'll bet she wouldn't even mind mending them for you."

"What good would that do? Jimmy'll just beat me up again."

"Probably."

"It ain't fair."

Silence fell between them, and Nathaniel thought about all the times at Harrow before he'd learned how to fight, when he'd faced the headmaster with his uniform torn and bloody, all the times he'd been punished for fighting when he'd never even had the chance to throw a punch. Life was seldom fair.

"Nathaniel?"

Billy's voice pulled him out of the past. "What is it, Scrapper?"

Billy was gazing up at him, his freckled face thoughtful. "Remember that story ye told me about when ye was a boy?"

"Of course."

The boy's face hardened with determination. "I want ye to teach me to fight like Mr. Donovan taught ye so's I can defend meself. Will ye teach me?"

Nathaniel leaned forward, resting his forearms on his knees. He should have known this would happen. He briefly considered all the ramifications. Mara wouldn't like it. She didn't approve of fighting.

He knew the boy's father was also a factor. He suspected that Calvin Styles's reaction would be less than favorable if he discovered Nathaniel had befriended the boy, and he was much more likely to find out if they spent even more time together than they already did.

"Billy, I'm not sure that would be a good idea."

"Why not?"

He hesitated, hoping he could make the boy understand. "Your father wouldn't like it if I taught you how to fight."

Billy snorted. "'e would, too. 'e's always tellin' me I ought to fight back when they beat up on me. 'e says I'm a coward."

Nathaniel could have cheerfully killed Calvin Styles at that moment. "No, you're not a coward," he told the boy. "Those boys know how to fight and you don't, that's all." He shook his head. "Billy, it's not the fighting your father would disapprove of. It's me."

"You mean 'cause you punched 'im?"

Nathaniel stared at the boy in surprise. "You know about that?"

Billy shrugged his thin shoulders. "Of course. Everybody knows."

"Do you know why I did it?"

"Some people are sayin' it's cause he pushed Mrs. Elliot." Billy paused, then added, "'e used to push me mum around, too."

Nathaniel sighed. God, sometimes, it was an ugly world. "You know that's wrong, don't you? Pushing women around?"

"Yea." Billy nodded. "Me mum told me. But me dad says you punched him 'cause yer a bloody bastard."

Nathaniel didn't know whether to laugh or admonish

the boy for swearing. But when he saw Billy grinning up at him, he couldn't help chuckling. "I can see how your father might think that," he admitted. "And that's why he won't like it if I'm the one who teaches you how to fight."

"I won't tell 'im we're friends or about you teachin' me," Billy promised. "I won't tell nobody. Please."

"If he finds out, you could get into trouble."

Billy thought about that for a minute. "I don't care," he finally said, looking back at Nathaniel. "I still wants ye to teach me."

Nathaniel knew he shouldn't get deeply involved in the boy's life, but when he looked down into Billy's bruised, determined face, he knew it was already too late.

Damn it all, the boy needed his father, not a substitute. But Nathaniel doubted Styles would ever be any kind of a father to Billy, and the boy was in desperate need of someone to fill that role. He remembered his own childhood, and the pain of having a father who had not been there for him.

"All right," he agreed before he could stop himself. "We'll deal with your father when the time comes. But Mrs. Elliot isn't going to like it either, so don't say anything about this to her. I'll tell her myself."

"All right, Nathaniel," the boy agreed, looking up at him with such a worshipful expression, Nathaniel nearly groaned. Being a father, even a substitute one, was a huge responsibility. He hoped he could live up to it.

"Are you out of your mind?" Mara's teacup hit the saucer with a clatter as she stared at Nathaniel across the table.

He'd been right. She didn't like the idea at all. He

grinned, savoring the battle to come. He was coming to enjoy their mornings of tea and debate. Slathering cream on his scone, he said, "Mara, you saw for yourself what that boy did to him yesterday. It happens to him all the time."

"Why does he have to learn to fight? Why can't he just walk away?"

"That's not always possible. His pride is involved here, and he has to be able to stand up to those other boys. He's learning how to be a man."

She sniffed, unimpressed. "It's a little early for that, don't you think? He's only eight years old. Besides, learning to fight doesn't make you a man."

"Not by itself, no. But the fact remains that he gets beaten up by other boys who aren't going to stop tormenting him just because he walks away. If he knew how to fight, he could defend himself. He needs to learn."

"What Billy needs to learn is how to read." Her crystal gray eyes sparkled with determination as she looked at him over the teapot. "He should be in school, not fighting with hooligans in back alleys."

"I agree. But he doesn't want to go, and neither would you if all the other children teased you. He needs to develop some confidence."

"And fighting is the way to gain it?" She shook her head. "No."

"I don't recall any objections like this when I came to your defense," he pointed out. "That was fighting, too."

She flushed and lowered her gaze to her gloved hands. "That was different."

He studied her for a moment, just for the sheer pleasure of watching her blush. "How is it different?"

"You weren't setting an example for an impressionable young boy." She lifted her troubled gaze to his. "He might learn the wrong sort of lesson."

"I didn't learn the wrong lesson when I was a boy.

I've promised Billy I would teach him, and I will," he said firmly. "Would you have me break my promise?"

She bit her lip and looked away. "I suppose not," she murmered finally.

"I'll make sure he knows fighting is a last resort, only to be used for defending himself or someone else."

With a sigh, she set down the pieces of the scone she had torn apart. She wiped her fingertips together to brush away the crumbs. "I don't think—"

"Nathaniel?" A voice broke in and had both of them turning toward the door as Michael entered the room. "We've got a problem."

"What is it?" Nathaniel asked.

"Our tin's not here yet. It was supposed to arrive this morning, but deliveries are usually made by nine. It's half past, and I'm concerned."

Nathaniel looked at Mara. "Didn't Halston's promise our tin by this morning?"

"Yes, they did." She rose to her feet. "I'll go to Halston's and see what's going on."

He nodded. "Remind them that if they can't get our orders here on time, there are other tin suppliers who would be happy to have our business."

"Don't worry, I will. It's probably just a minor delay."

But the delay proved to be more than minor, as Nathaniel discovered when Mara returned from Halston's London office an hour later.

"Monday?" Nathaniel stopped making adjustments to the conveyor belt he and Michael were working on. "That's five days from now."

"It seems they are having some labor troubles at the tin mines in Cornwall," she explained. "They apologized profusely, but it's still going to be five days."

Michael shook his head. "We won't be able to get tin from any other supplier sooner than that."

Nathaniel let out a frustrated sigh. "Without tin, we can't do anything. This is going to put us behind schedule."

"We'll catch up," Michael promised. "I'm sure we'll be able to make up the time somehow."

Nathaniel was not so sure. He remembered how delays and disasters had crippled him once before, and a tiny shimmer of disquiet ran through him. He shook it off with his usual optimism. Coincidence, he told himself firmly. It was just a coincidence.

21

Nathaniel kept his promise to Billy and began teaching the boy to fight. During the week that followed, he showed the boy many of the fighting techniques Donovan had taught him. Billy learned how to ward off a blow coming at him from any direction, and he learned where and how to hit. But on a Sunday afternoon in late October, with the sun shining and a crisp autumn breeze blowing, Nathaniel decided that Billy needed lessons of a different sort.

He asked Mrs. O'Brien to pack a picnic lunch, then he went to Cheapside and made several purchases, including a large cardboard box. He returned to his flat and set to work. When his project was completed, he put the items he'd made into the box and took them to the factory, picking up the picnic lunch from the landlady on his way. He sat on the bottom step of the fire escape and waited for Billy. When the boy arrived, Nathaniel announced that they were taking Mrs. Elliot on a picnic and showed the boy what he had made.

Despite his continual urging not to, Mara still spent most of her Sunday afternoons working in her office, and he knew they would find her there. Nathaniel let Billy carry the box and he followed with the picnic basket, arriving just in time to see Billy place the box on Mara's desk.

"Look what Nathaniel done!" Billy pronounced as Mara stood up.

"What Nathaniel did," she corrected, looking in the box. "What's this?"

Nathaniel watched from the doorway as she lifted one of his creations out of the box and stared at the item of wood and newspaper doubtfully.

"It's a kite," Billy told her. "Nathaniel made 'em. They've got string and everything. See?"

He lifted a roll of string out of the box and held it up for Mara's inspection. "We're goin' to fly kites today. Won't that be smashin'?"

She lifted her gaze to Nathaniel standing in the doorway, and a smile tugged at her lips. "A picnic, too, I see. Well, I'm sure you'll have fun."

"You're coming with us," he said firmly, crossing the room. "It's a perfect day for kite flying." When she opened her mouth to protest he added, "If you don't come with us, some of Mrs. O'Brien's culinary delights will go to waste. You wouldn't want that, would you?"

Her smile widened at the snare he'd laid for her. "That would be a shame," she admitted and set the kite back in the box. "Let's go."

They took a cab to the West End. Thirty minutes later they stood by the water of the Serpentine in the center of Hyde Park, where Nathaniel removed his jacket, rolled up the sleeves of his shirt, and took one of the kites out of the box. He then set the picnic basket in the box to keep the wind from carrying it away and proceeded to give Billy his first lesson in kite flying.

Mara shaded her eyes with one hand and watched him race across the grass with joyous abandon. The sun glinted off the water behind him as he ran, holding the kite aloft until the wind caught the paper sail and lifted it out of his hands. The kite soared upward, and Nathaniel spun around swiftly, running backward and letting out string as he watched it climb toward the white clouds scattered across the blue sky.

"Look at that, miss!" Billy cried, pointing skyward. "It's flyin'!"

Mara wasn't looking at the kite. She was watching Nathaniel, who now stood a dozen feet away, staring at the kite above with a smile on his face.

He took the greatest pleasure in the most basic things, she thought. Scones with cream, trains and kites, and Sundays in the park. Once, she'd thought him to be like James, but now she knew he wasn't like James at all.

Unlike her late husband, Nathaniel was a man of strong determination, willing not only to dream, but willing to work hard to make those dreams come true. Yet, he was able to set his work aside and take a boy kite flying. She suspected he did it for his own enjoyment as much as for Billy's. To Nathaniel, there was a time for work, but there was also a time for play.

He brought the kite back down, then helped Billy make it fly again. Mara sat down on the grass and watched them launch it, the man's long strides shortened to keep pace with the those of the boy as they ran across the clearing between groves of elm trees.

"Let it go, let it go!" Nathaniel shouted, and Billy did so. The kite swooped up and caught the breeze, climbing into the sky as Billy gave a shout of delight and Nathaniel's triumphant laughter rang out.

"Let out more string. We want it to go higher." Nathaniel moved to stand behind the boy, showing him how to keep the kite in the air.

Mara wrapped her wool cloak more tightly around her shoulders to ward off the crisp breeze and watched, enjoying the sight, knowing how much Billy needed days like this, how much he needed a man in his life who would be a good influence on him. Nathaniel was good with children, and she wondered if perhaps that was because he still had a bit of the child within himself.

Once Billy knew how to guide his kite and keep it up in the air, Nathaniel walked back over to her, tugging at his waistcoat to straighten it.

"I think he's having fun," she commented when Nathaniel reached her. "So am I, just watching him. This was a good idea."

He lifted another kite out of the box and waved it in front of her with a grin. "It's your turn."

"Oh, no. I'll just watch."

He shook his head. "No, you won't. You have to try at least once." He held out his free hand toward her, refusing to take no for an answer.

She took off her cloak, then removed her bonnet. She tucked the hat beneath the heavy folds of her cloak to keep the breeze from carrying it away, then grasped his hand and allowed him to pull her to her feet.

They walked over to the starting point by the huge elm tree. She took the kite from his hand and held it aloft just as she had seen him and Billy do. Then she grasped the string in her other hand and looked at him for guidance.

"Just start running. When you feel the wind pull the kite, let go."

She took a deep breath and started to run. But, although Billy had managed to launch his kite on his very first try, Mara was not so successful, and when she released the kite, it somersaulted in the air and crashed to the ground several feet behind her.

Mara came to a halt and turned around. Nathaniel stopped beside her and they watched the breeze carry her kite across the grass until it was stopped by the string in her hand. "What did I do wrong?"

He walked over to the kite and picked it up. "If you're going to get it up in the air, you have to run faster."

Mara sighed and looked down. "That's easy for you to say," she said, holding one hand to her corseted ribs. "You're not the one wearing a skirt."

His gaze moved down the black folds that whipped toward him in the breeze and back up to her face. "I see your point. I'll send it up for you."

"No," she said with determination and grabbed the kite. "No. I want to try again."

He followed her back to where they had started, watching as she grasped the front of her skirt just below her waist and tucked the fold of fabric into the waistband, hitching up the hem to expose the tops of her high-button shoes. Nathaniel studied her leather-clad ankles appreciatively for a moment, then let his gaze travel upward, imagining a pair of slender, shapely legs beneath that skirt.

She looked up and caught him watching her. "Why are you looking at me like that?"

His smile widened. "Never mind," he said with a shake of his head. "Remember, when you let the kite go, start letting out string immediately. I'll tell you when to stop. Ready?"

She nodded, took a deep breath, and tried again.

Nathaniel ran alongside, watching her. The wind

whipped past her, and the coiled chignon of her hair came tumbling down to fly loose behind her.

The kite left her hand, caught the breeze, and soared skyward.

"Keep letting out the string," he reminded her. He watched thick cotton thread slide through her gloved fingers, allowing the kite to climb as they slowed and finally came to a stop.

He picked up the spool at her feet and handed it to her. "You did it," he said, enjoying the sight of something lovely and rare—a wide, full smile that curved her lips as she lifted her face toward the sky.

"I did, didn't I?" she gasped, out of breath and laughing as she took the spool from his hand. "That was wonderful! Can we do it again?"

The wind caught her hair, sending long tendrils whipping across her face, and she brushed them back with her free hand. "I lost my hair comb," she said between panting breaths and glanced down at the ground.

"I'll find it," he told her. "Watch your kite," he advised, "or it's going to tangle up in those trees."

He went in search of her comb, and Mara tried to follow his advice. But despite her best efforts, the wind carried her kite over the tall elms nearby, causing the string to snag on the branches, and the kite came crashing down.

She sighed and began walking in that direction. Kite flying was more complicated than she'd thought it would be. Pausing a few feet away, she brushed wisps of hair out of her eyes and gazed ruefully up at the bit of newspaper and wood caught on a branch of the elm in front of her.

Nathaniel joined her there several minutes later. He glanced up at the kite tangled in the leaves about thirty feet above them, then gave her a teasing look of censure. "That didn't take long."

She smiled apologetically. "Sorry. I've never done this before."

"Really? I never would have guessed."

Mara made a face at him. "You didn't find it?"

"No." It was a lie. Her comb was in his pocket. But he looked at her with the wind tangling her long hair, and he wanted it to stay like that, loose and tumbled.

But he wasn't to get his wish. She set down the spool of string in her hand. Pulling all her hair over one shoulder, she separated it into sections and began weaving it into a braid.

She turned her head to find him watching her. Their gazes met, her hands stilled, and her eyes grew wide. For several seconds, they looked at each other, and he knew she was sensing what thoughts had run through his mind when he'd looked at her ankles. Slowly, he reached out his hand.

She sucked in a sharp breath as he grasped one end of the ribbon at her throat. He rubbed the ribbon between his fingers for a moment, his eyes never leaving hers. He tugged, freeing the bow and slipping the strip of black silk from her collar.

Still looking at her, he took the end of the braid from her fingers with his other hand and wrapped the ribbon around the thick plait. His knuckles brushed her breast, lightly, as he tied the knot, and he felt her tremble.

He forced himself to let go. Forced himself not to think about undoing the braid again and tangling his hands in her hair and making her tremble. He lowered his hands and turned away, toward the kite tangled in the trees. "We can't leave it there," he said, breaking the silence. "Good thing it's not way out on a limb."

He moved toward the tree. It took her a moment to realize his intent. "You're not going up there?" she asked, following him in some alarm.

"Of course." He reached up and grabbed the sturdy branch a few feet above his head. In one quick movement, he pulled himself up onto the tree limb and began to climb.

"Nathaniel, come down," she ordered, watching him continue his ascent through the branches. "It's not worth it. You could fall and get hurt."

"Me?" He paused and grinned down at her amid the leaves. "As a boy, I used to climb trees all the time. We had this huge oak tree at our estate in Devon and my favorite thing to do was sit up in that tree and read. I could climb it with two books and a bag of apples, so this is easy by comparison."

"You're not a boy any longer," she reminded, thinking sometimes he tended to forget that fact. "You might be too heavy."

"I'll be careful," he promised and climbed onto another branch.

Biting her lip, she watched him move from limb to limb until he reached the kite. It took him several minutes to unfasten the string before he pulled the kite out of the leaves and sent it flying toward her. The kite caught the wind and swooped over her head, hitting the ground about ten yards behind her.

She paid little attention to it but kept her gaze fixed on Nathaniel, watching as he began climbing back down. When his foot slipped and threatened to send him tumbling to the ground, she couldn't help giving a startled gasp. But he grabbed the branch above his head and paused long enough for her to catch her breath, then continued his descent.

He did not come all the way down, however. Instead, he settled himself on the lowest limb several feet above her head, facing the opposite direction. "I can see Kensington Gardens," he commented over one shoulder. "Let's have the picnic up here. The view is quite splendid."

He was teasing her. Wasn't he? With Nathaniel, she never knew for certain. "Nathaniel, please come down from there."

He lowered himself backward until he hung upside down by his knees, facing her. "You look different this way. Lovely," he added, "but different."

The man truly was mad. She stepped forward until her face was only a few inches from his upside-down one. "Nathaniel, come down this instant before you fall off and break something."

"I doubt that'll happen," he answered. "This limb is only about eight feet off the ground."

That wasn't reassuring. "Nathaniel . . . "

"Spoilsport." Even upside down, his eyes could tease. Before she knew what was happening, his hand reached out to rest on the back of her neck, and he swayed forward, closing the inches that separated them. He planted a quick, hard kiss on her mouth, then released her and swayed away again before she could even assimilate what he'd done. "You have to move."

Her lips still tingled from the brief contact, and it took a few seconds to realize he'd spoken to her. "What?"

"If you want me to come down, you have to move out of the way."

"Oh. Of course." She stepped back a few feet and watched him curl his body upward to wrap one arm around the branch. His legs slid off, and he jumped lightly to the ground. Smoothing back his ruffled hair, he turned around and smiled that special, reassuring smile. "Safe, sound, and all in one piece. Let's eat."

"Don't ever do that to me again," she said, but the impact of her order was negated by the answering smile that tugged the corners of her mouth.

"I can't make you a promise like that." Taking the

spool from her hand, he began winding string around it. "Given the opportunity, I just might do it again. I found it quite . . ." He paused in his task and glanced at her, his eyes still teasing. ". . . enjoyable."

Keeping his gaze locked with hers, he gave the string a tug and the loose end fluttered down from the tree. He continued to wind string around the spool, and the teasing gleam in his eyes disappeared. "I never make promises I can't keep."

He walked away, and her gaze followed him as he moved toward Billy, whose kite was still flying. She pressed the tips of her fingers to her lips and hoped with all her heart that this time he wasn't just teasing her.

Nathaniel left Mara at the door to Mrs. O'Brien's with the picnic basket, dropped the kites off at the factory, and took Billy home. The boy rebelled at the idea of going to bed, grumbling that he wasn't tired, but Nathaniel sent him up to his room, refusing to listen to the boy's attempts to stall.

The wind had picked up and powerful gusts stirred the trash and leaves that clogged the gutters as Nathaniel walked home. He pulled up the collar of his jacket against the chill as he passed the King's Head, and his steps slowed. He wondered if Calvin Styles was inside the pub.

Probably. If not this one, then the one around the corner on Goulston Street. He took Billy home every night, but he never saw Calvin Styles. Billy had said that his father was in the pub every night, and it seemed to be true. Nathaniel stood on the sidewalk outside the King's Head, sorely tempted to walk in and confront Styles about his son, but he knew it would do no good. He breathed a sigh, quickened his steps, and walked on.

He was becoming far too involved in Billy's life. He

wasn't the boy's father, and it was tempting fate to act as if he were. Styles hadn't yet discovered his friendship with the boy, but eventually he would. Nathaniel didn't want to think about what would happen when he did.

When he passed the factory on his way home a light in the office caught his attention, and he paused. It had to be Mara.

He went inside and found her bent over the ledgers on her desk, so preoccupied with her work that she didn't even hear him come in. He watched her for a moment, and he couldn't help smiling.

With her long braid hanging over one shoulder, and her tongue caught between her lips in concentration, she looked like a schoolgirl doing her studies, so serious and intent. He watched her and remembered her hair whipping behind her as she ran across the grass, laughing, with a kite in her hands. He remembered her eyes widening as he reached out to touch her.

He drew in a deep breath and entered the office as she looked up.

"Didn't I leave you at Mrs. O'Brien's?" he asked.

She bent her head over the ledger in front of her. "I had some work to do, and I spent the day flying kites, remember?"

She sounded so guilt-ridden, he almost laughed. To Mara, everything was a balance sheet, and to have a few hours of fun, she felt compelled to do an equal amount of work. Someday, he was going to make her see that life was not just debits and credits, even if it took him the rest of their lives to do it.

The rest of their lives.

"Flying isn't exactly how I'd describe it," he answered with a grin.

"I know," she said with a sigh. "It would appear I need more practice."

Teasing her was such fun, because she took everything he said so seriously and never seemed to realize when he was only having her on. He wondered if she'd ever figure it out. He looked at her earnest face. Probably not. They could spend the rest of their lives together, and she'd never be able to tell. She'd get that skeptical little frown between her brows that clearly said she thought him out of his mind.

The rest of their lives.

He tried to envision it. When the minister asked her if she would take this man, she'd look at him with that serious face, weighing all the pros and cons before saying yes. She'd try to plan their lives down to the last detail. She'd try to hide her vulnerabilities even when she knew he could see right through her. She'd fight with him over morning tea, reproving his extravagance with the cream and arguing with him over what was best for all their children, just the way they argued about Billy. Her lips would say no, even when her heart and her mind and her body said yes. And the maddening, contrary complexities of her would fascinate him for the rest of their lives. He was in love with her.

The rest of their lives.

He walked over to her desk and waited. He said nothing; he just enjoyed watching her. Finally she lifted her head. "What?"

"Nothing." He grinned at her vexed little frown, but he didn't move away. Then he took off his jacket and slung it over the back of the chair that faced her desk.

She looked up at him in some uncertainty. "Was there something you wanted?"

Yes. He tried to sound casual. "No."

She bent back over her work, but it wasn't more than a few seconds before she once again looked up at him. "Nathaniel, must you stand there?"

"Sorry." He circled around to stand beside her. Leaning down, he rested his forearms on the desk and looked at her. "Is this better?"

Her frown deepened. "No. Will you please go away? I can't work with you hovering around like this."

"Can't you? I'm sorry." He didn't move, and he wasn't sorry at all.

She tried to be so strong and independent, but if he kissed her, she'd go all soft and fluttery again. "I'm in love with you," he blurted out.

She didn't turn all soft and fluttery. Instead, she scowled at him and pushed back her chair, scraping it against the wooden floor. "That isn't funny. Stop teasing me."

He was right. She never knew when he was teasing and when he wasn't. "It's true. We're falling in love." He leaned closer. "Don't you think so?"

"I think you're out of your mind, that's what I think." She rose and circled her desk on the opposite side, watching him warily.

"Love does that to a person."

Her skeptical expression took on a hint of panic. "Nonsense."

"You don't believe me." He pushed aside the chair and followed her.

She retreated across the room until her back hit the wall beside his desk. "You're crazy."

"True," he agreed. She tried to get around him, but he lifted his arms and rested his palms against the wall, trapping her. "You want to know why?" He didn't wait for an answer. "It's your face."

Astonished, she froze, staring up at him. "What's wrong with my face?"

He tilted his head to one side as if giving the matter serious consideration. "Well, for one thing, it's your chin."

Her chin lifted. "What about it?"

"Stubborn," he pronounced. Leaning down, he kissed the dent in her chin, then pulled back. "Very stubborn. And your nose."

She was beginning to look anxious. "What's wrong with my nose?"

He reached up and ran his finger down the bridge of her nose. "It's nice and straight," he conceded, "but it turns up at the end and gets impudent." He moved his hand to span her jaw and kissed the tip of her nose. "Right there."

Her lip trembled. "Don't."

"Then, of course, there's your mouth," he went on, running the tip of his thumb back and forth across her lips. "Very kissable."

He moved his hand to the curve of her neck and bent his head. His lips barely brushed hers before she made a tiny sound and turned her face away. "Stop it. Don't make fun of me."

"Is that what you think?" he asked, his lips against her cheek. "Trust you to question my motives and come to the wrong conclusion. You do that often."

She couldn't escape, so she took refuge in defense. "I do not."

"Yes, you do." He kissed her ear and felt her tremble. "You argue with me a lot, too."

"Perhaps it's because you're completely mad." Her feisty answer lost all its punch in the soft breathiness of her voice. "You say things you don't mean, and you give Christmas presents in July, and you dangle from tree branches and say I look lovely upside down. You're out of your mind."

He pulled back and looked at her. "What makes you such an expert on female beauty? You are lovely, even when I'm looking at you upside down. That's not easy, you know. Usually, people look rather ridiculous when viewed upside down. Imagine the queen, for instance, or—"

A choked sound came from her throat, a mixture of panic and pain and laughter. "Don't," she pleaded. "Don't make me laugh, don't make me feel like this."

"Like what, Mara? How do you feel? Like you're falling in love with me?"

She ducked beneath his arm. "Life is complicated enough. I can't fall in love with you."

Nathaniel turned, watching her practically run for the door, knowing he had frightened her. But he couldn't take it back. He wouldn't. "You're running away again. You're afraid, aren't you?"

"Yes!" she shouted at him, stopping halfway across the room and whirling around to face him. "Yes, I'm afraid!"

He began to walk toward her, slowly, as if approaching a frightened deer. "Of what, Mara? What are you afraid of?"

Her face twisted with anguish and uncertainty. "Everything. I'm afraid to feel, I'm afraid not to feel. I'm afraid of being alone, of not being alone. I'm afraid of you, of myself, of what will happen to me when you leave." She ducked her head. "I'm afraid of not being enough to make you stay."

He saw the tear, saw it fall, a crystalline fragment that caught the light just before it hit the floor. He loved her, he loved the soft and tender core that lay beneath the icy shell, loved the bravado that tried so hard to conceal the vulnerabilities, and he wondered how anyone could be so tough and yet so fragile. "I know about being afraid," he said gently. "I know because I'm afraid, too, Mara. I'm afraid of watching you run back inside yourself, back into that dark, secret self that makes you feel safe, where I can't reach you. Don't you see?"

He took a step closer, wanting desperately to hold her, wanting to be the armor that protected her. "But we can't spend our lives being afraid. We have the chance, Mara. The chance to love, to be happy. Chances like this don't come along often. When they do, you've got to seize them and hang on, because if you don't, they disappear forever. And they never come back."

He took another step toward her. "I'm not going to leave you. I'm not going to hurt you."

She flung her head back. "Yes, you will," she cried. "You won't mean to, but you will."

She grabbed her cloak from its hook in the wall and put it on. When she glanced back at him over her shoulder he could hear her breath coming out in little gasps. "I can't fall in love with you," she repeated. "And I don't want you to fall in love with me!"

She whirled around and ran out the door.

"Too late," he said to the empty doorway. Grabbing his jacket, he followed her out the door, to make sure she got safely home.

Calvin Styles wasn't drunk yet, but he was well on his way. He took two hefty gulps from his fifth pint of ale, gave the behind of the pretty barmaid a hard pinch as she passed by, and joined in on the chorus of a lusty song with the group of sailors at the table next to his.

It took him a moment to realize the singing had faded away and the pub had gone suddenly quiet. He looked up to find all heads had turned in the direction of the door, and he followed their gaze. A footman dressed in immaculate livery stood there, an expression of distaste on his face.

Styles scowled, hating servants who got above themselves. The bloke had probably been born within the sound of the Bow Bells, but now he dared to stick his nose in the air and pretend to be better just because he had gold trim on his jacket and a few shillings in his pockets.

He and everyone else in the King's Head watched the man move through the room to the bar. He said something to the proprietor in a low tone, and Matty Fletcher nodded his head in reply, pointing in Styles's direction.

Styles turned his head, trying to figure out what Matty had pointed to, but when the footman crossed the room and came to a halt at his table, Styles realized it was himself.

"Calvin Styles?"

The man spoke with care, but Styles knew his guess had been right, and he grinned. Cockney, sure as froth on a pint. "Aye," he answered. "Who the bloody 'ell are ye?"

The footman tossed a guinea on the table and met his eyes. "My lord would like to have a word with you," he said. "Outside."

Styles eyed the gold coin on the table, then shrugged and picked it up. Rising to his feet, he shoved the guinea in his pocket. "Lead the way."

The footman turned away, and Styles followed him outside to the closed carriage waiting at the corner. There was no insignia, but Styles knew the luxurious carriage had to belong to a very rich man.

The footman opened the door and gestured for Styles to step inside. He did and found himself facing a handsome blond gentleman, whose white silk cravat and manicured hands made his lip curl with contempt.

"Mr. Styles, I would like to employ you," the man said with a smile of perfect white teeth.

Styles sat up straighter on the leather seat, and his contempt for the man before him fled at the mention of a job.

"I want you to do something for me," the man went on, "and I will pay you very well to do it."

Twenty minutes later, Styles was back inside the King's Head spending the gold guinea he'd been given, and looking forward to all the gold guineas that were going to come his way in the near future.

He lifted his pint and saluted his own good luck. He loved a fight, and he loved getting even. And a wealthy toff was going to pay him a bloody fortune for doing both. Calvin Styles was a happy man.

22

Mara awoke the following morning with a smile on her face. She sat up in bed, remembering how glorious it had felt to run across the grass with the kite in her hand, the wind on her face, and her hair flowing loose behind her. A few months ago, she wouldn't have dreamed of doing such a thing.

She'd kept herself under rigid control for so long, but yesterday in the park she'd been carefree, laughing, and truly happy for the first time in a long time. Because of Nathaniel.

Before Nathaniel had come, her life had been predictable and uncomplicated. And joyless. Then he had breezed in like a whirlwind, with all his brashness and enthusiasm, with his passion for living. He opened her mind to new ideas and made her reevaluate the old ones. He opened her heart to new feelings and made her aware of all she'd been missing. She could feel something within her turning toward it like a flower toward the sun.

His upside-down face came before her eyes, and her smile widened. Only Nathaniel would do something like that, hang by his knees from a tree limb and kiss her. Only Nathaniel would blurt out declarations of love like that, bluntly, without thought.

Her smile faded. She leaned forward, hugging her bent knees. He couldn't possibly mean what he said. Could he? Love wasn't like that. It didn't just happen. It didn't just fall in one's lap like manna from heaven. Did it?

She thought of James and tried to remember how she'd felt when she'd loved him. She hadn't felt like this, twisted inside out by doubt and uncertainty. Had she?

She groaned and tossed back the sheets. She rose from the bed and began pulling clothes out of the armoire. The man was mad, that was all there was to it, and he was beginning to make her the same way.

She bathed and dressed, trying to put last night's episode out of her mind. He didn't mean it, she told herself. He might have felt a momentary affection for her after the day they had spent together, but that was all.

As she tied a fresh ribbon around her neck, she tried not to remember how he had pulled a ribbon from beneath her collar the day before. As she brushed out her hair, she tried not to remember how he had tied that ribbon around her braid. But the memory of how his hand had brushed against her and made her tingle would not go away.

We're falling in love.

Ridiculous. She opened her window and dumped the soapy water from her bath out into the alley below, then shut the window and vowed not to think about it again.

You're lovely.

Balderdash. She took a peek in the mirror over her

washstand, and her ordinary face stared back at her. The man was blind.

She lifted her hand to nibble uncertainly at her thumbnail, then slowly rotated her bare hand, staring at the reflection, at the white, shiny patches of skin that she never looked at because they were ugly. Ugly, painful reminders of a past she could not change, of a daughter who was dead, of her failed marriage and her forgotten dreams. With a tiny sob, she turned away from the mirror. She'd never felt more inadequate in her life.

She put on her gloves and her bonnet and pushed thoughts of love out of her mind. Then she left the lodging house and walked to the factory. There was no place for romance in her life, she told herself as she unlocked the front door. She didn't like it. She didn't have the time. She wasn't any good at it.

By the time Nathaniel arrived with their morning tea about thirty minutes later, Mara was hard at work. She had pushed those crazy thoughts aside, but the moment he entered the room, whistling, with the tray in his hands, all her doubts came flooding back.

Did you mean it? The question hovered on the tip of her tongue as they sat down at the table and she poured their tea, but she couldn't ask. When she handed him his cup of tea she found him watching her with those perceptive eyes, a smile lurking at the corners of his mouth. It didn't seem to bother him at all that she'd bolted at his declaration of love.

She felt defensive. He was looking at her as if he knew what she was thinking and was waiting for her to ask the question uppermost in her mind. Instead, she asked another. "Why do you always look at me as if you're trying to read my mind?"

His smile widened. "Why does it bother you?" he countered.

It irritated her that he looked so pleased with himself. "It doesn't," she lied.

"Good," he said. He pulled a scone from the basket between them and began to slather cream on it. "Because I like looking at you."

"Mara?" Michael's voice interrupted any reply she might have made and had both of them turning toward the stairs as the engineer entered the room. "Mara, the first load of tin is finally here from Halston's, but now they're saying they need to be paid."

A puzzled frown knit her brows. "But when I met with them, they agreed to give us thirty days' credit. So did all our suppliers, for that matter. Why is Halston's suddenly demanding cash on delivery?"

"I don't know," Michael answered. "Can you come down and talk to them?"

"Of course." She set her napkin beside her plate and rose to her feet, then followed Michael out the door.

Nathaniel watched her go, feeling shimmers of disquiet. Thoughts of love vanished from his mind as much more disturbing ones took their place. Halston's had delayed their tin shipment, putting them nearly a week behind schedule. They had originally agreed to thirty-day credit, and had suddenly changed their minds. A pattern was forming, and it made Nathaniel very uneasy.

He went downstairs. By the time he found Mara in the warehouse, she was in a testy debate with the delivery man from Halston Tin.

"But we were promised thirty days," she said. "Why are you going back on your terms?"

The man shrugged. "Ma'am, I don't make the decisions. I was told to deliver the tin and pick up the money. No money, no tin. That's all I know."

"This is ridiculous! I—"

Nathaniel interrupted her by laying a hand on her shoulder. "Pay him."

She looked up at him in astonishment. "What?"

He nodded. "Pay him. We have the money in our account."

"That's not the point."

"It doesn't matter. This man said he doesn't make the decisions. Pay him." Nathaniel turned away. "I'm going to Halston's."

The owner of Halston Tin Supplies was unavailable. The secretary gave him the excuses. New company, not enough credit established elsewhere, not enough reliable references, no knowledge of agreements with Mrs. Elliot. He listened to the man ramble on and felt the eerie chill of watching the past repeat itself and the frustration of seeing no way to stop it.

Why? Nathaniel left the tin company and waved aside the cab that rolled past, preferring to walk back to Elliot's. As he walked, the question kept running through his mind. Why?

Other new companies managed to secure credit. Joslyn Brothers had seen no problem loaning him seven thousand pounds, but suppliers couldn't give him thirty days? It didn't make sense.

This would throw a spanner in the works. He and Mara had budgeted the money from the loan very carefully, and timing was critical. If he had to pay every supplier up front, he'd run out of cash before money from train sales came in. Without credit, they wouldn't be able to purchase any additional supplies. Train production would come to a halt, promised orders would not be delivered, and they'd be in the suds.

Just like before. Nathaniel came to a halt on the sidewalk, so abruptly that the man walking behind him almost careened into him. The fellow stepped around him with an irritated glance, but Nathaniel hardly noticed. *Just like before.*

He thought back to those frustrating days in St. Louis when delayed shipments and demands for cash up front had eroded his capital, when he'd spent all his time and energy just trying to stay afloat, when he'd stood by helplessly as everything he'd spent years working for fell apart and his dream disintegrated before his eyes.

He'd held himself responsible, certain that his inability to obtain credit stemmed from his own lack of credibility. He'd thought the delays were just bad luck. But what if that were not the case? What if it had been Adrian? Suppliers could be bribed, even from thousands of miles away. Deliveries could be intercepted.

Street traffic flowed around Nathaniel, but he stood on the sidewalk like a rock in a stream, oblivious to all of it. Now that the idea was in his head, Nathaniel had the sick, certain feeling it was the truth.

Adrian. He should have known, he should have seen.

He knew Adrian had always been a bully, picking on those weaker than himself for the fun of it. But when their grandfather had given Nathaniel a place in the company, when he had proven to their father that he had brains and ability, Adrian had come to see him as more than just a bothersome little brother to torment for entertainment. He had begun to see him as a threat.

Nathaniel had never thought of himself as much of a threat, but he saw it now through Adrian's eyes, too clear to ignore.

Adrian, who couldn't stand not being the center of attention, belittling him and telling lies about him to their father. Adrian, who couldn't stomach the idea of his brother as a partner, forcing him to choose between his dream and his ethics, forcing him to sell out. Adrian, who couldn't stand seeing him succeed, bribing suppliers and delaying deliveries, forcing him out of business. Adrian, who couldn't come up with an innovative idea to save his life, trying all the same tricks he'd used before. It all made perfect sense.

This time, it wasn't going to work. Nathaniel resumed walking, but at the corner, he turned, heading for Finch's office. His instincts told him he was right, and he wanted to know what he could do about it.

"Nothing."

Nathaniel stared at Finch across the desk, dumbfounded by his answer. "What do you mean, nothing? He destroyed my business!"

Finch was unimpressed. "What evidence do you have?"

"I don't need evidence to know one plus one is two." Nathaniel leaned forward, placing his palms on the desk. "The same things that happened before are starting to happen again."

"You have one similar incident. That's all."

"Two," Nathaniel corrected. "It can't be a coincidence."

"I agree, it looks suspicious. But without actual proof, you have no legal recourse."

"What kind of proof?"

"Witnesses. Suppliers who would testify that they were bribed. What supplier would be willing to do that? The solicitor sighed. "To be honest, I'm not even sure that would be enough. Adrian is a viscount, and he would be tried by the House of Lords. I doubt they would take the word of a tin supplier over that of your brother."

Nathaniel straightened away from the desk. "I know Adrian is behind it all," he said, slamming one fist into his palm. "I just know it."

Finch shook his head. "I doubt the House of Lords would be willing to take your word for it."

Nathaniel knew he had no evidence that Adrian was responsible for what had happened. But that didn't mean he was going to allow it to happen again. "Finch, I want you to investigate. See if you can get that evidence."

"I'm not qualified for such a task."

"Then find someone who is."

"All right. What are you going to do?"

"I'm going to continue with business as usual, of course. And I'm going to watch my back. There's nothing else I can do."

"Is that wise? If what you suspect is true, and you continue with your plans, problems will only escalate. But you haven't become Adrian's competitor yet. You could stop making trains—"

"I'm not going to be bullied by my pompous, arrogant ass of a brother."

"Nathaniel, aren't you forgetting something? You have a partner, you know. Mara does have some say in this, and I know she would not wish to continue this venture, given the additional risks."

Nathaniel knew it, too. He pushed Mara's fears to the back of his mind. "I will not allow Adrian to do this to me again."

"Even if Mara's future is at stake?"

"I'll tell her, in my own time and in my own way. In the meantime, I want you to find me some of that evidence you keep talking about."

He strode out of Finch's office without another word. He might not have legal recourse, but success was the best revenge. He was going to succeed, he was going to compete with his brother head-on, and he was going to win. He'd tell Mara what was going on, but nothing was going to stop him. Not even her fears.

*   *   *

While Nathaniel was out, other suppliers made their deliveries, and of all the companies that brought materials to the factory that morning, Harvey & Peak was the only one willing to honor the agreements Mara had made with them weeks earlier. All their other vendors had demanded cash on delivery. With Nathaniel gone, Mara had no idea what else to do and had paid them. Afterward, she sat down with Michael in the office, and they discussed the situation. "I don't understand it," she said.

"You're certain they understood you were expecting thirty days' credit?"

"Of course they did, Michael. I would never pay cash on delivery."

He leaned back in his chair. "Is this going to be a problem in future?"

"I hope not," she answered. "We can't afford it. We've got to have thirty-day terms or we won't be building any trains."

She glanced up to find Nathaniel standing in the doorway, leaning with one shoulder against the jamb. She'd been so preoccupied, she hadn't even heard him come up, but his expression told her he'd heard their discussion.

"Did you talk with Halston Tin?" she asked him.

"Yes." He entered the office, but he did not elaborate.

"What did they say?" she asked as he walked past her desk.

"I don't want to talk about it," he snapped and entered his laboratory without another word.

Startled, she stared after him. A quick glance at Michael told her that he was just as surprised as she by Nathaniel's testy answer. She started to rise, then hesitated, at a loss. His abrupt manner and terse words were so unlike him, she didn't know what to do. She sank back down in her chair.

He came out moments later and headed for the door. "Michael, have we got all the materials we'll need to get out our Christmas orders?"

"Yes. I've already got the men started on the locomotives."

"Good. I want the first one off the line today."

"Today?" Michael turned in his chair to look at the other man.

"Yes, today." He paused in the doorway. "I'll be gone for the rest of the day," he said and walked out.

"What about Billy?" she called after him.

"I'm sure you can find something for him to do," he called over his shoulder as he started down the stairs.

She and Michael exchanged bewildered glances.

"What's the matter with him?" the engineer asked.

"I don't know," she murmured. "I wonder what Halston's had to say."

"Nothing good, obviously." Michael rose. "If I'm going to get the first train off the line today, I'd better get back downstairs."

Mara nodded absently, her mind still on Nathaniel. It simply wasn't like him to behave this way, and it worried her. She had come to rely on his optimism and confidence to carry her through when things went wrong. But what about when his optimism deserted him?

When Billy arrived, he was confused and hurt by Nathaniel's absence. Nathaniel had promised to teach him some new fighting moves today, and his failure to keep his promise was a keen disappointment to the child.

"He has some important work to do that he hadn't expected," Mara explained, wrapping an arm around

Billy's shoulders and pulling him closer to her chair. "I'm sure he hasn't forgotten."

She studied the boy's downcast face, knowing how much it hurt when promises were not kept. A delay of one day could seem like a lifetime to an eight-year-old, but she was certain Nathaniel would not break his word. He wasn't that kind of man.

Since her debate with Nathaniel about the fighting, she'd done some thinking about the situation, and she had come to the reluctant conclusion that he was right. Billy couldn't be persuaded to go to school if it was going to be a source of torment and hurt. Until he developed some confidence, school was simply not feasible. She still wasn't convinced that fighting was the best way to develop his confidence, but the fact remained that the boy had been assaulted several times, and Nathaniel was doing exactly what he'd said he would, teaching the boy to defend himself.

She tightened her arm around Billy's shoulders, wishing she could bring a smile to his face. "I have some things to do today, and I need your help."

He lifted his head. "You do?"

"Absolutely." Mara rose to her feet. She had to think of something important to do that Billy could help with. She took him by the hand and picked up her reticule. "Come along. We don't have time to dilly-dally."

"Where are we going?"

I have no idea. Mara didn't say the words aloud. Instead, she answered, "I guess you'll just have to come with me and find out."

With Billy in tow, she left the office and headed down the stairs, racking her brain to think of something for them to do. She'd spent many afternoons entertaining her daughter, but that had been a long time ago. Besides, she had no idea what an eight-year-old boy would consider fun. Dolls and tea parties were probably out of the question. Billy had told her how he and Nathaniel had spent their Sunday afternoon a couple weeks before, but she doubted she'd be any good at spitting cherry pits and playing football. And given her limited kite-flying abilities, that wasn't a good idea either.

She stopped on the production floor long enough to tell Michael she was taking the rest of the day off, and she couldn't help smiling at the stunned expression on his face.

"But you heard Nathaniel. He wants the first train out today. And he said he's going to be gone all day."

Mara smiled. "I have come to have great confidence in your abilities, Michael. I trust you."

Leaving the astonished engineer staring after her, she turned away and headed toward the front door, hand in hand with Billy, still trying to think of a way for them to spend their afternoon.

But as they left the factory, Michael's words came back to her, and those words gave her an idea. Nathaniel wasn't the only one who could come up with special surprises, she decided.

Nathaniel turned down Whitechapel High Street just as the church clock chimed half past six, tense in body and tired in spirit. He'd spent the afternoon calling on their other vendors, and he'd found the Halston Tin story repeated over and over. Suppliers who'd had no problem extending them credit a week ago were suddenly refusing to do so. He was more certain than ever that Adrian was responsible, and he had never felt more frustrated in his life.

Beckett was at his usual post on the corner. Nathaniel stopped for a moment. "How's your leg, Henry?"

The old man bent down and rubbed his knee where it joined the wooden peg. "Achin', guv'nor, and that's a fact," he replied mournfully.

"Isn't that ointment helping?"

"Aye," the old man replied, with the usual melancholy sigh. "But not tonight. There be a mighty storm comin'."

Nathaniel glanced up at the black, starless sky as another gust of wind whipped a lock of hair across his brow. "I think you're right. Don't get caught out here when it starts."

"I was just packing up the cart to 'ead for me lodgings, guv'nor."

Nathaniel nodded, bid the coster good night, and turned toward the factory. He opened the front door, wondering what the hell he was going to tell Mara, but he came to a halt in the doorway, all his worries forgotten at the sight that met his eyes. Everything had been shut down for the day, but no one had left. Instead, he saw the men clearing away equipment and moving tables toward the center of the room. The women were hanging brightly colored streamers and chatting like an excited flock of magpies.

Nathaniel saw Michael leaning over one of the tables and fiddling with his gramophone, a beautiful girl beside him, tendrils of dark hair peeking from beneath the kerchief she wore, and a picnic basket in her arms. She had to be Rebecca, Michael's bride-to-be. Mrs. O'Brien stood near the couple, removing baskets piled with food and cases of beer and lemonade from a wheelbarrow and arranging them on another table.

His gaze scanned the room until he caught sight of Mara, and he smiled, watching her. She was about a dozen feet away, up on the ladder they'd installed that led up onto the mezzanine, tying a huge red bow around the rail and trying to get it just right.

Billy spied him standing in the doorway. "'e's 'ere!" the boy shouted and raced across the floor, dashing around the tables and people that blocked his path, to throw himself at Nathaniel.

Heads turned to look at him as he automatically wrapped an arm around Billy's shoulders and continued to stare at the sight before him, completely astonished. He looked up at Mara on the ladder, who was looking down at him, smiling. "Surprise!" she called down to him.

He lifted his hand and gestured to the chaos. "What is all this?"

He watched her climb down from the ladder, and he managed to catch a pleasing glimpse of a stocking-clad leg below the hem of her black skirt, a leg as shapely as he'd imagined, before she jumped off the ladder's last step. Her skirt swirled down over her high-button shoes, and Nathaniel felt a twinge of disappointment, wondering if she were going to climb ladders again anytime soon.

"It's a party," Billy told him. "We're celebratin'."

"We are?" He looked at Mara, still quite confused.

She nodded, her eyes sparkling with mischief as she approached them.

"What are we celebrating?" he asked as Billy pulled him by the hand, leading him toward the center of the room.

Mara followed. "Michael got the first train off the line today."

They halted in front of one of the tables, and Nathaniel looked down at the very first piece of concrete evidence that his dream was coming true. Painted dark green, with red trim and brass wheels, the locomotive sat atop a velvet-covered platform. A white card had been centered at the edge of the platform, nestled amid the red velvet. Written on it in Mara's perfect handwriting were the words, "Chase-Elliot Toy Makers, London, 1889."

"I ordered a brass plate," she explained, pointing at the card. "Until it comes, this will have to do."

"It's wonderful," he said, unable to quite believe it. "Thank you."

"Don't get too excited," Michael told him across the table. "We don't know if it runs yet. We can't test it until the paint dries."

He grinned at the other man. "It better work, or I'll have to have a long talk with my engineer."

Again he looked down at the locomotive, and a sweet mixture of joy and triumph flooded through him. His optimism began to return. Somehow, they would get through this. Tomorrow, he would begin finding alternate suppliers. Adrian couldn't bribe everybody. What happened today would happen again, and Nathaniel knew he had to have other suppliers ready to step in.

He looked up at the crowd of people who had gathered around the table. "I don't know what to say. I'm truly overwhelmed."

"Save the speeches," Michael advised. "Let's eat."

Everyone laughed, and the crowd began to gravitate toward the tables laden with food. Michael introduced him to Rebecca before they, too, walked away, sitting down at one of the tables to eat the kosher dinner she had brought.

Billy tugged at his shirtsleeve. "C'mon, Nathaniel. I'm hungry."

Nathaniel laughed. "You're always hungry," he answered and pointed to the food. "Go on, Scrapper. We'll be along."

Billy didn't need any further encouragement. He whirled around and ran to Mrs. O'Brien, asking her to fill a plate for him. The landlady happily complied, and Mara and Nathaniel watched his eyes grow round with delight as she piled a variety of tidbits onto his plate.

"It takes very little to make that boy happy," Mara murmured.

Nathaniel glanced at her. She was watching Billy, a tender smile on her face. She should have children of her own again, he thought, loving her with all his heart. The past months had brought about many changes in her. She was becoming softer, sweeter. She was as strong-minded as ever, but he knew the fear and bitterness that had been so prevalent when they'd first met were slowly fading away.

His gaze moved to the prim line of her collar and he thought of the night he'd unfastened the button at her throat and massaged her neck. He remembered again the soft warmth of her skin beneath his fingers, felt again the yielding in her tense muscles, and savored again the sheer pleasure of watching her enjoy the massage.

As if she sensed him watching her, she turned to look up at him. He said nothing, but she must have seen something in his expression because her smile faded. Her cheeks suddenly grew pink, and she ducked her head, clasping her hands behind her back and shifting her weight from side to side.

He wanted her, all of her, not just as a business partner, but as the woman he woke up with every morning. He wanted her, not just for one night, but for all of his life. "Was all this your idea?" he asked, feeling the need to say something.

"Yes. Everyone has been working very hard, and I felt that we all deserved a party." She looked up, and a tiny frown of concern knit her brows. "I'm afraid it was rather frivolous of me, wasn't it?"

"Very. I'm going to have to keep an eye on you."

"It will pay off in the long run," she said as if to console herself, and her frown disappeared. "After all, positive morale of the workers is important, don't you think?"

"Definitely," Nathaniel agreed, trying not to grin.

"I got a very good price on the food from Mrs. O'Brien," she went on. "And I got all the streamers secondhand in Petticoat Lane."

Nathaniel listened, loving the way she rationalized an expense she considered frivolous and reassured herself that she'd gotten a bargain. She was changing, but Nathaniel hoped she didn't change too much. He loved her just the way she was.

23

He made her waltz with him, right there on the production floor, in front of everyone. "You danced very well," he told her as they walked up the stairs of Mrs. O'Brien's lodging house a few hours later. "You didn't stumble once, and you actually let me lead."

"I wish you hadn't done that," she mumbled, stepping onto the landing and into the pool of moonlight that spilled through the window at the end of the hall. "They'll talk about us."

She walked the few steps to her door, and he came to a halt behind her as she fumbled in her reticule for her key.

"Mara, I hate to be the one to break the news to you, but they're talking about us anyway."

"They're not!" She shoved the key into the lock and turned her head to glance over one shoulder at him, giving a soft sigh. "Oh, dear."

"It's your fault. If you wouldn't wear your heart on your sleeve . . . "

"What?" She gasped. "Of all the ridiculous—" She broke off, seeing his grin. "You're teasing me again," she said, but he noticed the uncertainty in her voice, and he leaned closer.

"I wish you would," he murmured, placing his hands on her shoulders.

She took a sharp intake of breath. "Would what?"

He could smell the lilac scent of her hair, feel the softness of it beneath his jaw. "Wear your heart on your sleeve. Give me some idea that I'm not completely out of my head."

"You are out of your head," she retorted, not quite managing to put the proper amount of disdain in her voice. She leaned forward to grasp the door latch, trying almost desperately to free herself from his grip.

But he refused to release her. His hands tightened on her shoulders for an instant, then he turned her slowly around.

He looked into her face, loving the vulnerable tremble of her lower lip, the sign that betrayed her feelings no matter how hard she tried to hide them from him. He lifted his hands to cup her face. "I love you."

She shook her head within his hands. "No, you don't."

"Yes, I do. I want to hold you, protect you, cherish you. Forever."

He felt the change in her like the whisper of a chill wind, saw the slight twist of disbelief that touched the corner of her mouth. He could almost hear what she was thinking. Had James said these things to her?

Damn the armor she could put on at will. He wanted to wrap his arms around her and kiss away that cynical smile. He wanted to hold her and touch her, make her soft and breathless and fluttery, make her forget James Elliot and all his broken promises. But he couldn't destroy a ghost. He drew a deep breath, and his hands fell away. "You don't believe me."

"No." A flat, unemotional, honest answer.

"Why is it so difficult for you to believe that I love you?"

"What do you know about love?" she demanded. "You've never been in love." She looked up at him, and he saw something in her face, something apprehensive and unsure. "Have you?"

"Yes," he answered swiftly. "Twice."

"Oh, forgive me, I didn't know you were such an authority on the matter." The caustic comment was meant to sound indifferent, but it didn't. It sounded jealous, and both of them knew it. He grinned down at her. She pressed her lips tightly together and fell silent.

"The first time was Rosalyn Underwood," he said, leaning one shoulder against the wall. "Beautiful girl. She had red hair and green eyes. We were married," he went on, watching the rapid changes flit across her face. Disbelief, astonishment, dismay. "We had six children. Three boys and three girls. I owned a toy factory and was very successful, we had a lovely house in the country, and we loved each other madly."

She opened her mouth, then closed it again with a sound of agitation.

"In my dreams," he added. "I was fourteen, she was twelve."

She punched him, a light, frustrated jab in the shoulder. "I asked a serious question. I'd hoped for a serious answer."

"I am serious. I was in love with her, as madly and passionately as a stuttering adolescent schoolboy can be. I don't think she knew I was alive." He sighed. "Still . . . I couldn't help myself."

"And the second time?" Her voice was cool, but there was a quavering edge in it that told him more clearly than any words her indifference was pretense.

"Ah, the second time." He paused, thinking about the second time, long enough ago that the pain was gone, and only the distant pleasure remained, like warm coals after the fire had gone out. "Mai Lin."

Her name sounded almost unfamiliar now as he spoke it aloud.

"Who?"

"Mai Lin. She was Chinese." He met Mara's eyes. "She was my mistress for three years, from the time I was nineteen until I was twenty-two."

"Oh." She seemed at a loss for words, and he recalled the day he'd given her the abacus, the day she'd assumed mistress was what he wanted her to be. "What happened?" she finally asked.

"When I went to America, Mai Lin stayed behind. I asked her to come with me. I asked her to marry me. She refused."

"I don't believe it!"

"I'm flattered," he said, "but it's true. She said no."

"Why?"

"Several reasons. She didn't want to leave London. She said someday I would regret marrying her, that my brother would shun me and we'd never be able to make peace—as if I cared what Adrian thought!" He paused for a long moment, then he said, "But the real reason was that she just didn't love me, and she said I would never be happy with less. She was right, I suppose."

"Where is she now?"

"I don't know. Probably still living in Limehouse. I

haven't seen her since I came back, Mara." He smiled down at her. "Just in case you were wondering."

"I wasn't," she said, so indignantly that he knew it was a lie.

He moved to stand in front of her again and left Mai Lin in the past. "It seems I have a serious character flaw," he confessed. "I seem to have this habit of falling in love with women who don't love me back." He reached out and ran one finger lightly down her cheek and across her lips. "But I keep hoping."

"Don't," she said, her voice a fierce whisper. "Don't."

He stroked her jaw, felt the tiny muscle there flex beneath the tip of his finger. "I love you."

"Stop saying that!" She stepped backward through the doorway into her flat and balled her hands into fists, staring up at him, her whole body trembling. "You're not in love with me! You just think you are, with all your poetic, romantic notions. You don't love me."

She slammed the door in his face.

He was an absurd man. Charming, daft, absurd. She didn't want him to say things like that, with all that promise in his voice. She didn't want him to touch her like that, with all that open tenderness that left her standing raw and defenseless amid the pieces of her armor. She sank down into a chair, buried her face in her hands, and sat in the dark, listening to his footsteps as he went up the stairs, trying to turn her heart into ice.

She strained to remember all the times James had told her how much he loved her, all the times he'd made promises, all the times she'd felt the pain of betrayal and the wrench of loneliness. But just now, those memories refused to come, refused to fuel her bitterness.

All she could seem to remember at this moment was

Nathaniel. He came before her eyes, all tawny gold, so joyously alive, a shaft of sunlight piercing the dark prison where her heart was locked away, revealing her—what had he called it?—her dark, secret self.

Despite her denials, to him and to herself, she loved him, and that was her greatest fear: to love him, to fill her empty heart and her lonely soul with him, and to have it not be enough, to watch him walk away from her and take his light and laughter with him, leaving her alone again. She didn't want to be alone again, with only her dark, secret self for company.

Nathaniel heard the footsteps outside his door, and he lifted his head sharply, listening. The latch rattled, and he straightened in his chair, hopeful, tense, waiting.

Slowly, the door creaked open.

He'd drawn the shutters when he'd come in, and the room was dark except for the glowing coals in the grate, but Nathaniel knew it was her. Accustomed to the darkness, he could see her slender form as she entered the room and closed the door behind her. He could hear the soft sound of her breathing, he could smell lilacs and feel the sharp quickening of his own senses.

"'She walks in beauty, like the night.'"

His voice, sudden in the silence, startled her, and she jumped backward, her back hitting the closed door with a thump. "Nathaniel?"

"Yes." He said nothing more.

Her eyes adjusted to the darkness and found him. He was sitting in a chair across the room, his shirt a pale patch of white against the leather back of the chair. He made no move, and the silence lengthened.

"I decided I wasn't sleepy," she murmured, suddenly

feeling ridiculous. What was she doing here? But she knew the reason.

A peculiar sound escaped him, a laugh and yet not. "I understand."

"You aren't sleepy either?"

"No."

Another silence. "Perhaps you might play your violin, then?" she suggested, ashamed that she sounded so timid.

"No." A few seconds passed. Then he spoke again. "Why did you come up here, Mara?"

Did you mean it when you said you love me? The question hovered on the tip of her tongue, unspoken. Suddenly uncertain, afraid of rejection, she stood there with her back against the door, wishing he would take the lead, wishing he would show her what he wanted her to do. If only he would come to her, hold her, if only he would smile and tell her again that he loved her, everything would be all right. But he made no move at all. He sat, rigid in his chair, watching her and saying nothing, and she realized he was waiting.

Waiting for her to come to him. She turned her head away. She looked at the floor, the ceiling, anywhere but at the man watching her.

Why couldn't she just say it? Why couldn't she just walk over to him and wrap her arms around him and say the words? *Nathaniel, I love you, I trust you, I need you so. Love me.*

She finally looked at him again. He was still waiting.

Slowly, she began to walk toward him. If only she could say the right thing, do the right thing, he would make love to her. Somehow, the door would open, and all the feelings locked inside her would come tumbling out, released from the prison she had made so long ago.

With her gaze still locked with his, she came to a halt beside his chair. She opened her mouth, closed it again, and sank to her knees. With trembling fingers, she reached out and placed her hands on his chest.

He drew in a sharp breath and leaned back. Her fingers, awkward in their gloves, fumbled with the buttons of his shirt. But he gave her no help, and by the time she reached the third button, she knew this wasn't going to work. She yanked hard and his shirt button went flying. She heard it skitter across the floor, and she knew she was making a mess of things. Her fingers faltered, her lip trembled. With an anguished cry, she wrenched back and jumped to her feet, ready to flee, her courage gone.

"Mara, don't! It's all right." He leaned forward and caught her by the waist, pulling her onto his lap. "It's all right. Don't go."

"I'm no good at this," she cried, turning her face into his shoulder. "I knew I couldn't do it."

"Of course you couldn't do it. Not alone." He entwined his fingers in the knot of her hair. He pulled out the pins to free her hair, and tossed them aside. Tangling his fingers in the long dark waves at her temples, he brushed his thumbs back and forth across her cheeks. "But I wanted you to take that first step alone. I had to see if you truly wanted this."

She lowered her head and hunched her shoulders, trying to hide in his embrace, wanting to die of embarrassment. "I wanted it to be perfect. I wanted to . . ." A slight pause. ". . . seduce you."

Her choked words made him smile. Mara, always seeking perfection in an imperfect world. He leaned closer. "If you insist."

She shook her head, missing the teasing caress in his voice. "It's no good."

"It could be." He tilted her chin upward and bent his head until his lips brushed hers. "It could be, Mara," he said against her mouth, "but it has to be both of us. Together, don't you see?"

She shivered at the feel of his mouth on hers. Her hand flattened against his chest, and she ached with the longing to feel his bare skin beneath her fingers. "Love me, Nathaniel," she whispered.

"I do." He slipped one arm around her shoulders and the other beneath her knees, then rose to his feet, cradling her against him.

He carried her into the bedroom and set her down on her feet beside the bed. He lit the lamp on the bedside table, and she had to resist that temptation to run, to hide before all her inadequacies were revealed.

His gaze locked with hers for only a moment, then lowered as he lifted one of her hands in both of his. He turned her palm upward and his fingers moved to her wrist, to the row of buttons on her glove. The top button slid free, and she jerked her hand back, realizing what he intended to do. But his hands tightened, refusing to release her, and a sound escaped her, a tiny protest. She stretched her free hand toward the lamp on the bedside table, but it was just out of her reach. "Nathaniel, the light."

He shook his head and freed another button. "Only lies need the dark, Mara. Leave it on."

"No, Nathaniel, I can't," she whispered. "Please put it out."

He unfastened the last button, then his fingers slid to the tips of hers. One by one, he tugged at the ends of her glove, then pulled it off of her trembling hand and let it fall to the floor. She tried again to pull away, but his other hand closed over her wrist, capturing her naked hand, refusing to let her hide it from him.

"I don't want you to see," she mumbled, hating her scars.

"I already did. Remember?" He opened his hands, exposing her deepest vulnerability to his gaze, cradling her hand in both of his as he might hold a trembling bird, waiting to see if it would fly away. She remained perfectly still, too anguished to move.

He slowly lowered his head. He pressed his lips to her palm where burning timber had seared her skin and left its mark, his kiss a balm to heal wounds that lay much deeper. The sweet, piercing beauty of that kiss shattered her hard and brittle heart, tearing a sob from her throat.

His arms came around her instantly, held her tightly. "Lovely," he murmured, kissing her cheeks, her mouth, her throat, anywhere his lips could reach. "My lovely Mara."

She reached up, entwining her arms around his neck, wanting to explain what his gesture meant to her, but there were no words that could explain. She buried her face against his chest, loving him so much, unable to say it.

He pulled her arms down and stripped away her other glove, letting it fall to the floor beside its mate, then unbuttoned the cuffs of her shirtwaist. He unhooked the clasp of her pendant watch and laid the heavy, silver-backed timepiece on the bedside table. Then he grasped the ribbon at her throat and pulled it away from her collar. His intent expression made it seem as if undressing her were the most important thing in the world, and she scarcely noticed the ribbon flutter to the floor.

He looked up at her then, looked at her with all that open tenderness as his fingers undid the first button of her shirtwaist, then the second, then the third.

His knuckles brushed against her breasts and then her ribs as he worked his way slowly down to her waist. Through layers of fabric, she felt the heat of his touch. A tiny gasp escaped her with each button he unfastened.

He pulled the shirtwaist away, and the cool air hit her bare arms. She shivered with the chill and the heat, like a fever, and she slid her trembling arms around his waist as he moved even closer and lowered his head. He kissed her shoulder just beyond the lace edge of her corset cover, then turned his head to trail kisses along her throat to her ear as his hands slid around to the small of her back and undid the hooks of her skirt.

She felt the light scrape of his teeth, and she realized he was actually nibbling on her earlobe. She gave a little cry and clutched at his shirt, bunching fabric in her fists as she felt her knees buckle. His hands caught her waist to steady her, and she heard his soft laughter in her ear.

Dazed by what he was doing to her, lost in the sensation of his warm breath in her ear, she hardly noticed as he continued to unfasten more buttons, more hooks, and more ribbons, until her corset cover, corset, skirt, and petticoat were lying in a careless tangle at their feet.

His hands slid up her bare arms to her shoulders and he gently pushed her down until she was sitting on the edge of the bed. Then he knelt down in front of her, pushing aside the discarded garments. He lifted one of her feet in his hands and let it rest on his thigh.

"I don't suppose you happened to bring that handy little buttonhook of yours?" he asked in a voice that was not quite steady as he looked up at her.

She opened her mouth to speak, found she could not, and wordlessly shook her head, staring down at the seam of his trousers, at his arousal which was obvious beneath the gray fabric.

"Damn." He bent his head and began to unbutton her shoe by hand. She stared down at him, and reached out toward his bent head, curling one hand in his tawny hair that felt like threads of silk between her fingers.

He pulled off her shoe and tossed it aside, then took her other foot and repeated the process. He lifted one of her stocking-clad feet in his hands and lifted his head to look up at her.

"Do you remember the other day when we went kite flying?"

Startled by the unexpected question, she let her hand fall to his shoulder. She nodded.

"You hiked up your skirt so you could run faster," he said softly. "And I was looking at you, and you asked me why I was looking at you like that." His lids lowered a fraction, and he stared at her through half-closed eyes as his fingers caressed her instep in a slow, circular motion. "I was looking at you and thinking of this."

He slid his hands up her legs to her knees to unfasten her garters. "And this," he added, rolling down her stockings, his palms burning her skin through the silky fabric.

Stunned by his confession, she watched him remove her stockings and toss them aside. His hands, brown against her skin, slid back up her legs.

"And this." His fingertips caressed the back of each knee just beneath the lace edge of her drawers. She could only stare at him, mindless little gasps of pleasure escaping her at the feel of his hands stroking her and the knowledge that he'd been thinking about doing this to her long before now.

He straightened up on his knees and grasped her hands, pulling them to the front of his shirt, silently telling her he wanted her to try again what she had begun in the other room.

Her hands shook as she pulled the braces off his shoulders, then yanked the tails of his shirt out of his trousers. She pulled the shirt off his wide shoulders and leaned forward, pressing a kiss to his bare chest.

Freed from the shirt, his arms came up. His fingers raked through her hair as she pressed her lips against his skin. She could feel his heart hammering against her mouth. Tentatively, she touched him with her tongue.

"Oh, God." His voice was a low, agonized rasp in the silence. His hands tightened into fists in her hair as she pressed butterfly kisses across his chest. His breathing grew labored, but his body stayed motionless, his muscles tense and hard beneath her lips. When her tongue tasted him again, he let out a sharp exclamation, and pulled her head back to stop her.

His hands left her hair and reached for the hem of her chemise, yanking it upward. She raised her arms toward the ceiling, allowing him to pull it over her head.

"You're so beautiful." He reached out, cupping her breasts in his palms, teasing her nipples to hardness with his thumbs. She heard herself, heard her own soft sounds of agitation. Her hands reached for him, grasped his arms, felt his skin and the hard smoothness of muscles beneath. Her hands worked, opening, closing, involuntarily pulling him closer.

He moved at her command, using his body to part her legs as he pushed her gently. With her feet still on the floor, she fell backward into the soft mattress, felt herself yielding to the sweetness of it.

Leaning forward, he slid his hands up into her hair, and he bent his head. He kissed her breast, his tongue grazing the tip in slow, coaxing circles. She was acutely aware of every place his body touched hers: his hands in her hair, his arms pinning hers to the mattress, his mouth at her breast, his waist between her thighs. She arched upward against him, her hips pressing closer, wanting him with a sudden desperation, but he was just out of reach.

He lifted his head and she cried out, her arms straining against his, wanting to hold him, keep him there. But when he turned his head and opened his mouth over her other breast, she felt his hands slide out of her hair, moving downward to her hips, and she got her wish. She wrapped her arms around his shoulders, her fingers raking upward to clutch at his hair, pulling him closer, but it still wasn't enough.

His hands paused at her waist and untied the string of her drawers. He pulled away from her again, moving backward on his knees, tugging at the garment, and she realized what he wanted. She closed her legs and lifted her hips, enabling him to remove her drawers. Then he rose to his feet and lifted her fully onto the bed. Without the heat of his body close to hers and the magical feel of his hands on her, she became aware that she was lying naked before him and the light was on. She closed her eyes, turning her face away, embarrassed and completely vulnerable.

She heard his boots hit the floor, a sound that was very familiar. She squeezed her eyes tightly closed, feeling again all her inadequacies, feeling herself withdraw, feeling the rigidity coming over her by degrees. She wasn't any good at this. He would realize it. She would disappoint him.

Standing beside her, he ran his hand over her body from thigh to chin. She stiffened under that long caress, knowing full well his observant eyes missed nothing. Grasping her chin in his hand, he turned her face toward him. She reluctantly opened her eyes.

He was leaning over her, naked and unashamed, not looking at all embarrassed or disappointed. "Mara, sweetheart, you have to move over," he said, his breathing uneven, his voice unsteady. "Unless, of course, you want me to climb over you, which could be fun, I admit . . . "

Hastily, she slid toward the wall, the cotton sheets cool and smooth beneath her. He joined her on the bed, stretching out full length beside her. She could feel his arousal against her hip, and she knew what would come next.

But again, he surprised her. Lying on his side, he reached out and spread his fingers across her stomach. She lifted her head and stared at his hand, a hand large enough to touch both her hipbones at once. Her stomach quivered inside at his touch.

He looked up at her, and their gazes met as his hand slid lower, parting her thighs. She gasped, her eyes widening in astonishment as he touched her most secret place, where not even her husband had dared to touch. She closed her eyes again and fell back, shocked by the scorching intimacy, thinking wildly that she ought to stop him from doing that. But the caress of his fingers was so exquisite and delightful that she found herself arching toward his hand instead of away, and she forgot all about feeling inadequate.

She'd been a married woman, she'd thought she had some experience, but not this. Not like this. That had been a brief look exchanged at the dinner table, and later a fumbling in the dark, a lifted hem and a quick, furtive coupling, followed by a longing only slightly relieved and a vague disappointment. But, oh, God, never like this.

She felt that she must be burning alive. He stoked the fire within her even hotter, and she began to move with his hand, unable to stop herself, unable to stop the whimpers that escaped her. He bent his head and kissed her, capturing the tiny sounds in his mouth, until the caress of his fingers turned them to soft, shuddering moans. The pleasure of it washed over her in waves, higher and higher.

He pulled back slightly, his breath warm on her cheek, and the movement of his hand changed, until only one finger touched her, tracing a tiny little circle with the tip of his finger. Everything seemed to explode inside her, fragmenting, and she cried out, an ecstatic, wordless sound.

She heard his reply, a low, masculine sound of urgency, just before he moved to lie on top of her. She felt his weight, his long, lean body heavy and hard against her. He trailed kisses across her skin, tiny kisses along her exposed throat, across her collarbone, to her breasts and back again, murmuring incoherent phrases between each one as if uttering complete sentences were beyond him now. "Soft . . . Mara . . . beautiful . . . love you . . . "

His arms slid beneath her back, he settled his weight between her thighs, and he entered her with a sudden, hard push that sent the air rushing from her lungs. Her arms and legs wrapped around him, and she felt the heavy fullness of him inside her, felt the luscious slow slide and thrust as her body yielded, accepted, embraced.

She tangled a handful of his hair in her fist and caressed his back with her other hand, feeling the muscles of his back flex beneath her touch. She pressed her face into his shoulder, kissing his hot skin as she matched his rhythm, a slow deliberate cadence that made her ache.

"Nathaniel." The desperate, impatient whisper escaped her, a plea for release, for surcease, for completion.

When it came, her head fell back and she said his

name again, not a whisper this time, but a startled, strangled cry of exultation.

His breathing came harshly now, and he quickened the pace. His body pressed hers into the mattress with the rough, frantic motion of passion finally unleashed.

"Love you always," he groaned and the thrust came again, the final one. His body jerked in an explosive tremor, lingered into tiny shudders, then stilled. He sucked in great gulps of air and fell against her, burying his face in her hair. "Promise."

Mara heard that whispered word, and her arms tightened around him. She savored the feel of his body, the lovely heaviness of him, but she wished he had made her no promises, because she was still very much afraid that he would never keep them.

24

Nathaniel didn't realize that he had drifted off to sleep until he awakened. But all vestiges of sleep disappeared instantly at the feel of Mara lying beside him.

He felt alive, in every part of himself, intensely aware of everything, the counterpane across his hip, the softness of Mara's long hair in a tangle across his throat and her cheek in his shoulder, the sound of her deep, even breathing. The room was pitch-dark, but he could feel her small hand splayed across his chest in an involuntary gesture of trust.

Despite the warmth of her legs tangled with his beneath the bedcovers, he felt the chill in the air around them. He grasped an edge of the counterpane, pulling it over both of them, smiling as he felt her snuggle closer to him with a little sigh, still fast asleep.

His arm tightened beneath her head and his hand moved to caress her shoulder in aimless circles as his lips pressed against her hair.

She stirred again, rubbing her thigh against his. Lust rocked through him, and he slowly rolled on top of her, pushing her hand out of the way.

She awoke instantly, her body stiffening at the feel of his weight. He moved against her, savoring the way she felt. Lush, warm, and so enticing.

She shifted beneath him and said his name, a little squeak of protest that held a hint of panic. But when he rose on his elbows and opened one hand over her breast, her head fell back and she made the sweet sound of acquiescence. He kissed her lips, he nuzzled her throat, he caressed her until he felt the yielding of her form, the willing arch that beckoned him with irresistible, feminine force and sent him to the place beyond all reason.

Then he entered her, felt the quick convulsions deep within her as she closed around him. A visceral sound escaped his throat; he felt the unbearable tension rise and peak, hurling him over the edge. He climaxed in a rush that left him falling into a languorous aftermath, like sinking into a bed of feathers. He gave her a long, lingering kiss, then rolled to one side, taking her with him.

His arms tightened around her, then slowly relaxed, and he settled into lethargy. He felt drugged by the warmth and softness of her, wrapped in a sated peace. Just as he drifted off to sleep, he whispered in her ear, "We can be married before Christmas."

When he woke again, the first thing he felt was the emptiness, and he knew before he opened his eyes that he was alone in the bed. The feeble light of a typical English dawn filtered in around the closed shutter, casting an anemic glow over the room.

He turned his head and saw Mara sitting on a stool beside the armoire, clad in her chemise and drawers, her remaining clothes in a neat pile on the floor beside her. In profile, her face was hidden by the curtain of her hair.

He rolled to his side and leaned on his elbow to watch as she lifted one slender leg to put on her stocking, toe pointed and knee bent in a graceful arc. He watched her pull it slowly over her calf, knowing the sight was now his to enjoy, wanting to begin every morning of his life with it.

"You know," he murmured sleepily, "there might be a better sight for a man to wake up to than that, but I can't imagine what it would be."

His voice, drowsy and satisfied, flustered her. Her fingers fumbled with the garter, and although he couldn't see her face, he'd have bet his last quid she was blushing. Without looking at him, she scooped up her corset and rose, turning her back to him as she began to fasten the hooks.

She kept her back to him as she dressed. At first, he thought she was just embarrassed, but as he watched her, his drowsy senses began to sharpen and he realized something was very wrong. He tossed back the covers and rose from the bed. She heard his approach and stiffened, her fingers stilled in the act of buttoning her shirtwaist as he came up behind her and wrapped his arms around her waist. He kissed her shoulder. "Good morning."

"I have to go," she mumbled, head bent, all her attention on fastening buttons, putting up all the barriers he'd stripped away the night before, barriers he thought he'd destroyed. "It's nearly seven."

He didn't reply. Instead, he pulled back her hair and turned his head to kiss the side of her neck. She slid out of his hold and bent to reach for her skirt. She pulled it over her head, buttoned it. With her back to him, she pulled on her gloves. She still would not look at him.

Dread filled him, and he reached for her, held her tight. *Not now,* he pleaded with her silently as he felt her inexorable withdrawal like water through his hands, knowing he couldn't hold her tight enough to stop it. *Not again, not ever.* "What's wrong, Mara?"

"Nothing. I have to go to work. We both do." She brought her hands up between them and tried to push him away, a bit more forcefully this time.

"Nothing?" His arms tightened. "Mara, why are you doing this? Last night, I thought—" He broke off, feeling like an utter fool.

"Last night was a mistake," she said, but she didn't look in his eyes. She stared past his shoulder at some vague part of the room behind him.

"A mistake," he repeated in disbelief. Anger rose within him, sudden, hot, vital, at the way she couldn't even meet his eyes, couldn't bear to look at him. "I wasn't the one who went to your room. You came to me, remember?"

"I shouldn't have!" she exclaimed, pressing her gloved hands to her flushed cheeks, finally looking at him, her eyes wide with dismay and—what hurt him more— regret. "It was very wrong of me. I don't know what I was thinking, to behave so shamelessly. And James not even dead half a year."

He seized her hands, dragged them down, held them tight in his. "When did James's ghost visit us?" he asked. "I thought last night it was just the two of us in that bed."

She pressed her lips tightly together and didn't reply.

He looked into her face, studied her closed expression, and frustration fueled his anger. "There it is again."

"What?"

"That damnable armor you use whenever you want to hide what you're really thinking and feeling. It won't work. I know what's going through your mind. You're as easy to read as a book. You came to me last night because you needed to believe me. You needed me to love you, to say it, to mean it. I did. I do. I love you."

"Words, words, words. I'm sick of words of love. Don't you understand? I had eight years of words from James that didn't mean anything. He did what he pleased, when he pleased, and never asked me what I wanted."

"I'll ask. What do you want? Do you want me on my knees, bleeding, with my heart in my hands?"

"I want to be left alone!"

"No, you don't. If you did, you would never have come to me."

"I wish I hadn't."

"Why? Because I showed you how it could be with us? When did it happen, Mara? When during the night did I get classified, labeled, and filed away like a page in your ledger, dismissed as just another man to hurt you?"

She tried to jerk free, but he held her fast. "I'm not like James. How many times do I have to say it, how many ways do I have to prove it before you believe me? You wanted me, but you're too stubborn to admit it, even now, even to yourself. And whether you realize it or not, whether you admit it or not, you need me. Want, need, love. It's all part of the whole."

"I don't need you," she said, shaking her head, fighting him with all she had. "I will never allow myself to need anyone again. I can't bear it." Her voice broke. "I can't bear it. Why can't you understand?"

"Do you think I don't?" he demanded, his voice rising with his own frustration, refusing to hear the pain and fear in hers. "I understand perfectly. There was a time when I liked James, but do you know what I think of him now? I hate him. I hate him because he was the one who hurt you, he was the one who was always leaving you, but I'm the one who's getting all the blame!"

He took a deep breath. "I love you. For that, I am condemned."

She yanked her hands out of his and took a step back.

"You want what I can't give you. You want all of me, every piece of my soul, my heart, my mind, my body. I can't give them to you. I won't!"

She whirled around and ran from the bedroom. He started to follow her, but he suddenly realized he was naked. With a muttered curse, he fell back onto the bed, and he heard the front door slam. She was gone.

Foolish woman, when would she stop running away? He wasn't James, damn it all, but she still couldn't trust him. He'd been certain last night that she loved him, but now he wasn't even certain of that.

He rubbed a hand over his eyes and sighed, wondering if perhaps it were he, not Mara, who was the fool.

Mara tried to tell herself that she was a strumpet. She'd gone to him, she'd lain with him, she'd let him do things to her that her own husband had never done. Just the memory of his hands on her made her burn. She studied her face in the tiny mirror above her washstand, wondering how she could look exactly the same when she felt so different.

She should be ashamed of what they had done, but try as she might, she felt no shame. She couldn't see herself as a strumpet. All she felt was the aching sweet happiness of loving him and the horrible panic of needing him, warring within her for control, each trying to overpower her.

The rightness of it was the thing that frightened her the most. When he'd held her, and kissed her, and touched her, it had felt so right. Lying beside him, feeling the safety and warmth of his arms around her had been like coming home. She loved him, and she hated the power that love gave him, the power to give her a home, the power to take it away.

It surprised her now, when she gazed at herself in the mirror that she should look so calm, when everything inside her was in tumult. All the ramifications, the possible consequences, raced through her mind. Nathaniel had said he loved her, but what did that mean? James had said the same, and what had love brought either of them?

When he'd mentioned marriage, the panic had come over her like a shower of icy water. After the love died, marriage was a trap. She didn't want to be married again, not ever. Then she thought of a home again and wavered. Did she?

What if there were a child as a result of last night? Until this moment, that thought hadn't even occurred to her, but now that very real possibility made her sick with dread. If there were a child, they would have to marry. She sank into a chair with a miserable little moan, wrapping her arms around her ribs. "Oh, God," she whispered, "what have I done?"

The thoughts swirling around in her head were making her dizzy, and Nathaniel was making her crazy. She wanted to run back to him. She wanted to scream, she wanted to weep.

She didn't do any of those things. She took some deep breaths. She got to her feet. She went through the motions of getting dressed with methodical precision, trying to regain some semblance of order within herself as she donned fresh clothes and put up her hair. But when she left the lodging house and walked to the factory, the questions and doubts still swirled round and round in her mind, and her emotions were so tightly strung, she felt that if someone touched her, she'd snap.

She unlocked the front door and stepped inside the factory. But her steps faltered and her thoughts dissipated into numbness at the sight before her. All three steam engines had been dismantled and the pieces lay on the floor, a montage of pistons, connecting rods, and crankshafts. The place looked like a junkyard.

She heard a clinking sound and jumped, turning from side to side in a desperate search for the noise until she realized it came from herself. She was shaking so badly, it rattled the ring of keys in her hand.

The keys fell from her fingers. She walked forward slowly, staring at the mess as if in a dream. She glanced toward the door Boggs had put in that led through assembly, and she began walking that way without thought.

Assembly had been completely ransacked. Train parts and half-completed locomotives lay scattered everywhere. Crates had been opened and overturned, their contents dumped on the floor. She retraced her steps, moving like an automaton, until she was back on the production floor.

Her shaking legs gave way, and Mara fell to her knees. Right before her, she could see a swath of red velvet and a smashed locomotive and a white card. She began to whimper.

Rooted to the spot, her body rocked like a willow in a storm until shock set in, and she jumped to her feet, her teeth chattering, her body chilled, and her breath coming in little gasps. Blindly, she ran for the door, stumbling over pieces of the steam engines. She grabbed the handle with a shaking hand and jerked open the door.

Leaving it hanging open, she raced up the street. She dodged around the pedestrians that crowded the sidewalk and ignored the odd stares she received, wanting only to reach Nathaniel, wanting only to cling to the man she'd run from in fear half an hour before.

She stumbled up the stairs at Mrs. O'Brien's until she was at his door, and she flung it open, trying to call his name, but unable to utter any sound beyond choked little whimpers.

Nathaniel was getting dressed, tucking the ends of his shirt into his trousers, when he heard the sound of his door hitting the wall with a bang.

"What the hell?" he muttered, fastening his trouser buttons as he strode toward the bedroom door.

Mara collided with him in the doorway, falling heavily into his arms. "N . . . n . . . n . . . "

"Mara?" Her incoherent syllables and the way her body shook in his arms told him something terrible had happened, and he held her close. She gave a shuddering sob and clung to him, burying her face against his chest.

"S . . . s . . . some . . ." She couldn't say it.

"What is it? What's happened?" He pulled back, and his hands closed on her shoulders. Her eyes were wide and glassy. "What happened?" he repeated, his heart jumping in alarm at the shock in her eyes.

She tried to answer, but she could only stammer out tiny sounds. The tight fabric of her control was unraveling; she was coming apart in his hands.

He pulled her back against him, holding her tight. "It's all right," he murmured against her hair. "Take deep breaths. Slow and easy."

He could hear her rapid breathing and feel the panicky rise and fall of her breasts against his ribs. He waited, listening as her breaths deepened to a more steady cant, his fingers moving in soothing circles against her spine as he pulled back again to look into her face. "Tell me what happened."

"S . . . somebody broke in . . . into the factory," she choked.

His hands stilled for a second, then resumed their reassuring strokes. "Are you all right? You're not hurt?"

She nodded to answer the first question, then shook

her head to answer the second. She swallowed hard, fighting to regain control, and went on, "I went in and f . . . found it. Oh, Nathaniel, it's a mess!"

He maneuvered her gently to the bed and sat down beside her on the edge of the mattress. He pushed back a loose wisp of hair from her cheek. "It's all right," he murmured, his fingers brushing gently across her cheekbone to tuck the tendril of hair behind her ear. "Don't move. I'll be right back."

She took a deep, shuddering breath and nodded. He rose to his feet and went into the front room, returning a moment later with a bottle of brandy in his hand.

He uncorked it and held it out to her. "Here. Take a good swallow."

She took the bottle, lifted it to her lips, and obeyed. She coughed, made a grimace, and thrust the bottle back at him. "That's terrible."

"Glad you like it," he returned, relieved to see color begin returning to her face. He corked the bottle and set it down. After a few more minutes, when she had stopped trembling, he gave her cheek a caress and said, "Stay here. I'm going to go take a look."

He left the flat and went down the stairs, heading for the factory. When he walked inside the building, he came to a halt and stared at the dismantled steam engines with dismay. In the warehouse, his dismay turned to a sick feeling in his gut as he stared at the havoc.

A sound caused him to turn around and he saw Mara standing there. "I thought I told you to wait in my flat."

She lifted wide gray eyes to his face. "I'd rather be with you," she whispered and wrapped her arms around her ribs. An admission of need. He opened his arms and waited.

She walked toward him, stepping carefully amid the things on the floor, and came into his embrace, curling against him, seeking comfort and answers. "Why?" she whispered. "Why would somebody do this?"

Nathaniel knew why. He glanced around at the mess. His feelings of shock changed to a deep shimmering anger. Yes, he knew why. He also knew who.

"My God, what happened?"

A shocked voice from the doorway caused both of them to turn in that direction. Michael stood there, staring at the scene in astonishment.

Nathaniel's lips tightened. He pulled gently away from Mara and looked into her face. "You're certain you're all right?"

"Yes."

He took a step toward the door. "Michael, send for the police and notify the insurance company. If the police allow it, start getting this place cleaned up. Make a list of anything that's damaged or missing. We'll need it for the insurance."

"Where are you going?" Mara asked.

He didn't answer that question. "I'll be back later," he said and walked out the door.

It was a few minutes past nine when Nathaniel entered Avery's Athletic Club. He passed through the foyer, shaking off the restraining hand of the clerk who said that only members were allowed beyond the receiving area. The man muttered something about finding the manager, but Nathaniel paid no heed.

He passed the changing rooms and Turkish baths, heading for the squash courts. He interrupted three squash matches in progress before he found the one he sought, and he took a great deal of satisfaction in seeing Adrian miss the volley as he caught sight of him standing in the doorway.

"Well, now," Adrian drawled. He faced Nathaniel, peering at him as if he were an interesting insect under a magnifying glass. "What have we here?"

Nathaniel looked over at the younger gentleman on the other side of the net, acknowledging Baron Severn with a slight nod. "Excuse us, please."

The baron must have sensed the tension, for he dropped his racquet and hastily left the room.

"Predictable as ever, aren't you, Adrian?" Nathaniel stepped onto the court, letting the door slam shut behind him as he came to a halt several feet away. With his feet planted wide apart, he studied his brother. "Still playing squash every morning. Nine to eleven, regular as sunrise. But that's not surprising. You never did have any imagination."

Adrian didn't move, but there was an answering challenge in his eyes. "B . . . but I t . . . try s . . . so hard," he mocked.

Nathaniel ignored the taunt. "What, no warm welcome for the prodigal returned?" he asked. "No desire to renew the family ties?"

His reference to Adrian's visit to the factory wasn't lost on his brother. "Lovely woman, Mrs. Elliot," Adrian commented. "It made me realize that having a woman as a partner has certain . . . advantages."

The slight pause made his meaning clear, but Nathaniel refused to be drawn. "Leave her out of this, Adrian. We both know this is between you and me. She has nothing to do with it." He took a deep breath and went on, "I know what you're trying to do. It won't work."

"I'm glad to see you've finally managed to get rid of that ridiculous stutter." Adrian began turning his racquet over and over in his hands. "But you still have that irritating habit of rambling on about nothing, little brother. I don't know what you're talking about."

"Of course you don't. How much did you pay them? Probably not enough, considering the fine job they did last night. You always did pay your employees too little."

"Are you accusing me of something?"

"Don't play games with me, Adrian."

"But I love playing games with you, Nathaniel. I always win."

He hefted his racquet and tossed it to his brother, an unsporting toss that sent the racquet spinning toward his head. Nathaniel lifted both hands and caught the racquet, then lowered it to keep his gaze locked on Adrian. "Not this time."

"You've changed. You're not quite as clumsy as you used to be."

Adrian was afraid. The sneer in his voice had a hollow ring, and his contemptuous gaze barely hid a glimmer of fear. Nathaniel recognized all of his brother's taunts for what they were. The simple posturing of a bully.

When they were boys, Adrian's constant ridicule had eroded his confidence, making him feel inadequate and foolish. Those feelings had carried over into adulthood, when he'd left England at twenty-two still intimidated by his brother. But, as Mara had pointed out only yesterday, he wasn't a boy any longer, and ten years away had changed his perspective. Now, he faced Adrian unshaken by the taunts that had shattered him as a child.

"Yes, I have changed. And the old tricks don't work any longer. If you want to throw your money away on petty schemes to ruin me, then do so, but they'll be futile. I will not let you destroy my business."

"Still trying to compete with me, aren't you?" Adrian sighed and shook his head. "When are you going to realize you can't win?"

Nathaniel's jaw tightened. Ten years ago, he would have realized it. He would have caved in. He would have walked away rather than fight Adrian. But now he didn't move. "Never."

"I was wrong. You haven't changed at all. You're still as pudding-headed as ever."

"I guess so."

Adrian gave him a pitying look. "Make it easier on yourself, little brother. Pack it in and go back to America."

Nathaniel couldn't resist a taunt of his own. "Why should you care that I'm here? You must be afraid of the competition."

Adrian shrugged, but Nathaniel saw through his brother's nonchalance. "The way I see it," Adrian continued, "you have two choices. The first is to retreat now while you still can."

"And the second?"

"Prepare yourself for war."

Nathaniel tossed down the squash racquet like a gauntlet, but his gaze never left his brother's. The racquet landed at Adrian's feet, and the clatter echoed in the empty gymnasium. "War it is."

Without another word, Nathaniel turned and left, vowing that this time, there would be no retreat. There would be no surrender.

He walked all the way back to Whitechapel, and by the time he reached the factory, he had a plan. He knew what he had to do. He just hoped it would be enough.

When he arrived at the factory, workers had already begun cleaning up the mess, Percy had gone for the insurance representative, Michael had started putting the steam engines back together, and Mara's shock had worn off. He found her in the warehouse, directing workers with brisk efficiency as they put train parts back in their proper boxes.

She glanced up as he came to a halt beside her. "Whoever did this tried to break into the safe."

Nathaniel sucked in a deep breath. Not only did Adrian intend to destroy him, he intended to steal his invention as well. "The train?"

"The train, the track, and the design specifications are intact. They didn't get the safe open, but the office was ransacked. They must have gone looking for another copy of the design specifications when they couldn't get the safe open."

"Was anything else taken?"

"Yes, the beam of each steam engine is missing."

Another way to delay him. Cleaning up the mess and replacing the beams would take at least three days. "What did the police say?" he asked.

"Apparently, the vandals went up the fire escape and forced open the door into our office. They also went out that way."

"They?"

"Inspector Carlisle thinks that in order to do this much damage, there must have been more than one, and they were probably here for quite some time. Michael agrees with that."

Nathaniel nodded. "Yes, dismantling the steam engines couldn't have been done quickly, even if there were several of them."

"It couldn't have been done quietly either. I can't understand why we didn't hear anything last night."

An ironic smile touched his mouth. He leaned closer. "Can't you?"

She blushed but didn't reply.

Nathaniel took another glance around. "Besides, this room is on the opposite side of the factory from us and there was quite a storm last night."

"The police said they would make inquiries in the

neighborhood. Whoever did this was trying to break open the safe to steal the train. That I can understand." She lifted her hands helplessly. "But this? This is senseless vandalism. Why?"

It wasn't senseless, and Nathaniel knew it. It was a delay, exactly what Adrian wanted, knowing that delays could cripple him. He turned away abruptly. "I'm going to help Michael put those steam engines back together. We need to get things back to normal as quickly as possible."

He left her there and set to work, but he knew he was only postponing the inevitable. Mara deserved to know the truth. He had to tell her what Adrian was up to and how he planned to prevent the scheme from succeeding, but he knew that when he did, she would ask him to stop. The woman that he loved would ask him to abandon the dream that was his life. And giving up his dream was the one thing Nathaniel could not do, not even for love.

25

By that evening, the factory was in some semblance of order. But due to the parts missing from the steam engines, production would be delayed another three days until they could get replacements.

Nathaniel and Michael spent their afternoon rebuilding the steam engines as best they could, while Mara worked in the warehouse. Billy came to watch Nathaniel and Michael work. When the factory closed and all the employees left for the day, Nathaniel took the boy out for a bite to eat, then took him home. Mara went up to the office and started straightening up the mess there.

When she'd finished, she sat down in her chair with a tired sigh. It had been an exhausting day, and she had managed to keep the impact of what had happened at bay. But now, when the factory was quiet, when it was dark out and she was alone, the shock and fear began to seep back into her bones.

She felt violated, invaded. She rubbed her palms up

and down her arms, wishing Nathaniel would return. A thump outside on the fire escape made her jump out of her chair with a startled cry, but when she heard a loud meow and a scratching sound, she drew a deep, shaky breath of relief. Algernon.

She opened the door, and the kitten strutted inside, a tiny and obviously dead mouse in his mouth. He dropped the prize at her feet like a sacred offering, then strolled past her and curled into a ball under her desk.

Mara stared down at the stiff gray rodent with distaste. She kicked it out onto the fire escape and shut the door, still shaking. She wanted Nathaniel to come back. If he were here, she wouldn't be jumping at every little sound. She'd feel safe.

She had no idea what she would have done this morning if he had not been there. There would have been no strong arms to hold her, no safe haven to protect her.

Yet, she had run from his arms, from his protection, only moments before that, frightened by the intensity of other feelings, overwhelmed by needs and desires she had never even imagined. She wrapped her arms around her ribs, feeling the misery and confusion well up inside her, as if she were being ripped in half by her own warring emotions.

The loud bang of a door downstairs interrupted the quiet, and she turned her head sharply toward the doorway of the office. Holding her breath, she waited, listening to footsteps on the stairs. It wasn't until Nathaniel entered the room that she let out her breath in a rush of relief.

He carried a steamer trunk on his back, and he took it into his laboratory, giving her a nod of greeting as he passed. She followed him and watched in puzzlement as he set down the trunk. It hit the floor with a thud.

"What's that?" she asked.

"I've brought over some of my things," he said, pointing to a cot that had been set up against the far wall. A wooden chair and several crates stood beside it. "I'm going to sleep here from now on."

She stared at the cot and realized that he was completely serious. "You're moving in here? But why?"

He pushed the trunk against the wall to get it out of the way. "After what happened last night, you have to ask?"

"I thought we agreed—"

"We did, but what happened last night changes things. I want to make sure it doesn't happen again."

She paled. "You think something like this might happen again?"

"I'm certain of it."

"What makes you so certain?" she asked.

He had to tell her. Honesty and trust. Wasn't that the litany he chanted to her? Nathaniel walked over to one corner and grasped the back of the chair. He pulled it out a few feet. "Sit down. I want to talk to you."

She didn't move. "What makes you so certain?" she repeated.

He circled around to face her over the back of the chair. "Sit down."

Something in his voice told her not to argue. She walked over to him and took the offered chair, as he sat down on one of the crates against the wall. He rested his forearms on his knees and stared down at his clasped hands for a long moment without speaking, then he looked up at her. "Did I ever tell you that my brother and I were partners once?"

She knit her brows in puzzlement. "No. What does that have to do with—"

"My father died when I was twenty," Nathaniel interrupted. "In his will, he left nearly half of Chase Toys to me."

She settled herself more comfortably in her chair. "I thought you said your father didn't have a very high opinion of you."

"He didn't, when I was a boy. He ran Chase Toys, but my grandfather owned it. When he died, my grandfather left it to my father with the stipulation that I be made chief engineer. My father had no choice but to bring me into the firm. I left Cambridge and went to work for Chase Toys. I was nineteen."

He turned his head and stared off into space, remembering. "We had to work together, and my father began to see that I had some good ideas. Adrian was in his last year at Cambridge, so I never saw him, and my father and I developed some mutual respect. That spring, Adrian graduated and came into the company as well. You can't imagine what that was like."

"Yes, I can."

He glanced up at her in surprise.

"I met your brother, remember? A very arrogant man."

Nathaniel acknowledged her comment with a wry smile. "At first, I don't think Adrian considered me a threat to his position. He was the heir, groomed to take over. I don't think he realized our father would ever take me seriously. But when he came into the firm, he saw how our relationship had changed in his absence, and I think it was then that he truly began to hate me. My father died that summer and left nearly half the company to me. Adrian and I became partners. It was a failure from the start."

"What happened?"

"It was the worst two years of my life. If I made a decision, Adrian countermanded it. If I designed a new toy, Adrian refused to manufacture it. He constantly undermined my authority, refused to compromise, and there was nothing I could do. All my life, I'd wanted to be a part of the company, but even after all that had happened, I was still excluded."

"That's why you were so insistent on having fifty-one percent of Elliot's," she murmured. "So I couldn't do to you what Adrian had done."

"Yes. I wanted to have control, because when Adrian and I were partners, I had none. He made all the decisions, and I could only stand by and watch him slowly send Chase into ruin. Finally, I couldn't take it anymore. Adrian offered to buy me out. I took the money and left for America."

"I still don't understand. What does all this have to do with the vandals that broke into the factory?"

"Let me finish." He sighed and leaned back against the wall behind him. "At first, I didn't know what to do. I wandered around for several years, temporarily lost at sea, as it were, trying to figure out what to do with myself. I knew I could never be a part of Chase Toys again."

"So what did you do?"

"I worked for a few toy companies to support myself, but I started working on my own ideas again, at night, until I had enough new inventions for a product line of my own. Then, I took all the money I had and started my own toy company. It failed after a year."

"You told me about that," she reminded him gently.

"Yes, but I didn't tell you why." He took a deep breath. "I kept having problems. Suppliers wouldn't give me credit, shipments of parts kept getting delayed, toys shipped to customers would never arrive. I kept pouring more and more cash into the business, but I finally ran out. The problems bankrupted me."

She stiffened. "I see."

"I just didn't want to start over." He paused, then

added quietly, "All my life I'd been told I was a failure. I finally believed it, and I became convinced that success just wasn't in the cards for me."

She reached out and placed her hand over his. He looked at her and saw understanding in her eyes. He felt a glimmer of hope. "James came to see me. He said he wanted to talk about my ideas. I laughed at him, and told him to leave me alone. He didn't. He told me he wanted to manufacture some of my inventions and proposed a partnership. He believed in me when I didn't even believe in myself. Do you have any idea how much that meant to me?"

He didn't wait for an answer, but went on, "So, we agreed to be partners. James didn't have any capital, of course, and neither did I. To raise the money, I sold the patents on many of my inventions, except the train, of course, and the toys you saw in my flat that day. Then I came to London. You know the rest."

She started to speak, but he pulled his hand from hers and lifted it to stop her. He wanted to finish this, he had to finish it. "At first I didn't see the connection. But when our suppliers started demanding cash on delivery, I began to see what was happening. It was too much of a coincidence that a man should face the exact same difficulties twice."

"What are you saying?"

"It's Adrian, Mara. I think he was responsible for what happened to me before. Suppliers demanding cash up front, delayed shipments, lost product. He's bribing suppliers to delay shipments and refuse us credit. I think he hired someone to break into the factory."

"What? But why?"

"To make things difficult. To delay us. To prevent us from filling orders by Christmas. He can't stand the thought that I might succeed."

"Because we're a competitor?"

"No. Because I'm his brother."

"He hates you that much?"

"Oh, yes." He paused, not knowing how to explain. How could he make her understand what life with a brother like Adrian had been like? "My brother and I never got along. He was always a bully, and when we were boys one of his favorite pastimes was tormenting me."

He looked up at her. "He did it because I let him. As a boy, I never had the courage to stand up to him. Rather than fight, I would walk away. If I got a toy for Christmas, and he wanted it, he took it. Because I let him. When we were in school, he'd destroy my textbooks. Pour ink on my papers. That sort of thing. Because I let him."

"We have to tell the police."

"I've already spoken to Finch. I don't have any evidence, but I've asked him to have the matter investigated, hoping he can find some sort of proof that Adrian is behind what's been happening here."

"But if you don't have evidence, what makes you think your brother is responsible?"

"I just know it. Call it instinct." In spite of everything, her skeptical expression made him want to smile.

"Oh, God." She bent her head and buried her face in her hands. "What are we going to do?"

"We're going to go on. We're going to succeed in spite of him."

Mara opened her mouth to protest, but he forestalled her. "Mara, listen to me. If Finch can find proof of what Adrian's been doing, we can bring charges against him. In the meantime, we have to get our trains into stores. Once the trains start selling, we'll have enough revenue that delays and vandalism won't cripple us. Finch is bound to find something linking Adrian to what's been happening to us eventually. Adrian can't cover his tracks forever. We just have to hang on until then. We have to fight."

"No." She jumped to her feet, and he knew what she was going to say. "We can stop."

This was the moment he had known would come, the moment he dreaded. Nathaniel lifted his gaze to hers and saw the shadows in her eyes. "I can't," he said.

"Yes, we can." She turned away and began to pace back and forth across the room. "We haven't spent all the money. We can go back to making dynamos and generators again. We can repay part of the loan to Joslyn Brothers right now, and make arrangements to repay the rest over the next few months."

He listened to her suggestions, heard the desperation creep into her voice as she paced, and he wanted to give in. He wanted to wrap his arms around her and agree to whatever she asked of him. But slowly, he shook his head. "And let him win? No."

She stopped pacing to look over at him. "Nathaniel, your brother is a viscount. He's influential. He's wealthy and powerful. Even if Finch found evidence, what if it isn't enough? We can't fight him. We might make it through Christmas, or even the first year. But eventually, he'll destroy you." Her voice rose in panic. "He'll destroy both of us. We have to stop now."

"Don't you understand?" He rose to his feet, wishing he could make her see that he couldn't do what she wanted. "I've walked away every time Adrian has tried to intimidate me. I've let him win, I've let him steal away every hope and every dream I ever had. I will not do it again. If I fight him, he'll back down just like any other bully."

"You can't be certain of that. What if he doesn't? It

isn't just your own livelihood you're trifling with. It's mine, and that of all the other people who work here."

"And what would have happened to the livelihoods of all these people if I hadn't come along?"

"Nathaniel, please don't do this. I know how much making trains means to you, but—"

"No." He cut her off in midsentence. She might know, but she could not understand. This wasn't just about trains, this was about his life, his future. If he gave in to her fear, if he let Adrian win, he would face the same battle again and again for the rest of his life. Adrian would never allow him to succeed at anything. If it wasn't trains, it would be something else. He could build dynamos, or make liver pills, or explore Africa, and it wouldn't matter. If it looked like he was going to succeed, Adrian would try to stop him. "I will not let my brother do this to me," he said stubbornly, walking toward her. "I cannot."

He walked past her, unable to look at her and see the fear in her eyes as she asked him to give up the only thing he had ever wanted.

But she followed him, walking over to where he stood and put a hand on his arm. "You told me you loved me."

Don't. He didn't want to hear her say it. *Don't make me choose.*

"Was it just words, Nathaniel?" she asked, her soft voice cutting through him like a knife. "Or did you mean it?"

The future he'd envisioned for them passed vividly across his mind, morning tea and lively debate, soft kisses and nights of lovemaking, waltzing with Mara, flying kites with her, watching her pull on her stockings. "I meant it," he finally said.

"Then stop this now. Give it up."

He closed his eyes, and he heard her play her last card.

"Do it for me."

The idyllic picture shattered like a breaking pane of glass. He opened his eyes and turned to face her. "I can't."

"Yes, you can," she whispered raggedly, dropping her hand to her side.

He shook his head, watching her shoulders droop. "No. He'll try what he tried before, but this time it isn't going to work. I'll circumvent him every way I can, but I won't give up. I'm going to fight."

"With what?" she asked. "For how long?"

He didn't reply, and she turned away with a sound of frustration. Then she suddenly turned back to look up at him again. "You said you first began to see that your brother was responsible yesterday?"

He nodded and watched the icy mask steal over her features. When she spoke again, her voice chilled him. "You knew about this before you . . . before we . . . oh, God."

He knew what she meant. "I was going to tell you, but with the party last night, I didn't get the chance," he said, knowing it sounded like the poor excuse it was. "I was afraid of this," he confessed, reaching for her with a sudden desperation. "I was going to tell you what I suspected when I got back yesterday, but I knew you would look at me just the way you're looking at me now. I kept putting it off all evening, hoping for the right time, hoping to find the right way." His words tumbled out in a rush, trying to stop the inevitable condemnation. It was too late. "Mara, I love you."

"Words again." She pulled back, out of his hold. "You truly love me? Then give this up."

He shut his ears to the pain in her voice. All he could feel was his own. "What about you?" he countered. "You know how important this is to me. You wouldn't ask me to give it up, you'd stand by me and help me find a solution. If you truly loved me."

"It isn't the same thing."

He folded his arms across his chest. "Yes, it is."

"No, it isn't." Her eyes were cold, so cold, like ice on a millpond. "I never said I loved you."

He sucked in his breath as if she'd punched him in the gut, but it was his heart that felt the pain. Her words hung between them, a wall he could not break down. "No, you never did. I guess you never will."

He tore his gaze from hers and walked away. "We are not going to stop," he said, striding for the stairs to the roof. "We are going to make trains, I'm moving in here, and we will not discuss it again."

"Don't I have any say in this?" she demanded. "Partners, remember?"

He halted with one foot on the stair and squared his shoulders, but he didn't look at her. "Fifty-one percent versus forty-nine. Remember?"

"I remember."

He forced himself not to listen to all the bitterness in her voice. "It's late. You'd better go home."

He started up the stairs, but her voice stopped him again.

"Nathaniel?"

He gritted his teeth. "What?"

When she didn't answer, he glanced back at her.

"Aren't—" She cleared her throat and ducked her head, shifting her weight from one foot to the other. "Aren't you going to walk me home?"

His heart hardened, and a blessed numbness washed over him. "No. You're an independent woman. You don't need me. You said so yourself."

She raised her head, and he saw the pain in her face before she turned away and left the office. He'd succeeded in hurting her as she had hurt him, but he felt no sense of triumph.

He went up the stairs, telling himself that he no longer cared what she did. But up on the roof, he stood at the corner and leaned over the parapet, watching her walk up the street and enter the lodging house. He looked at her window, telling himself she was not his responsibility. But he remained standing there until her light came on and she was safely inside her room.

Mara wanted peaceful sleep, but all night, her own bitter words kept repeating themselves in her mind like the rhythmic lash of a whip.

I never said I loved you.

She hadn't meant to say it. But the words had come tumbling from her lips without conscious thought, born of fear and panic and the desperate need to retaliate. They had wounded him deeply, and she felt ashamed now.

He hadn't deserved that. Her words had been thoughtless and cruel, and she wished she could take them back.

I never said I loved you.

Trying to sleep was futile. She got out of bed, shivering at the chill in the air as her bare feet hit the floor. She walked to the window, and the dim light that filtered down into the alley told her dawn was breaking.

She looked up to the third floor of the factory. The lamps were lit, and she could see his silhouette, black against the light behind him. He was playing the violin.

She watched him, almost able to imagine that she could hear the music. But the only thing she heard was the bitterness of her own voice.

I never said I loved you.

She turned away from the window and began to dress. She had to go up there, she had to face him. She couldn't hide in her room all day. But it was nearly an hour later before she finally left her room and walked to the factory. Her footsteps dragged as she climbed the stairs to the second floor. He was still playing the violin, and the music floated down to her, a poignant and lonely melody.

She halted in the doorway. He was still standing by the window behind her desk, and the morning sun caught the polished wood of the violin as he drew the bow across the strings.

He wanted her to believe in him with absolute faith, expected her to follow him with absolute trust, demanded that she love him right or wrong. There had been a time when she could have done it, a time when her heart had overflowed with love and dreams. But that time was gone. Her heart was empty. She could never love like that again.

She wasn't capable of it anymore. She was too cynical, too proud, too afraid. It was too late. She watched him from the doorway, listening to the melancholy tune he played, and her throat clogged with longing. *Why?* she cried out silently. *Why couldn't you have come when I could believe in your dream, when I had more than an empty heart to give you?*

He caught sight of her standing there, and the music stopped. Slowly, he lowered the instrument in his hands.

She struggled for something to say, but she knew she'd already said enough. Her words of the night before hung between them as they looked at each other, neither of them able to forget, neither of them able to relent. The silence lengthened.

I never said I loved you.

His lips tightened, and he turned his back to her. She

pressed one clenched fist to her lips. Behind her hand, she whispered, "I love you."

But he didn't hear her soft confession. A sob rose in her throat, and she stifled it, watching as he walked away, disappearing into the other part of the room without a word, without a backward glance. Mara watched him go, and the pain fractured through her. Too little, and much too late.

Later, during the lunch break, she went out to get a bite to eat for herself, and she thought about asking if he wanted her to bring something back for him, but when she descended the stairs, she caught sight of him having a sack lunch with the workers in the break room.

She paused on the stairs and watched him for a moment through the doorway as he sat talking with the men and women at the table. She thought about joining them once she'd purchased her lunch, but suddenly Nathaniel looked up, laughing. His smile remained for only the briefest moment, then he caught sight of her on the landing, and it faded away.

She waited, but he made no gesture beckoning her into the room, and she knew she couldn't join them. Nathaniel didn't want her there. He didn't want her at all.

She continued down the stairs. When she had purchased her lunch of cold tongue and an apple from Mr. Beckett's cart, she turned and retraced her steps, not pausing to glance into the lunchroom on her way back up the stairs. She ate her lunch at her desk and tried not to care that she ate it alone.

26

By tacit agreement, Mara and Nathaniel avoided each other. She stopped coming into the office early; he stopped bringing morning tea. During the day, she stayed upstairs and watched their cash balance dwindle; he stayed downstairs and watched toy trains come off the production line.

He still spent one hour each evening giving Billy lessons in self-defense. After he had taken the boy home, he resumed work on the production floor with Michael far into the night, while she worked at her desk. He no longer walked her home, but whenever she passed by him on her way out, she knew he followed her far enough to see her enter Mrs. O'Brien's. He was still concerned for her safety, but that gave Mara little consolation because the rest of the time he hardly noticed her at all.

Billy became their only link, traversing the stairs a dozen times a day to report to each of them the everyday happenings of the other. He sensed the tension in the air and knew something was wrong, but his curious inquiries met with no response from either of them. "We're both very busy," became the phrase Billy heard more than any other.

Nathaniel found alternate suppliers, and any vendors that had promised credit and reneged on that promise found their delivery refused. Although the situation provided continual delays, with a bit of ingenuity and a lot of help from Michael, he didn't get too far behind. Mara had scoffed about his use of Lord Barrington's name with Mr. Abercrombie, but the earl proved to be a genuine friend, and allowed Nathaniel to use his name as a reference to get new suppliers every time he was forced to turn away a delivery.

Nathaniel went to the local police station and spoke with Inspector Carlisle himself. The inspector assured him that they were investigating the vandalism, but they had no leads as yet. Nathaniel told Carlisle his own theory about the incident, acknowledging that he had no evidence to support it. The inspector confirmed what Finch had already told Nathaniel, explaining that without proof there was little they could do, but he promised to have his men patrol the area more frequently at night.

Mara grew more tense with each passing day, waiting for Adrian to make his next move. She worried about bankruptcy and dreamed about fire. She fussed over the account books and refused to authorize any unnecessary expenditure. She kept herself informed of every decision made and every problem that came up. She reverted to her old habit of putting tuppence in her tin bank every day, wanting to have at least that if they went bankrupt.

Mara stared down at the little tin bank in her hand. These rituals had once provided her with a feeling of security, but now they gave her surprisingly little comfort.

During the past week, she and Nathaniel had exchanged

scarcely a dozen words. She set the tin can down on her rickety table and sank into a chair. She rested her elbow on the table and her chin in her hand, staring at the door of her flat, remembering the first time she had seen him, standing there motionless, yet burning with energy and life.

Restless, she pushed back her chair and rose. She wandered around the room with no particular purpose in mind, and it was only a few moments before her aimless steps found her once again at the table.

She glanced at the pendant watch that hung around her neck. It was barely seven o'clock in the morning. With Nathaniel sleeping at the factory, she couldn't go in yet. It was too early.

A dull ache began in her midsection and spread through her limbs. When she did go in an hour from now, she'd find him on the production floor with Michael, too busy to give her more than a polite greeting. She'd give him an equally polite reply, then she'd go up to the office, he'd stay downstairs, and that would probably be their only conversation during the entire day.

No. Mara shook off her dark mood with sudden rebellion. There had to be a way that they could bridge this chasm between them, a way they could compromise. She didn't know what the solution was, but she knew one of them had to take the first step.

Twenty minutes later, Mara walked up the stairs of the factory, balancing a laden tea tray from Mrs. O'Brien's kitchen in her hands. "Nathaniel?" she called, entering the office.

He appeared in the doorway, shirtless, a towel slung around his neck and a bit of shaving soap on his chin. He lifted one corner of the towel and slowly wiped away the dab of soap, but he said nothing. His eyes studied her with that piercing intensity.

Looking at him, she longed to toss aside the tray and hurl herself into his arms, to feel him hold her, to tell him she loved him. She took a deep breath and walked over to the table, shortening the distance between them. She set down the tray. "I thought we might have tea," she said. "I thought . . ." She paused and glanced at him, hoping to see him smile.

He didn't.

She tried again. "I thought we might talk a bit."

"What is there for us to talk about?" he asked.

There was something in his voice she'd never heard before, a cold chill that stabbed her like an icicle. She clasped her hands behind her back and looked down at the table, trying to gather her defenses, trying to put on the armor that had once protected her from hurt. But just now, she couldn't seem to find it. "I don't know," she whispered.

She heard his heavy sigh, and she raised her gaze to his face, waiting.

"I can't," he said shortly and turned away. "I have an early meeting."

"Nathaniel, wait!" she cried.

He turned slowly around. "What?"

"I'm sorry about what I said," she whispered. "I didn't mean it."

"Didn't you?" The corners of his mouth lifted in a smile that held no amusement, no teasing mischief. He slowly shook his head. "It doesn't matter anyway. I won't give up my dream for you, and you won't give up your fear for me. So, where does that leave us?"

"I don't know."

"Neither do I." He went back into the other room without another word.

She bit her lip and sank down in the chair, staring at the extra pot of cream she'd brought just for him, knowing he was right. There was nothing for them to talk about. Even if she told him she loved him, it wouldn't matter.

She heard his footsteps, and pride stiffened her spine. She straightened in her chair and poured herself a cup of tea. It took everything she had, but she managed to keep her face expressionless until he had walked past her and left the room.

Only after he had gone, only after his footsteps no longer echoed on the stairs and she was alone, did she allow the desolation and loneliness to overwhelm her. She lowered her face into her gloved hands, loving him for being the man that he was, hating him for not being the man she wanted. But most of all, she hated herself for the pain she had caused him and the fear that made her unable to take it away.

She was not the optimist Nathaniel was. She had no illusions that he could win against his brother's wealth and power. Adrian would destroy what they were trying to build, and Nathaniel would go off to seek new dreams. He might even ask her to follow him, but she knew she could not live that life again. So she would remain here, left to rebuild her life, alone again.

Nathaniel would not be beside her to lighten the burdens. He wouldn't be there to tease her or make her laugh or provide a strong shoulder she could lean on. He wouldn't be there to boost her spirits with his smile or remind her of the magic in everyday things or hold her when life seemed unbearable. He would leave, and that was the most unbearable burden of all.

Nathaniel went downstairs, trying to harden his heart. He'd never been very good at that. But he couldn't have stayed with her, couldn't have borne sitting across from her and drinking tea, loving her without being loved in return. He would not be a beggar, craving one smile, one kind word from a woman who had ice water in her veins. She might truly be sorry for what she'd said, but apologies didn't just make everything better.

It made him angry, this effort of hers to make peace after she'd sliced him wide open. And it hurt. God, it hurt, like salt in the wound.

He'd tried so hard to earn her trust, but it was all for naught. He wanted her love, but it was a futile desire. He never learned. Once again, he wanted too much, hoped too much, expected too much.

A man's reach should exceed his grasp, or what's a heaven for?

The words of Robert Browning echoed through his head, and he wondered wryly if he ought to have them carved into his headstone when he died. He'd had a fleeting glimpse of heaven a week ago—a heaven where Mara loved him and looked at him with faith in her eyes, where his dreams became reality and she stood beside him. But that brief glimpse of heaven, of desires fulfilled and sated peace, was gone now, and Nathaniel knew it was farther from his grasp than it had ever been.

The days of November went by, and the tension built. Continual delays plagued them, but Nathaniel and Michael worked nearly round the clock to keep production from getting too far behind. Nathaniel knew that Mara worked long hours as well, keeping tight control over the expenses, but he also knew she was only doing it because she had no choice.

They hardly spoke to each other. The chasm still lay between them, so deep and so wide that it seemed there was no way to cross. There was nothing that could bridge the differences between them, not even love. There was no way to take back the hurtful, angry words that had been spoken. There was no compromise.

*   *   *

Adrian watched Owen Rutherford leave the study. He took a cigar from the box on his desk and snipped the tip. He then reached for his gold lighter and leaned back in his chair, staring at the polished walnut panels of the door with unseeing eyes.

The news that the private investigator had brought him came as no surprise. Rutherford had confirmed that Nathaniel was digging himself in deeper and deeper, just as Adrian had expected he would.

It had been expensive but not difficult to persuade suppliers that his business was more vital to their interests than Nathaniel's. Styles, too, had proved to be very valuable and had been well paid for his efforts. Now, Nathaniel was scrambling, working day and night, unable to keep production on schedule, plagued by the continual delays and aggravations Adrian put in his path, laying out more and more cash just to stay afloat. Everything was going according to plan.

A slight knock diverted his attention, and he watched the door open.

Honoria walked in, looking chubbier than ever in lemon yellow silk. "Adrian, I thought that man would never leave. Tea is waiting." When he made no move to rise, she gave him an inquiring glance. "Aren't you coming?"

He suppressed a sigh of impatience. "Of course, my dear. I just have a bit more work to do."

She circled the desk to stand beside his chair. "You work too hard. Everyone has arrived, and we are awaiting our host."

"Honoria, please occupy our guests. I'll be in shortly."

"Very well, but after we're married, I'm going to provide you with so many distractions, you'll find it much harder to spend all these hours at your desk."

"My dear, just your presence is distraction enough. I must say, you look lovely in yellow."

Her round blue eyes widened. "My, my. I shall have to wear it more often then."

She walked out of the study, pausing long enough to give him a smile, then departed. The moment the door closed, she vanished from his thoughts.

When Nathaniel had confronted him on the squash court, Adrian had been a bit concerned and more than a bit surprised that his brother had actually figured out he was responsible for all the little inconveniences plaguing Chase-Elliot. That had worried him at first, but over the past few days, he'd revised his opinion on the matter.

When he had forced Nathaniel's company in America to go bankrupt, his little brother hadn't had a clue where all the bad luck was coming from. That had been satisfying because the plan had succeeded, but it was even more satisfying to destroy Nathaniel when the other man knew who was behind his destruction and why. The only thing Nathaniel had not yet figured out was that he was powerless to stop it.

Adrian knew that only a week remained before Nathaniel had to deliver his trains, and his capital was nearly gone. It was time to make his move, the last move in the game. Checkmate. He smiled and lit his cigar.

For the first time in his life, Calvin Styles had money. Fifty guineas were tucked in his pockets, a bloody fortune, and he planned to have a good time spending it. He bought himself a set of clothes. Dressed in his new finery, he strolled into the King's Head, enjoying the stares he received.

Matty pulled a draft of ale for him. "What ye all fancied up for?"

"Had a turn in me luck, Matty, and I'm celebratin'. Made meself a bit o'money, and there be plenty more t'come."

"I'll be damned." Matty set the pint of ale in front of him, and listened as Styles explained about the rich toff who'd hired him for a job.

"Doin' what?" another voice called out. "Bein' a wanker?"

Everyone laughed, but Styles was in too good a mood to let Alfie Logan's insult bother him. He bought drinks for everybody in the pub, including Alfie. He cornered Molly for a kiss or two, and he got roaring drunk. But by the time he was ready to leave, he hadn't spent more than a tiny fraction of the fortune in his pockets.

He downed the last of his ale and tossed a guinea on the table. He winked at Matty. "Keep the change, mate. I've got plenty more where that came from."

When he turned away from the bar and headed for the door, Alfie Logan stepped in his path.

"I want the money you owe me."

Styles laughed. "C'mon, Alfie. Ye knows I paid ye weeks ago."

"You didn't. You still owe me five quid, and I want me money."

The pub quieted as the two men faced each other. Styles was drunk, but he knew perfectly well he'd paid Logan back. He set his jaw stubbornly. "I paid ye just after Michaelmas. It ain't my fault ye lost it gamblin'. I don't owe ye any more. So sod off."

"You never paid me, Cal. You're a liar."

"Nobody calls me a liar."

"I just did."

With those words, several things happened at once. Chairs scraped against the floor as people scrambled to get out of the way; Matty Fletcher yelled, "No fights in my place!"; and Styles slammed his fist into Logan's jaw.

Logan fell back and crashed into a table. Styles sensed his advantage and moved forward, ready to pound the other man into pulp. But before he could take another swing, Logan came up, a knife in his hand.

The knife sank between two of Styles's ribs. He let out a gurgle of surprise as Logan pulled out the knife, but before he could knock the weapon out of the other man's hand, the knife went in again, higher this time. Calvin Styles was dead before he hit the floor.

Matty Fletcher went out the back in search of a policeman, but by the time the officer arrived, the pub was empty, Alfie Logan had disappeared with his five quid and a bit more, and the remainder of Calvin Styles's fifty guineas had found their way into the pockets of several King's Head patrons.

Mara was still working in her office about nine o'clock that night when Inspector Carlisle came to see her. Percy, who was also working late that night, brought him upstairs, then went back to work, leaving them alone as the policeman explained the purpose of his call.

"I'm afraid Billy isn't here, Inspector. Nathaniel—Mr. Chase—took him home about an hour ago."

"I've been by his place, but he wasn't there, ma'am."

"I think they were stopping for ice cream first." Mara looked up at the inspector worriedly. "Is Billy in some sort of trouble?"

The policeman shook his head. "No, I wouldn't say that."

His enigmatic words made her even more concerned. "What is it?"

When he didn't answer, she went on, "Mr. Chase and I have taken an interest in the boy."

"Yes, ma'am," he agreed, shifting his weight from one foot to the other. "I'd heard that. I'd hoped to find him here."

She gestured to the chair opposite her desk. "Perhaps you would care to sit down and tell me what this is about."

"Thank you, ma'am," he said and took a seat. He slumped forward, twirling his hat in his hands. Finally he looked at her. "The boy's father is dead."

"What?" Mara straightened in her chair. "How did this happen?"

"He was stabbed during a fight in the King's Head about two hours ago."

She sucked in a sharp breath. "Are you here to tell Billy?" When the inspector nodded, she asked, "Would you like me to tell him for you?"

He seemed relieved to hand the responsibility over to her. "Thank you, Mrs. Elliot," he said and rose to his feet.

Mara also stood up. "I'll show you out."

He waved her offer aside. "Don't bother. I'll find my way."

"Very well."

"I'll send one of the Salvation Army ladies to collect the boy tomorrow. Is there somewhere he can stay tonight?"

"He can stay with me at Mrs. O'Brien's," she answered before the rest of his words sank in. "The Salvation Army?"

"Yes, ma'am."

"What will happen to Billy?"

"An orphanage, if he's lucky, but it'll probably be the workhouse, I'm afraid. He's got no other relations, near as I can tell."

The workhouse. She shuddered, and everything

inside her rebelled against it. She couldn't let that happen to him. "Would it be possible for me to keep the boy?" she asked, without taking time to think about it.

"What?" The policeman stared at her. "You want to adopt him?"

"Yes," she said firmly. "If that would be possible?"

"I don't see why not. It's most generous of you, but I'm not sure it's wise. Pardon me, ma'am, but these street urchins aren't a desirable lot. He'll give you no end of trouble."

"Thank you, Inspector," Mara answered, "but I've quite made up my mind."

"Mrs. Elliot—"

"I advise you not to argue with her, Inspector."

Both of them looked over at Nathaniel standing in the doorway. He glanced past the policeman to her.

"When Mrs. Elliot makes up her mind, she can be quite stubborn about it," he added.

The inspector put on his hat. "Ladies is like that, sir." He turned to Mara. "Good evening, ma'am. And thank you again."

He walked toward the door, and Nathaniel stepped back from the doorway to let him through. "What happened?" he asked, falling in step beside the inspector as they went down the stairs.

Carlisle told him.

"Nasty business," he commented.

"As you say, sir. But these fellows can't always think straight after a few pints, and Alfie Logan's especially mean after he's had a few."

Nathaniel fell silent for a moment. Then he paused on the stairs and asked, "Where did Styles get this money he was throwing around?"

The inspector also came to a halt and nodded slowly. "That's the question, isn't it, sir? He was bragging about a rich toff who had paid him for a job, but he didn't give any details, and he didn't mention the man's name. Bit of a coincidence, eh?"

Nathaniel didn't think so, and when he met Carlisle's shrewd gaze, he knew the inspector didn't think so either.

Mara had to tell Billy about his father, but when she'd volunteered for the task, she hadn't thought about how hard it would be. Nor had she thought about the responsibility she was taking on by adopting the boy. As she considered these things now, the enormity of it all engulfed her.

"Do you want me to tell him?"

She looked up as Nathaniel came back into the office and walked to her desk. Taking a deep breath, she shook her head and rose. "No," she answered, circling her desk and walking past him. "I said I would do it, and I will. I'd better go now, before he hears it from somebody else."

He put a hand on her shoulder and gently turned her around. "You won't do it alone. I'm going with you."

Mara saw the steady determination in his blue eyes and felt an overwhelming rush of relief, gratitude, and love. Love, most of all. Never had she loved him more than she did at this moment. Impulsively, she stepped forward and walked into his arms, feeling the strength of him flow into her as he wrapped his arms around her. "Thank you," she whispered against his shirt.

He held her for a long time. When he let her go, he took her hand in his, and they made the short walk to Old Castle Street together.

Mara had not been back to Billy's flat since the first day they'd found him, but nothing had changed. The lodging house was still filthy, and she didn't need a light to know it. The smell was enough. They walked up the dark stairs silently and entered the small room at the end of the corridor.

Billy was in bed and did not awaken at the sound of the door creaking open or the sound of Nathaniel fumbling in the dark for the candle. But when Nathaniel lit the candle, he stirred.

"Dad?" he asked. He sat up, and his sleepy expression changed to one of bewilderment at the sight of the two figures in the room. "Nathaniel? Mrs. Elliot?" He raised one fist to rub his eyes, and he yawned. "What ye doin' 'ere? Me dad'll be mad if 'e sees ye."

Mara stepped forward and sat down gingerly on the edge of the cot. She took his small hands in hers. "Billy, I'm afraid I have some bad news."

He lifted his freckled face to hers and yawned again. "What?"

She glanced over her shoulder at Nathaniel, who remained motionless by the door, the candle in his hand. He nodded encouragingly, and she looked down at the boy again. "Billy, your father died tonight."

Billy stared at her, frowning in confusion. "Me dad?"

"Yes." There was no other way to say it. "He was killed during a fight in the pub a few hours ago."

Billy didn't speak, he just stared at her. She pulled one of her hands free and brushed back a lock of his hair. "I'm going to take you home with me. Is that all right?"

"I guess so." His voice was indifferent, devoid of emotion. "Me dad's really dead? Ye mean 'e ain't comin' back?"

"No." She gently caressed his cheek.

Billy's eyes grew round as he tried to accept the finality of this news. He turned his head toward the wall and stared at the silhouette of the flickering candle. "Me mum died, too. She didn't come 'ome neither 'cause they took her away. Dead's forever, ain't it?"

Tears stung her eyes, and she squeezed his hand. "I'm afraid so, love."

He looked back at her. "They goin' t'take me dad away, too?"

"Yes. They'll bury him."

"In the ground?" When she nodded, she saw a change come over his face. The bewildered innocence disappeared, and his expression hardened to angry defiance. "I don't care what they does with 'im. I hope they dig a real deep 'ole, and I 'ope the worms get 'im, I do! I do!" His face puckered, and he yanked his hand out of hers. But instead of jumping from the cot to run away as she thought he might, he suddenly hurled himself into her arms, sobbing. "I don't care what they does with 'im. I don't care!"

She wrapped her arms around his thin shoulders and held him tight as he clutched her shirtwaist and sobbed out his grief and fury. She rocked back and forth, helpless to do more.

Nathaniel came and knelt down beside the cot, facing her. She stared at him over the boy's head, seeing him through a blurry haze, and she realized she was crying, too.

Nathaniel said nothing. He just reached out his free hand and gently wiped her tears away.

27

Mara was awakened in the middle of the night by a frightened cry, and although it was a sound she hadn't heard in a long time, she knew instantly what it was. She was out of bed and down on the floor beside Billy's pile of blankets in a second.

"It's all right, sweeting," she murmured. He reached up his arms and she sat down on the floor to pull him into her lap. "Were you having a nightmare?"

"It was awful," he mumbled. "It was the worms."

"Worms?" One arm tightened around him, and she ran her fingers through his hair in a soothing motion.

He nodded and snuggled closer to her, shaking like a leaf in the wind. "The worms was eatin' me dad," he wailed. "I saw 'em."

She held him even tighter at the horrible images he had seen in his dream, images that would terrify anyone. "It must have been awful. But it was just a dream."

"They started eatin' me. It was scary."

"I know. Worms don't really eat people," she added, hoping she wasn't lying to him.

"They don't?"

"No. They eat dirt." It sounded logical enough.

"Oh." Billy seemed to accept her word for it. He said nothing more, but he was still trembling with fear.

She held him tight, rocking him. How many times had she soothed Helen in just this same way, chasing away dragons and monsters with hugs and soothing words. She used to hum to Helen, too. What was the song?

She rested her cheek against the boy's hair, and began to hum the melody of "Barbara Allen," feeling the fierce protective love flowing from her heart like water from a mountain spring. She kept humming until Billy's small body stopped shaking and his fists didn't cling so tightly to her nightgown.

She pulled back a little. "Feel better?"

He sniffed. "Yes."

"Good. Let's get you tucked in again."

"I don't want worms in me bed. Could we 'ave the light on and make sure they're not really there?"

She almost smiled. "Of course."

She stood up and fumbled in the darkness for the lamp on the table and the box of matches. Then she lit the lamp, turning the knob until the light was as bright as it could be and filled every corner of the room.

She turned and found Billy standing beside her, staring at her hands.

Her first impulse was to hide them, but she didn't. She remained still, her hands curled around the base of the lamp.

"What 'appened to yer hands?"

"I was in a fire once, and I was burned. Now I have

scars." She glanced at him and saw the thoughtful frown on his face.

"It's a bit like me, ain't it, ma'am?"

She watched him touch his fingers to the birthmark on his cheek. "Yes," she answered, "I suppose it is."

She grabbed the handle of the lamp and carried it to the twisted pile of blankets on the floor. She made a great show of searching for worms before she picked up the pile of quilts and moved it even closer to her own narrow bed. There, she spread them out, one on top of the other, until it was once again a mattress of sorts, then she pulled back the top one. "In you go."

He dived into his makeshift bed, and she pulled the quilt up to his chin.

"Do people say mean things to ye about yer hands?" he asked.

"No, Billy, because I wear gloves most of the time. But if I didn't, they probably would."

"Then it ain't the same as me after all." She looked at him in puzzlement and watched as he rubbed a hand over his cheek. "I can't hide me mark with gloves."

"No," she whispered and leaned over to press a kiss to the birthmark. "I suppose not. Good night, Billy."

"Good night, ma'am."

She carried the lamp back over to the table and turned it off. Then she stepped carefully over the boy, and climbed into her own bed. She closed her eyes, remembering the night Nathaniel had removed her gloves and taken down her barriers, leaving her nothing to hide her scars or shield her heart. She lifted her hand above the sheet and pressed her lips to the palm of her hand just as he done that wondrous night, wishing he could be beside her to do it again.

"Ma'am?"

Billy's voice broke the silence, and she reached down to give his shoulder a squeeze. "Yes?"

He grabbed her hand and clung to it. "Am I really going to stay with you from now on?"

"Yes."

"Bloody smashin'."

Billy fell asleep almost immediately. But when Mara woke the next morning, the boy was still clinging to her hand as if, even in sleep, he needed to know she was there.

She took him down to Mrs. O'Brien's kitchen for breakfast, and soon the landlady was happily cooking bacon, eggs, and toast. Billy watched, asking every few seconds if it was ready yet. Mara thought it a very good sign that the boy was so hungry.

Mara laughed. "Billy, it's going to be a few minutes yet. Why don't you go over to the factory and see if Nathaniel might want some breakfast?"

He was out the back door in a flash, and by the time Mrs. O'Brien was ready to dish up the food, the boy was back, dragging Nathaniel by the hand.

Mara gave him a smile of greeting, and he answered it with a smile of his own, a smile that gave her hope for the first time in days. No matter what the outcome of his battle with Adrian, she wished they could regain the closeness they had once shared.

They ate in Mrs. O'Brien's tiny dining room as if they were a family. Mara watched Nathaniel and Billy as they sat side by side and talked about trains. The landlady bustled around the table, refilling their plates, looking happier than Mara had ever seen her.

"I'm going to help the employees pack train sets today," Nathaniel told the boy.

"Can I be an em-ploy-ee, too?" Billy asked, pronouncing the word carefully.

"Of course. How about if you stand at the end of the line and check each train set to make sure nothing is missing? I'll pay you . . ." He thought for a moment, then said, "A penny per set. How's that?"

"Smashin'!" Billy swallowed his last mouthful of eggs and shoved back his empty plate, then jumped to his feet and started for the kitchen. "Let's go, Nathaniel. Time's a'wastin' and we got to go t'work. 'Bye Mara. 'Bye Mrs. O'Brien."

Nathaniel lifted his teacup, his eyes meeting Mara's over the rim. "I think I just officially hired him as an employee, partner."

Something fluttered inside her at the tone of his voice. "A part-time employee," she answered in a firm whisper. "He's going to go to school."

Nathaniel gulped down the last swallow of tea, and rose. He set the cup back in its saucer and gave her a mock salute. "Yes, ma'am."

She and the landlady followed them through the kitchen as far as the back door of the lodging house. There, she leaned in the doorway, watching Nathaniel being dragged up the steps of the fire escape by a very enthusiastic boy, both of them laughing.

"By Mary and all the saints, it does me heart good t'see that."

Mara glanced over at the landlady, who was standing behind her, peering over her shoulder. Once again Mara looked across the alley at Nathaniel and Billy and couldn't agree more. It did her heart good to see it, too, and she realized she'd been very wrong about herself.

Her heart wasn't empty at all. A man and a boy had somehow sneaked in, had managed to get past every barrier and wall in their way, and had filled her heart with love again, filled it until there was no room for fear.

*   *   *

Calvin Styles was buried the following morning in Tower Hamlets, the same public cemetery where his wife had been buried the year before. Mara and Nathaniel attended the brief graveside service with Billy between them. Emma Logan was also in attendance, looking much older and sadder than her twenty-five years. No one else came.

Billy's face betrayed no emotion as the body was lowered into the grave, but he squeezed Mara's hand very tight when they dropped in the first handful of dirt.

Afterward, Mara and Nathaniel had a brief whispered consultation and agreed that keeping busy was the best thing for the boy. It was Saturday afternoon and the factory was closed, but they set him to work checking the train sets already awaiting delivery, a task that occupied much of his weekend.

Mara bought a cot for him to sleep on and placed it right beside her own bed, just in case his nightmares returned. When they did, she was there to soothe him with a comforting touch or hug.

Monday morning, Nathaniel drafted a letter to all the retailers who had agreed to purchase train sets, informing them that trains would be delivered to their warehouses by Friday. Percy typed the letters, and Nathaniel sent Billy out to post them with enough money to buy stamps.

Proud to be in charge of something really important like letters and money, Billy raced to the post office and completed his errand. Eager to tell Nathaniel, he ran all the way back and turned the corner into the alley beside Elliot's at full speed. When he found Jimmy Parks and his friends playing marbles beside the fire escape, he skidded to a halt, his pride in his accomplishment replaced by a sick feeling of dread.

Jimmy spied him and swaggered forward, pushing the other two boys aside. "Well, if it ain't Spotty Face," he drawled and pulled at the brim of the too-small cap that sat atop his head.

Billy swallowed hard, knowing what he had to do. He faced the larger boy, spreading his legs wide apart in fighting stance just as Nathaniel had taught him, his heart pounding like a piston on one of Nathaniel's steam engines. "I don't like it when y'call me that, Jimmy. And I want me cap back."

Algernon was hungry. He made his demand for food known to Mara by sitting by her chair and letting out a series of loud and indignant meows.

"In a minute," she told the kitten, her fingers moving rapidly over the beads of her abacus. "I want to finish this first. It won't take long."

She continued adding up the column of figures. She had to finish the December budget today so that she and Nathaniel could make some decisions tonight about expenditures. Their cash balance was very low, and if they didn't cut their expenses somehow, they'd be overdrawn before revenue from the trains started coming in.

As she worked, she tried to remain oblivious to Algernon's protests. But the kitten meowed so loudly and persistently that she lost count three times and finally gave up.

"All right, all right!" She pushed aside her abacus and stood up, laughing in capitulation. "Food first."

Nathaniel and Billy often used the fire escape as a shortcut to Mrs. O'Brien's. Mara usually did not, finding the drop to the ground difficult to navigate in a skirt. Today, however, she decided expedience was more important than decorum. She opened the door onto the fire escape, but froze in the doorway at the sight in the alley below.

Billy was facing another boy as two others looked on, and she knew immediately what was happening. All her protective instincts came to the fore, and she stepped forward to start down the fire escape, but Nathaniel's words came back to her. *He has to be able to stand up to those boys on his own.*

She pressed one clenched fist to her mouth, and watched with all the fear and agony of a mother as the larger boy stepped forward and gave Billy a shove.

But Billy didn't move. He stood straight and unshaken, a frown of fierce concentration on his face. "I want me cap, Jimmy," she heard him say.

Jimmy lifted the cap and waved it in front of Billy, but when Billy tried to grab it, Jimmy jerked it back out of reach. "Come an' get it, Spotty Face."

Billy stepped forward and reached for it again. Jimmy pulled it back and moved to hit him with his free hand, but Billy was ready for that. He blocked the blow and slammed his fist into the other boy's stomach.

Mara bit down on her knuckles and watched in silent agony as the fight began in earnest. Jimmy threw himself at the other boy, but Billy stepped back and kicked him in the teeth. The blow sent Jimmy sprawling backward to the ground.

"Bloody 'ell." Jimmy got up and shook his head from side to side, dazed, but not yet defeated. Moving toward him to continue the fight, Billy locked his legs around the other boy's and pulled him down as well.

They rolled across the cobblestones, but when they hit the factory wall, Billy was on top. He gave Jimmy a solid punch to the jaw. "I've learned 'ow t'fight, Jimmy. Give in or I'll darken yer daylights. I swear I will."

Jimmy tried to throw him off, but Billy punched him again and he gave a grunt of pain. "'elp me, lads!" he cried, appealing to the other two boys for assistance.

The two watching the fight looked at each other and shook their heads. Davy Boggs seemed to speak for both of them when he said, "Not this time, Jimmy. Fight yer own fight."

"Bloody cowards!" he screamed back in fury. "I don't need yer 'elp anyway."

He managed to throw Billy off, but before he could get to his feet, Billy knocked him flat again. Fists clenched, he stood over his opponent, ready to go another round, if necessary. "Give, Jimmy! Say ye give."

The other boy stared sullenly up at him and didn't answer. But when Billy moved to begin the fight again, Jimmy held up his hands in defeat. "All right!" he shouted. "I give! I give! Stop punchin' me, ye bastard!"

Billy stepped back and allowed Jimmy to scramble to his feet. Keeping his eye on the other boy, he bent down to pick up the cap that had fallen during the struggle. He settled it on his head. "Get outta 'ere, Jimmy Parks, and don't never try t'fight with me again."

Mara watched as Jimmy Parks wiped the blood from his nose and turned away, running out of the alley, one of the other two boys right behind him. Davy Boggs was the one who remained behind.

Billy stared at him warily, but Davy made no move to fight. Instead, he said, "I didn't like what Jimmy's been doin' to ye."

Billy didn't relax. With fists still clenched and ready, he faced Davy. "If ye didn't like it, how come ye never 'elped me?"

Davy shoved his hands into the pockets of his

knickers. "Guess I never 'ad the nerve. I'm real sorry, Billy."

Abruptly, he turned and raced out of the alley, leaving Billy standing alone but victorious.

He looked up and found Mara watching from the top of the fire escape. Then he grinned and gave her a thumbs-up sign just as Nathaniel might have done. She gave a sigh of relief and mirrored the gesture. She smiled back at him, her heart threatening to burst with pride. The realization hit her with sudden force.

Nathaniel had been right all along. Some risks were worth taking, and some things were worth fighting for.

28

After his morning squash game, Adrian Chase visited his new bankers. Milton Abercrombie was flattered and pleased that Lord Leyland had deigned to visit the bank in person, but his pleasure quickly changed to alarm at the viscount's first words.

"I have come about a very serious matter, sir."

"Oh, dear." Abercrombie made a worried, fluttering motion of his hand. "Please sit down, my lord."

Adrian took the offered chair opposite the banker's desk. "This is a grave situation," he said, settling back in the chair. "I felt it required my personal attention."

"Is—" The banker licked his suddenly dry lips. "Is something wrong?"

"When I first came to you, I was confident that your bank would be able to provide me with investment opportunities that were both profitable and secure." Adrian looked down and studied his manicured hands.

"But I fear my confidence may have been misplaced. I have . . . concerns about your solvency."

Abercrombie was aghast. "We have been in business for over forty years, and there has never been a run on our bank. I assure you, we are one of the safest banks in England."

"Nonetheless, I feel compelled to discuss my concerns with you."

"Of course," the banker murmured faintly.

"You must understand, I will soon be responsible for a substantial fortune. When I marry in April, I will need to be completely satisfied that your bank is safe before I place any further investments with you."

Adrian Chase's money—or lack of money, if the rumors were true—was not crucial to the bank's business. But his future control of Honoria Montrose's millions and the promise that those funds would be funneled through Joslyn Brothers was another matter entirely.

Abercrombie hastened to put the viscount at ease. "My lord, you may be assured that we make our financial decisions very carefully. We would never put the investments of our clients at risk."

"Indeed?" Adrian leaned forward. "I find myself doubting that, sir."

Abercrombie's hands began to shake. "I am dismayed that you should feel that way. What has brought about these apprehensions?"

"I have recently been informed that my brother has taken a loan with your firm, and I know that he actually used my name as a reference."

Adrian knew nothing of the sort, but Abercrombie's reply confirmed that his guess was an accurate one.

"He mentioned you, my lord. Yes, indeed."

Adrian shook his head. "I cannot believe he had the gall."

"I . . . I'm not quite . . . quite certain I understand," the banker stammered, his uneasy feeling rapidly eroding into panic.

"My brother is an irresponsible fool, sir. When our father died, he unwisely left forty-nine percent of Chase Toys to Nathaniel. If it had not been for me, my brother would have bankrupted the company. Most of the difficulties I face today are a direct result of his foolish decisions."

"My lord, I had no idea!"

Adrian sighed. "It's not something I would wish to have widely known. I trust you will keep this information to yourself?"

"Of course, my lord. I shall be most discreet."

"I hope so. It would be most unfortunate if I were forced to take my business elsewhere. It would be even more unfortunate if, when I marry, I would be unable to bring my wife's investments here. I require discretion and safety from my bankers, sir."

"I understand, my lord." Abercrombie nodded several times for emphasis. "What can I do to reassure you that your investments and that of Lady Leyland would be completely safe here?"

Adrian set his jaw and hardened his expression. "Call my brother's loan."

"Oh, dear." The banker clucked like a distressed hen. "I'm not at all certain we can do that, my lord. It is not our policy to call a loan without cause. Perhaps—"

"Then let me provide you with cause, sir. My brother falsely used my name as a reference, because he couldn't possibly have gotten this loan any other way. Why, his own suppliers won't even give him thirty days' credit."

"What?"

Adrian was quick to press his advantage. "They are demanding cash on delivery, sir. It's appalling that your bank would be so gullible. East End tin vendors and brass foundries can spot a fraud more easily than you."

"Oh, my." Abercrombie's voice was a squeak.

"You can see, I'm sure, that this situation is at the root of my concerns. I have money on account with you and it frightens me that my money could be at risk because your bank makes poor decisions. I need reassurance that all my future investments with you will not be in jeopardy."

He paused to let those words sink in. Then he once again made his demand. "Call his loan."

Abercrombie straightened in his chair. "I understand, my lord. I'll see to it immediately."

Adrian smiled, a tiny, ironic smile of satisfaction. "Yes, I thought you would."

Later that morning, while Mara was working in her office, a messenger came with a letter from Joslyn Brothers addressed to both Nathaniel and herself. Puzzled that the bank would send a letter so urgent that it could not be delivered by post, she opened it and frowned in disbelief at the typewritten words. Her disbelief changed to alarm, then numb shock as she read the letter through several more times.

"You should've seen it, Nathaniel. Jimmy ran like a scared rabbit! An' I got me cap back an' everything."

Billy's enthusiastic recounting of the story interrupted her fourth reading of the letter as Nathaniel and Billy entered the office together.

Nathaniel noticed the expression on her face. "Mara, what is it?"

She turned to the boy. "Billy, I want you to go to Mrs. O'Brien's and get some milk for Algernon."

"Right now?" Billy frowned, puzzled. "We already fed

'im this mornin'. Remember? After me fight with Jimmy, you sent me for the milk—"

"Now."

The hard edge of her voice startled him. "Yes, ma'am." He departed without another word.

Nathaniel crossed over to her desk. "What's wrong?"

She thrust the letter at him. "Joslyn Brothers is calling our loan," she said, and as she spoke the words aloud, she began to shake.

"What?" He took the paper from her trembling fingers and read it quickly, then crumpled the paper into a ball and tossed it onto the desk. "That bastard," he muttered to himself.

"How did he manage it?" Mara rubbed her hand around the back of her neck, feeling a headache coming on, feeling the old, familiar panic. "Joslyn Brothers has an impeccable reputation. He couldn't have bribed them."

"Couldn't he have?" Nathaniel gave a heavy sigh and raked a hand through his hair. "I'm sure the idea of all Honoria Montrose's money coming to their bank in the future was incentive enough to cooperate."

"Who?"

"Honoria Montrose, the American heiress. Adrian's engaged to her. They're to be married in April."

"Oh, no." Mara groaned and buried her face in her hands.

Nathaniel stared down at her bent head, knowing he had to do something. Finch was still trying to find the evidence they needed to put a stop to Adrian's schemes. But to do that, the solicitor needed time, and time had just run out. Barely able to control the rage and frustration he had been keeping in check for so many years, Nathaniel turned away and headed for the door. "I'll be back later."

"Where are you going?" she cried, but he did not answer.

He walked out of the office, slamming the door behind him, and left the factory. He hailed a cab, giving the driver the address of the Chase Toy Company. He formed no strategy, he made no plan. His anger was in control of him now, and the only thought on his mind was wrapping his hands around his brother's throat. He found it a very tempting notion.

It was galling to see Adrian's secretary show no surprise at his arrival, but it was adding insult to injury when the secretary said, "Yes, sir. Lord Leyland has been expecting you."

He followed the secretary down the long corridor to the door at the end. After a soft knock, the secretary opened the door to announce him.

Nathaniel walked in, and Adrian rose from behind the polished mahogany desk. Nathaniel gritted his teeth at his brother's triumphant smile of greeting.

"Good morning, little brother. What brings you here?"

Nathaniel was in no mood for trite small talk. He yanked out one of the upholstered chairs opposite Adrian's desk and sat down, uninvited. "Let's forget the polite preliminaries, shall we? I told you before and I'll tell you again, it's not going to work."

"But of course it's going to work, because you're out of options." Adrian's smile widened as he leaned back in his chair. "When do you leave?"

"Leave? What makes you think I'm going anywhere?"

"You don't have much choice, do you? I heard that Joslyn Brothers called your loan. Your company is ruined, you're facing bankruptcy."

"I have no intention of going anywhere," Nathaniel said through clenched teeth. "I'll get the money somewhere. Your plots and schemes are not going to ruin me."

Adrian's eyes narrowed. "They already have. Pack your bags and be on the first ship out of Dover. Face it, Nathaniel. You just can't win."

"That's it, isn't it? Always a need to prove to yourself that you're a better man, a more successful man, a more brilliant man than I. You set up this competition between us the day I was born, and it's an obsession with you." His lip curled with contempt. "You're sick, Adrian. Sick, obsessed, and rather pitiful, actually."

Adrian did not react to the taunt. "My reasons, my motives are not at issue here. You will leave England, Nathaniel, and you will never come back. In addition, you will give me your word that you will never go into competition against me again."

"What?" Nathaniel gave an incredulous laugh and stared at his brother. "Do you really believe I would make you such a promise? And what makes you think my word is worth anything anyway?"

"Really, little brother, you're so childishly honest, so ethical, it's almost embarrassing." He paused, then gave Nathaniel a pitying smile and added, "You see, I know you. I know that if you give me your word, you won't break it."

"You're right, I wouldn't. But it doesn't matter, since I'm not going to." He returned the smile with a bland one of his own. "Go to hell."

Nathaniel saw the rage flicker in his brother's eyes, the only sign that his words had any impact.

"I can see I have not made the situation clear to you," Adrian said softly. "I can understand your ridiculous stubbornness, it's so typical of you. You'll hang on to your idiotic notions until the end of your days, even after I've proven time and again that you will never be able to compete with me. But would you really sacrifice your lovely partner by your stubbornness?"

Nathaniel felt dread clench his insides. "What do you mean?"

Adrian clasped his hands together on top of the desk. "Let's remove the gloves, shall we? If you don't give up this stupid train idea, if you don't leave England, if you don't stop competing with me, I will not only destroy you, I will destroy her." His eyes locked with Nathaniel's. "If you find the money to pay back Joslyn Brothers, I'll simply bide my time and find another way. It's that simple. With my future wife's money, I will have unlimited resources. I'll destroy this little company of yours eventually."

Nathaniel shook his head. "I'll stop you. What you're doing is extortion and blackmail, and I'll find a way to prove it."

"Who would believe you?" Adrian leaned forward. "You see, Nathaniel, your reputation precedes you. Every man of influence in London knows what a bizarre eccentric you are. Your accusations will merely be regarded as the ramblings of a madman."

For the first time in his life, Nathaniel found himself cursing his own careless disregard for society and all it represented. "It doesn't matter what you do to me. And I'll take care of Mara."

"How?" Adrian countered with a complacent smile. "I'll make certain you won't be able to find a job as an errand boy. What kind of future will you be able to offer Mrs. Elliot then? Will you condemn not only yourself to a life of poverty, but her as well?"

Nathaniel stared at his brother, knowing Adrian meant what he said. His mind worked furiously, desper-

ately, but he could see no way out. Even if he could think
of a way to prevent this crisis, Adrian would simply find
another way. Mara had tried to tell him that, but he had
refused to listen, had refused to admit defeat when it
was staring him in the face. He'd been fooling himself by
thinking Adrian would back down. Now, looking into
his brother's hate-filled eyes, he knew that was purely
wishful thinking.

If he kept fighting, Mara would be the one to lose.
She'd lose the company she had worked so hard to build
and the security that meant so much to her. With Adrian
dogging his heels, there was no way he could provide a
life for her. He thought of all that her husband had put
her through, all the pain and fear, and he knew he could
not do that to her. There was only one way out.

"All right, Adrian," he said abruptly, before he could
change his mind. "You win." He ignored the gleam of
triumph in his brother's eyes, and went on, "You've told
me you want me to leave England. I will. You've told me
to promise that I won't make toys anymore. I give you
my word, I won't. I agree to your demands." He straightened in his chair and leaned forward. "Now, let me tell
you what I want in return."

"What you want?" Adrian's brows rose in surprise.
"You're hardly in a position to make demands."

"Leave Mara alone. I want your word that you'll leave
her be, that you won't interfere in her life in any way.
Ever." Nathaniel set his jaw. "I intend to keep a close
watch on her to make certain you keep your word. You
break your promise, Adrian, and I swear, I'll drag you
through hell and back."

"An empty threat. What can you do to me?"

"Anything I can think of. You, of all people should
know how inventive I can be. If you do anything to
Mara, if any convenient misfortunes occur in her life, I

swear, I'll come after you. I'll start up another toy company, and if you bankrupt it, I'll start another. I'll torment you until the end of your days."

"And break your word?"

"For Mara's sake, I'd break my word to the devil himself. Don't underestimate me, Adrian. You've done that before, and it's always cost you." He leaned back in his chair. "That's my offer. Take it or leave it."

Adrian was silent for a long moment as he considered Nathaniel's offer. Finally, he nodded. "All right. She's no threat to me in any case. For the sake of convenience and expediency, I promise you I will not interfere with Mrs. Elliot's life in any way, provided she never goes into competition against me. As long as she goes back to making her little dynamos or whatever they are, I'll leave her be. I give you my word. Are we agreed?"

"Not quite. There's one other minor point to be settled."

Adrian gave a sigh of long suffering. "What?"

"You will pay off the loan to Joslyn Brothers in full."

"You must be joking!" Adrian said, clearly astonished. "Why should I?"

"Because I still have something you want."

"You've already agreed to give me everything I want."

"Not quite everything," Nathaniel answered softly. "What about the train, Adrian?"

Adrian stiffened, and Nathaniel pressed his advantage. "I'll bet you're foaming at the bit to get your hands on my train."

The other man made a grimace of distaste at the description. "It has possibilities, yes."

"Possibilities, hell. It's a surefire money-maker, and you know it. How long have toy makers been struggling to design sectional track that doesn't send the train flying off the rails when it hits the curves? It's been a couple months since you learned I had a sectional track, and I'm sure you put your engineers to work on it right away. I'll bet they still don't have the geometry right. Trust me, it'll take them years. I want that loan paid off, Adrian. If it isn't, Mara will still be forced into bankruptcy. I won't let that happen."

"In exchange for the train, I'll tell the bank to reverse their decision. She won't go bankrupt."

"Not good enough. My price for the design specifications and the patent is seven thousand pounds payable to Joslyn Brothers, Limited."

Adrian pulled his lower lip between his teeth and stared at him for a long moment. "Very well," he finally agreed. "When you bring me the patent, you get the money. I'll wait at my home in Mayfair."

"I'll have my solicitor draw up the papers signing over the patent to you, and he will bring them to you there. He will also pick up the draft. I'll be on a ship out of Dover, remember?"

Nathaniel rose. Adrian held out his hand to seal their bargain, and Nathaniel took it.

He could see all his dreams crumbling into dust. After leaving the building, he paused on the front sidewalk and stared at the factory where many of his dreams had begun so long ago, where they now ended.

He shoved his hands in his pockets and walked up Tottenham Court Road, looking for a cab that would take him to Finch's office in Bloomsbury. He felt sick at heart, but he knew that he'd done the only thing possible. Mara's future was now secure, and that was all that mattered. Once the loan was paid off, her company would be solvent. Once he was gone, she would be no threat to his brother. She would be safe, and her future would be secure. Somehow, he'd find the money to hire private detectives so he could be sure she remained that way.

For himself, Nathaniel made no plans. He was adrift

once again, cut off from his dream. He was in love with a woman he could never have. He had just traded away his dreams and his future for her security. To protect her, he would have willingly given his life. Perhaps he had.

29

Mara stared at Finch in astonishment. "He's what?"

"He has signed over his control to you, and he has forfeited all rights to the company." The solicitor handed her a stack of documents across the desk. "He made a deal with his brother."

"I don't believe it!" she burst out, rising from her chair. "Nathaniel would never leave me in this kind of trouble."

"His last action as controlling partner was to sell the patent on the train to Adrian for a draft of seven thousand pounds payable to Joslyn Brothers. As soon as I take these documents to Lord Leyland and pick up the bank draft, the company will be yours alone, free of debt and unencumbered."

Mara took the papers, but her gaze remained on the man before her. "You went along with this crazy scheme?"

"Mara, he insisted. He wanted to be certain you would have security."

Security. There had been a time when that had been all that she wanted or expected from life. It seemed so tame now, so unutterably dull.

She looked up at Finch. "Is my signature required on these documents?"

"No. Based on your partnership agreement, Nathaniel has the power to do this without your authorization. However, as part of the deal, Lord Leyland insists on your promise not to make toys or go into competition against him."

"I see," she murmured. "How convenient for him."

"He demanded that Nathaniel give him the same promise. Nathaniel agreed." Finch paused, then added, "He also made Nathaniel agree to leave England and never come back."

"Leave?" she whispered. "He's going to leave?"

Finch nodded, and she lowered her gaze to the papers in her hands, staring at Nathaniel's scrawling signature on the first document, recognizing it even though her hands were shaking so badly, all the other words were a blur. She set down the papers and sank slowly back into her chair, unable to speak, her mind unable to muster the clarity required to form words.

Finch sat down in the opposite chair. "You'll be all right, my dear. You and the little boy. Nathaniel saw to that."

Yes, she'd be all right. She'd have safety and security. Billy would be all right. She'd be able to see that he never went hungry or wore ragged clothes again. They would survive. They would exist.

Once, that would have been enough. But Nathaniel had come along and changed all that. Existing was no longer enough. She wanted to fly kites. She wanted to dance and laugh and get married and have more children. She wanted Nathaniel.

Haven't you ever wanted anything so badly, you were willing to gamble all you had to make it happen?

When he had first asked her that question, her answer had been no. But now, when she asked herself that question, the answer was yes. It was time to risk it all. Abruptly, Mara rose to her feet. "Where is he?"

The solicitor shook his head. "I don't know."

"He wouldn't leave without telling me," she murmured, hoping it was true. "And he'd have to pick up his things."

She thought about it for a few moments and made several quick decisions. "Finch, I have to go out for a little while. On my way down, I'll send Michael up here, and I want you to tell him everything you've told me."

She gathered up the documents the solicitor had given her and shoved them into her portfolio, then headed for the door. "The two of you are to wait for Nathaniel, and when he arrives, keep him here until I return."

"What are you going to do?"

She didn't reply because her answer would have alarmed the solicitor.

She was going to jump off a cliff. She could see the edge before her and she knew it was a long way to fall if she failed. She didn't care. She was going to jump off that cliff and grab for castles in the air. She could only pray that Nathaniel would be there to catch her.

Adrian went back to his home in Mayfair and waited in his study for Nathaniel's solicitor to arrive. He had promised Honoria he would spend the afternoon at Kensington Gardens with her, but he'd sent an apologetic note canceling those plans. Savoring victory over Nathaniel was more enjoyable than strolling through a rose arbor with his vacuous fiancée.

He occupied his time making plans for his new train, and he found that quite a pleasant diversion, but when several hours had gone by and Nathaniel's solicitor had still not arrived with the documents finalizing their deal, he began to grew restless. What was taking so long?

He stoked the fire in the grate. He browsed through the bookshelves but found nothing there to occupy him. When the clock struck five and a maid brought him tea, his restlessness grew into annoyance. How long did it take to draw up some simple business documents?

He paced back and forth, ignoring his tea, and he began to feel uneasy. What if Nathaniel had changed his mind? What if he'd found some fool to rescue him? Adrian thought about those possibilities for a moment, then discarded them. No, Nathaniel had given his word and his hand on the deal, and he wouldn't jeopardize the woman's safety. No, he wouldn't back out now.

Adrian's complacency returned. He sat down on the sofa to enjoy the crumpets and China tea before they got cold, but he had barely poured himself a cup before the butler came in to announce the arrival of Mrs. Elliot.

"Mrs. Elliot?" he repeated in some surprise.

"Yes, my lord."

Impatiently he set down his cup. It didn't matter who had brought the papers. All that mattered was that they had finally arrived. "Send her in," he ordered and rose to his feet.

"Very good, my lord." Lovett withdrew, returning several moments later with the woman. She entered through the double doors of the study carrying with her a worn leather portfolio.

Adrian met her gaze. The haunting quality of her that

had struck him on their first meeting was gone. Her eyes were cold, her face expressionless, giving little indication of what she was thinking or feeling, but he had the impression she was somehow taking his measure. It annoyed him.

He turned to Lovett. "That will be all."

The butler gave a bow and departed, closing the study doors behind him.

Adrian smiled at Mara as he walked toward her. "Good afternoon, Mrs. Elliot."

She gave a short nod but did not reply.

"This is certainly a pleasure. Would you care for tea?"

"No."

He gestured to the sofa and chairs around him. "It's quite cold today. Please sit down by the fire and be comfortable."

"I'd rather stand."

He was making an effort to be courteous and her icy tone was quite irritating. The least she could do was show a bit of civility. After all, he hadn't done anything to her. Her stupid little company was still intact. He discarded formalities. "I believe you have something for me."

"Yes." She pulled a sheaf of papers out of her portfolio, but when he reached for them, she did not hand the documents to him. Instead, she hugged the papers to her breast and looked up at him. "You have the money?"

"Of course. I'll write you a bank draft."

"Good." She glanced past him at the coal fire in the grate. "You were right, my lord," she said as she stepped around him and walked toward the sofa. "It is cold outside, and I think I will take a moment to warm myself."

She heard his impatient sigh as he walked to the desk and pulled out his bankbook. He reached for quill and ink and wrote out the draft.

She took a deep, steadying breath and glanced down at the orange coals burning in the grate. It was time to jump off that cliff. "Lord Leyland?"

He tore the bank draft out of his book and tossed down the pen. "What?"

"Your fire is much too low. I believe it needs fuel."

She bent down. Quickly jerking back the fire screen with one gloved hand, she tossed the documents into the grate.

With an outraged cry, he circled the desk and raced across the room. He dropped the bank draft and shoved her out of the way. Mara stumbled, but caught herself before she fell. As she straightened, she noticed a plump and pretty blonde woman, richly dressed, standing in the study doorway with her hands poised on the knobs as if she had just entered, a horrified expression on her face. Mara glanced at the viscount, but he was occupied with trying to reach for the documents, and he did not notice the woman.

His efforts proved futile. The hot coals had already ignited the papers, turning them into a ball of fire. He jerked his burned hand back from the flames with a cry of pain and fury as he whirled around to face her.

"You stupid chit! What have you done?"

Enraged, he lifted his hand to strike her, but Mara stood motionless, daring him to do it, and he slowly lowered his hand.

"This is a business deal between my brother and myself!" he shouted at her. "You are only his junior partner, and a mere woman, besides. You have no right to intervene!"

"Too late, my lord. I just did." Her eyes on him, she took two long steps back and bent to pick up what he had dropped. Then she straightened. "On your brother's behalf, I formally reject your offer," she said as she ripped the bank draft to shreds, which she then tossed in his face. "Bribe all the suppliers you can. Hire all the vandals you like. Use your fiancée's money to coerce the bankers to your heart's content. Nathaniel and I will not submit to your extortion and blackmail."

He took a deep breath. Brushing the scraps of paper off his shoulders, he met her gaze, and she could see the rage in his eyes. "You have made a very serious mistake, my dear, and you will live to regret it, I promise you. You have just destroyed Nathaniel and yourself."

She knew he was probably right. But at this moment, she just couldn't find it within herself to be afraid. Her heart was too full of satisfaction for that. She smiled at him. "Well, my lord, I am only a woman, after all," she said sweetly. "We can be quite silly, you know."

"Adrian?"

The voice had both of them glancing toward the doorway, but Mara's gaze shifted back to Adrian, who was staring at the woman in shock and dismay.

"Honoria, my dear," he said awkwardly. "What are you doing here?"

So, this was Adrian's wealthy fiancée. How delightful. Mara moved toward the doors, and the woman stepped aside to let her pass.

"Good afternoon, Miss Montrose." Mara gave a nod and a smile to one of the world's wealthiest women before she walked out of the room.

"What is going on?"

Honoria's demand caused Mara to pause a moment outside the study. She could not hear Adrian's reply, only the smooth, low pitch of his voice.

But his soothing tone seemed to have little effect on the woman. "Don't patronize me, my lord. You were going to strike that woman. And what is all this talk about extortion and blackmail and coercing bankers with my money?"

Mara smiled. Crossing the foyer, she left Adrian Chase to explain the situation to his fiancée as all his well-laid plans burned to ashes.

When Mara returned to Whitechapel, she found no one at the factory, so she went to Nathaniel's flat. Without bothering to knock, she walked in. Following the sound of voices, she walked to the bedroom and found Nathaniel packing, Michael pacing, Finch quietly watching, and Billy crying. Everything was in quite a muddle, and none of them noticed her arrival.

"I don't know why yer leavin', Nathaniel." Billy glared at him from his perch atop the huge mahogany bed, his eyes filled with angry tears. He punched one of the pillows. "It ain't fair."

Nathaniel tossed his shaving kit into the open trunk on the floor. "I have to go, Billy. I'm sorry, but there's nothing I can do about it."

"Yes, there is." Michael stopped pacing and turned toward him. "You can stay here and fight."

Nathaniel tossed another shirt into the trunk. "I can't do that."

Michael turned to the solicitor. "Can't you persuade him?"

Finch leaned one shoulder against the wall and folded his arms across his chest. He shook his head. "I'm afraid not."

The engineer gave a snort of disgust. "This is ridiculous. I can get you the money to pay back the loan."

Nathaniel stuffed a handful of socks into a corner of the trunk. "It doesn't matter."

"Of course it does, if Joslyn Brothers is calling your

loan. Listen, my Uncle Hiram's wife has a third cousin, Jacob, who knows Solomon Leibowitz, the moneylender. He'll give you a loan. I'm sure of it."

"Why?" Nathaniel slammed one drawer of the wardrobe shut and opened another. "Because I'm such a good credit risk?"

"That's not your fault. Adrian was responsible for all that. Solomon Leibowitz would love the chance to get back at Adrian for his refusal to hire Jews. I'm sure of it."

"I told you, it doesn't matter." Nathaniel lifted a bundle of clothes out of the drawer and dumped them haphazardly into the trunk. "I can't fight him forever. I won't put Mara through that. It's too risky."

"But—"

"No." Nathaniel slammed the lid down on the trunk and shoved it aside. Then he opened another and began to fill it with more of his belongings. "I won't risk Mara's future."

Mara coughed, and all three men turned to find her standing there. "Don't you think I have something to say about it?" she asked.

Billy jumped off the bed and ran to her, wrapping his arms around her legs. "Nathaniel says 'e's leaving. 'e says 'e ain't comin' back."

She brushed a hand over Billy's hair, but she kept her gaze on Nathaniel. "Yes, I know what he says. But he's not going anywhere."

Michael stopped pacing. Finch straightened away from the wall. Billy sniffed. And Nathaniel stopped packing.

She looked at him and lifted her chin stubbornly at the scowl he gave her. Their eyes met for a moment, but he said nothing. Instead, he turned and grabbed a handful of cravats and ties out of the drawer.

She turned to Michael. "Would you and Mr. Finch

please take Billy out for some ice cream? I want to talk to Nathaniel alone."

The two men left the office with an unpacified Billy between them.

Mara turned to Nathaniel. "Packing already, I see?" she whispered painfully. "Were you planning to say good-bye before you left? Or did you feel a letter would suffice?"

He continued tossing clothes into the trunk without even looking at her. "I wouldn't leave without saying good-bye."

"Why are you doing this?" she asked.

The question was so soft, he barely heard the words. He stopped packing and stared down at the shirt in his hands. "You know why," he answered. "Finch said he explained it all to you."

"He did, but I want to hear it from you. Tell me why."

"I'd hoped Adrian would back down if we could get the trains out on time. I was wrong. He would have destroyed the company. You would have lost everything. I couldn't let that happen."

"Michael said he could find us a moneylender."

"That's not the point." He threw the shirt into the trunk and faced her. "If I don't stop, it won't end here. You realized that long before I did. He'll keep after us until he succeeds in bankrupting us. This way, it'll only be me that's affected. You'll be secure. I've made sure of that."

"How noble of you."

Her sarcasm caught him by surprise. He lifted his head and looked at her, only to find her crystal gray eyes sparkling with anger.

"So that's it, then?" Her voice began to shake, and he could hear pain behind her anger. "It's getting too diffi-cult here, so it's time to move on?"

"That's not it at all!"

"Isn't it?" She strode forward until she was a mere foot away. Tilting her chin, she looked up at him. "You came to London with a dream. You filled my head with it, you made me believe it, you made all of us believe it. And now, you're just going to turn your back on us and leave it all behind?"

"You're the one who asked me to stop all this in the first place!"

"Yes, and it was a mistake. I was wrong. I let my fear control me, and I wanted it to control you." She watched him shake his head from side to side, and she reached up, cupping his face in her hands to stop his denials before he could say them. "Don't you remember what you told me? You said we can't spend our lives being afraid. We have to grab what we want and hang on. Well, I'm hanging on, Nathaniel Chase, and so are you. You aren't going anywhere, except back downstairs to finish making those trains. We don't have much time. We're supposed to deliver them by Friday."

"We can't do that. Haven't you been listening to me? I've sold Adrian the patent on the train so that Joslyn Brothers could be paid."

"Well . . ." She lowered her hands and clasped them behind her back. She ducked her head and shifted her weight from one foot to the other. "You didn't sell Adrian the train. Not quite."

"What do you mean?"

She lifted her head and gave a little cough. "I . . . umm . . . I sort of threw a spanner in the works."

"Mara, what have you done?" he demanded.

She told him.

"I don't believe this," he muttered when she'd finished. "Are you out of your mind?"

"Probably. Love does that to a person."

He didn't take in her confession of love or the fact that she was using his own words against him. He folded his arms across his chest and glared at her. "What you've done changes nothing."

"Yes, it does. We'll deliver our trains to the stores. We'll go to this Solomon Leibowitz and get a loan to pay Joslyn Brothers. When the money from the trains comes in, we reinvest it in the business and keep going."

"And then what happens?" he asked and grabbed her hands tight in his. "Assuming we do get the money to pay back the loan, then what? What happens when Adrian finally succeeds and we lose it all?"

"We start over." She took his hands in hers, entwining their fingers. "Together."

She felt his hand tighten around hers at the word before he slowly pulled back and stepped away from her.

"Then Adrian will eventually bankrupt us again," he said. "What kind of future would that be? James all over again. I love you, but I would have nothing to offer you."

She looked up at him, wondering how to make him see that her future meant nothing without him. "Words again. Why do you love me, Nathaniel? What is there in me that you love so much that you would sacrifice all your dreams for my sake?"

He raked a hand through his hair. "How do you expect me to answer a question like that? How am I supposed to explain?"

"You have said I'm lovely. So, is it my beauty that you love?"

"Not only that." The words came out slowly, as if each one caused him pain. "It's so much more than that."

"What then? My warm heart? It was cold and empty and bitter before you came. An unlovable heart, to be sure."

"No." He shook his head. "Not to me."

"My courage, perhaps?" She choked out a laugh. "I, who have spent the past four years hiding from the world?"

"You do have courage. You are a very brave woman."

"Indeed? I don't feel brave at all. I find the idea of spending the rest of my life without you a terrifying prospect."

"If I'm gone, Adrian won't bother you. You'll have the means to support yourself and Billy."

"You would abandon him, too?"

"He'll have you to care for him. His future and yours will be safe."

"Safe?" She considered that for a moment, then she nodded. "Yes, I suppose so. I'll endure, I'll save my pennies in my little tin bank, and I'll wear gloves to hide my scars. I'll try to be a good mother to Billy. I'll hold him when he cries, I'll put on a brave face, and I'll be strong for him. But, tell me, Nathaniel, if you leave, who will be strong for me?"

She wrapped her arms around her ribs as she felt herself splintering apart. "Who will fill me with hope when all I feel is despair? Who will fly kites with me when I feel chained to the ground and make me laugh when I want to weep? Who will give me upside-down kisses and dance with me and fill my heart with joy? Who will give me dreams to strive for and music to soothe me to sleep? Who . . ." Her voice broke, and she turned away. She lowered her head to stare at the floor, watching the tears fall unchecked to form dark circles on the wood.

"Who will keep me from turning into a bitter, lonely, dried-up shell of a woman?" she whispered. "Because that is what I was before you came, and that is what I will become if you leave."

She fell silent and waited, not daring to look at him,

unable to breathe. The silence seemed to last an eternity, before she heard him take a step toward her. Then another. Then another.

His hands fell on her shoulders, and she let out her breath in a soft little sob of hope as he turned her around. He brought one hand to her cheek, but she did not look up.

"I love you," she said, her voice shaking. "And I need you more than you could ever know. Don't leave me."

She squeezed her eyes shut, but the tears did not stop. She waited, hoping this one wish came true. *I'm falling, Nathaniel. Please catch me.*

He bent his head and kissed away tears one by one. "I won't leave you, not ever. I love you. God only knows what kind of life we'll have."

She opened her eyes. She looked at him and saw the promise in his eyes. "We'll have a life together," she whispered and rested her cheek against his chest. She leaned into his strength and felt his arms wrap around her. Now, when everything they'd worked for was falling apart, now, when all the plans were unraveling, now, she felt safer than she ever had in her life.

"Mara, did you really tear up the bank draft and throw it in Adrian's face?"

She lifted her head to find him smiling down at her with all that open tenderness. "Yes," she answered. "And Honoria Montrose saw the whole thing. Your brother is going to have a lot of explaining to do."

He pulled her back against him and kissed her. "What a pity."

30

The letter arrived in the post the morning after his confrontation with Mara Elliot. Adrian stared down at the note in Honoria's childishly round handwriting, unable to believe the words even as he read them. He'd thought her satisfied by his explanations of the scene she had witnessed, but obviously he had been mistaken. He read the letter again, and he knew his mistake had been a fatal one.

Viscount Leyland, you are a man of some admirable qualities, but the scene I witnessed yesterday forces me to reconsider our engagement. I cannot, in all good conscience, marry a man who would deliberately set out to ruin his own brother, whatever his reasons. Further, I am appalled that you should use my name and influence for such dishonorable purposes.

I have sent a statement to The Times social register announcing the dissolution of our engagement by mutual consent. Should you choose to contest that statement and bring a breach of promise suit against me, I am bold enough to say that it will be futile. I'm certain that you would not wish to have my investigators explore the matter of your fight with your brother too deeply.

I am journeying to Paris forthwith. Please do not try to contact me. I feel there would be no point to a conversation between us. It would only be painful and embarrassing for us both. My regrets. Miss Honoria Montrose.

P.S.—I have enclosed your ring.

By the time he finished reading the letter again, Adrian's disbelief had chilled to cold rage. Of all the impudence! That fat, American cow lecturing him on honor when she'd had the gall to inform the social register of *The Times*. God, the news would be all over London by this afternoon.

He crumpled the letter into a ball and tossed it across the study with a curse. What was he going to do? Without the promise of Honoria's money, his creditors would be swarming around him within hours.

He reached one hand toward the bell pull, intending to ring for tea, but changed his mind. Walking to the sideboard, he reached for one of the crystal decanters there and poured himself a whiskey instead. To his disgust, he noticed his hand shook as he lifted the tumbler to his lips.

He leaned back against the sideboard. All he could think of was the scandal, the humiliation. The sound of shattering glass startled him, and he realized he'd thrown the tumbler against the wall.

Adrian spent the day in his study, striving to find a way out. Lovett informed the constant stream of bankers and solicitors who came calling that his master was unavailable as Adrian sat behind his desk, composing letters to influential acquaintances. He tried to grasp what had happened as he scrawled words on paper. How had all his carefully laid plans gone awry?

It was all Nathaniel's fault.

The realization came to him and he paused, his grip tightening around the quill pen in his hand. Of course, Nathaniel was to blame. Adrian jabbed the point of his pen into the palm of his hand, icy rage numbing the pain.

It was all Nathaniel's fault.

If it hadn't been for Nathaniel, none of this would have happened. If Nathaniel hadn't come back to England, if he hadn't dared to go into competition against him, if his impudent chit of a mistress hadn't come along and ruined everything with Honoria, Adrian knew he would not now be facing ruin and disgrace.

It was all Nathaniel's fault.

Adrian repeated those words to himself as he stabbed his palm with the point of the pen again and again, drawing blood, not even feeling the pain. All Nathaniel's fault.

Nathaniel stood beside the cart in the alley behind the warehouse. "Two hundred trains to Whiteley's and three hundred to Gamage's," he told Boggs. "And be careful. God knows what my brother might try."

"Right-o, guv'nor." Boggs swung up onto the cart beside his son, Alfred. "It'll go rough on yer brother if he gets in our way." The workman pulled at his cap. "We'll be back in an 'our or two for the next load."

Nathaniel gave him a thumbs-up gesture as the cart loaded with crates of trains lurched forward. He watched it roll down the alley and disappear around the corner. Then he walked back into the warehouse.

He paused beside the table where Billy, Davy, and Millie Boggs, and all four of Emma Logan's children were checking train sets under Emma's watchful eye. He paused beside Emma's chair. "How's things in here?"

"Smashin'!" Billy closed the lid on another case and set it aside.

"Emma?"

The woman looked up from the train set she was checking, and she smiled at him. "They're working 'ard, sir. You can trust me on that."

"You're a good supervisor, Emma. Keep this up and I might have you out on the production floor, supervising the men as well."

She laughed. "I don't think Mr. Lowenstein would be 'appy about that."

"Probably not." He grinned and walked away.

He made his way through assembly, where women put trains, pieces of track, batteries, and sheets of printed instructions into wooden cases and stamped them with the Chase-Elliot trademark. As he passed by, he paused often to give a compliment or make a suggestion, knowing there were many long hours of work ahead and that a little encouragement went a long way.

They had until Friday to get those trains delivered, and Nathaniel would feel better once the trains were out of the factory and safely in the stores, just in case Adrian tried some new scheme.

He entered the production floor, stopping occasionally to watch the men as they cut sheets of tin into pieces, molded them into locomotives, passenger cars, and train stations. Again, he took every possible opportunity to give a compliment or exchange a joke or two as he made his way to where Percy stood.

The secretary looked worried. Nathaniel paused beside him, and the two of them watched as welders soldered locomotives together. "Are you all right, Percy?" he shouted over the din.

The secretary gave him a dubious glance. "I don't think I have the qualities necessary to be a good supervisor, sir," he yelled back.

Nathaniel grinned and took another look around. "I don't know, Percy. Everyone seems to be working very hard. I think you're doing fine."

Percy shook his head. "I'll be glad when Mrs. Elliot and Michael return."

"Me, too." He clapped Percy on the shoulder. "I'll take over. It's getting pretty late in the day, and no one's taken a break. Everybody's probably getting hungry and thirsty. Why don't you go find Mrs. O'Brien and have her bring sandwiches and jugs of water for everybody?"

"Yes, sir." Percy departed, grateful for the change of duties, and Nathaniel went up to the mezzanine where he had a better view.

He leaned against the rail and watched the work going on below as he waited for Mara and Michael to return from their meeting with Solomon Leibowitz. When they came through the front doors a few moments later, Mara immediately looked up to see him watching her from the mezzanine. Even from his position thirty feet above her, he could see her wide smile as she nodded emphatically and waved a slip of paper at him.

He smiled back at her and made a thumbs-up gesture to show he understood. The slow, sweet warmth of satisfaction washed over him, even though he knew it might not last. Leibowitz had obviously agreed to give them the money to pay off their loan, but Nathaniel had reneged on his deal with Adrian, and he knew his brother would not let that pass. Still, he couldn't regret what they had done. He just hoped Mara would never come to regret it either.

They paid off Joslyn Brothers that afternoon, and Nathaniel's worries eased somewhat. The following evening, Finch brought the news of Adrian's misfortunes to their attention, and Nathaniel's worries eased a bit more. Finch brought the huge stack of newspapers to the factory with the dry pronouncement, "Adrian's in a bit of trouble." The announcement that his engagement had been broken had made the morning newspapers, and the news that creditors were calling in all his debts made the evening editions.

Busy with getting trains out to stores, Nathaniel and Mara didn't take the time to read all the articles, but a quick scan of *The Times* gave them the important points. Adrian was bankrupt, all his assets had been confiscated, and his former fiancée was in Paris, refusing to comment on the reasons for her broken engagement. Although Mara and Nathaniel suspected what had really happened, they didn't care about the details. They just breathed a prayer of thanks, went back to work, and hoped their troubles with Adrian were over.

Adrian's letters to Lord Ashton, Lord Fitzhugh, and Lord Severn were answered with gushing sympathy and regretful refusal. Times were difficult, what with passage of the Reform Acts and fixed rents making money so scarce. Without assistance, Adrian knew he was doomed.

Desperate, he telegraphed to Honoria, but a coldly

polite reply from her lawyer was his only answer. Over the next few days, he contacted every business and social acquaintance he knew, but without the promise of marriage to a wealthy heiress to back him up, he had become a very bad risk. He received a great deal of sympathy, but no assistance, and with every sympathetic pat on the back he received, Adrian's hatred for Nathaniel grew.

Creditors made good on their promise and began confiscating his assets. The Mayfair house, with all its contents, was first. Adrian stood helplessly by as bank clerks swarmed over the house like an infestation of ants; he watched as workmen marched his furnishings out the front doors; he listened as all his possessions, including his beloved art collection, were auctioned off in the forecourt to the delight of the curious onlookers peering through the gates. Each time the auctioneer cried, "Sold!" and pounded his gavel, the crowd cheered, and Adrian's hatred for Nathaniel grew.

Chase Toys came next. All the equipment was auctioned, all the inventory confiscated, the building put up for sale. He walked through the vacant factory, and the voice of his father echoed through his mind, imagined tirades of what a mess Adrian had made of the company. With each reprimand, each recrimination, Adrian's hatred for Nathaniel grew.

Creditors could not take the entailed estate in Devon, but they stripped it of all its valuables. They took the villa at Brighton. They took his stocks, his bonds, the ring he'd given Honoria, and all his other jewels. They took away his influence and his reputation.

But they could not take away his pride, and they could not take away his hatred. Adrian sat on an empty crate in the empty mansion in Mayfair, the shreds of a letter ordering him to vacate the premises scattered across the bare floor and an empty bottle of whiskey in his bandaged hand. Creditors had shut off the gas jets and had taken all the crystal lamps, so he sat in the dark, flicking his gold lighter and planning Nathaniel's death.

Mara and Nathaniel were too busy making trains to spend much time contemplating Adrian's problems. They changed their bankers to Kaplan & Sons, and spent their time delivering trains. By Friday evening, all orders for the Christmas season had been filled but one.

Mara placed the last box on the cart and watched as Nathaniel climbed up beside Boggs. "I'll be back in a couple of hours."

"I'll wait for you here. I've closed the factory and sent everybody home. I've given everyone tomorrow morning off. With pay."

He gave her a surprised glance as he took the reins. "Mara, I'm not sure that was very practical of you," he said gravely.

She looked up at him, and the light of the street lamp at the end of the alley revealed the troubled expression on her upturned face. "Well, they all worked so hard, Nathaniel. Sixteen hours a day for the past three days."

"Mara—"

"I thought it would be good for morale. A Christmas bonus, and—"

"Mara, I was only teasing you."

"Oh." She bit her lip. "I never can tell when you're doing that."

He grinned and snapped the reins. "I know."

Nathaniel and Boggs made the last delivery to Harrod's. They unloaded five hundred trains, and Nathaniel tucked the receipt of delivery in his pocket, once again feeling the satisfaction of success. They'd done it. They had defied Adrian, they had delivered their trains, they had managed to circumvent all the obstacles in their path. He and Mara deserved to celebrate.

He sent Boggs home, asking him to take the rented cart back to the livery on his way. He went upstairs to Harrod's toy department, unable to resist taking a look at the Christmas offerings of his competition and unable to resist gloating a bit. Nothing anyone else offered could compare.

There were a few products from Chase Toys on display, but Nathaniel knew that once those were gone, there would be no more, for he knew creditors had already taken the company and had auctioned off everything. Although Adrian was getting exactly what he deserved, Nathaniel was not happy that his grandfather's legacy should come to such a pathetic end.

He left the toy department and wandered through the rest of the store, purchasing a bottle of champagne from the wine department, two crystal goblets in the china and glass department, and finally, a box of chocolates and a pint of greenhouse strawberries in the grocery. He smiled to himself as he paid for his purchases, knowing Mara would lecture him on the impracticality of buying expensive, out-of-season strawberries.

He then left the department store and was immediately enveloped in the thick fog that had descended over the city. A boy appeared in front of him, emerging from the mist as if out of nowhere. "Get ye a cab, guv'nor?"

"Yes, thank you."

The boy raced toward the curb, and even though the street was less than a dozen feet away, he disappeared from view, lost in the fog.

He knew that these street children spent many long hours standing in front of stores to find cabs for those who could afford them and were experts at the task, but it surprised Nathaniel at how quickly the boy was able to obtain one for him, given the weather. Within three minutes, the child had returned with a cab, and Nathaniel gave him a well-earned sixpence.

The boy gaped at the tip, six times the amount he usually received. "A tanner? Thank ye, guv'nor."

Nathaniel climbed into the cab and placed the bag containing his purchases on the seat beside him, as the carriage moved up Brompton Road at a slow crawl. He leaned back in his seat, knowing it was going to take ages to get to Whitechapel and trying to curb his impatience. He wanted nothing more than to be with Mara and celebrate their success. It had taken him a long time to see his dream come true, but it appeared fate was going to make him wait just a little bit longer before he could enjoy it.

While Nathaniel was out, Mara made preparations of her own. She left Billy with Mrs. O'Brien and went up to her flat, where she bathed with lilac soap. She put on her nicest white shirtwaist and lace collar, and her best winter skirt, a soft, plum-colored merino wool. She wrapped a towel around her shoulders and washed her hair, shivering as she leaned out the window to do it. She then dried it with a towel and piled the damp tresses atop her head.

When she had completed her toilette, she fetched fresh water, then went back down to Mrs. O'Brien's. She sent Billy upstairs to take his bath. He grumbled about it, saying it hadn't even been a week since the last time she'd made him take a bath, but he did as she bid him, and when he came back down, she was pleased to note that he'd even remembered to wash behind his ears.

The two of them returned to the factory, left a lamp burning by the front door for Nathaniel, and went upstairs to wait for him in the office. They played checkers while they waited, but after about an hour, she saw Billy's head nodding in exhaustion as he leaned over the checkerboard. It had been a tiring day for the boy, and she knew it was time to put him to bed.

She ignored his sleepy protests as she tucked him into Nathaniel's cot. She smiled down at him, watching as his eyes closed. "Good night, Billy," she whispered and bent to place a soft kiss on his cheek. She straightened and started to turn away, but Billy's voice stopped her.

"Mrs. Elliot?"

"Yes, Billy?"

He opened his eyes. "It's been almost two years since me mum died. I'm startin' to forget 'er."

Mara knelt beside the cot and gently reached out and brushed the lock of hair back from his forehead. "Well, two years is an awfully long time." To an eight-year-old, it could be an eternity.

"Do ye suppose a boy could 'ave two mums?"

"I suppose so."

He plucked at the edge of the sheet. "Since I'm goin' t'be livin' with you from now on, can I call you mum?"

Mara's heart constricted with a joy so powerful it was almost pain. "Of course you can, sweeting," she choked out and wrapped her arms around him.

She held him until she felt his arms relax, then she gently pulled away and went back into the office. The clock struck nine, and she began to worry. She walked to the door and stepped out onto the fire escape, but the fog had become so thick, she couldn't even see the light of the street lamp at the end of the alley. No wonder he wasn't back yet. She closed the door and sat down at her desk to do some work while she waited.

When the clock struck ten, her worry began in earnest, and wild thoughts shot through her mind. What if he'd had an accident in the fog? What if Adrian had done something? Adrian wouldn't do anything violent. Would he?

Restless, she shut the ledger before her and began to pace. She was wondering if perhaps she should inform the police, when a slight sound caught her attention.

"Thank God," she breathed and raced out the door. "Nathaniel?" she called as she started down the stairs.

She received no answer. She paused on the mezzanine and took a look around, but the lamp she'd left downstairs by the door provided almost no light at all and she could see nothing but the faint outline of the railing.

"Nathaniel?"

She heard no sound. She turned around and started to head back up the stairs, when a sudden noise caused her to jump just as something brushed her leg. She gave a startled cry. Algernon answered with a meow.

"Oh!" She bent over to pick up the kitten. "Algernon, you silly cat, you frightened me nearly to death."

She lowered her head to rub her cheek against his soft fur, when suddenly she was grabbed from behind. A hand came over her mouth, muffling her startled scream as Algernon fell from her arms and let out a loud, indignant wail. The hand covering her mouth pulled her head back, and she felt something cold and flat press against her throat. The blade of a knife. She heard herself begin to whimper behind the sweat-damp hand.

Hot breath fanned her cheek and a voice spoke softly in her ear.

"Mrs. Elliot," Adrian said, "it's a pleasure to see you again."

31

Nathaniel paid the cab driver and unlocked the front door of the factory as the cab rolled away. He could see lights burning in the third-floor windows, but the ground floor was pitch-dark. He made his way across the production floor, but memory was not a reliable guide and he bumped into a few tables before he reached the stairs. With one hand on the rail, he started up.

At the mezzanine, he heard a faint squealing sound and paused. He heard the scraping flicker of a lighter, and lamplight illuminated the far corner of the mezzanine. He drew in a sharp breath at the sight revealed to him.

Mara was seated behind Michael's desk, facing him. Adrian stood behind her, one hand tangled in a handful of her long hair, the other holding a knife poised across her throat. "If you move, I'll kill her."

Nathaniel stared at his brother, wondering what the hell to do. "A knife, Adrian?" he said, striving to keep his voice steady. "Isn't that a bit too unsophisticated for you?"

"They took my pistols, you bastard, and everything else I own," he answered, keeping the knife at Mara's throat and his gaze on Nathaniel.

"I heard about that. I'm sorry."

"Sorry?" Adrian screamed the word in contempt and fury. "A knife was all I could get. If I had a pistol, I'd shoot you down like a dog."

"I see." There was no way he could get to her. Nathaniel waited, trying to think past the hammering of his heart.

Moving slowly, Adrian sat down in the chair behind Mara's, keeping the knife at her throat. He nodded to Percy's desk directly opposite. "Sit down."

Nathaniel obeyed, then leaned forward in the chair and spread his hands wide. "So, now that you have us both here, what's next?"

"You're going to make your will. There's a pen and ink on that desk."

"My will? Leaving my share of Chase-Elliot to you, of course."

"Damned right. As well as everything else you own." He jerked Mara's head back a little further and the blade of the knife touched her throat.

Nathaniel drew a deep, steadying breath. "Really, Adrian, you must be joking. I can't write worth a damn, and you know it."

"Just shut up and do what I say!"

"He's right, my lord." Mara's voice intruded softly, and Nathaniel could hear the slight quaver in her voice, the only indication of her fear. "You know he has horrible penmanship."

He looked over at Nathaniel. "Then you'll write it, Mrs. Elliot."

He wrapped the strands of her hair more securely around his fist. He leaned back, his gaze on Nathaniel. "Do it."

"All right." She reached for the quill and ink on Michael's desk. "I have to get paper out of the drawer," she said, her eyes meeting Nathaniel's as she slowly moved to open the right-hand drawer of Michael's desk. He knew she was planning something, and he tensed in his chair, praying she wouldn't try anything but intending to be ready if she did.

"Do you really think this is going to work?" Nathaniel asked, his eyes still on Mara as he spoke. "No one is going to believe it's legal."

"They will! This company is going to be mine. I'm going to take everything you have as payment for what you've done to me!"

Nathaniel knew that his brother's spirit was broken. Everything that mattered to him—his money, his possessions, his power—was gone. He'd always been arrogant and cruel, but now, when his misfortunes had sent him into madness, he was almost pathetic. And very dangerous.

"What's goin' on?"

Billy's sleepy voice from the stairs broke the silence, but Adrian was the only one who paid attention. Distracted, he straightened, and the hand holding the knife moved away from Mara's throat.

Nathaniel saw a flash of metal as she moved, and he was over the top of Percy's desk before the letter opener in her hand sank into the vulnerable skin of Adrian's wrist.

Adrian screamed as the knife flew from his hand. He released his grip on Mara's hair, and she instantly swung around in her chair with all the force she had, hitting him square in the jaw with her fist.

He staggered back, and Nathaniel was on him. Mara scrambled to get out of the way, running across the room to Billy, who was holding Algernon in his arms and staring in wide-eyed terror at the scene playing out before him. She pulled the boy against her skirt, turning her head in time to see Nathaniel swing his fist. The impact of the blow sent Adrian flying backward against Michael's desk, knocking over the lamp. Kerosene spilled and fire ignited. Mara watched in horror as flames licked greedily at the engineering diagrams spread out over the desk top. Within seconds, the desk was on fire.

Fire. Mara began to shake with fear. In her mind, she could hear Helen screaming, she could almost feel the floor caving in beneath her, and she forced herself to blot it out. Helen was dead, and she had to think of Billy now, she had to get him out of here. She started to pick him up, thinking to run, but she could not leave Nathaniel. She bent down. "Billy, listen," she said, grabbing him by the shoulders, fighting off waves of panic. "Listen to me, sweetheart. I want you to get out of here."

"I'm not leavin'," he said, hugging Algernon tightly. "What if Nathaniel needs 'elp?"

"I'll help him. You have to go get the firemen. There's no time to argue." She shoved him toward the stairs. "Now! Run!"

Billy ran toward the stairs, pausing to give her a doubtful glance, and she waved her arms, urging him to go on. With the kitten in his arms, he disappeared down the stairwell.

Percy's desk had also ignited, and the center of the room was a giant ball of fire. Flames were already devouring the wooden floor, and it would be only minutes before the entire mezzanine was engulfed. She felt the heat at her back as she raced across the mezzanine to the rail in time to see Nathaniel give Adrian two quick jabs in the ribs. Then she looked down to see Billy running across the production floor, his way lit by the flames upstairs. She waited until he was out the door, then turned her attention to the two men who were grappling against the rail, each struggling to gain the upper hand.

Mara cast a frantic glance around, but she found nothing to use as a weapon. Adrian's knife was somewhere in the center of the raging fire. There was no way she could get to it. She started toward the two men, but without a weapon, she knew she would only get in Nathaniel's way.

Adrian managed to break free of Nathaniel's grasp. He took several steps back, then flung himself at his brother. Mara watched in horror as the impact sent both of them over the rail.

Nathaniel heard Mara scream his name as he felt himself going over the rail of the mezzanine. He grabbed desperately for something to hang on to as he fell and managed to hook one arm around the rail. Adrian hurtled past him into empty space. Nathaniel gripped the rail with all his strength and watched his brother plummet toward the ground.

The steam engine directly below broke Adrian's fall, but he sprawled over the machine like a limp rag doll, motionless, his head twisted at an unnatural angle, his neck broken.

Nathaniel grimaced and turned his face away, but he had neither the time nor the inclination to grieve. He swung one leg up, wrapping it around the top of the railing, and hoisted himself up. He rolled over the rail and let go, hitting the floor of the mezzanine with a groan of relief, drinking in great gulps of air, coughing when the smoke filled his lungs.

Mara was kneeling beside him in an instant. "Thank God!"

"Are you all right?" he asked as he sat up. She nodded, and he glanced around. All he could seem to see was fire. "Where's Billy?"

"I sent him down when the fire started. He's outside. He's safe."

Nathaniel rose, grabbed her hand, and turned toward the stairs, only to find their way blocked by a wall of fire. The flames had spread to the stairs, and the enclosed stairwell had acted like a chimney. The wooden staircase was completely engulfed in flames. They could not go up and they could not go down. He pulled her to the opposite side of the mezzanine, but the ladder had been unhooked and now lay on the production floor. "Damn it! He took the ladder down."

"Nathaniel, what are we going to do?" Mara shouted over the roar.

"I have no idea," he shouted back, coughing as he inhaled more of the thick smoke. He glanced around, but no brilliant plans came to him.

"Think of something." She looked up at him anxiously, twisting her hands together. "You're the inventor. Can't you think of something?"

He glanced over the railing. The smoke made his eyes water, and he rubbed an impatient hand across them, trying to see. His attention caught on one of the pulley ropes hanging from the ceiling beam. A quick glance down told him one end was attached to a winch. The other end dangled in midair, the hook on its end a perfect stirrup. But the rope was too far out. He couldn't possibly jump for it. He looked up at the ceiling again.

"I have an idea," he said, and pointed to the rope. "We climb down."

"Are you crazy? How are we going to reach it?"

"We have to crawl to it from the ceiling beam."

He looked at her, and he could see her eyes were glazed with panic. Her whole body was trembling. "No," she choked, glancing down. "I can't!"

"Mara, listen to me." He grabbed her shoulders and gave her a little shake. "It's either that or the fire. There's no other way. Take off your skirt or it'll get in the way."

She hesitated, glancing over the rail, then back at the fire.

"Trust me." He squeezed her shoulders, planted a quick kiss on her lips, and released her. "C'mon. Get out of that skirt."

She pulled off the garments as he said, "I'll lift you. Grab the beam and pull yourself up until you can get one leg over. Roll up onto the beam so you're lying on your stomach. Understand?"

He could see her trembling. He knew she was terrified, but he couldn't let her fall apart now. "A letter opener, for God's sake!" he shouted as he grabbed her around the waist, lifting her toward the ceiling. "Of all the idiotic things to do. What were you thinking of?"

His ploy succeeded. Instantly, she forgot her panic and got defensive. "Well, it worked, didn't it?" she shot back, reaching up to grab the beam.

"You're damn lucky it did," Nathaniel said, waiting until she was lying along the length of the beam on her stomach. Then he jumped and grabbed the beam himself. He pulled himself up and stretched out, facing her, the pulley rope they needed to reach about two-dozen feet behind him. "He could've slit your throat."

"Well, he didn't!"

They faced each other, lying on the beam like a pair of panthers on a tree limb as the mezzanine below them collapsed, shooting sparks in all directions. He began to move backward on the beam, inching toward the pulley, and she followed his lead, scooting forward on her stomach.

She started to look down, but he spoke again to stop her. "Don't look down. Look at me."

"I'm scared!"

"I know. Imagine we're climbing a tree."

"I've never climbed a tree."

"I can see I'll have to take you tree climbing at the next opportunity." He glanced back to see how far they had to go. At least a dozen feet.

"That punch to his jaw wasn't bad," he said, starting to move backward again. "How did you manage it?"

"You taught Billy how to fight, remember? I paid attention."

"You're a good student." A fit of coughing overtook him, and he paused until it subsided. He could feel the heat of the fire intensifying, and he knew they didn't have much time.

"How much farther is it?"

"Only a bit," he lied. "We're getting married before Christmas."

"You might at least ask me first."

"I'll get down on one knee and propose when we're safely on the ground. Will that suit?"

"Yes."

They were above the pulley. He reached down, fumbling until he could grasp the thick rope. He pulled until the hook at the end hit the wheel.

"What do we do now?" she asked, watching him.

He met her eyes. "I'm going to climb down."

"No!" she cried. "Don't leave me!"

"I have to. Listen to me. I can't lower you down from up here. The rope's too thick for me to keep a good grip. I have to climb down. When I get to the bottom, grab the hook and put your foot through it as if it were a stirrup. In order to do that, you'll have to sit up on the beam. Once your foot's secure, hang on to the rope and swing off, so you're standing with your foot in the hook and the rope in your hands. I'll lower you with the winch."

"Why can't I just slide down?"

"You'll shred your hands, and your gloves won't protect you. We don't have time to argue. For once, just once, do what I tell you. All right?"

She swallowed hard and shook her sweat-damp hair out of her eyes. "All right," she whispered.

He hefted the rope, holding it securely in both hands. Before he could roll off the beam, her voice stopped him.

"Nathaniel?"

"What?"

"I love you, and if you fall and break your neck, I'll kill you."

"I'll keep that in mind." He slid off the beam and wrapped one leg around the rope. Suspended in the air, he paused and looked up at her. "Before Christmas," he said firmly and began to descend along the length of the rope, hand over hand. Mara peered over the edge and watched him through the smoky haze, her heart pounding in her breast, unable to draw breath until she saw him reach the ground.

When he was on the ground, he let go of the rope, and she saw him give her the thumbs-up sign. She reached down and grabbed the hook, doing exactly as Nathaniel had instructed her, giving herself no time to think. Once she was in a sitting position, with her foot in the hook and the rope grasped firmly in her hands, she knew she had to jump off. She gathered her courage, and said a brief prayer, then she closed her eyes and slid off the beam.

She fell several feet, and her heart seemed to leap into

her throat, but the rope went taut and she halted with a jerk, swinging in midair. She clung tightly to the rope and kept her eyes closed, fighting a wave of nausea.

She felt herself moving down, and she knew Nathaniel was lowering her with the winch, but she didn't have the courage to look. It seemed an eternity, but finally she felt her foot hit something solid.

She opened her eyes and found herself on the ground, Nathaniel standing in front of her.

"We did it!" she cried, jerking her foot free of the hook to wrap her arms around his neck with a sob of relief that ended in a choking cough.

"Damned right, we did! And splendidly, too." He pulled back and grabbed her hand. "Let's get out of here."

They raced across the production floor, dodging between tables and equipment, and left the burning building. They stumbled into the street, coughing and gasping for air.

"I think," she choked, "we make a pretty good team."

"I think you're right, partner." He pulled her away from the factory, leading her across the street to where a crowd had gathered. Billy raced forward to meet them, sobbing, Algernon still in his arms.

"I was goin' to go back in and get you, but they wouldn't let me!"

Mara fell to her knees in the middle of the street and wrapped her arms around him, kitten and all. "Are you all right?"

Billy nodded and looked up at Nathaniel. "I weren't worried," he said suddenly and sniffed, his cheeks wet with tears. "I knew you'd get out."

"Of course you did." Nathaniel reached out and ruffled his hair as Mara wiped the tears from his cheeks and kissed him before rising to her feet.

The crowd began to gather around them. Someone handed Mara a blanket and she took it gratefully, suddenly remembering that she wore only her shirtwaist and drawers.

With the blanket tied around her waist, she leaned back against Nathaniel, and felt his arm slide around her as they stared at the burning factory. Billy stood beside Nathaniel, holding Algernon and clinging tightly to the man's free hand.

Heat had burned away the fog surrounding the building, and the three of them stood at the front of the crowd, watching as the steam-powered fire engines of the Metropolitan Fire Brigade began to pull up in front. Firemen instantly set to work. It was too late to save the factory, so they concentrated on wetting down the surrounding buildings to prevent the fire from spreading.

The roof of the factory fell in, and Nathaniel leaned down to murmur in her ear. "I hope you remembered to pay the insurance premium."

She glanced up at him, looking affronted at the very idea that she would neglect something so important. "Of course I did."

A slow smile curved his mouth as he turned her in his arms. He brushed a patch of soot from her cheek. "My practical Mara. I love you."

"I know," she said and curled her arms around his neck. "But then, I've always suspected you were a crazy, rainbow-chasing dreamer. How am I ever going to keep up with you?"

He lifted her in his arms until she was off the ground. "By holding on to me very tight and never letting go."

Her arms tightened around his neck. "I can do that," she said and kissed him.

"So, when are ye gettin' married?" Mrs. O'Brien's

voice demanded as she pushed her way to the front of the crowd and faced them, hands on hips.

"As soon as he asks me," Mara answered.

"Do I really have to get down on one knee?" he asked.

She smiled wickedly. "You promised."

He sighed and set her on her feet. He grasped her hand and bent down until one knee touched the pavement. "Mara Elliot, you asked me once why I love you, and I couldn't find the right words to explain, but I'd like to try again. I love you because you never know when I'm teasing you, and because you try to save gift wrap, and because you take everything so seriously, and because you can't fly a kite worth a damn, and because you have the prettiest eyes I've ever seen, and because of so many other things, it's going to take me a lifetime to list them all. So . . ." He paused and took a deep breath, then added in a rush, "Will you marry me?"

She smiled down at him, loving him with all her heart, her mind, her body, and her soul. "Yes, Nathaniel, I will."

He rose and pulled her back in his arms for another kiss as a cheer went up around them. Just before his lips touched hers, he added in a whisper, "And I love the way you put on your stockings."

He started to kiss her, but he felt Billy tug at one leg of his trousers, demanding attention. He pulled back but did not release Mara as he looked down at the boy. "What is it, Scrapper?"

Billy frowned up at them. "Does all this marryin' and kissin' stuff mean I'm goin' to 'ave a mum *and* a dad?"

"You bet it does," Nathaniel answered.

Billy grinned, hugging Algernon even tighter. "Bloody smashin'!"

32

Christmas night was clear and cold. Moonlight streamed across the huge mahogany bed that nearly filled the bedroom of Nathaniel's flat. Mrs. O'Brien's lodging house was finally quiet, after three weeks of hectic activity.

In the wake of Adrian's death, all his business activities had been investigated. With Finch's help, Inspector Carlisle was able to present evidence of Adrian's connection to the vandalism at his brother's factory. In addition, it was discovered that not only had Lord Leyland tried to use extortion and blackmail to ruin his brother, but he had also used those same tactics in the past to force other competitors out of business. The rest of London society was still in shock three weeks after the news made the papers, but Nathaniel and Mara had not been surprised at all.

Adrian had made no will. Nathaniel, as his closest relation, would have inherited his property, but there had been nothing to inherit. Creditors had taken all that he owned, from his Rembrandt masterpieces to his last box of matches. The only thing left was the entailed estate in Devon, stripped bare of all its furnishings, and the title, both of which passed to Nathaniel, who reacted to the news that he was now a viscount with an unimpressed yawn.

The trains had proved to be as successful as Nathaniel had predicted. All the retailers who had purchased Chase-Elliot trains reported within days of delivery that their inventory was gone, and all had demanded more. Nathaniel and Mara had gladly rented a vacant building and all the necessary equipment, and with Michael's help, they'd been making trains at a frantic pace right up until December 22, the day of their wedding.

The ceremony had been held at St. Andrew's Church, making Nathaniel the first viscount on record to be married in Whitechapel. Mara had worn a lovely ecru silk dress that Rebecca had made for her, Emma had been her bridesmaid, Billy hadn't fidgeted at all in his fancy clothes, and all the employees of Chase-Elliot had attended.

It had been the happiest day of her life, even though Nathaniel had, of course, arrived late at the church and worried her to death. But he'd smiled that special smile as he'd watched her walk down the aisle, and she'd forgiven him instantly. He had looked at her as they spoke their vows with so much love in his eyes, she knew no other woman in the world was as blessed as she.

Christmas Eve had come next, with wrapped presents being hidden all over the lodging house, and plenty of kisses beneath the mistletoe that had been mischievously hung in doorways by Nathaniel and Mrs. O'Brien.

And today, Christmas. A very special day for Billy, who had never received a wrapped Christmas present in his life. Roast beef, Yorkshire pudding, and trifle, the exchange of gifts, and stories of St. Nick and sugar plum fairies had entranced the boy. It was nearly midnight before Mara and Nathaniel finally tucked him into bed, paying no heed to his protests.

"I was very proud of you," Nathaniel murmured as they lay in bed. "You ripped the paper off every single one of your presents."

"Not very dignified of me," she replied. "I should be dignified. I'm a viscountess now." She glanced over at him. "Are viscountesses allowed to fly kites and climb trees?"

His arm tightened around her. "Only when accompanied by viscounts."

She smiled, snuggling close to him beneath the thick counterpane and resting her cheek on his shoulder. She closed her eyes and listened to the even rhythm of his breathing. She was Nathaniel's wife, next year's orders for trains were already pouring in, and despite the fire, they were actually going to make a reasonable profit. She couldn't be happier.

She began making plans. If the weather was good, the new factory would be finished by April, and the insurance would cover nearly the entire cost. They'd reinvest most of the train profits back into the business, of course, but by autumn, there would be enough money for them to purchase a London house. Knightsbridge, perhaps, or Kensington.

She pictured it in her mind. A nice town house, with blue shutters and window boxes of red geraniums. Nathaniel had lost most of his equipment in the fire, but his furniture and books would soon fill their house.

They would spend August in the country, since Nathaniel now owned the estate in Devon. Billy would love that. He and Nathaniel could climb trees to their heart's content. Mara decided she might even give tree climbing a try.

Income from rents would maintain the estate and perhaps provide a bit of extra income, if she were careful with the finances. By next Christmas, they ought to have a nice sum in the bank and a secure future ahead of them.

"Parlor furniture."

Startled to hear his voice when she'd thought him asleep, she lifted her head from his shoulder and looked at him. "What?"

He nodded absently, staring up at the ceiling. "Yes, and maybe some window seats. There would have to be other furniture, too. Wardrobes, and rocking chairs. Kitchen utensils, too."

She frowned in bewilderment, listening as he rambled on about furniture. "Kitchen utensils?" she echoed.

"Mmm . . . Bookshelves. Books, too, of course."

Was he making plans for their house? She continued to study him doubtfully.

"Paintings, maybe some potted ferns, coat trees."

"Nathaniel?"

Lost in thought, he didn't answer, and she reached out, grasping a handful of his tawny hair to give it a gentle tug. "Nathaniel, what are you talking about?"

He looked at her. "Dollhouses, of course," he answered, surprised by her confusion. "We sell the basic house, then offer all the furnishings for sale by the piece. Think of the opportunities."

She groaned—visions of a secure future and a tidy bank account disintegrating—and leaned down until her face was inches from his. "One dream at a time, Mr. Chase," she said and kissed him. "One dream at a time."

Winner Take All by Terri Herrington

Logan Brisco is the smoothest, slickest, handsomest man ever to grace the small town of Serenity, Texas. Carny Sullivan is the only one who sees the con man behind that winning smile, and she vows to save the town from his clutches. But saving herself from the man who steals her heart is going to be the greatest challenge of all.

The Honeymoon by Elizabeth Bevarly

Newlyweds Nick and Natalie Brannon are wildly in love, starry-eyed about the future...and in for a rude awakening. Suddenly relocated from their midwestern hometown to San Juan, Puerto Rico, where Nick is posted with the U.S. Coast Guard, Natalie hopes for the best. But can true love survive the trials and tribulations of a not-so-perfect paradise?

Ride the Night Wind by Jo Ann Ferguson

As the only surviving member of a powerful family, Lady Audra fought to hold on to her vast manor lands against ruthless warlords. But from the moonlit moment when she encountered the mysterious masked outlaw known as Lynx, she was plunged into an even more desperate battle for the fate of her heart.

To Dream Again by Laura Lee Guhrke

Beautiful widow Mara Elliot had little time for shining promises or impractical dreams. But when dashing inventor Nathaniel Chase became her unwanted business partner, Mara found his optimism and reckless determination igniting a passion in her that suddenly put everything she treasured at risk.

Reckless Angel by Susan Kay Law

Angelina Winchester's dream led her to a new city, a new life, and a reckless bargain with Jeremiah Johnston, owner of the most notorious saloon in San Francisco. Falling in love was never part of their deal. But soon they would discover that the last thing they ever wanted was exactly what they needed most.

A Slender Thread by Lee Scofield

Once the center of Philadelphia's worst scandal, Jennifer Hastings was determined to rebuild her life as a schoolteacher in Kansas. She was touched when handsome and aloof Gil Prescott entrusted her with the care of his newborn son while he went to fight in the Civil War. When Gil's return unleashed a passion they had ignored for too long, they thought they had found happiness—until a man from Jennifer's past threatened to destroy it.

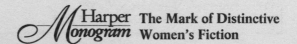